MOUNT ROYAL

there's nothing harder than love

MOUNT ROYAL

there's nothing harder than love

a novel by

Basil Papademos

Tightrope Books
17 Greyton Crescent
Toronto, Ontario. M6E 2G1
www.tightropebooks.com

Edited: Halli Villegas
Cover design and photograph: Fernando Pereira
Cover model: Araina Nespiak
Typography: Dawn Kresan
Author photograph: Alison Campbell
Printed and bound in Canada

We thank the Canada Council for the Arts and the Ontario Arts Council
for their support of our publishing program.

Canada Council   Conseil des Arts
for the Arts   du Canada

ONTARIO ARTS COUNCIL
CONSEIL DES ARTS DE L'ONTARIO

Library and Archives Canada Cataloguing in Publication

Papademos, Basil
Mount Royal / Basil Papademos.

ISBN 978-1-926639-43-7

I. TITLE.

PS8631.A628M69 2012   C813'.6   C2012-901805-8

In memory of Henry Gaines & Tony Albano

ONE

The sun crawls over the east-end tenements, utterly exhausted and barely able to drag itself out of another night. Getting home, I see a couple of Hassids in stained white coveralls unloading a van at the fishmonger's on my corner. One of them grins at me, wagging his head.

I climb the long staircase to our apartment. Everything's quiet. When Jane stormed out a few nights ago, she again swore to never return, but I half-expect to find her sprawled under the duvet, auburn hair spread across the pillow. Checking our bedroom, nothing. I flop onto the bed and catch a trace of her body's scent. Thirty-six and she's finally allowed herself to go out and devour the whole fucking world. Thinking of those sharp blue-green eyes dissecting it all so easily, I wonder if I'll ever see her naked again.

I know chances are pretty good Jane won't be coming back this time, but shit—she *should* come back. She's come back before. We've had some great fights in this apartment. Real crockery smashing, wall busting mêlées as the guy downstairs bays like a wounded dog.

Our place is a huge, high-ceiling pad that's dirt cheap. It takes up the top two floors of an old tenement a couple blocks off The Main. Yeah, it's drafty, has barely any furniture and the water pressure's worthless, but the rooms are grand, with crumbling stucco molding and ornate peeling wallpaper. It's an incredible luxury—the large salons Jane can hurl ashtrays across, bowling alley hallways where we roll and wrestle and tear one another's clothes off on the floors of the empty rooms upstairs. Who needs a bed.

Best of all, Mount Royal looms right out the front windows, its eastern face maybe a mile away. And down here under our mountain it feels like an Open City, that wartime Casablanca kind of idea when civic leaders declare their town is sitting out this fight and the walls won't be defended. Sure, armies can wander through to drink and fraternize, but no guns and definitely no marching. Commanders on all sides issue strict orders nobody will be raped, murdered or molested; nothing will be blown up, and people's belongings won't be seized. That makes the atmosphere relaxed and holiday-like; everyone sleeps in a lot, no annoying air raid sirens.

With its ancient buildings and broken, beautiful streets, Montreal is one of the last big Western cities where you can live in tarnished opulence without needing some idiotic job—which is why so many musicians, students, career welfare bums, and alleged artists gravitate here. Few of the low-rent Anglophone ex-pats who live around The Main speak more than rudimentary French, but we all vote for those xenophobic Separatist loons. Our strategy is meant to keep them in power and encourage the continued "flight of capital." This insures the economy stays deep in the shitter, and our two favorite words remain posted on those big red and white signs you see on every street, all over town: *À Louer.* For Rent.

As I lie around wallowing the phone rings a couple times, stops, then rings again. It's the code used by Al Polo, fellow rent-exile from Hogtown. To see him, you could easily imagine Al riding a penny-farthing, one of those old bicycles with the giant front wheel. Although he claims to be an actor, Al's real talent is an uncanny party radar. He can find a gathering of booze, drugs, people, and noise on a dead Tuesday night in the middle of January. It might occasionally be something like a bunch of second-rate hairdressers, but more often than not we'll end up at a mindblowing free bar and hot crowd soirée you'd normally only see in a movie.

"No time to be sleeping, Johnny."

"Yeah… So where were you last night, Al?"

"I left early. Too many skinheads and off-island rustics. Listen, I've just received an important communiqué. Aunt Byron is coming to town."

"Aunt Byron? Really, when?"

"No ETA established. However, judging from our conversational subtext, I predict two weeks."

"So is this a visit er… what?"

"Unknown at this time. Byron plans to conduct some highly classified research. Our assistance will be required."

"Uh huh… How's he doing with the big switcherama, nothing's grown back? They say the body never forgets—phantom feeling and so on."

"First of all, it's she, and her transition has gone beautifully. No complications. Now it's simply a matter of emotional support and psychological reinforcement. And Johnny, keep the stupid jokes to a minimum, will you, please?"

Al's coming on as if he'd used the scalpel himself and is worried about a malpractice suit.

"Sure thing, Herr Polo. So, Hennessy tells me you nailed down some extra gig."

Like everyone, Al cheers up when he can talk about himself. "That's correct. I have been engaged to perform in a television commercial featuring incontinence bags. The elderly are a major growth industry, my friend. I strongly urge you to invest now."

"Old people. They're a fucking embarrassment. Exterminate the brutes!"

"You're a real tonic, Johnny. Nevertheless, it is a situation, which allows me to practice the thespian arts as a paid professional, along with procuring some samples for Mama. Now, let me paraphrase from the script." Al must be pretty excited—sounds like he's getting to his feet. "All right then," he comes back on. "I portray a man who strides past in the out-of-focus background, along a walkway in a well-manicured park. Perhaps he checks his watch, a furrowed brow, critical issues on his mind. Meanwhile, a very attractive elderly couple, in full possession of their faculties, waltzes happily in the foreground, eyes a'twinkle."

"'Eyes a'twinkle'? Holy fuck, Polo. So what's this war crime pay?"

"Ten dollars per hour—cash. Time and a half after eight hours."

"Ten bucks an hour. Christ, you're a dupe."

"Don't be naïve, Johnny. Show business is all about favors and connections."

"Show business?"

"Yes, show business. For example, Karen at Ace Talent, the agency in the Cooper Building—she's assured me that if I play along on this advert, I'll be a shoo-in for full union scale and in-focus on *EcoKidz Rock*."

"All right, I'm sitting down. What's *EcoKidz Rock*?"

"It's an award-winning CBC television series. A team of young sex-abuse survivors get into little adventures saving the environment."

"Where's my machinegun."

"Oh, keep your hair on. I have to go. Mama has already begun her daily campaign of harassment. Perhaps I'll see you at Tony's."

As old lady Polo yaps in the background, Al hangs up and I recall how a few years ago, when we still lived in Hogtown, he'd been one of the first to decipher where that place was really headed. In a matter of hours, Al had packed up and left for Montreal in the dead of night. He threw Mama in a wheelbarrow and they slipped past the guard towers, razor wire and mine-fields along the Quebec-Ontario border.

I'd been stubborn enough to stick it out during the final days of the First Developer War, driven from stylish loft to furnished room to un-heated hovel. After being overrun by good looking, credit-worthy ground troops, I rolled up my life in an old rug and arrived in Montreal during a February blizzard. Al and Mama Polo were living in a huge, ramshackle flat at the north end of L'Esplanade. He'd stood in the doorway wearing a floor length Ayatollah nightshirt and bobbed his head with that knowing smirk. "Welcome to our island refuge, Johnny."

The moment I hang up somebody starts riding the door buzzer, going crazy on the thing. I run down ready to flip out. It's Hennessy. His usu-ally crafty features are sweaty and distressed. He skips around me and heads upstairs, starts to rattle on about some government yenta who wants to be double-teamed. The Hen says he's haggled her up to a hundred and fifty bucks over the phone, but she gets right of first refusal upon seeing the merchandise in person. With almost zero endorphins in my blood, the idea of performing three-way sexual calisthenics with some extra feisty stranger holds about as much appeal as a steak knife colonoscopy.

"She'll slam the door in our faces," I tell him. "You look like stepped-on cat shit. Christ, your skin's not even brown. It's gray."

Hennessy adjusts his oversized bowler and brushes off the ragged black suit. "You aren't exactly appetizing either, you know. I wouldn't vomit on you if I was paid."

"Well, that would depend on how much, wouldn't it?"

"If you have any bright ideas, Johnny, I'm listening."

"Okay, okay. So where is this hot-to-trot character?"

"Outremont. She's a doctor, part of the inner sanctum at the Ministry of Culture."

"Inner sanctum of my ass. Will she write for us?"

"She's not that kind of doctor."

"What the fuck? I've never understood this pretentious academic bullshit. What good is having Doctor in front of your name if you can't write a goddamn narcotics prescription? It shouldn't be allowed. It's phony advertising."

Hennessy sighs at my kvetching. "Can we go now?"

When we get to Outremont the deal seems like it might be okay. Nice Modernist box house with mellow Nordic box furniture. The quasi-doctor bureaucrat doesn't gack at the sight of us. She wears a black cat-suit, which isn't the best outfit for her short, wide physique, but what the hell, the woman's pleasant enough as we sit in some sort of ante-room, chatting. Who knows, maybe she'll do most of the work. But then we find out what she really wants is to have us double-team her husband across his home-office desk while she plays audience and jerks off with some adult toys. I glare at Hennessy. He gives me a weak shrug. *Oops.*

Hubby's a snarky, cavey chested middle-aged guy. He's already down to nothing but a pair of blue and white Y-fronts and has patches of gray hair on his shoulder blades. "Where did you find these two specimens? They look like refugees from a palliative ward."

"You wanted something street," his wife bitches at him. "So I found you something street."

"Yes, Montreal street. Not pox-infested Calcuttan gutter!"

He turns up his nose, looks away and points at the door. The doctor lady walks us out. She gripes under her breath, offers a few mumbled apologies and fifty bucks as compensation. After we score from Benny the Bike Thief, Hennessy runs off to a sociology class at Concordia: *The Housebroken Dog As Consumerist Metaphor in Late 20th Century Western Society.*

TWO

Having procured a few hours of relief, I begin walking home to get some shut-eye, but fuck it—sleep's overrated. Time to be pro-active and think of the future—like six or seven hours from now, when the heebiejeebies will be crawling up my ass again. So I bolt on the sunglasses and head toward Tony's, the artist and part-time dealer—see if I can roust him out of his latest drug coma and try to cadge a little reserve supply.

At Duluth, I cut over to L'Esplanade and walk along the side of Fletcher's Field. There's still some early mist on the mountain. A young white urban pioneer watches me warily from the door of her gorgeously renovated Victorian townhome. This reconstituted groover comes down the walkway, dragging a high-fashion toddler. She makes a show of locking the tall, stainless steel gate as they leave, then points her key fob at a new Volvo wagon I'm shuffling past. The car's alarm issues a loud double squawk, verifying it's armed. The woman marches away with her offspring and goes into a nearby daycare. I wait a couple minutes then take a few steps backward and use a hip-check to break off the Volvo's passenger side mirror. The car instantly begins to shriek. Nobody pays attention. I'll have a bad bruise, but it's worth it to see a pair of twisted holes in the door metal where the screws have torn out. I catch the mirror before it hits the sidewalk and carefully place it on the roof of her car.

Finally making it to Tony's warehouse just north of the park, I'm covered in sour sweat, practically wheezing. I pound on the big double doors and yell that it's me. He stomps across the floor and lifts the crossbar while putting on a cornball robot voice. "Dis-en-gaging." Tony turns the deadbolt as if breaking the seal on a pressure chamber. "Ptshhhh. Clearance-authorized-for-agent-Johnny. Enter."

Tony's an expansive guy, easily given to absurd and theatrical outbursts. He's hirsute and proud of it. His hairline begins a couple inches above his thick brows and dense brush covers almost his entire body, front and back. The guy can fucking well comb the hair on his fingers and toes.

His studio is a huge rectangle with wall-to-wall windows at one end. Pieces of plywood, disemboweled machinery and other found junk are left wherever they were dropped. Once in a while he does manage to slap together a painting or collage and they're not bad, a kind of colorful Haight-Ashbury vibe.

Al Polo and Hennessy are already here, sitting around Tony's big office desk littered with various tools and trinkets. Al is sunk into the shabby black suit jacket he's worn since 1976, bony legs crossed tight—the cut-rate Mephistopheles. He claims to simply enjoy the company. Al's thing is obscenely expensive brandies, cognacs, malts—and lots of them, an alcoholic with fantastic pretensions. The Hen's slumped back in a typing chair, legs sprawled out, nodding on a narco-valium mix.

"Aren't you supposed to be in class?" I poke at him.

"I am," he says without opening his eyes. "I signed in and now I'm there in spirit."

"Are you ever," I mutter and grab a seat next to Tony, try to ease in on him. "So, Toneski, what's happenin'?"

"It's May Day."

"Lotta continua," Hennessy murmurs.

"Lemme guess," Tony grouses and puts on his Slavic peasant shtick. "You coming here to my houz with no dinars."

"C'mon, just something small till I work things out."

He rubs his fingers together and leans toward me. "Tonsko need many dinar—now!"

"Gimme a break with the goddamn dinars, will ya?"

14

"Fuck man," he crabs, dropping the Shmengie act. "What am I, your private perfumed ass wiper? Can't you get some money off Jane?"

"She's still not back."

"Oh yeah? So what did ya do to earn all this extra drama?"

"It's personal."

"That's right," Al throws in. "Something personal called the old dumparoo."

"Fuck you, Polo. You don't have that inconvenience living with your mother, sitting on her lap every night, eating perogies."

"At least she never runs away," Al replies, stroking his goatee.

"Just do me twenty bucks worth," I keep bugging Tony. "Cheques are due soon."

"*Not* possible."

"Fuck 'not possible'. After all the cash I give you?"

"All the cash you give me? What about all the cash you owe me? I can't do anything because I don't have anything. You think this is some kinda hobby?"

"All right, already," Hennessy snaps, eyes popping open. "Can't we go one bloody day without hearing about your-"

"You shut up!" Tony yells at him. "In case it slipped the deformed piece of gray matter you have left, this," he gestures with both hands. "What I'm doing here? It happens to be a felony! Y'know, jail, prison-"

"Keep it down," Al crabs from behind yesterday's Gazette.

"Keep it down? You wanna tell The Man to keep it down? He's coming here this morning and I'll have to French kiss his hairy ass and pray he lets me re-load even though I'm like four hundred short cuz I carry all you fucking deadbeats!"

Al tunes him out while he savors one of his stinky French smokes. Hennessy drifts back into a quiet nod, Tony's noise remote as distant traffic. He turns on me. "Why don't you get out there and raise some goddamn venture capital!? Where's your entrepreneurial spirit, for chrissake?"

"Yeah, yeah, I'll get right on it."

Tony's got to have a bit stashed, but he's keeping that in case he'll need to hunker down and wait for The Man, who could take ten minutes or ten hours or all day or who the hell knows. Even if The Man shows up soon, he'll give Tony tiny bits, just enough to make up the money he owes, and then, if Tony's a good little halfwit, give him a larger count to work with. In other words, it could be days before The Tone can front again. I look to Hennessy. Without raising his head, he pulls his empty pockets inside out.

Leaving Tony's place, of course I run into The Man when he steps out of the elevator. His broad smile lights up the corridor. The Man's about five foot five and wide as a doorway. He has a steroid-induced muscular bulk that makes his dark eyes bug out like a goiter case. The Man comes on warm but probing. The Man remembers all names, phone numbers and old debts. Occasionally, when the mood is right, The Man's big hand sweeps before the debtor and the obligation vanishes. But if the fates are on the rag, The Man may don a pair of deerskin gloves with pockets of sand sewn into the knuckles.

"Johnny..." he lubes me. "Johnny the Carp. So, how's Tony been treating ya?"

I'm not sure what to call him. *Mister Man? Sergeant Man?* "Uh, not bad... Guess he has his problems." I instantly regret opening my mouth.

"Problems?" The Man turns an ear toward me. "What kinda problems?"

"Well... uh... it's tough to keep things in line, right."

"Things? What things?"

"Uh... y'know, his coming up short sometimes, I guess. I dunno..."

The Man frowns at the floor between us. A power saw screams from a workshop down the hall then stops. "Short," he repeats and his eyes snap up to mine. "You gotta number, Johnny?"

"Me?"

"Yeah, you." He taps me on the chest with his middle finger. "A number where I can call ya. You got something like that?"

"I... uh... don't have a pen on me."

"We don't need a pen." The Man's eyes focus on my lips as I recite the number. He looks me up and down. "So, how much you owe us now?"

I'm ready to break into a run. "Em... 'bout two hundred bucks, but I'll be-"

"Not too bad at all," he cajoles, enjoying my dread. "A real stand up guy."

The Man continues down the hall, leaving behind a waft of peppery cologne. I watch the wide back, the rock-hard ass flex in the stone-washed jeans. When he reaches Tony's door, I make for the stairs.

Actually, that wasn't too bad. No dire threats or stairwell beatings. Maybe The Man's thinking about a little personnel shake up after all of Tony's financial debacles. I'm instantly absorbed in a rich fantasy: good money, solid career, some local status, all my troubles resolved… But fuck. That asshole won't call. He'll freak on Tony yet again and Tony'll get his shit together for a little while then its rinse and repeat. The Man's nice-guy act was just a casual warning because he's heard I've been scoring on Park Avenue the odd time with Benny the Bike Thief. Aw, screw him. What's a lousy two hundred bucks next to the piles of loot I've given that walking gland?

I drag my ass down Clark, completely bereft; wrack my brains over how to drum up some gelt. My credit's burned with anybody I know who'd have an extra twenty bucks hanging off them. Jane would give me a kick in the nuts rather than a fiver—even if I could track her down. My recent streak of thefts from downtown record stores and trendy bookshops has attracted far too much heat so that's out for a while. This whole thing's worse than the tyranny of food. You can't just consume a finite amount and be done with it forever.

At the corner of Marie-Anne, I see Slim sitting in the window of a tiny café with another woman, a shave-headed young dyke she's been banging lately. I can't figure out what she sees in this baby chimp. Slim's shoulder-length, bleached blonde hair comes straight down from under a backward Oakland Raiders ballcap, torn and faded oversized jeans belted and bunched tight at her thin waist. I sidle up and notice a book on their table, fourteenth-century English social history. On the cover there's a painting of serfs or somebody being horsewhipped.

Slim vaguely re-introduces her pal then scowls up at me. "You're a mess."

"Thanks."

She pulls me down by the sleeve and whispers into my neck. "Come over to my place in an hour or so. I got something." Her little tattooed chimp friend angrily lights a cigarette. I grin at her and shuffle off, high on anticipation.

I met Slim a couple years ago. Since then we've gotten pretty tight and regularly cheat on our respective partners with one another. I'd first seen the back of her from a distance, at a shithole bar on Lower Saint-Denis where she was working. She had really short hair then and I'd thought she might be a teenaged boy. When I realized she was a girl with a boy's narrow hips and taut little butt, I got pretty fucking excited. Hennessy was with me and he kind of knew her so I pestered him into making the intros.

The three of us ended up in bed a couple times then I ran into her a few weeks later when I'd left Jane at home late one night to go out to The Main for smokes. Slim was with a gang of drunks on the sidewalk in front of the Bar Saint-Laurent at closing time. She led me over to the mountain. It was still late winter and we fell into a rolling tussle up behind Etienne-Cartier's monument, among the trees, in the snow, to scratch and claw at each other in the dark and get soaking wet, hair full of icicles. She took me back to her place to defrost, a sprawling attic slum on the top floor next to Schwartz's Deli. I hadn't seen such a long, lean body on very many women. Those small, perfect breasts, deep green eyes and a dissolute beauty that always reminds me of Charlotte Rampling in *The Night Porter*. Her high cheekbones and thin lips underline a supremely indifferent surface, impenetrable as buffed granite. While we'd been screwing, Slim mentioned her boyfriend, a guy called Warren, was asleep in one of the other bedrooms. She told me he was a big-brain at McGill and she'd goaded him to the hilt, but he refused to react. No matter how many men or women she dragged home, Warren was impervious. I admired him.

I kill some time by cuffing a couple packs of Marlies at Mario's Duty-Free Depanneur then loiter at the magazine racks in the lobby of the 4040 Building. I'm reading a touching memoir of Michel Foucault's attempts to suck and/or fuck every male grad student in Hogtown while researching *The History of Sexuality*, when Warlock appears at my elbow. An upper-class WASP anomaly in this shtetl full of cast offs, he's a member of the moneyless Anglo gentry. Warlock sports slicked-down hair and dresses like a

Depression Era banker. He stands next to me, breathing. I give him half a sneer. "Haven't the Frogs thrown you into the camps yet?"

"That's been postponed," he replies with his glib little air. "I have agreed to learn to speak the historically valid dialect of French known as Quebecois, along with a smattering of Joual. That's the colloquial parlance used by working class folk of rural French-Canadian descent."

"Fucking collaborator."

"I try."

"Okay, then. How about a demo?"

Warlock shrugs modestly and clears his throat. "Bon joor, mez ah-mee."

I wait but that's it. "Wow, you're a regular Frère Andre."

"Thank you," he acknowledges with a short bow. "By the by, Johnny, I happened to see your *wife* on The Main late last night—or very early this morning, if you prefer." His shiny face closes in on me. "She seemed rather relieved about something, hm…?"

"I'm so glad I ran into you."

I put the magazine back and leave him standing there, aglow with malice. The Main is smog-choked, packed with discount shoppers and squeegee punks, delivery trucks blocking traffic. I turn into the stinking alleyway beside Schwartz's smoked meat house and press the button next to a steel plated door. When the buzzer sounds, I struggle up two flights of rickety stairs littered with junk mail.

Slim's place looks different than the last time I was here. Maybe the latest boyfriend has been swapped for a new guy—or a roommate. In the kitchen, the snazzy glass table is gone, replaced by an old door held up by a couple of sawhorses. The living room is furnished with a scavenged psychiatrist's couch, mismatched chairs and a wood-plank bookshelf filled with paperbacks, busted phones and camera equipment. A couple of blown-up black-and-white prints are tacked to the wall—so huge I can't tell what they are. *Park Porn—M. Ant.* is written on them in red magic marker.

I find Slim in one of the bedrooms, just out of the bath. Her hair drips, lean polecat body wrapped in a beach towel. She mutters a greeting while ducking into the room's sloped corners to sweep out dust and debris. She dumps a pan full of hair and furballs into a trashcan then drops her ass onto the bare futon on the floor. I watch her peel away crusty condoms stuck to the orange-crate nightstand. She holds them over a lit match. Each one sizzles and flames before she lets it fall into an ashtray. The burning latex and petrified sperm give off an acrid plastic odor. I plop down next to her and she lays a pair of tiny packs between us.

"You're a peach," I smile and begin to set things up.

"So... Warlock told me Jane still hasn't come back."

"She will."

"Enjoy it while it lasts, Johnny. You're pretty miserable when she's around."

"Yeah, well, so's she. That makes us even."

Slim lights a cigarette, smoke curling from her lips. "That English guy who was staying here, Trevor, he's gone too. Went kinda crazy on me."

"I'm not surprised. You seem to have that effect on people."

She leans back on her wrists, ankles crossed. "Trevor," she says again, both amused and fed up. "He told me he had nightmares about you."

"I'm flattered."

"You should be. I think he had a big crush on ol' Johnny."

"Are you trying to be funny?"

"When do I ever try to be funny?" Slim gets up and grabs a small square of foil off the bureau. It has a hardened brown puddle on it. She fires up a lighter and heats the underside. As the puddle liquefies, she uses a foil tube to inhale a few hits. I watch her undo the towel and let it fall to expose purple and gold bruises on that tight ass of hers, down those long legs.

She turns and sees the empty little folds of paper next to me, scowling as I do the shot. "Fuck, Johnny, do you have to be such a pig? I hope you're not going to nod out on me." Her pupils have contracted to pinheads, eyes almost completely green.

"What about you? You're high as a fuckin' kite."

Slim stands over me, looks down with a mean little smirk. "I'm a girl. I've got a button."

I barely run my fingers up between her legs, get a hint of how wet she is. She begins to sway back and forth ever so slightly. I take her knees and raise my chin. Her pussy lands right on the tip of my tongue, perfectly balanced. She tastes of soap and heat. Slim groans deep in her throat as my tongue curls in and she grabs a fistful of hair, grinds against my mouth, thighs trembling, then reaches down for herself. The momentum builds fast. Within a couple minutes I feel her tense and shudder, a bit of come washing over my lips. Man, it sure must be nice to have that tiny button.

"That wasn't too bad," she grins, hanging onto her pussy with both hands. She wrinkles her nose at me. "But I want the big one. Y'know, the backbreaker."

Slim drops to her knees, straddles me and opens my shirt. Her teeth latch onto my shoulder. Fuck—her bites really hurt, deep incisions that bring up a flash of anger and a smear of blood. She's drawn toward earlier wounds, to re-open them. She undoes buckle and button and zipper, yanks off my boots and pants and my two-dollar Montreal Expos wristwatch, throws it across the room and cackles happily when it smashes to bits.

"C'mon," she mutters, turning her ass toward me.

I smack it hard. She yelps when I take a bite then lick the two red arcs left behind. "You know why the Quebecois do it doggie style, doncha?"

"Yeah, yeah," she drones at the old chestnut. "So they can both watch the hockey game. C'mon, already..."

I drag her up by the hips and those long fingers snake down to play with us. She looks round at me. "So you think you can come?"

"I dunno. I'll try..."

"Yeah, let's... it'll be good..."

See, when you're not too high, your entire surface lights up, every pore shimmers with a smoky, electric lust. But the thing is—having a serious, head-busting orgasm while under the influence also becomes a deeply potent contradiction, a monumental struggle where you must pound the absolute fuck out of each other. Every muscle and tendon screams at the limit, and you can sense it's right there, just out of reach, inching closer then it recedes, cockteasing yourself into lunacy. If you're with a woman who hasn't used, then sure, she can come and come again and yet again and she thinks, yeah, okay, it's great and all, but how long is this going to take? He's still fucking the living hell out of me and I'm getting kind of sick of it. I've got to get up and go to work in the morning.

But Slim's got nowhere to go right now so we're soon curled chest to back as the motion builds and it all drives into a red horizon. I yank on her bleached hair and she laughs with frustration, her voice skipping along. "Fuck, man, this feels so good... I really wanna come. Fuck!..."

And that little button does help her tremble out another partial convulsion. But it also makes the deeper itch worse so she rolls over to face me, pulls me back in and the room whirls. I'm engulfed as those green eyes glare and urge me beyond the dying flesh, the river of isolation. Slim knows she must sweet talk me, purr to me, keep me working. "C'mon, baby, you can do it. Yeah, c'mon, fuck me. Fuck me."

We burn with friction as our pubic bones bash, deep bone bruises that will hurt for days. Slim's knees come up high to squeeze my ribs, one hand dug into my neck, the other snaking between us, jacking herself to our rhythm. She's all the way off the bed now, ass against my thighs while I hold her up by the tail and slam into her. I'm on the verge of a stroke or a heart attack as we snarl into each other's mouths and our fucking becomes a frantic reaching then finally—finally bodies and souls shattered and shrieking and the back of my head blown away...

HO-lee shit... My heart thumps in my ears as we roll apart, sweat soaked and utterly wrung out. I can barely raise my arms. While it all slowly subsides in trembles and twitches, Slim shows me our come mixed together on her fingers. "Congrats, baby."

Good thing I have enough of a functioning brain filter left. It intercepts my vocal chords before I can gush a load of maudlin nonsense that would instantly turn me into a big fucking drag, one more dipshit guy who won't leave her alone.

THREE

I'm wandering down The Main a couple hours before sun-up when
Hennessy prances out of the Bar Saint-Laurent. As usual, he's dressed like a
nineteenth-century anarchist, all in black and topped with a leather newsboy's cap. His sweet, devilish grin lights up when he sees me. I watch him
push through some hotheads crowded around the stairs leading up to the
bar. All of them dolled up in tight shirts and toreador pants, they're hostile,
but also seem kind of hopeful. Hennessy's happily drunk and comes up on
his toes to lay a wet smooch on my neck.

"Relax, Romeo," I hold him off. "What's going on up there?"

"Samba marathon."

"I didn't know you like Samba."

"I don't. I'm carrying out important research for my anthropology thesis,
The Cross-Cultural Maternal Obsessions of the Traditional Male Immigrant."
He tosses his head at the grim-faced bunch behind him. "These poor lads,
they're waiting for the horsy but randy and well-employed white lady who
will take them away from all this yet remain relatively submissive—at least
in public."

"Sounds tragic. How you fixed, ya got anything?"

Hennessy rubs against me and exposes his sharp little teeth. "Does the
Pope wear skirts? Perhaps we could trade something."

"Like what?"

"Like what else?"

"Nah, not tonight. I think my prostate's broken."

"Mine's not," he beams then waves it off. "But romance can wait. Right now, we have a social call to make. Al Polo told me about an apocalyptic lease-breaking party in Griffintown. It should be peaking by the time we arrive." But then he stops in his tracks and holds up a hand. "Wait just one second, *Monsieur*." His finger circles at me. "What are you doing off the leash? Hasn't that harridan wife of yours come running back yet?"

"No—and don't call her that."

"Really...?" he asks, all sly and malicious. "So... how long has it been?"

"Five nights. She's never stayed away this long."

Hennessy tugs on his lapels and preens a bit. "Oh, you're better off without all the *dramatae*, my friend. And methinks 'tis far preferable to be a kept man."

"Get off my back, will ya? Besides, you're not that well kept. Heidi's a miserable hag. I don't know how you haven't killed her in her sleep."

"In the immortal words of Captain Hugh Abercrombie, 'a barnacle must cling to any passing ship.'"

As we turn a corner onto Saint-Cuthbert, Hennessy pulls me into an unlit doorway and opens his jacket to show off a row of loaded syringes. They're lined up like pens and the nut's even got them in a plastic pocket protector.

"Jesus, you come prepared."

"Boy Scouts," he says, handing me a fit. "One of the truly positive influences in my life." He whips out a mini-maglite and shines it on the thirty units of caramel colored liquid. "One-twentieth of a gram per dose. More than enough to perk up your spirits."

I flag a good vein on the topside of my wrist. We switch round and he does a faithful scab on the back of his hand. Our mood lightened, we grope each other and laugh stupidly. The little cockteaser squeezes my leg between his thighs and I feel him get hard. We've been flirting and fucking around for about a decade now, from the early days in Hogtown when we shared a girlfriend—a brilliant, black-eyed woman called Wander.

The Hen flags down a taxi and orders the driver to head for the old port. In the back seat, he curls up under my arm and coos like a baby fruit. The cabby floors it away from green lights and blares the horn at nothing. He glowers at the rearview as we race toward the river. Knots of night crawlers are still out, along with whooping gangs of frat house beasts.

But everything falls silent south of that monument to Neo-Fascist architecture, the Palais des congrès. At the bottom of Peel Street, the driver refuses to go any further so we get out and walk into the unlit laneways of Griffintown's derelict warehouses. Some are bombed-out Victorian skeletons while others remain fairly intact. Shouts and music beckon from the party a ways off, but closer to us, sinister figures move in the shadows. I feel for my exacto-blade then see a pair of skinheads stripped to the waist, human tattoo parlors with cue-ball heads. They grapple with one another while a gaggle of onlookers yell drunken curses and a beer bottle explodes on the cobblestones. Both combatants are blood splattered and foam at the mouth. A pug-faced female of their tribe flits around them in torn fishnets and a tattered wifebeater. She spurs on the struggle with a torrent of guttural Joual.

"Ah, yes," Hennessy points as we give them a wide berth. "Here we have a fine example of the Franco-Saxon mating ritual. Observe the rutting cow as she circles the competing bulls. This allows them to catch enticing whiffs of her scent and thus further provoke their battle to prove genetic supremacy." He bats his lashes. "And win her heart."

A noisy crowd mills around the doors to the party building. We work our way up a dark staircase full of smoke. It's jam-packed with more skins, metalheads, hippie punks, groovers of various ilk coming and going, along with the odd wino who happened by. The railing's torn from the wall, huge holes booted through the plaster that now litters the steps.

The cavernous third floor loft condemned to this evening's devastation is blacked-out but for a few red spotlights. The Nils *Call of the Wild* booms from a stack of PAs powered by gas generators. Under a dense cloud of hash smoke, a mass of bodies rolls and sways to the music. Thick, sweaty heat sucks the air out of the place. Every window's shattered, frames smashed to kindling. It appears the vortex is centered on the cash bar somewhere at the other end. A few couples, bodies wrapped around each other, go at it while standing against the wall. A pair of lanky women near the door slow dance with their shirts off. Thumbs hooked into one another's belt-loops, both of them wear big sunglasses and face the ceiling, both of them high as fuck.

Al Polo is nowhere in sight. No doubt he already scoped this shindig, rated it B minus then moved on. Hennessy grabs a handful of my ass and gives me a filthy grin. He's flush with drugs and money. We take a ride back to my place.

FOUR

In the past several weeks I've pillaged every record shop and bookstore from Bonsecour to Beaubien and Sainte-Babette du la trou d'cul immaculée. But I almost got nabbed during my last foray on de Maisonneuve and it scared the living shit out of me. Some pimply-faced security gonad had me by the arm, but I broke free and skedaddled through the busy mid-day traffic. Al Polo said afterwards he saw a photocopy of my face on a few record store bulletin boards.

"You looked like a billy-goat wearing sunglasses and a dark suit jacket."

So it's time to try a different tack, at least until things cool down. I get on the phone to locate an aspiring coke kingpin I know, one Ziplock. I'm not really a coke guy. Sure, I'll do the odd speedball, but not as a steady diet, so blow would be an ideal moneymaker. This Ziplock character has occasionally made vague offers to front me eightballs I can break up and retail in the generic pubs and discos along MacKay, Crescent and Bishop. Just stand over a urinal and proposition potential customers. Usually drunk, this variety of weekender hardly ever balks at the inflated price. Of course, they always look at you bleary-eyed and ask: "Is it any good?" *No, stupid, it's phosphate free drain cleaner cut with dried pus. Wanna try some?*

My standard sales rap goes like this: "Good? You josh me to the extreme, sire. It is la fucking bomba. Blow the ol' reptilian sub-brain right out your anesthetized asshole!" Fortunately, it's a rare suburban bozo who's ever done real blow. So these mooches go into a stall and snarf up a line of what is actually industrial speed cut with dextrose, benzocaine to numb out the nose and a trace of coke, if only to keep the Advertising Standards Board from yapping. They come back out with bulging eyes and grinding teeth. I greet them with a bad Spic accent: "Welcome to Colombia, Señor!"

After eight or ten fruitless calls, I go out and try to hunt down the budding Pablo Escobar in person, roust a few bars and cafés along The Main. No Ziplock. Nobody's seen the little bullshit artist.

Sneezes begin to hit me in bunches as the first pangs rear up. Stomach cramps, vice-grip migraine, everything smells acrid. The world takes on a fierce, unfiltered clarity. Faces, cars, houses, all of them defined too sharply. People's expressions convey a severe meaning. I'm light-headed, manic but exhausted, in danger of crash landing on Planet Jones where a single gulp of the atmosphere gives you a black depression, listless panic and exploding bowel syndrome. Thank god for the genius who invented sunglasses.

Some old-timers call it *The Monkey*. A monkey on your back, they say. Feed The Monkey—you have no choice. But it's not just about being addicted to some man-made venom. That's the most obvious route to putting your head in the Monkey yoke. You can live like an ascetic vegan monk devoted to spiritual awakening and it won't matter. Everything you've bought into becomes The Monkey. Your stupid career, your endless obligations, your moronic colleagues, your mate, your kids, your parents. Despite your volunteering and caring and community-building, you can't get away from the shitty little voice in the back of your head that repeats: *I am a complete fraud.*

You don't remember when it all began because there was no beginning. Sure, there were a few doubts during your youth, but things have progressed as they should. Privately, you even became a little smug. *I've got this shit figured out*, you told yourself. *Life isn't all that hard if you know what you're doing.*

But one fine fucking day a few cracks appear. A crap economy gives you a financial hemorrhoid. Not lethal but no fun either. Then you're called in to take a browbeating from some jerk ten years your junior, sitting across a bank branch desk like he owns the place. Next you're plagued by a spate of domestic squabbles and get punished with several fuckless months. To top it all off, those sullen kids of yours, they treat you like a senile joke—and no way you're allowed to say dick. By that point you're so far in, it's not easy to dump The Monkey. So you withdraw into fantasies of being alone, beautifully alone. No family, no mortgage, no fiscal hamster wheel. Giddy with excitement, you take the first tentative steps toward off-loading some of these gratuitous operating costs.

That's when you finally see the true, unvarnished Monkey and it is nauseating. He hangs on like a fanged leech and discharges the vile stench of pure methane farts. You try to work up some of the old righteous anger and fling Monkey off, tell him to go back to the fucking trees. But Monkey's too flabby to climb a tree. Instead, he guilts you with sentimental crying jags, nostalgic for those horrible, nameless pop tunes you once sang together. You tear Monkey off your neck and try to drown the crazy fuck in the tub. But he turns himself inside out so your hands are full of nothing but raw guts and noxious feces.

Monkey slithers out of the tub and along the floor until he finds the phone. An entrail reaches out like a finger and deftly dials the correct number. Monkey says he'll call in a few favors, if you get back into harness. He promises to one day sit in a room and type the collected works of Shakespeare, even if takes a thousand years. Monkey appears on late-night TV and demonstrates a portable lobotomy saw on several satisfied customers. Monkey makes it impossible to resist 365 easy payments of just $3.29 each.

I should go home, have a good cry and knit myself a comfy old straight jacket. But Monkey's snarls and screeches force me to continue down Saint-Urbain, past the ranks of curving wrought-iron staircases toward the McGill Ghetto. The university's spring term has been over for a couple weeks now and without the usual herd of undergrads, everything around here seems deserted. Beneath the gray skies, these narrow, heavily treed side streets of dignified greystones and walkups have a menacing, Victorian air—straight out of Jekyll and Hyde.

I think about breaking into cars but have no idea how, so instead make my way along Milton to The Word, a musty little used bookstore with a low ceiling and an illustrious rep. They're supposed to have some rare editions that might be worth trying to rip off. It's dim enough to appear closed, but I try the door and walk in. A gnomish clerk peeks up from a small crowded counter at the rear then dips his head again. The place smells of damp and old print. Obsolete textbooks and yellowed paperbacks are stacked to the rafters. A table of ancient magazines and oversized art tomes fills the middle of the room.

The only other customer is a woman. She's got her back to me and, holy Christ—it looks like Jane... My heart begins to hammer as I move in for a side view. It's gotta be her—copper-colored hair, scuffed black leather coat and short-nailed hands... yeah... it is her... no... it's not her—someone younger, maybe twenty or so. The girl's head is bowed over a book of Bukowski poems. Perhaps a student forced to make up an elective: *Inveterate Assholes in Modern Literature. Discuss.*

She glances at me without expression. For an instant I see her superimposed on herself—Jane fifteen years younger. But without the crow's feet that have begun to form at her eyes, no bitter twist of the lip. I inch along the shelves, my fingers trace spines. I catch a hint of her washed scent.

"Uh, sorry for staring... I thought you were somebody else."

"That's all right," she replies warily, closing the book.

"Um... your name's not Jane, is it?"

"No," she answers with a sidelong frown and moves toward the clerk.

I strain to hear their small talk while she pays. The girl turns to leave, stops for a moment and appraises me coolly. Crouched by a bottom row, I blink, eyes watering. She goes out and comes past the bookstore window, but pulls up suddenly, checks both ways then squints back into the dark shop. I run outside and she looks at me, eyes vivid and blue, her young face hard as plastic. "Could you walk with me?" she blurts. "There's a guy following me."

I snap round, expecting a cowled ghoul to lunge for my neck. But across the street an aging academic looking hipster glares at us from behind tiny round specs. Tall and balding, with a trimmed beard, the Range Rover/ Eddie Bauer proto-pederast.

"Do you know him?"

She shakes her head stiffly. "No. He was following me before I went into the bookstore. I guess he waited till I came back out."

I'm not sure if I should believe her. Recent studies would indicate other-wise. Perhaps he's a jealous sugar daddy, or maybe the English lit Prof who insists on payment for the influential grad school reference. More likely, they're in this together, a careful plan to bushwhack some hapless bohunk. After the trap is sprung, you regain consciousness in a filthy, rat-infested basement, naked and disoriented, all body hair shaved off. You feel a raw gash on your forehead then realize your ankle's chained to a radiator.

We cross at the corner and go south on Aylmer toward the far-off noise and traffic of Sherbrooke Street. She looks back and I follow her glance, but the stalker's gone. Maybe he's holding his breath behind a wall somewhere ahead; laying in wait with a razor honed surgical instrument, ready to unleash him-self. You never know the depth of rage behind those Greenpeace facades.

My back aches, legs heavy as running in a nightmare. I check between parked cars and up laneways. Low-hanging branches brush my face. Car horns cry from the surrounding city. At an ivy covered rowhouse, a long white face peers from behind a curtain then quickly withdraws. I suck in a gasp. The girl shoots me a worried look. "You okay?"

"Yeah, just great."

A few cars slowly idle past, the drivers' faces in shadow. They bend low to inspect the female at my side, their dowser wand pricks drawn to the faint tremor of human fright. When we reach Sherbrooke, she looks past me while getting into a cab. "Thanks."

The taxi pulls away into the dense traffic. I walk east, sapped by my own impotence of letting her go without a word or a phone number.

As a last resort I decide to hit Octavio's fruit stand at Pine and The Main, front some codeines off him. But on my way, I get trapped on the west side of Lower Park Avenue by a parade of flag wavers. The weird thing is, not many people watch, just some curious bystanders and no one has any idea what's being celebrated. Some guy shouts senseless feedback through a bull-horn. Cops prevent anyone from crossing, but I'm ready to make a run for it when the colorful procession climaxes with a giant float of a hydro-electric dam escorted by serious looking men dressed as beavers.

Finally getting back to The Main, I turn the corner at Pine and see Octavio slouched in front of what is basically a rotting plywood lean-to. He's all gold chains, wide stance and no-nonsense machismo, but the bald spot and coke-bottle glasses leave him kinda squirrelly.

"Hey, Jorge Hard-on," I catch him. "Why so limp?"

Octavio's jowly face swings round. "Johnny," he crabs then horks into the street. "Fuck you, man. You're free as a wino. My life's got the runs." He goes to the curb and lightly pats the roof of his car. "This Celica, I got the turbo, fully loaded, almost five bills a month to carry her, but I need this fuckin' car, tabernac'. I'm a fag's asshole without it."

"Oh yeah? So what's that make me?"

"A cocksuckin' queer, I'd say. C'mon, buy some blow, the faggot's friend. Twenty-five bucks a quarter GR—but no deal on quantity. The wop who rents me this stand—he won't cut me a break, tabernac'."

"Naw, coke's for squares. Cuff me some threes, will ya?"

Octavio glances around then rummages in the pockets of his tracksuit. He pulls out a cigarette pack, dumps out some white pills and counts thirty into my palm. "Okay, that's all I can do ya," he says. "And you gotta pay me on cheque day, right?"

"Yeah, no probs."

I hate these fucking codeines—useless to shoot. They do straighten you out—barely—but make your skin crawl and everything tastes and smells medicinal. Still, it's better than shitting out your lungs. I toss down five of them. "I guess you never got any more percs or dilaudids, eh?"

"Fuck, no! It's the wop, câlice! He won't let me do the hard stuff. Strictly blow, hash and low-grade bullshit like these threes." Octavio shakes his head bitterly. "Fuck, Johnny man. You don't know the shit I gotta eat, every fuckin' day!"

"Must be your bad karma. Still paying for those past-life crimes. Like when you were the village idiot back in the Azores and raped all those chickens."

He grunts and picks up a leprous looking orange, rolls it in his hands. "It's no joke, man. I tell the wop, lemme move up, fuck. Says he's doing me a favor anyway renting me this stand, but I got a chick now. You seen her, long brown hair—'member?"

"Yeah… isn't she screwing that Waspafarian DJ at the Bifteck?"

Octavio threatens a backhand. "Shut the fuck up, man! Crystal's very clean. I didn't just peel her off The Main for a coupla lines of blow." His eyes, big as a bullfrog's behind the thick bifocals, search round to the car. "If I'm gonna keep her, I need the Celica. I won't meet a babe like her if I'm taking the fucking bus."

"Like you always tell me, 'Tavio, don't get hung up on some broad."

He eyes me with a crooked grin. "You mean like your chick, Jane? Yeah, I heard she dumped you. Must be a real drag you don't have the hard-on to keep her."

"Fuck you, hamster dick! I've fucked more women than you've sold bananas!"

"That just proves it!"

"Proves what!?"

"Gettin' a lotta broads don't mean shit. Just shows you can't keep any of them interested. Nowadays, you gotta talk to a woman, let her say how she wants it."

"Holy Christ, 'Tavio. What are you, Joe Feminist now?"

"Hey, at least I'm not scummin' around like you—or worse, like the fuckin' wop! Always gettin' them model chicks on Saint-Denis with the blow and cash he makes on my fuckin' back!"

"Don't burst a nut. This is still a money-making operation. But you could use more variety of fruit."

"Oh yeah? Howz about I round up half a dozen pegboys for ya? Sound good, Johnny?"

"Ah, you took the cock right out of my mouth."

Octavio snorts and loosely grapples with his nuts as I walk away. Eating a couple more codeines, I mull over this crap about Jane. She's gone five seconds and even a jack-off like Octavio gets the drop on me. What the hell did she do, rent a billboard? Letters twenty feet high: WARNING—*Johnny is a creep. I dumped him because he is a liar, a coward and a lousy lay.*

FIVE

Everything feels like it's on rewind. I waste the next few days casing potential shoplifting locales, but merchants are especially vigilante during the last week before welfare cheques arrive. The Main is stripped to the bones. So out come the part-time whores, the pawnshop guitars and half-assed B&E's, the petty thieves and semi-logical conjobs. Pennies and nickels have long been rolled up and bottles cashed in. Gut wrenching shrieks echo across our fair arrondissement.

These goddamn codeines scarcely keep the shits at bay so I go down to Octavio's shack, thinking a couple hash joints might help, but his place is shut up tight. I drift over to the Bifteck, see if there's anyone around I can hit up for a few bucks, a drink, something. It's 2 p.m. and the place is dead. The bar's lit only by the sun streaming all the way into the back.

A cross-addicted boozehound called Hernav sits with Savva Grudtsyn, the rubber-faced Russian who's seen much better days. They're the only patrons and their table is empty. Both sniveling and hunched over, they hug themselves and rock slightly, demand cigarettes the moment I join them. "Sorry, ladies."

"Every month same boolshit," complains Savva in his good but heavily accented English. "We suffering like dogs because of cultural prejudice, victims of basic Western hatred of all Eastern influence—deeply racist."

"Let's go to Izzy's drugstore," winces Hernav, fighting a bout of cramps. "See if he'll front us some twos at least."

"Get real," I tell him. "Everybody east of the mountain's been harassing Izzy for days now. I was there this morning. He's put down the gate."

Hernav's face snaps to attention. "Oh, Christ!" he panics. We watch him scramble through the tables and chairs, rush into the can and slam the door. Sandy the waitress suddenly looms over us. She gives the table a cursory wipe.

"Will you tell Hernav not to block up the john again?"

Savva sits up and raises a finger. "I go to steam bath. To cleanse glandular system is possibly helpful."

As we leave, I pound on the men's room door. "Hey, Hernav, management says don't clog the toilet!" A long quavering fart is followed by his high, tortured wail.

Savva nods seriously. "I believe he understand."

Personally, I don't buy the steam bath theory. I've tried it and you end up drained of all toxins. Just what I need—a fresh start. But I do accompany Savva up The Main and crossing Pine, we see Octavio's still AWOL. Hopefully, the dumb fuck isn't taking a phone-book beating in some Champ-de-Mars interrogation cell.

The slight incline going northward feels steep, but it's time to be determined, jaws and sphincters clenched tight. I consider hitting up Al again. Better still if I can catch Mama Polo while he's out, she might take pity on me. Those old moujik bags always have a few twenties wrapped up in a wrinkled hankie pinned to their girdles.

Across four lanes of traffic we see one of Tony's regulars, big Cro-Magnon browed Ruthie, getting rousted outside the Rossy's Discount, no doubt for shoplifting. Some sales geeks and geekettes are frisking her up against a parked car. Savva goes to step off the curb, but I grab his arm. "Where the hell are you going?"

"Lotta Continua!" he shouts, fist raised.

The Rossy's goons glare across The Main at us. "Stop that!" I say and pull him along. "We'll end up hanging from the same lamppost."

Getting to Manoir de Polo, I press the bell and hear his old mother yammer in Lithuanian. Al shouts something back. Fuck, he's home. His silhouette appears through the doily curtain as he comes down the hall and opens up. Al's head is wrapped in a pair of giant bug-eye sunglasses. He wears a ratty silk bathrobe over street clothes, his few pale hairs stuck out sideways. He mutters something and retreats down the hall.

I follow him into the rear parlor, stuffed with every kind of figurine and candy dish, bawling Virgin Marys all over the mantle. The house smells of boiled cabbage and an old woman's drawers. The kitchen door opens a crack and a pair of myopic eyes peek out.

"Alfonsus?" his mother pleads and burbles something in their tongue.

Al grumbles a few words then grabs the knob and pulls it shut. He painfully eases himself into a lumpy old wingback and pours out a few fingers of something that resembles diabetic urine.

"What the hell are you drinking?"

"I'm not even sure anymore." He takes a sip, eyes screwed shut and forces it down. "It's purported to be some sort of peach liqueur. One of the primates at the Bar Saint-Laurent manufactures it. Three dollars per half gallon, on credit. Which means, no, I don't have any more money for your disgusting habits—and neither does Mama."

I pick up the glass and take a whiff. A pungent shoe polish odor makes my head snap back. "Jesus, Al! I know you're an alcoholic and everything but this stuff is poison."

"And what? The toxic scum you ingest is made of twenty-seven different herbs and spices?"

The parlor door slowly opens and Mama Polo pushes in with a tray. Al's arms flop to his sides. "For the love of god…"

"Jooz ant kek for you ant yor frent," Mama smiles. "It is okay, Alfonsus?"

She's a stout little matron, about five feet tall with a bun of white hair and a sweet round face. "Hello, Mister Yonee. Hows are you? You liking jooz ant kek?"

"Yes, thank you, Missus Polo, very nice of you."

Al grunts at her and vaguely waves at the coffee table littered with old newspapers and gossip mags. His mother sets down the tray and returns to the door, hands clasped at her waist. He gives her a curt dismissal and she quietly withdraws.

"Why you so hard on her, man? That's your mother. Here she is dying for grandkids and all you can worry about is your fucking Courvoisier habit."

Al eyes me as he twists a cigarette into a black ebony holder. "All right then, darling. How about I get you pregnant?" He lights his smoke. "As I was going to say before your biological alarm clock went off, I've heard from a fairly reliable source that Tony isn't long for the retail trade."

"Yeah, yeah. That's the rumor every time he fucks up and The Man blows a gasket. They'll be playing footsie again soon enough."

"In other words, you and Tony's other clients have once again abused his terms of credit and he's experiencing a severe cash flow crisis. Very loyal of you, Johnny."

"Gimme a break. He shouldn't cut the shit if he expects loyalty. Besides, you gotta tune in to the big picture, Al. Y'know, the global perspective."

"Oh, really? And I suppose you're going to fill me in?" He settles back, glad I'm winding up for a bit of absurd distraction, get his mind off the DTs for a few minutes.

"It's obvious. Somewhere in the Middle East right this second a CIA station chief stares at a map of the world. Next to him is some bearded towelhead, right? So this JJ Angleton intelligence character just stands there and ponders the map, little red pins stuck in all these big Western cities. After a minute, the Arab says to him: 'Tell your Ivy League faggots back in the Beltway the West will not receive one more grain of product until the 4.6 trillion you owe is in the Brunei account. No more FRONTS!'

Of course the CIA moron—an alcoholic ex-quarterback—he shits his Brooks Brothers suit. 'C'mon, Sharif! We gotta have the stuff! Otherwise, there's gonna be pump action madness, cities in flames—the coons, the spics, the slopes, the faggots, the malcontents. You don't realize how heavy this is!'

'Silence!' the Arab screams at him. 'I warned you and your Langley sodomites not to dilute the product or risk a tidal wave of defaulting accounts! Now you have reaped what you have sewn, Anglo-Saxon fools! You have until midnight tomorrow. Lucky for you this is a holy day, Sahib.'

So this CIA jack-off—he paces around, wonders what the hell to do, right? 'In the '70s' he bitches, 'they had us strapped over an oil barrel, ass wide open. Now *this*, the fucking Saracen cocksuckers!'"

"Nice theory," Al nods. "It may just play out that way, depending on how badly Tony has displeased his master."

"Well, I wouldn't bet real money on it."

"Nevertheless, being an impartial observer, I would only warn you not to fall into the same trap."

"No way. I'd be much more dedicated than Tony, but fuck that, it's a goddamn pipe dream. Any more news on Aunt Byron? How's our oversized she-male adjusting to the dickless life?"

"Shut up, Johnny. Byron has been a woman for some time now, your moronic humor notwithstanding."

"Well, I for one can't wait to see what *she* looks like now."

"*She* is not going to do a strip-and-show just for you."

"Get off it, Polo. You're acting like some jealous boyfriend."

"Nevertheless—"

"Will you stop saying 'nevertheless'?"

"Very well, then. I consider it an act of unsurpassed bravery."

"More like unsurpassed idiocy. Now he's just a guy without a dick. Have you seen Hennessy?"

"Your boyfriend was just here, actually. I understand he's down at Prince Arthur trying to drum up a little rough trade."

I choke down the rest of my cupcake, drain the OJ and stand up. "Okay, I'm going."

Al suddenly breaks into a cold sweat. He wipes his brow with a tattered hanky. I wonder if I should call Poison Control. "My Lord," he coughs and glances at the Virgin Mary wall clock. "Approximately twenty-two hours until cheques arrive."

I pat him on the shoulder. "Hang in there, Alphonse. I'll come by with a decent bottle if me or the Hen can raise any scratch."

He doesn't reply. Reaching the front door, I hear a garbled shriek and the sound of a glass shatter against the wall. Outside, I run into his mother as she sweeps the front steps. The old woman clutches her broom and dredges up a little good cheer.

"Good bye, Meestar Yonee. You are vorking today?"

"Oh, yes. Very much 'vorking.'"

"Alfonsus," she says softly, smile sunk into her wrinkles. "Why Alfonsus no vorking?"

"Alfonsus is sick," I try to console her.

"Alfonsus alway sick."

SIX

After the Outremont humiliation with the quasi-doctor and her spiteful spouse, I'm not too keen on trying to put out, but maybe I can land something easy; a jovial old duffer in a late-model American land barge. A local variant of the British model that puts on the old school tie and kilt, bellows the marching tune of the Queen's 14th Fusilier Guards while I administer a sound thrashing with his favorite cricket bat. *Rathah invigorating, I dare say, what?*

I find Hennessy loitering under the door canopy of a low-rent apartment tower. He's in another version of his torn-up ragamuffin gear, lovely half-caste features faded to a sickly yellow in this drab weather. He puffs on a joint and hands it to me as I pull up next to him.

"Any action?"

"For those two." His eyes spit needles at a pair of suede-colored spic kids that flounce at the stop light. A comely strain of Native-Latino mix with high cheekbones and full mouths, they resemble young Hennessys and toss heads of long black hair, flash deadly white teeth at the passing cars. Playful, over-the-shoulder glances size up makes and models slowing down to browse. I lick my lips. "Oooh, yeah… Paco and Luis. Don't you worry, they'll be snapped up in no time."

"Bloody immigrant labor. They're stealing our jobs—undercutting the market."

"But you've gotta admit, that's some premium candy-coated ass. Not even legal."

A pearl-white coupe dips out of the traffic, stopping beside the two kids. Paco bends from the waist, hands on hips, and greets the driver while Luis keeps an eye on the street. After a brief haggle, they bop round to the passenger side, climb in and the coupe slips back into the stream of cars.

"Okay, they're out of the way," I tell Hennessy. "Go ahead, you've got dibs. And cheer up, for fucksakes."

"Why bother?" he glooms.

"It's all right," I try to coax him, hoping he'll do the heavy lifting for both of us. "We'll score afterwards, then go to my place—play a little monkey-eat-banana. C'mon, whaddaya say?"

He's not having it. "It's only a matter of time. Hordes of these young peasants are showing up to do people's pets for the price of a hot meal."

"Take it easy, will ya? There's still marks that appreciate a senior score."

"Sure, all they want is some conversation, a nice literate prostate massage."

"Jesus Christ, man. You're not even thirty. Imagine how I feel."

"I'm going to try for psych welfare again," he decides. "It pays better than minimum wage."

I leave him slumped against a post and cross the street, hover near a bus stop feeling incredibly foolish. When I look back Hennessy's gone. The rain's begun to fall harder. A half hour goes by without so much as a cursory once over. Dark figures sit behind the wheel. Grim managers in a big hurry, no time for a good stretch done cheap. It'd be sweet to get a woman for a change. Some health club, tanning salon nut in hubby's two-seater. She gets a spontaneous urge to slum and there's Johnny, waving.

This is useless. I'm wet and shivering, drops of cold rain run down the back of my shirt while I give myself a painful hard-on waiting for a centerfold to rescue me. As I'm stewing away, it takes me a moment to notice the shark-nosed Porsche idling at the curb, wipers thumping. When the passenger window glides down, I make my move and instantly recognize the mark. It's that aging ginger-haired hipster who'd tailed the girl in the bookstore last week. Christ, this really is a tiny town. I open the door and get in. He ogles me in a curious way from behind the gold-rimmed John Lennon specs. His thin-lipped little mouth is moist and pink in the middle of a well-kept beard.

"So, what are you up for?" he asks.

"Anything at all," I yawn, sure this old dog doesn't remember me. "My specialty's booting down closet doors. Eighty bucks."

The hipster perv nods thoughtfully and doesn't quibble. He puts the car into gear. "Very well. We'll go to my home. It's nearby. I have a fairly simple proposal." He looks me up and down again. "You seem to be in good condition."

"Yeah, good enough. You need a workout?"

"Of sorts." He veers around a stalled truck and makes a hard right onto Sherbrooke. "I assume you're experienced. There is no time for training."

"Don't worry," I assure him and pull out my cigarettes. "You'll get off just fine."

"Please," he raises a hand. "No smoking in the car."

"Sure thing," I say and light up, blow the first drag in his face.

He turns north on Durocher then goes up to Milton and parks near the bookstore. I wouldn't be surprised to see the girl he'd stalked. She's probably waiting at his place.

"Here we are," says the Perv and leads me around the side of a stately old townhouse. He glances in both directions before slipping in the key then hurries me through the door. "I don't normally do this during the day," he smiles. "I usually find evenings are preferable."

The creep's patter is already getting on my nerves. He sneaks me through the place as if we'll get in trouble with his parents. We go down a richly appointed hallway with refinished Empire furniture and plenty of fussy chachkas. The Perv shows me into a study lined with books, floor to ceiling. Leatherbound sets and yards of paperbacks, binders and oversized litho editions. A big hardwood table covered with hand-written notes and open legal volumes sits on a blue Persian rug. He switches on an antique floor lamp. A pair of wingbacks face an unlit fireplace. The cornball Sherlock Holmes set up. I turn toward him. He's got his tweed sports jacket off and straightens some papers on the table.

"So, what'll it be? Time's sweet, as they say."

"So it is, so it is…" the Perv muses while tapping his chin. "Quite simply, I'd like you to assault me."

"What?" I can hardly believe my luck. "No kidding?"

"No, not at all. As if I've been sitting here hard at work and say… you've broken in. Or perhaps I owe you a significant sum of money. Significant to you, I mean—and since I have avoided payment for too long… Well, the rest is something I'm sure you're quite familiar with."

"You smug little faggot. What the fuck do you know about me?"

"Very good, very good," he blushes.

I'm suffering a fullbore mindfuck, dopamine receptors howling to be filled and this pumped-up shitheel thinks I'm gonna play act his pencil-dick fantasy. I swipe all the papers off the table, fling one of the big-ass law books at his head.

"Wait!" he ducks then reaches for his notes. "I didn't mean that you should-"

"Should what!?" I take a fistful of his shirt. "Should split your fuckin' head open and clean out this dump?"

I smack him across the face, send his glasses flying. He cringes and whimpers; soft, unworked hands try to defend. His craven fear throws me into a wild, fuming spin. An attack of leg spasms makes me wince. "You disgusting old faggot! I'm gonna break your fuckin' balls!"

I drive a knee into his groin and he doubles over with a breathless moan. It's like some ridiculous old wrestling show. I grab what's left of his ragged fringe of orange hair and hurl him into the wingbacks. He sprawls onto the carpet as chairs and knick-knacks tumble. I kick aside little soapstone Inuit hunters, arms and heads snapping off.

"My glasses," the Perv begs. "Could you please help me find my glasses?"

"Yeah, they're right here," I point.

When he reaches for the specs, I stomp on them and catch his fingertips. He yowls with pain. "That's not nice of you," he simpers, curled up against a bookshelf and sucking on the bruised digits.

I heft a gold and white, two-foot tall vase. "Hey, dogshit, what's this thing worth?"

He squints, tries to recognize what I'm holding. "Oh-um—please, that's very rare and—"

I hurl it at him, two handed. It shatters just above his head, leaving him covered in shards. "Even rarer now, pops."

I go over and grab his ear, drag him to the couch. He's going "Ow! Ow!" and hangs onto my wrist lest his ear get torn right off. I sit down to catch my breath with pops at my feet.

"So tell me," I say and squash my smoke onto his bald dome. He lets out a sharp cry while slapping away the embers. "What gives you the cash to have this set up? You somekinda swindler, a shrink maybe? A head fucker, is that it?"

"No—no," he sputters, still rubbing his noggin. "I'm—I'm in the public service."

"Fascinating."

A terrified noise jumps from his throat when I snatch him by the beard. The trembling, freckled hands cling to my fist as he rises off the floor. His fey resistance almost gives me the giggles. "Wha- what are you going to do to me?" he whines. "I didn't intend this to be so—so uncontrolled. I think you'd better-"

"Shut up!" I yell and pull him nose-to-nose. "Why were you following that girl in the bookstore?"

I love the shock in his eyes. "H-How do you know?"

"How do *I* know?" I straight-arm him in the chest. He does an impromptu backward somersault—the gimp athlete showing off. "I know everything about a parasite like you."

The Perv collects himself on his knees, panting with all the exercise. "Then—why *was* I following her?"

"Because you're a spineless old leech who can't handle the sight of ripe young flesh full of ripe young life. You dried-up old bloodsucker, it must make you nuts a babe like her wouldn't piss on you if your hair was on fire. At least not for less than three or four hundred bucks."

Pops approaches cautiously, on his knees. "M-may I fellate you now?"

"No, you may not fellate me now!" I give him a hard boot to the ribs. He groans and collapses, goes fetal, lays there whimpering. "Hey fuckhead, stop feeling sorry for yourself and c'mere."

Face wet with tears, he struggles to all fours and crawls over, flinching as if I might let him have another kick. "Let's see some cash."

Christ, I'm such a bonehead. I almost forgot. It would have been just like Johnny Jerkoff to walk out of here without a dime. Pops slowly pulls out a brown leather wallet. I grab it, count exactly two hundred and five dollars, fold the bills into my shirt pocket and reward him with a solid backhand. He cries out and falls aside. A wave of euphoria rolls over me. I threaten another smack. "Why, I oughta…" He shrinks away, eyes squeezed shut. But really, I'm glad this is winding up. My stamina's had it, dragged down with chest pains. "Listen, Sir Arthur Conan Wasperton the Fourth or whatever the fuck you're called, sorry I didn't use the cat'o'nine tails and iron spike dildo on ya, but I've had better days. Maybe we can do this again sometime. No hard feelings, okay?"

He hiccups in reply. On my way out, I turn and the Perv is suddenly on his feet. He reaches down to right a chair. "You're very good," he says and pulls a protective cup from the crotch of his pants, along with some street-hockey pads from his ribs and chest. "Not the best, certainly, but quite acceptable. Authentic, actually. Real temper. Though, I suppose, like any aging athlete, it's difficult to maintain certain em—standards."

He begins to clean up, collects papers off the floor, whistles a jolly little tune. My hand freezes on the doorknob. A vein of fury rushes up the back of my skull. He takes another pair of glasses from a desk drawer, puts them on and glances at me. "That's all. You may go."

"I may what?!"

I get ready to go another round. This time I'll beat his shriveled old ass for free. The door pushes open. A heavily tanned musclehead with a spiky black crew cut is at attention, fish eyes lowered at me. The Perv smiles at us. "Please show the gentleman out, will you, Antonio?"

"Very good, sir," replies the goon. His big soft lips form a greasy curl. "This way, please."

We pad down the carpeted hallway, Antonio a step behind on my right. At the side door he reaches past and opens it. "See ya round, tough guy. Don't OD on all that cash."

Once outside, I take a close look at the money. It feels real enough. Shit! That freak got right inside my Jones like a malignant breed of Santa Claus. What a technique! He reamed me good and I did all the fucking work. I should come back with a shrapnel grenade. *Hey, Antonio, wanna play a little handball?*

I hit the depanneur down the street and buy three large bottles of decent red. Grabbing a taxi, I stop by Al's house and get the driver to honk half a dozen times. Al finally appears at the door and I hold the booze out the cab window. He takes the bottles with shaky hands then uses one of them to make the sign of the cross and give me a Papal blessing. "Indulgentiam, absolutionem et remissionem."

He turns and goes back inside without another word. I tap the driver on the shoulder and wave a twenty in his face. "Mount Royal and Clark! And step on it!"

The guy burns rubber down to Rachel, hangs a couple of rights then roars up Henri-Julien. I mumble my own prayer that Tony, the useless idiot, has his shit together. Arriving at his place in record time, I don't bother with the anemic elevator and bolt up four flights of stairs, two at a time. Tony swings open his big double doors and I march in, out of breath.

"Ah, the mighty Johnny," he welcomes me. "Enter—only if you have money, that is."

I flash my bills—but his sole visitor stops me short. Fuck me—it's the girl from the bookstore last week, the one the Perv had been stalking. Christ, maybe she really is somehow tied to him. But there's no way she could have followed me or known I was coming here. She eyes me without comment.

Tony's laying on the charm. The studio is cleaned up for a change, but with just enough haphazard junk left lying around to make it seem genuine. His color-crazed paintings are strategically placed here and there to give the maximum casual impression. I take a seat at his big desk and reach for my smokes.

"This is my esteemed colleague, Johnny," he says by way of introduction. "Well, most of the time he's esteemed." Only he laughs. "And this is Morgan, a friend of Warlock's."

She stops chewing her gum. "We're not really friends. I met him at a booze can a while ago."

"I stand corrected," Tony responds with a little dunk of the head.

Geez, him and his gentlemanly act. The fool deserves a big zetz. He's freshly shaven, thick hair combed, eyebrows trimmed and wants me out of here quick so he can continue *The Great Seduction*. But Tony's always had this one major blind spot; no clue when a woman just isn't interested. And if she does show even the vaguest curiosity, he'll instantly forklift her onto a diamond-encrusted pedestal and smother her feet in kisses and rose petals, worship the very air she breathes, then bellow some operatic heartbreaker about his eternal *amore*. The strange thing is, Tony's not stupid and not a bad looking guy. Well-read, funny, good company—but dumb as a post when it comes to this one thing. He fusses over Morgan, brings her tea, rifles through his little corner kitchenette for some "special cookies."

"Johnny's from Hogtown," Tony calls over to us, the ever-gracious host making useless conversation. "It's an amazing city. Have you ever been?"

I don't know what he's talking about. He hates Hogtown. We all do. "Tony," I say. "I gotta go."

He comes back with the goddamn cookies on a plate and sets them down. Morgan ignores his bustling. Tony resumes his seat and takes a sip of tea, making one of those preposterous *bellissimo* gestures with thumb and forefinger pinched together. "Mmm! Excellent blend," he says, then gets down to business. "First, what you owe."

I slap the money onto his desk and he foregoes the Slavic peasant shtick. The bonehead doesn't realize that doing his Shmengie routine might actually make this Morgan girl laugh and relax a bit. Instead, he's going for the slick but sincere drug dealer act. "Now, what else can I help you with, Johnny?"

I lay down more cash. "A quarter GR."

"Ah," he patronizes. "When it rains it pours, eh?" I watch him eyeball the count, being a bit generous to impress Morgan. He dumps the shit onto a small square of paper and folds it up.

One more dumb cliché and I'm going to pull a Don King and beat him to death with a chair. He goes back to his tea then taps me on the leg. "Johnny, don't you think Morgan resembles that beautiful young actress, Jennifer Aniston?"

"No," I say, dead serious. "She's way better looking. That Hollywood hairbag has a chin like Oscar Bonavena."

Morgan rolls her eyes then primps her wild bed-head mane.

Tony lets out a short barking laugh. "Who's Oscar Bonavena?"

"Argentine boxer," I reply, eyes locked on Morgan's. "Shot dead in a Reno cathouse. Ali TKO'd him in the 15th round at Madison Square Garden in 1970."

"Oh," Tony nods, as if this means something to him.

The three of us sit there for a few minutes not saying anything. Tony fidgets, then digs a fat Fidel Castro stogie out of his desk. He lights up the stinker and leans back, thumb hooked into a belt loop like he's Jim Backus or somebody.

"Okay," I say and get to my feet. "See ya later." I turn to Morgan. "Good to meet you."

She doesn't reply.

"Drop by any time," Tony offers. "If you have money! Ha ha!"

I resist slapping the cigar out of his mouth. Twenty minutes go by while I hide up the street behind a parked truck—don't want the Tone to scan out his window and see me hanging around waiting for this Morgan chick, then lay on some future passive-aggressive punishment like cutting my stuff with baby laxative. I figure there's no way she's going to stay much longer, no matter how polite she is, and I'm right. She comes out, chin lowered and catches me sneaking a look from around the truck.

"You're stalking me, right?"

"How'd you guess?"

Morgan looks up Clark Street. "C'mon, we should talk." She takes my arm with the easy gesture of an old girlfriend. "It's funny we've never met at Tony's before. I've been coming by for a few weeks now."

"I guess he's keeping you all to himself."

"The poor guy. He really needs a girlfriend."

"Don't we all."

"Yeah, he mentioned your girlfriend left you." She says it like I've lost a leg.

"She's my wife, not my girlfriend."

Morgan squints, head angled up at me. "Tony said that too. You keep calling her your wife even though she's not. You really want to marry her that bad?"

"It's complicated."

"Isn't it always?"

"Well… I can't say we ever got along that great, but the fights were really intense and—"

"Yeah, yeah, so was the sex. I know the drill; Too bad it has to work that way but nothing good is free. I just don't get the 'wife' hang up. You got kids with her or something?"

"No, but we had a really fucked-up abortion."

"Sounds depressing."

"Yeah, it is. So what's the deal with you and that pervert at the bookstore?"

"There's no deal. Like I told you then, he followed me and waited till I came back out. He's just some creep."

"C'mon, I'm not that stupid. You could kick the shit out of an old fruit like him."

Morgan's not so sure. "Maybe. I just got the feeling he wasn't alone or had mace on him or who fuckin' knows. His vibe was pretty hardcore. Besides, I liked how nervous you got. You were practically shaking."

"That's cuz I thought you were my wife—but my wife from like ten or fifteen years ago, a long time before I knew her. It's hard to explain."

Morgan stops and regards me curiously for a few moments. "Wife schmife, you're just looking for a way to avoid."

"Avoid what?"

"I dunno, a reasonable everyday thing with somebody—a fucking *relationship*. Not that I'd go for that myself—it's totally bogus. But you're one of these guys who gets piney and weepy about shit you really don't want. I think it's called Risk Averse Idealism or something."

"You make me sound like a simpering fag."

She shrugs. "That's not always a bad thing. I mean when it's called for."

"Thanks for the tip…"

"Anyway, from what Tony says you were totally miserable with this wife of yours."

"Yeah… I guess… But it felt kinda legit, y'know. Like a serious thing. You're living with somebody, you go out for groceries together, plan shit, see your families, all that crap."

"Wow. Like a real grown-up and everything."

"Yeah, sorta."

"I can think of better things to do with my time."

"Well, I'd never really lived with a woman before Jane. I mean like a come-home-to-this-one-person kind of living together. Knowing all their shit—good shit, bad shit."

"Yeah, a pipe and slippers to go with the hypes and spoons."

"Okay, so I never got the total hang of how it works. So what, I can still miss it."

"You just miss the idea of the thing—like every other asshole on the planet."

"Christ, you're mouthy."

"It's my job. Don't take it personally."

When we reach the corner of Saint-Joseph, Morgan sticks a pair of fingers in her mouth and lets out an ear-piercing whistle. A taxi slams its brakes right in front of us. She gets in but I hesitate. "Well?" she says from inside the cab. "Are you coming?"

"Should we really do this?"

"Don't worry, Johnny. I don't wanna be your girlfriend."

"No… but should we even get to know each other?"

The driver's head pivots round. He's had it, as if I'm his third birdbrain already today. "Monsieur," he implores, palms together, "s'il vous plaît…"

Morgan glances at him then back to me. "C'mon, Johnny, don't be scared. We'll see, okay? You can always leave."

I get in and she gives the driver her address. He pulls a U-turn, goes a few blocks over to Park Avenue then heads north. The street's packed with traffic, it's damp and stinks of diesel fumes. We sit in silence for a while as the car crawls along.

"How old are you?" Morgan asks.

"Thirty-two. Why?"

"Tony said you were older."

"How much older?"

"He didn't say exactly. Around forty."

"What an asshole. That guy is so desperate he's lying about my age."

She smiles at my pique. "I like Tony. He's honest."

"You just mean he's obvious."

"Now don't you be an asshole."

"At least I didn't tell you he's sixty or something. Did you believe him when he said I was forty?"

Morgan's shoulders slump. "God, you're conceited. No, I didn't believe him."

"Why not?"

"I dunno. Forty-year-old guys are usually less screwed up than you—or screwed up in a different way."

"How do you know how screwed up I am?"

"You think Tony's obvious?"

"Forget it."

"Yeah, good idea. We're here."

Morgan's apartment is north of the mountain, up near that ancient, beautiful Rivoli burlesque theater turned porno house, turned alt-band venue. Her place is above a boarded-up Chinese restaurant. While she fumbles for the keys, a Greek shopkeeper a few doors down eyes me with the usual smallholder's contempt. A flash of temper makes me want to beat the crying shit out of him. It's a mathematical certainty this aggressive illiterate has been eyeing Morgan's ass since she moved in. Now the little puke's giving me attitude because he pays a few bucks in taxes and doesn't get tail any better than the mustachioed barrel-on-wheels waiting to ambush him at home.

"Don't say anything," Morgan warns, catching the play. "Just get inside."

She opens the door and shoves me through. We go upstairs and Holy Christ—this woman lives in a certified dump! Makes me look like Madame Benoit. It's a minefield of clothes, books, magazines, paintings, drawings, cassettes, rotting pizzas, half-drunk beers, broken furniture, burgeoning ashtrays and hell only knows what else crammed into several rooms. Good thing it's big.

Morgan throws some stuff off a cigarette-burned leopard print couch then makes room on the coffee table. Small talk is stowed, implements readied and medication administered. Within a few minutes we're both slouched back, eyes half-shut and sated as a couple of well-fed cats.

She peels off her black tights then reaches over and takes my hand. "There's something I've got to tell ya."

I get suspicious. "What?"

"The guy at the bookstore…"

"Yeah… what about him?"

"He's a john."

"Fuck, I knew it!"

"You didn't know shit."

"But I was right!"

"You're just naturally paranoid."

I smack my forehead. "I'm such a putz! You used me for some role-playing bullshit, right?"

"Take it easy. He was long gone by the time you and me got to Sherbrooke."

"So why did you bother with all that?"

Morgan lets out a mischievous little snicker. "I guess I'm just cruel. I was kinda getting off on how freaked out you were."

"I wasn't that freaked out."

"Yeah, sure you weren't. Anyway, I only saw him that once and all he did was jerk off in front of me. Easy money, but then he follows me and keeps calling my answering service, leaving these weird messages full of bad poetry. The guy's obsessed."

"Him? The way he lives? I don't believe it."

Now it's Morgan's turn to sit up and take notice. "You fucking whore!" she yells and whacks my leg. "You've been in his place! You met Antonio?"

"Yeah, the bootlicker," I brag. "Your Perv buddy wanted to get smacked around—paid me two bills."

"Any sex?"

"Naw, just our little slapfest. But that was only a mild appetizer. A hard-core vünder-fag like him? He must go to incredible lengths to have his calloused old prostate tickled. I'll bet once things get rolling, he drags out the heavy artillery. Y'know, fires up some Russian Sovremenny Class 300-horse-power body dildo. Within minutes the entire apparatus heats up, hydraulic hoses bulge, drive belts whine, noisy as a battle tank. Foul black smoke belches from the exhaust stack hung out a window and pretty soon some nosy neighbor calls the fire department. So those big jocks boot down your door and find you strapped into this thing with a baboon's head up your ass. Compromising, no?"

Morgan's eyes and mouth are wide open, astonished. She cackles hard, screams and pounds the couch. "What the fuck are you talking about?! You're fucking ridiculous!" We both laugh like fools.

"All right," I say, catching my breath. "I think we can get to know each other."

She kneels next to me, barelegged, laughter still bubbling out of her a bit. I pull her close. She shifts up the black mini and I try to get between her legs, but she puts a hand on my chest. "No, I don't want any cock right now. I get enough of that."

She lays out on the couch and puts a heel on the edge of the coffee table. Her other leg hooks over the back. She smiles and closes her eyes, hands on the inside of those luscious white thighs. I imagine my eyeballs popping out on springs as the crotch of my pants explodes.

I go down on my knees and slowly lick along the ends of her toes, then from arch to heel. She giggles quietly as my mouth slides over her ankle, gradually moves up the curve of her calf, then across that delicate tendon at the side of her knee and really slo-mo up her thigh to loiter for a while at the softest, the awfully softest part, lingering and getting kind of high on her, feel her pubic hair brush against my lips and nose. Morgan nuzzles her ass into the couch, legs inching apart as I hang about here and there, slip downtown with kisses and lewd mutters, dawdle back up. She lets out a warm little sound and I feel her clit harden against my tongue—then taste her sudden, intoxicating spice.

"Tell me about my pussy," she murmurs, eyes shut and grinning to herself.

"Hmm… let's see… It's a good and kind pussy…" I say between licks and kisses and tickles. "A sweet and lovin' pussy… A far-reaching pussy… Oooh… I'd say a brave and passionate pussy… Maybe a loner pussy, but willing to work… A self-starter pussy…"

She grabs my hair, begins to rock against my mouth. "You're right, Johnny… We can get to know each other."

I stop and lay my chin on her pubic bone. "Is this why you brought me here?"

Morgan meets my eyes with a little shrug. "Somebody said you give pretty good head."

"Somebody? What, like somebody in the street?"

"Don't be stupid. I heard about you at Tony's, from a couple of women I ran into there. Don't worry, nobody made a big fucking announcement or anything. One of them just mentioned it in passing."

"What do you mean 'in passing'? What's her name?"

"I don't remember."

"Well, what did she look like, the one who said I give great head? Or did they both say that?"

"One said it, and she said 'pretty good', not 'great'." Morgan pushes my face back down. "Okay, Johnny, I think it's time for you to shut up and concentrate."

Sometime later we're passed out on the couch, naked and entwined when there's a weak rap at the door and a pleading little voice calls Morgan's name. She raises her head a couple inches and listens with an annoyed frown. "For fucksakes…"

"Who the hell is that?"

"It's this broad, Lindy. She's got the mail slot open."

"Who's Lindy?"

"I saw her bummin' change in the Jean Coutu doorway a few days ago and felt sorry for her. So I gave her my address and told her to drop by sometime."

We hear the pathetic injured bird voice again. "Hello? Morgan?"

"You women, always falling for some lost dog."

Morgan sits up and shuffles through the crap on the coffee table, lights a smoke. "Let's wait a few minutes. Maybe she'll go away."

But Lindy doesn't go away. If anything, her calls become more insistent—a tiny, tortured animal squawking for help. Morgan's finally had enough and gets to her feet. "Fuck. I'll let her in for a little while." She digs though a laundry hamper and puts on a long black t-shirt while I get into my pants and shirt, begin to collect our paraphernalia. "Don't bother," she says, going down to open the door. "She's here for a shot."

In a few moments I hear them coming back up, this Lindy character kissing ass. "Thanks so much. It's totally cool of you. Man, I am so fucking sick."

"Yeah," says Morgan, already out of patience. "This is Johnny," she gestures at me as Lindy casts round nervously.

"I'm really sorry for intruding, you guys." She shivers in a flimsy monkey fur jacket, mousy hair hung in her face. Morgan clears off a big red armchair and quickly sets Lindy up with a small shot. I watch the chapped gray hands expertly prepare and draw up the dose, careful not to lose a drop. She suddenly pulls her t-shirt down to the nipples and quickly nails a hardened old vein in her left breast. The sight of the diaphanous, bonerack chest is dramatic as discovering a corpse at the opera. But, you do have to admire Lindy's ludicrous self-respect in the face of looking like she's a foot and a half in the grave, timorous little heart still beating. The old poodle must have been a saucy number a couple decades back. But since then… well, for sure there's a litter of brats left behind, social workers snatching them away before their eyes were open. And guaranteed there's a squad of brain-dead guys in the wreckage, men both feckled and feckless. I give her five minutes tops until we're subjected to her endless tale of woe; all the horrors visited, beatings suffered and privations accepted. Lies and truth garbled beyond recognition from having to con too many cops, counselors and parole bulls.

Used by Satanic morons for sacrificial blood rituals? Mutilated baby corpses scattered far and wide in unmarked graves? Really!? You too!?

SEVEN

Cries of 'Hallelujah!' can be heard from Mount Royal to Rue Saint-Denis. It's finally cheque day and the weekend millionaires are out in force. I go to the Olympic Torch Burger Souvlaki at Rachel and Clark to meet Morgan. I owe her a few packs so I've already been up to see Tony and grabbed for both of us.

The Olympic Torture, as it's known, is your traditional long and narrow spoon, famed for its grease-spill breakfast special. There's a counter with stools along the left side and some decayed red vinyl booths opposite, a few tables scattered in the back. On the wall above the booths is an out-of-perspective mural depicting what I've always assumed to be the owner's village. A big gray vent box near the ceiling has been worked into the painting as some kind of power station beside the village church. At the mural's bottom right-hand corner in large white letters is the artist's name, PETROS, and his phone number.

The owner is a grim-faced peasant, wide gut packed into a dirty apron. Everyone calls him Mister Jimmy. At three in the afternoon the diner's dead empty but for a sleazy little guy perched on one of the stools. He wears a horse-blanket suit and an elaborate comb-over hairdo. He complains loudly in Greek and picks at his ear with a long pinky nail then contemplates the findings. I grab a table in the rear to wait for Morgan.

"What you wanting?" Mister Jimmy asks from behind his cash register.

"Coffee."

The comb-over dude adjusts his nuts while he spins round to glower at me. Mister Jimmy comes over and practically slams the cup and saucer onto the table. "You no eat?"

"I'm waiting for a friend."

He grumbles something and goes back to his post. Of course I don't let on I *speaka their lingo*. No use trying to get chummy with these small business fascists who usually belong to the Hitler-Should-Have-Finished-The-Job school of Jew hating. Once they realize I'm a member of their tribe, they'll turn on the interrogation light and demand to know surname, village of origin and political sympathies.

After the two of them return to their bitching, I unfold the sports section someone left behind and listen in: "As I was saying," Comb-over starts up in his fairly hickish Greek. "This was a country. Now, forget it. They let in every kind of black and Mongol. Anyone's bound to get lost in this chaos. Remember when we came? Remember, Jimmy? The Anglos were still in command. You had to respect the police. Today, the Hebrews and Gauls are in control. It's everywhere, my friend, disease and faggotry running loose."

Mister Jimmy nods sadly while topping up his pal's coffee. "My son," he laments. "Thirty-three and unmarried, spends his days driving around in that car. Powerful enough to drag away a house. Who knows what'll become of him."

"Be grateful you don't have any daughters," Comb-over confides. "We had to send our Soula to Greece to find a husband. Here, she turned into a wild beast, losing her Greek and taking up with a French hoodlum she was ashamed to bring home. Her mother nearly died of grief and worry. I had to listen to it all. 'Your daughter! Your daughter!' Whenever Soula behaved like a mad dog she was my daughter. What didn't we give her? Closets full of clothes, enough shoes for an army of centipedes. We satisfied every whim. Soula wanted dancing? Bring in the Russian swindler with a painted face. Then it was antiques. We filled the house with expensive lumber. Then a car—brand new—and who made the payments? Who worked night and day like a mule? I'd get home exhausted and find them at each other's throats—mother and daughter on the verge of murder." Comb-over wags a finger. "No, you can't have two grown women in a single household. Impossible."

He stops and lights a smoke, sighs at the brazen infamy of it all. "Finally, after our little doll gave up university and wanted to see a psychiatrist, I decided I don't need another thief in my pocket. So I paid Soula off—and Jimmy, let me tell you—she responded to the treatment very well. We bought her a beautiful apartment in a respectable part of Athens. We worry less about her over there, at least she's in Greece. In time she'll settle down and find a suitable husband. My sister lives in the same building and she's got a few good prospects. I don't care what he is—as long as he's Greek."

"One of our Atticans wouldn't be bad," Mister Jimmy allows. "But what if she takes up with a Macedonian, or a Spartan? Or worse, some Thracian savage?"

"What can I do?" Comb-over pleads, hands out. "I'll be glad if she doesn't end up with a Catholic—or an African!"

Mister Jimmy gazes out the window of his dive toward the mountain. "No, Costa. It's not like in our day. Now men are held hostage by wives and daughters, always being threatened with their infidelity and lechery if he doesn't pay up. You lay a hand on them, they'll find ten Jew lawyers who'll take your last dollar and have you thrown in jail."

They lapse into silence after their soliloquies, now somber as pallbearers. I want to say something but there's no point in blowing my cover. Instead, I begin to read about the Canadiens' unlikely playoff run. A commotion suddenly erupts on the sidewalk outside the floor to ceiling window next to my table. It's Al, Tony and the Hen. They're elated with our monthly good fortune; the reassuring news the regime is still solvent. Tony and Hennessy shout happy nonsense. The Tone gives me the cocksuck gesture—a fist pumping at his mouth while he sticks his tongue in and out of his cheek. Hennessy makes a V with his fingers then wags his tongue between them, international sign language for eating pussy. Al stands by and shakes his head at their sheer idiocy, but does concede a slight smile. Playfully jostled, he makes with a drinking gesture to indicate they're going to the liquor store and will stop in on the way back. With a few more noisy huzzahs, the three of them continue down Clark Street.

I return to the Canadiens' scoring summary, but within a few minutes, Vern, aka The Raging Skull, stomps up to my table. Big and angular, his chinless, balding mug is tilted sideways. He sits down and wipes his mouth on the back of a huge, veined hand.

"Been on the trails?" I ask as Mister Jimmy sets a coffee in front of him.

"Down in Hogtown for a month. Quack puts me in detox. My old man paid for a fancy rehab so I can start grad school in the fall. Real fuckin' trip."

"Hogtown or rehab?"

"Both."

"Y'know, Vern, cleaned up you almost seem human—likeable even."

"Don't insult me, J."

"So, how is the straight life?"

He lights one of my smokes then winces and claws at his unshaven jaw. "Got stuck in this group therapy bullshit. I'm not for the holding hands and huggin' thing. Just gets me horny. Anyway, the holy fartcatchers running the place got on my nerves so I went AWOL."

"How long were ya in there?"

"Twenty-seven days."

"So you must be fairly clean."

"Clean enough. Quick reduction cure on valium and some other shit."

"So what," I try to deflate him. "You'll be begging fronts again in no time."

"You oughta know, Johnny. Like Burroughs said-"

"No, not the Burroughs. Please?"

"Yeah, yeah..." Vern peers round the place and eyes a noisy team of over-built secretaries that have commandeered a nearby table. They eat these huge garbage pail salads. A pork-faced monster among them checks us out. "Jesus," Vern scowls. "Blue eye shadow."

"What's wrong with blue eye shadow?"

"Gimme a break. Anyway, look at the size of that ox. Try to pitch her onto a bed and crack—there goes a disc. Next thing ya know, Maria and her big tits are pushing ya down the sidewalk in a wheelchair."

"Will ya keep it down? I come in here all the time."

Vern drains his coffee and raises the empty cup at the Greek. He leans in close and drops his voice. "So…uh… word is Tony's fucked up one too many times and The Man's gonna deep six him for real."

"Yeah, why don't you ask Tony yourself?"

"Still owe that asshole for a front."

"I guess that's why he's in shit with The Man."

"Fuck off. Tony's an oil burner. Shouldn't dance all over the stuff if he expects to get paid."

"Okay, so it's not news," I admit. "He can't handle the responsibility. His screw-ups are putting a serious strain on the whole community."

"No fuckin' kidding. He'd forget what a useless retard he is if it wasn't stamped on his forehead. Guy needs a pager with a goddamn bullhorn on it that screams, 'Hey, STUPID, call the number NOW!—and won't shut up till he does. Some beeping, vibrating little plastic box? Way too subtle for him." Vern studies his empty cup. "So, who ya thinks gonna get the job when The Man finally ditches the ol' Tone?"

"Maybe The Man will hold an election. Better sharpen up your campaign speech."

Vern smiles broadly, shows off those yellow horse teeth. "Too bad The Man's a Neanderthal with no appreciation for the democratic process, eh, Johnny? Anyway, chances are he'll go with whoever's the cleanest and that happens to be me. 'Sides, I already know the business and all the customers. I'm fuckin' perfect."

"Yep, you're a natural," I say as Morgan barges in wearing battered knee-high biker boots, Medusa hair now dyed fire-engine red. She parks herself next to me and pulls through her bag. I make the intros.

"I've heard about you," she says, eyes narrowing at Vern.

He shrugs. "Who hasn't."

I slip her three packs.

"Usual shit?" Vern snoops. "Help out an old friend, Johnny?"

"Gonna remember my kindness, Hassan-i-Sabbah?"

Morgan stops rummaging. "What are you guys talking about?"

"How bad's Tony?" Vern pries.

She's guarded. "Tony's all right. Kind of messed up, but he'll survive."

"Yeah," Vern grunts. "Till The Man beats him to death with his bare hands. No big loss. Tony's ugly with a capital *UG*. Don't want him breedin' with anything."

Morgan squeals with delight, an infectious noise that turns a few heads. For a brief instant her youth rises up, fresh faced and irresistible. "That's pretty loose talk coming from you, gorgeous!"

The snappy comeback gets Vern all revved up. He pulls in his chair and turns serious. "I gotta sit here and look at you? Might as well let ya know. Money. Eileen Ford or any of those places. Walk in. They'll see it too. Go. Just like you are. They love this semi-punk glam bullshit. Get signed up right away. Got ya doing covers and big name spreads in no time. Fashion fags? Drool all over ya."

Morgan gives me a look then turns back to Vern. "So you gonna be my agent, Svengali?" She gets up, bumps him with a swing of her hip then goes toward the can, tools wrapped in a black bandana.

"Shit must be pretty clean," Vern chuffs, goggle-eyed at Morgan's ass. "Hasn't harmed her features any—fuckin' tasty."

"She's young. Her body can take it."

"Yeah… and what a body. But still, no raccoon eyes? She been living in a goddamn greenhouse er what?"

"Vegetarian."

"Oh," he nods then gives me the hairy eyeball. "So, uh… you banged her yet?"

I don't reply and think of Morgan's bed, a lot of cheap candles burned to daylight. Vern gets solemn while staring at the door to the women's toilet. "Chick's right into you, man." He reaches over, fist nudging my chin. "Big cred, J. Big fuckin' cred."

"You haven't been alone with a woman for quite some time, have ya?"

"Can ya tell? Her bod looks nice 'n' tight. Guess it would be if she's only twenty or—"

"Take it easy, will ya? Don't jerk off on my sleeve."

The Greek comes by and pours us more coffee. "You wanting food?"

"Not yet," I say. "Soon."

He frowns at Vern. "You eat?"

"Hm… Wanna make me an egg-white omelet?"

"I no hev."

"Forget it then."

Mister Jimmy goes away with a hostile mutter.

"C'mon," I bug Vern. "Have something."

"Like what?"

"How about a jar of liver?"

"For breakfast?" he plays along.

"Better than no girlfriend at all."

When we get out of the Olympic Torch, Vern goes looking for Tony while Morgan heads off to a life drawing class at Concordia. She's working on her BFA in fits and starts—mostly fits. I walk down to Mario's Duty-Free Depanneur. His tall, lanky brother Harry is behind the counter. They're a pair of Caribbean East Indians and act as neighborhood patrons, bankers, tabkeepers and gossipmongers. Their shop's a rickety jumble of dusty cans, beer fridges and cases of cut-rate toilet paper. Harry's baby-faced but wily, usually wearing a big sassy grin. He's got his feet up, perusing a Carib skin mag. "Whachoo tink?" he asks, letting the center fold fall open.

"I'm not crazy about the big fake boobs—or any kind of giant boobs."

"What's wrong with da big boobies?"

"No, I can appreciate a nice rack as much anybody but personally, I just prefer something a little more proportional."

"No wonda everybody tink you gay."

I hand him some money. "Gimme a carton of Marlies before I buttfuck ya—and take forty clams off my tab."

Harry snorts out a laugh as he gets to his feet and reaches down a trap door in the wall behind him. He wraps the smokes in newspaper, shoves them at me then adjusts my balance in a dog-eared notebook. "Oh, Johnny Johnny," he starts up. "I got me trouble with *le petit functionaire*. The fella come round and want me to pay back taxes!" He makes with a girlie scream and sticks out his ass. "I say to da man, 'Monsieur, I don't play dat way!'"

"Hey, c'mon," I grin while lighting up. "At least the guy's got good taste."

Harry zeroes in on me. "So… what's dis I hear about your Janey leaving you high and dry once more?"

"Christ, not you too." Harry hasn't finished chortling when Warlock minces through the door. "Aw, for fucksakes," I groan. "If it isn't Good News Gideon himself. Got another story about running into my wife?"

"I may. I'm sure I've seen more of her lately than you have."

Harry points a finger-gun at me. "Right through de heart, Johnny. Every time, right through de fucking heart."

EIGHT

I come through the door, pissed off, the phone ringing. I grab it, ready to tear a piece off whoever's calling. "Yeah, what!?"

"Johnny…" croons The Man. "How's Johnny the Carp? Huh, how are ya?"

He softens me up with plenty of warm lubricational vibes. "How am I? I'm ready."

"That's nice. I'm glad you're ready cuz I'm ready for you to be ready. Isn't that nice?"

"It's nice."

"Busy right now, Johnny?"

"Not unless it would be nice for me to be busy right now."

"Can I buy you a drink, Johnny? Would that be nice?"

"Very nice."

The Man abruptly drops the schmooze. "La Cabane in half an hour." He hangs up and I put down the phone, nervous as a young bride. What should I wear? Should I shave?

The story on The Man is despite being dark enough to look like a second-rate Maghrebian greaseball he's actually Polish and his real name is Stary Samobójca. But he gets off on his moniker and Tony even played him the Lou Reed song, but it didn't make much of an impression. "*Nice song. Too bad the guy's a fruit.*" The Man is reportedly connected to the Rock Machine, an upstart bike gang that's been going toe-to-toe with the fearsome Quebec Hells Angels and has actually won a skirmish or two.

The bar's like a morgue in the early evening. I sit in the old section with the ersatz log cabin décor. The waitress approaches all cute and friendly, but I get the sudden urge to do something vulgar—grab her ass. She picks up my low-brow waves and goes cool, sets down the vodka tonic I order from as far as she can reach.

Guaranteed she's a committed girlfriend. Grimly shackled to some introspective mumbler. One more miserable couple fucking through a thick coating of latex and spermicide and rubber kisses and quick-hot-foot-to-the-toilet-before-any-leaks-out. Sentenced to an apartment full of groovy gewgaws that ends up as a standard police blotter scenario after somehow inciting the homicidal rapist tendencies in the quiet guy in the ground floor pad who keeps to himself and isn't any trouble and wouldn't harm a fly and always pays his rent and once gave her boyfriend's car a boost. Aw, Janey, your absence makes the heart grow cankers.

The Man glides in and instantly fathoms my brainless hostility. "Girl trouble?" he asks, taking a seat. The barmaid seems reassured by his appearance. Big, clean-cut and obviously lethal if necessary, but otherwise polite and a pleasure to serve—and maybe he's brought along my muzzle. She smells an excellent tipper and sways her darling ass over to us as if The Man sits alone. He may dress like a Park Ex thug done good, but The Man's not some big-mouth Gino who'll snap his fingers and yell for attention. No, The Man can even handle non-heteros—such as the one working behind the bar, wearing colorful eye make-up.

"Hey, buddy, nice dress," he mutters through his smile after sending the girl off with an order for bottled beer.

"You may like to know," I tell him, "there's a big difference between being gay and committing a homosexual act."

"I know one thing," The Man grins a mile wide. "As long as there's assholes, there's gonna be queers." And with that he shifts gears, folds his big paws on the table and hunches forward. "I've got an idea."

"Oh, yeah?"

"Yeah," he nods happily. "It's an idea about Tony. He started out good when he took over from that cocksucker Aaron after the moron OD'd. Business moved along without missing a beat. You remember."

"Aaron was the pioneer," I reminisce. "He opened up The Main." I think back to when the neighborhood wasn't awash in poison.

"Yeah, right. Everybody forgot about that jack-off ten minutes after he was dead."

"Not exactly. People still mention him."

"Who, the ones that got scabies off the dirty fuck? Anyway, the point is, Tony's lost it, using a ton of the shit himself then cuts it with goddamn vitamins, tellin' me it'll do the customers good!" The Man sits back, exasperated. "Like holy fuck!"

The waitress returns with his beer and he instantly lays on the sugar. "Merci, mon cher."

She smiles shyly then actually looks over her shoulder at the goon while walking away. I guess for someone like this Kamouraska hayseed, The Man exudes nothing but cash and class.

"So you and me," he goes on. "Us—together—we're gonna keep all of Tony's good customers from going to other players, right?"

"Uh, my wife... She... uh-"

"Your wife? What's your wife got to do with any of this? You tellin' me you'd rather play house than make money?" He brings his face right up to mine. "Or you gotta clear everything with your wife like you're some little pussy faggot? Anyway, didn't she dump your ass?"

I look out the window then back to him. "Naw, my wife—well... Forget it. You're right, I'm in. It'll be a piece of cake."

"You sure? I figured you to be half a step up from these other mooches."

"Fuck yeah. We'll straighten this shit right out."

The Man sips his beer and studies me for a few moments with those bugged-out eyes then puts a Russian Roulette finger to his temple. "Now, to be totally clear, if you, Johnny—if Johnny gets smart and tries to rip me off, I-will-fuck-you-DEAD." His generous smile quickly reappears. He lays a pager on the table, and a sheet of paper with a bunch of names and numbers. "Okay, at the top here—that's the new pager number." He points at the list of customers. "These are the good people. Call and let them know things'll be working again after ten tonight. Give 'em the new number and say everything's gonna be great and no more Tony bullshit."

I pick up the little black rectangular box and press the button on top. The personal code of the most recent caller shows on the read-out. "Can this be traced?"

"No, it's a pirate." He leans back, grinning at me. "So, Johnny, we're partners now. I'm even gonna cancel your debt. Isn't that nice?"

Butterflies flap around my guts. "Yeah, very nice."

The Man chuckles and thumps my arm. "Don't worry, buddy. The bottom line is customer service. Don't be ignorant with people, don't make them wait too long and don't burn 'em." He whips out a cell phone, pulls up the antenna with his teeth and flips it open. "Okay, I'm calling the pager."

"Fuck, that thing's pretty small. No more Maxwell Smart shoe-phone, eh?"

"I got it in New York," he brags while entering the digits. "Just came out a couple weeks ago." In a few moments the pager buzzes and his number appears. "All right, memorize that then erase the fuck out of it." The Man stands up and leaves some money on the table. He glances about and checks his watch. "I gotta go reload. I'll call you around nine and we'll get started. Phone those people on the sheet then burn it." He sticks out his hand and we shake. "Oh," he remembers and slips me a small baggie. "Here's a starter bonus—on the house. It's the new stuff, uncut—so don't go apeshit."

It looks to be just over a gram—a sweet little bundle.

As nightfall comes on, The Man struts out and the bar begins to fill with the dinner crowd, ordering La Cabane's famous mussels & draft beer special. I go into the can and do a shot then hit the pay phone with a bunch of quarters. I nod out pretty hard for a couple minutes with my head against the wall. Man 'o' Manischewitz, this shit's gonna have some serious fans. Starting on the list of regulars, of course there's plenty of bleating and lowing when I explain the situation; that normal operations won't resume until approximately ten o'clock this evening.

Regrettably, Sir/Madam, this temporary suspension of service is unavoidable. After our—ahem—recent corporate restructuring, there will be a general tightening of credit, no more deficit financing on the backs of reputable clients such as yourself. No more here take this discman and my leather jacket and I'll be back in an hour with the cash for sure man please c'mon you gotta help me out.

All right, but not just the discman and the jacket. You can also leave your shirt, pants, shoes, house keys, cigarettes, the gum in your mouth and then fine, okay, see you in an hour.

I ease fears and offer repeated reassurances that each of them will be the first I'll phone when the tap's turned back on. Some threaten to go elsewhere, but the promise of uncut bliss convinces almost all to husband their resources and wait it out. A woman known as the Sphinx is the final check mark on the list. Mysterious as hell, she actually calms my nerves. Tony said she never raises her voice, never a cross word or unreasonable demand. She makes a Zen master seem like a jabbering nervous wreck.

Coming out to the front of the bar, I see Slim wander in with her latest dudeski. He's a rebuilt musicologist gone urban cool. His name's Bob, of all things, a vested yokel that's grown a little phony-tail. I've heard he's on a first name basis with the chief door apes at the hottest clubs. He takes Slim along as an all-access pass to private album launch parties and exclusive interviews with taciturn, ego-heavy art rockers. Bob works hard. He maneuvers to get caught in candid magazine shots with Slim on his arm.

And she sure does wash up well, an effortless switch from old and busted jeans to raw-edged sophistication in her little black dress—the elegant jawline, the white-blonde hair and fiery green eyes—she requires no cosmetics. Slim sits at the bar while Bob takes a table with the rapidly ascending Dred Blanc, rag-headed leader of *The Fuss*. Bob will collect incisive quotes and awe-inspiring anecdotes then spiel long and earnest in Montreal's weekly alternative paper, *The Mirror*.

I go over and join Slim. "So, how's it going with Bobbo? Charity drive winding down or what?"

She gives me a lopsided smirk. "Shut up, Johnny."

"I'm taking over from Tony."

"Way to go," she deadpans. "When's this supposed to happen?"

"Right now. I've got a nice sample—uncut."

That makes her swivel round and shove a knee between my thighs. Bob shoots us distracted looks. He can't concentrate on the interview that's supposed to turn into a powerful indictment of the local alt-music scene. I can see the hot vein of doubt wind round his throat. Dred Blanc instantly picks up on it, quickly cuts off Bob's exclusive and goes over to join his band, who sit around drinking shots and beer. I'd seen Slim and Bob on The Main a couple days ago. Bob's worried face had scanned over the shoppers and sidewinders. He'd peered up the street as if there was a place they could go where Slim would wear his license plate, but she'd only lanked along beside him, not doing anything to prove he was more than random.

He shuffles over to us, hangdog, grumbles something to Slim with an aggressive whisper then goes off to try to exercise damage control with Dred and his crew. After a minute, Slim tugs on my arm. "C'mon, let's go."

I'd bet serious money once we left, Bob looked around from his intense one-on-one with *The Fuss* and was gutted to see the two empty bar stools. After-action reports will verify he pulled a face while Dred and his band half-sung, half-talked a sneering, off-key version of *Slip Slidin' Away*. Bobbo's street cred is instantly napalmed. *Okay, you, back to covering the environment beat.* He eventually works up the nerve to demand answers and storms across the street. Slim's got my cock in her hand when we hear the door buzzer go off repeatedly with long angry bursts. I look up. "What the fuck…"

"Just ignore him."

Bob starts to pound. *Bam Bam Bam.* Then silence. He'll scramble into the overgrown lot behind Schwartz's Deli just in time to see Slim's light go out. Without the sheer stupid bollocks to boot down doors or come up the fire escape, Bob returns to the bar to drink and stew and occasionally gaze up at Slim's attic. He runs through everything he'll tell her, all the razor sharp afterthoughts that would cut her to the quick if she actually gave a shit.

Slim wriggles out of her dress, the best piece of clothing she owns, and carefully puts it on a padded hanger. Underneath she wears nothing but panties. No lacy bra or silk stockings or frilly garters or any of that shit is necessary. She looks down and examines the length of her body with a shrewd appraiser's eye, judging the minutes that drag along the flesh, indomitable force of gravity working on anything left alive. She once told me her few stretch marks are from taking the pill too young.

She's descended from Scottish jailbirds given a new lease on life in the colonies to go forth and build the suburbs from whence their willful daughters may emerge. Leaving home, she took along a memento of finding Pops alone in the midnight basement, pants around his ankles, old fleshtone magazine held at his belly; part of the collection he'd thought so well hidden, never to suspect she'd added a headless shot of her own body.

She sat at her teenage vanity table and studied the adolescent breasts in the mirror, worried about her thin lips and limp blonde hair and regretted never seeing the desperate shadowy men her step-mother had warned were right outside the window in the empty fields across the road, the step-mom who'd forced to her to use a pad instead of a tampon.

Her main indictable offense was reading too much and correcting inane and erroneous statements made at the dinner table. This resulted in ultimatums that would mean no more speechless meals of canned ham, rice-a-roni and re-runs of *The Tommy Hunter Show*. There would be no more five dollars in an unsigned greeting card for coming home with straight A's. No more grounded for six weeks at a time for crimes never even considered, to lie in her room, endlessly jerk off and wonder about those desperate shadowy men. Now, a decade after crossing the river to the Open City, she still has no trouble coming. It's what to do with the guy afterwards.

Slim slides off her panties and squats next to me on the bed. I chuckle at Bobbo's dramatics. "That guy's probably crying at the bottom of your stairs right now."

She exhales hard. "Bob's ridiculous. He thinks I'm orgasmic because of him."

"So what are you gonna do with the poor slob?"

"I dunno. Too bad he can't relax, he's got a nice cock on him."

She leans into me, her index finger traces down my chest and finds a small black bruise beside my right nipple. There's a nasty hemorrhage under the skin.

"This one looks new. Is Jane back?"

"No, it's Hennessy's."

She pushes on it to bring up a jolt of pain. "Must have really hurt."

Slim moves on and gravitates to her favorite scar, the one running down my ribs. "Hi there," she murmurs and begins to nip and bite and tear open the scab.

Afterwards, we're sitting in her kitchen, pretty much naked and drinking beer, cruising on a good, clean nod, bullshitting some more about Bobbo. Even from way in the rear of Slim's apartment, we can hear the over-loud, booze- and drug-fueled conversations on the sidewalk outside La Cabane and Bar Saint-Laurent across The Main. Mixed with the summer night's traffic, it's a familiar, reassuring noise. But then there's a soft knock at the back door fire escape. Slim squints at the interruption. "Shit. I hope it's not Bob."

She goes to answer and for paranoia's sake, I reach back and pull a big carving knife from the dish drainer. When she opens up, I catch sight of a young guy with curly black hair, acne scars and a scraggly bit of beard, most of it below the jaw line—the hairy chinstrap. He wears a formless blue windbreaker, as if he's here to read a meter. The doofus carries a small bouquet of cheap convenience store flowers. Slim wears nothing but my long-tailed shirt. I've got on exactly one sock, a paint-splattered American Devices t-shirt and her ex-boyfriend's Montreal Royals ballcap.

The guy at the door, his face erupts with stunned elation until he notices me in the background. His mouth turns into a big trembling O. Slim pushes away the proffered flowers with an eviscerating nasal boredom. "I'm busy."

He slowly backpedals. She closes the door and sits down.

"Who is that?"

"Some guy. I met him at one of the bars. I think his name's Gamil."

"Slim, you gotta cool it with the mercy fucks."

She slowly lays her forehead in her palm. "Yeah, I know..."

An hour or so later I get dressed and going out the side door into the laneway, I almost trip over the Chinstrap guy. He's sitting on the stoop and jumps to his feet. "What are you doing?" I confront him. "She's not gonna be too happy with you loitering down here."

"Uh… I, uh, just want to talk to her," he says with a slight Joual accent. "Are you her boyfriend?"

I'm in no mood for this asshole ruining my red letter night. "C'mon, man. She fucked you once or twice. Isn't that enough? If she wants to see you again, she'll find you. Don't stalk her."

"I am not stalking her!"

I poke him in the chest. "You fuck with her and you're fucking with me, tu comprends? So take my advice and piss off."

The guy bridles and jacks himself up, as if he's ready to throw down. "You cannot tell me what to do!"

Now I'm really not in the mood. I slap him, hard. My palm stings. He reels backward and grabs his face with genuine shock. I snatch a dusty wine bottle from a case of empties by the door, smash it against the laneway wall. "Get the fuck away from here and don't come back, you small time piece of shit. I'll slit your fucking throat!"

He glares at me, still hanging onto his precious mug, scoots off then yells back, "You are ignorant! Read Céline, if you can read! Read the quatrains! Nostradamus knows who I am! He wrote about me!"

Oh, he's one of *those* guys. The war-book-reading, Illuminati and UFO-obsessed, Star Trek-loving creep who never got laid in high school and wants the whole fucking world to pay for it.

"Time to go home, Chinstrap! Your boyfriend Hitler's waiting for his blow job!"

He cocks an imaginary pump action shotgun, fires it at me then shouts, "Boom!"

Passing pub crawlers gape and laugh. A taxi idling by playfully honks. I'm tempted to go after him, but he's broken into a trot, already a good thirty feet away. I stamp my foot as if to give chase. Chinstrap jack-rabbits and he's gone, disappearing past a throng of half-cut frat dorks rolling down the sidewalk.

Goddamn Slim, balling these shitheads when she's too drunk and too high to see straight. I've always told her she's far too good looking to screw these lowbrow gomers. They can barely get laid for money, let alone get laid by some total knockout. It literally blows their minds. They become puppy dog psychos and believe her fucking them actually meant something.

After scoping the vicinity for a while to make sure Chinstrap's really gone, I head up to Tony's. Time to check out the results of his grim demise, etc. When I knock on the door, a strangled groan tells me to enter. The place is dark as a mineshaft and rank with the sour stench of bonehead regrets. Some of his paintings have been jammed into the window frames, tinfoil haphazardly taped over any gaps. Tony's curled up under a thin blanket full of burn holes, just another lump among his indoor scrapyard.

"Johnny," he croaks. "You got anything? I'm totally fucked, man." His bushy brows are raised in helpless agony. He's maybe six or seven hours away from apoplectic seizures, when his own guts will crawl out his ass and drag themselves away to die.

"You queered the deal, Tone. People are suffering."

"Yeah, primarily me." He blows his nose into a dirty sock. "The Man's re-organizing and I'm not part of his plans. The sadistic fuck really put the golden sombrero on me. I thought he was showing up to reload, but like a cold kick in the nuts, he takes the pager and says, 'Oh, by the way, you're fired.' I hate these boss-stooge relationships—they're really primitive."

"So who's taking over?"

He shivers and swallows hard. "No idea. So can ya do me anything?"

I'm about to give him a little taste of my sample when something big crawls out of the refuse behind me. Vern the Raging Skull emerges tall, gaunt and barefoot. *Jeezus...* Even just a few days back in the saddle and the guy looks like he was thrown bodily out of a Francis Bacon painting. His face is distorted, arms too long, a scary light coming out his eyes. Still, give him credit. Tony's wholly succumbed to withdrawal sickness—a creaky, blubbering mess, but Vern's made of sterner stuff. He fights off the agony with a visceral hatred. His open hand shoots out at me. "Ya got anything? I'm sick, y'know!"

"I got nothin'," I tell him and watch the long, knotted fingers slowly ball into a fist.

"Then how come you're not sick?"

"Slim got us a quarter," I lie. "Off Benny the Bike Thief."

Vern makes a face like he's caught a passing whiff of dogshit. "Yeah? So why's everybody say it's all fuckin' dry out there?"

"I guess Benny held some back for her. He's one of Slim's biggest fans."

"Well... you'll be sick soon enough. His shit's got no legs. And the bastard wouldn't front me no more—after all I done for him." He looks to Tony. "Hey, dickweed, why doncha stop playing Marat and go find us somethin'?"

Tony lets out a painful screech. "And why don't you get outa my house, you goddamn parasite!"

"Parasite, eh?" Vern stumbles through the gloom to the windows and peels back a piece of tinfoil a few inches. "Man... too bright." A streetlight illuminates his exoskeleton, the corpse he will always be. "Fuck... Nobody ever gives me nothin'." He pushes back the foil and returns, sour breath in my face. "You gotta smoke?"

I hold up my half-gone cigarette. "Just this."

"Gimme a drag."

I hand it to him. "All yours. Enjoy."

Vern's face glows orange as he takes a long haul. "So, who ya think's gonna be the new Man's man?"

"Not you!" Tony yells from his bed.

"Good question," I reply. "You tried calling the pager?"

Vern fakes a yawn. "Yeah, a few times. Still off the air. Guess he re-organizing. I'll call him later, see what's up."

"Go stick your head back up your ass!" Tony sobs. "You have to do it, Johnny! This shithead will go power crazy—worse than Pol Pot!"

"Fuck you!" Vern bellows at him. "'S all your fault!"

Tony grits his teeth as an ice-pick-in-the-guts spasm folds him in half. He throws up some bile into a plastic bag. "Oh, sweet baby raping Jesus.

Do it, Johnny! Nobody else. I know I screwed up, but remember how good I've been to you…"

Vern dismisses Tony's throes. "Guy's hysterical. How 'bout you and me, J? Approach The Man together. Partners, split hours, pressure, cover for each other. Teamwork."

"That'd be up to The Man. Why don't you have a chat with him and see what he says?"

"Yeah…" Vern stalls, searching for another tack. "You know him a bit better than me. He'd listen to you more."

"Okay," I say and throw him a curve. "You got his phone number?"

"Lost it," he parries. "Tony's got it, doncha, brother?"

I can feel Vern's fervent hope and prayer, his goal within sight. It must be a monumental struggle to keep sounding casual. Tony's panting very shallow, barely the strength to speak.

"You know I can't give it out. The Man's already fired me. I don't want him hacking my tongue out too. If The Man wants you, he'll find you."

Vern's flummoxed—no moves left. To encourage the disobeying of a direct order from The Man is straight-up suicidal and he knows it. I watch him suppress a boiling rage. His mind seethes, races into brick walls at every turn. He paces to the windows, tugs at his nose then begins to pick through an ashtray full of butts.

I go over and squat next to Tony, push away the sweat drenched hair stuck to his forehead. "You crazy shit. See all the turmoil you've caused?"

"Don't feel sorry for him!" Vern hollers from the other end of the studio. "Feel sorry for me! I didn't make this happen!"

"Listen," I whisper, leaning right up to Tony's ear. "It's a done deal. Get rid of that mooch. I'll be back at ten thirty or so to take care of you."

Tony's eyes fill with tears. "Really?"

"Really." I put a finger to his lips then stand up. "You guys hang tough," I say for Vern's benefit. "Things should be back on line soon."

"Yeah, thanks for the positive vibes," he gripes, his plans for world domination down the crapper. Going out the door, I wink at Tony. He gives me a weak smile then disappears under his blanket to count the moments.

I go south on The Main and cutting through Portugal Square, there's a pair of fat-looking northern vultures perched on the small gazebo. They tear at the bloody remains of a pigeon—a quick snack on their way to a summer of fun up in Ungava. Hennessy and his sugar momma Heidi appear at the edge of the square, coming north. She's a bitter, middle-aged harpy with a bad frizzy blonde dye job and these big stupid glasses. The Hen looks drawn and quartered. Heidi practically drags him up the sidewalk. He falls into my arms, a complete ruin, barely able to cough my name. "Johnny... Nobody's around and I can't find Benny... and Tony doesn't—"

"I've taken over from Tony. C'mon, I'll do you a taste right now."

He bursts into tears. Heidi's disgusted, armed crossed, completely fed up. Her chin gestures across the street. "Let's go into the Peanut Bar. I'll have a drink."

Helping the Hen into the can, I explain my little tête-à-tête with The Man while setting things up. Hennessy's so sick I have to play nurse and give him his shot before lining up a small whack for myself. And no matter how many times you witness it, the transformation is always astounding. The way someone goes from warmed over cadaver to slick and animated funster just a few seconds after the plunger goes down. Hennessy wraps his arms around me after we finish. He grabs my ass with both hands and grins madly, his saucy good looks now fully recovered.

"This is going to be so wonderfully wonderful," he chirps. "I just knew The Man would choose you."

He makes me blush. "No you didn't."

The Hen kisses my chin. "Of course I did."

When we go back out, Heidi's at the bar, drinking red wine. "Feeling better?" she sneers.

"Much," replies Hennessy, holding my hand in both of his.

"Lord," she groans. "Why don't you two just get married and move to the suburbs?"

The Hen raises his eyes to mine. "Don't imagine we haven't considered it. Ah... the man of my dreams..."

NINE

The first week after being appointed The Man's new kennel keeper has been a blur. I didn't realize how much running around was involved. No wonder Tony got lazy enough to let everyone come to his place and risk having narcs show up. It's a logistical nightmare, this care and feeding of our pack of mutts, mongrels and just plain old rabids. Although, there is the odd purebred, like Morgan. High-strung but also supremely skilled; she's the Type-A Border Collie of this bunch, able to efficiently corral the wallets of well-to-do wankers by the score.

After it became clear to the whole roster I do indeed begin responding to pager calls at 9 a.m. sharp, it's been an onslaught. I am, as The Man foretold, covering my own use and making money besides. When added to my welfare cheque, I can actually relax a little.

I've just serviced a flurry of midday calls when Psycho Savva Grudtsyn, the Russian Rogue pages several times in rapid succession. Odd since he's not the kind of no-class lowlife to go nuts bugging me. Savva takes his pound of flesh in other ways, like the endless diatribes about his vaunted Slavic roots. *Tragic Rodina! Incomparable Rodina! Ah, the mighty Steppe, Cossacks, the Gulag, Uncle Joe Stalin, twenty million dead, exploding TVs!*

It's the bloody saga that courses through Savva's badly scarred veins. He'll work himself into a torrent of Russian then switch back to broken English and greet visitors with the announcement he's a direct descendant of the original Constructivists. Savva will gesture dramatically at a photo torn from a Costakis catalog and hung in his living room; a black-and-white portrait of a wild-haired animal called Kazimir Malevich. There is no resemblance.

"He is spiritual father of Madison Avenue design principles. Ironic, do you not think, Johnny?"

"Yeah, very."

Ever since I've known Savva he's kept up a writer fraud. He did pen a thin novel entitled *The Return of Frol Skobeev*, published by a small press outside Hogtown. But that was more than two decades ago and there hasn't been a paragraph since. Nevertheless, even in his late forties, going gray and flaccid, Savva claims the writer shtick has been a boon. It's gotten him thousands in grant money, along with countless paid trips, conferences, panels, postings, adjudications and teaching gigs. Besides, he insists it's great for meeting women.

I'm around the corner from his spread above a shoe repair store on Duluth so I don't bother with the call-back. And there he is on his balcony, tracking me with a pair of giant Soviet binoculars. Easy to imagine him in the big fur hat, the greatcoat, AK-47 slung on his shoulder.

"Excellent capitalistic service," he says from the top step after pulling the long cord that runs down the stairwell wall and is hooked to the street-level door latch. It's a gizmo for those who are too lazy to go down and open up themselves. A common enough apparatus in Montreal, I've never seen them anywhere else.

"Johnny, you would be very good kulak."

"Thanks. So where's the fire, Savva? It's not like you to abuse the pager."

"I have excellent reason. Extremely spectacular woman is scheduled to arrive very soon. She will be here"—he checks his wall clock—"in precisely fifteen seconds. Synchronize watches please." Savva yucks at his own joke. "I am funny, no?"

"A real scream."

His big elastic face is lively and animated, long grayish-blonde hair strapped down in a tight ponytail. He's clean shaven for a change and looks pretty dapper in a pressed black suit and tie. "There is something abnormally clean about this woman," he says, as if faced with a baffling mathematical conundrum. "I must make sure she have very intense climax."

"Aw, Savva, you're such a romantic."

"Bah! Romance is for bourgeois."

"Okay, stud. How much you want to spend?"

He pulls out a nicely folded wad of twenties and fifties, hands over a hundred bucks then reacts to my surprise with a devious grin. "I have announcement, Johnny."

"Lay it on me, comrade."

"I have signed publishing contract with big house in Hogtown."

"Get the fuck outta here."

His hand comes down on my neck and massages it as he considers the happy implications. "Yes, Johnny, this publisher is owned by very intelligent, very fashionistic Anglo-Canadian woman. She come to Montreal on business—incredible sexual tension. Unfortunately, she is with husband and I can do nothing at the exact moment. But she send me thousand dollars for royalty advance. Also she help me get more money from government propaganda apparatchiks. Then she tell me I can send many invoice—for expenses."

"What expenses?"

He shrugs. "Pencils, fifty dollar. Paper, one hundred. Hat, one seventy-five. Things I need."

"You need a hat to write?"

"Of course. Yes… very mysterious people, these Canadians. I say to publisher woman, 'Listen, Savva is very honest. I am big addicted narcotics guy for long time, many years.' She only laugh, say nothing. Then she send cheque."

I'm pretty mystified myself. "So why send all this money to some Russian loser in Montreal who hasn't written shit in twenty years?"

"Please, Johnny. Count Lev Nikolayevich Tolstoy, he write *War and Peace* over fifty year period."

"No he didn't."

"Okay, not so long but very long time, I am sure."

"Anyway, Savva, you'd better enjoy the ride while you can. She must be totally hung up on you and in my experience, that doesn't last—especially when there's money involved." I trade him product for cash and watch as he prepares to cook his shot at the kitchen sink. "And go easy with this stuff. It's stronger than the last batch."

"So, tell me. Do you believe one-fifth of gram is adequate for my present purposes?"

"I'd say half that, unless you want to nod out and drool all over this babe you've got coming over. That'll charm the pants off her."

"Ach, women," he bitches. "I cannot believe the things I must do to make woman share my bed." Savva pokes himself in the chest. "This degrades me, Johnny."

He carefully removes his jacket, rolls up a sleeve, then flags a vein in his forearm and drives it home. He waits a few moments, as if listening to a very quiet radio broadcast. "Is good. Yes, is definitely stronger." His pupils f-stop down to almost nothing. Suitably high, Savva dumps his tools into a drawer, wipes blood from the puncture, does up his sleeve and continues with the tirade. "In the West, Johnny, women control everything. Men are nothing—small barking dog. In Russia, women are *women*."

"Aw, geez. Not this again."

"What!? Is true! Russian woman expect man to be *man*. They want he slap them sometime. Not hard. Is more symbolic. Not beat them to the death, but show woman who is man. If he not do this, Russian woman believe guy is ridiculous homosexual." He raises a finger. "I am going to write major political manifesto about this matter."

"No you're not."

"I swear it!"

"Yeah, sure."

"But this is secondary project. First I must complete novel for Hogtown publisher."

"You're not writing any novel."

"I am! Is big indictment of current socio-political conditions with powerful historical subtext."

"Okay then, what's it about?"

"It is about... em... us!" he declares with a wide sweep of his arm. "All of us!"

"All of who?"

"Wake up, Johnny! Famous American poetess whose name escapes me at this moment, she say all reading is now act of subversion, that book is act of subversion."

"'Poetess?' I thought that word went out ages ago."

"Do not be trivial. She is making reference to what Western intelligentsia categorize as 'outsider literature.' There is great media love for all degenerate filth. But do not worry. I will alter all names, dates and location of incident. Savva is not Chekist," he says with finality. "No."

"I'm relieved. So what's this opus going to be called?"

"Ah… it is called…" The doorbell rings before he's forced to think up a title. His eyes open wide. "Is her!" He hustles me out the back stairs. "I am coming now!" Savva sings aloud and rushes toward his date with destiny.

Turning out from the laneway onto Duluth, Al Polo pages. I hit a pay phone across the street. He's grave. "Aunt Byron is scheduled to arrive in just over one hour. Are you prepared?"

"Of course I'm prepared. How's he getting here, jet-powered casket?"

"Shut up, Johnny. Aunt Byron is coming by train—and remember, it's she. Now hurry up and come get me."

When I arrive at Al's, he's waiting in a rocker on the front stoop. He looks like an out-of-work mortician, hidden behind big insect-eye sunglasses. He hauls himself upright and straightens his tattered old cravat. "Hail a cab!"

Still showing a bit of the old drama, Aunt Byron is the absolute final passenger to come up from track level and I barely recognize him—*her*. There's no more sleek urbanite with plenty of jazzy style. She wears earth tones; corduroy pants, a hemp jacket and fucking Birkenstocks. Her look reminds me of those affluent, earth-loving dykes. I don't get why so many sex change cases go from being super-cool fashion plates as men, then after getting their plumbing rearranged, they become hard-bitten shrews who refuse to wear make-up and develop this really gross anti-style. Or going the other way, women get turned into guys and become stupid macho jerks.

Byron's also put on weight that even the six-foot-three frame can't hide. She's developed a fair-sized gut and the strong jawline has been weakened by a thick hammock of double chin, the hawk-like nose now far less defined. Her vibe has turned totally placid, the smart alec quip no longer poised on her lips. Christ, talk about de-balled. I put on my shades and check around to see if I know anyone.

Aunt Byron's tall bulk envelopes Al in a warm embrace and rocks him. After some time they part and look to me with benign smiles. I reluctantly give her an awkward hug and catch a nauseating whiff of sandalwood.

We all know each other from the pre-Developer War days in Hogtown, before Al and I fled to Montreal. Back then I'd been driving cab and hanging out at Norm's Open Kitchen, a rowdy dive on Dundas East. Al manned the midnight-to-dawn counter and Byron was a dandified limo driver who stopped by occasionally. He looked like a 1950s cabaret singer with pomaded hair and a satin-collared smoking jacket. When Norm's wasn't busy, we'd loiter by the cash register and speculate about who really did run the world. Masons in the Kremlin? Anti-Christ in the White House? No shit. These theories bound the three of us. Each new turn of events, whether local, national or global was shoehorned into our overall thesis, forming a complex and interrelated pattern, which of course appears entirely circumstantial to the brainwashed or uninformed.

But things didn't last because they never do. Al got sacked when Norm's was upscaled and I lost my license for repeatedly boozing behind the wheel. Byron vanished, leaving only a trail of rumors; he'd become the international chairman of the Julien Sorel Society, taught exo-psychiatry at the Mount Cashel School of Geloscopy, led the storming of the D.I. Mendeleev Institute, was in prison for intentionally running down a pair of especially irritating clients. After several years of silence, contact was re-established a few months ago when Al began to receive a series of cryptic cards and letters from various locales. Byron had developed some kind of agenda so a reunion was finally arranged.

TEN

I come-to in my bed, undressed, and remember something about Aunt Byron lying next to me. I'm not sure what time it is—really late, I guess. Only a few cars go by outside on Coloniale, headlights running up the wall.

Al Polo had come back here with us after we picked Byron up at the train station. I drank too much of Al's contraband supply of Nikka Taketsuru scotch and hit the floor. I do recall asking Byron why she got the sex change and she kept giving these stupid personal growth clichés. *"It is enough to know that the Being I nourish inside me is the same Being that suffuses every atom of the cosmos."*

I gave up trying to have an adult conversation somewhere around the eighth or ninth scotch. After Al went home, me and Aunt Byron talked about having sex, but I must have conked out. Either that or it's become a repressed memory.

Rolling out of bed, I stumble downstairs and find Aunt B in the kitchen. She's peeling a bowl of golden apples. There's a small tattoo on her hand, on the flesh between thumb and forefinger—the word *Arcanum*. More air-headed conspiracy nonsense, I presume. Her short hair is dyed light brown, with a classic Anne Murray side part. I sit up on the counter, naked, and light a Gitanes Al Polo left behind.

Byron hands me a slice of apple. "You were talking in your sleep."

"Oh, yeah, what was I saying?"

"Something about one of your women."

"Probably a nightmare."

"Don't be glib, Johnny. Dreams are just as important as the waking world."
I look at the ceiling. "Oh, god… not this…"

"Be cynical if you like, but years ago I lived across the hall from a Huron who was out on prison furlough. He told me time in jail is substantially contracted if you maintain a dream journal. One builds on these narratives and returns to them each night. It made his waking hours seem short and inconsequential. It's known as lucid dreaming."

I'm having a hard time taking her mumbo jumbo seriously. "That's all fine and dandy," I rasp, putting on a Newfie squaremouther accent. "But this savage friend a yars, he didna need to pay fur no room and grub while livin' as a guest of good Queen Bess, didee na?"

Byron stops her peeling and gives me a patronizing smile. "You still love to play the good Canadian, don't you? The hard-nosed Maritime graybeard. One of your favorite characters, isn't he?" She gets whimsical and goes back to the apples. Her chin drops, suddenly overcome.

I lay a hand on her shoulder. "C'mon now, darlin', no need to get gloomy. Maybe you'd better cut back on the estrogen."

I get dressed and go out to deal with a bunch of backed-up pager calls. Slim comes over at around three in the morning, hauling some quart bottles of Ville-Emard lager. She kicks off her black flats and tosses me three packs of Camel Lights. I introduce her to Aunt Byron. They barely exchange hellos, both immediately wary. Byron accepts a beer, but refuses any smokes.

Slim sits next to me on the couch, legs slightly apart, purple satin panties beneath a dark gray mini. Byron's eyes waver up and down the inside of her thighs with vague disapproval. There's a long awkward silence as a lead blanket falls over the room. Aunt Byron sits back, forehead damp, eyes now locked on Slim's.

"Whatever happened to key parties?" I laugh stupidly. My own words sound tinny and pre-recorded.

"Key parties?" Byron asks sharply.

"Yeah, I think they peaked in the '70s. Couples arrived at a party and the men would toss their car keys into a big bowl. At the end of the night, the women each grabbed a set of keys at random and went home with the owner. Y'know, 'Swingers.'"

Byron and Slim continue to glare at one another. "Or nudist parties," I go on. "Everyone leaves their clothes at the door. Pretty gross when you think about it. Straight out of an old Playboy magazine cartoon."

I reach out to touch Slim's leg. My hand comes down like an artificial limb. She pushes it away. Aunt Byron stands and stares out the front windows toward the big dumb crucifix lit up on top of Mount Royal. "The mountain is the key," she says, all portentous and dramatic.

I feel a headache coming on. Slim lays on the couch sideways, tuning us out. "The key to what?" I ask.

Byron continues to peer at the mountain then gives me a somber gaze. "*That* will become evident soon enough." It'd be no surprise if horror movie violins started up.

Thankfully, Aunt B soon gathers her stuff and takes a cab to Al Polo's. I lead Slim up to the bedroom. We begin to kiss and touch, but my girl's exhausted from all the beer and drugs and falls asleep, a hand under her cheek. I sit up in bed, stubbornly cling to consciousness. My eyes creep up Slim's long legs, over the reddish-blonde pubic hair and slender hips, along her bony shoulders to the supple throat. I try to get between her thighs.

"Stop it," she crabs and rolls away, trembling a little.

I get up in a huff and pull the duvet over her. Sitting at the bedroom desk, I attempt to read a letter I've been writing to my brother for the past month, doing time in some Florida air-base stockade. But the typewriter seems to float before me, letters distended. Too fucked up to focus, I fiddle with the dial on my cheap transistor radio, the airborne refuge obsolete white men seek out in the middle of the night. I roll along the static and hiss, pass through hysterical sports shows, moron-grade news loops, conspiracy nuts, bible thumpers, depresso golden oldies and vicious call-in hosts.

I zero in on a powerful transmission right down to its source—the shit-brown, nuclear-proof CBC bunker in Montreal's windswept eastern harbor, festooned with aerials and satellite dishes. Some white guy with a deep, educated tenor relates the tale of a notorious medieval Chinese tyrant called

Chou Hsin. He tells listeners Chou knew very well that to be morally exempt you observe and never take part, never get down with the concubine and do the fornicating yourself. A stud is always appointed to perform the actual labor. But that kind of mundane entertainment wouldn't have been enough for a character like Chou. The way the CBC guy tells it, an illiterate serf was dragged in and ordered to perform with a completely life-like object for the amusement and edification of Chou and his court. Hand tooled by master alchemists, the mechanical woman's flesh was warm to the touch. She also came equipped with a mellifluous voice and liquid brown eyes.

Some dirt farmer would leap between the thing's legs, unaware it's a sex toy, convinced he's being allowed to screw one of Chou's favorites. Wary at first, then gradually finding his rhythm, he bangs away proudly, adding little hip swivels and other bodily flourishes, which prompt a few rounds of polite applause. Of course pride turns to stark terror when he's trapped by the machine's loving embrace and hears his own bones crack as fat Chou and his cronies laugh uproariously. The mechanical woman's internal organs are a series of razor-honed gears which lock onto the peasant and spin faster the louder he cries.

The CBC host doesn't explain why he's told listeners this particular anecdote. He simply stops talking and there's a bit of dirgy piano, which fades into a station ID, followed by a weather report.

ELEVEN

There aren't many things worse than being caught in a suffocating nightmare. You can't force yourself to wake up, you dream you've woken, but then bizarre shit happens and you realize you're still asleep. You struggle for the light, moan and roll around, but finally give in and let it play out… forced to watch a redneck auctioneer with a wooden puppet's mouth rattle off meaningless numbers. He holds up a rat-sized creature by its long greasy tail. A reptilian thing, notch-backed, eyeless and limbless, hairless and toothless, but with a muscular forked tongue. A very rare species, it has been bio-engineered to do nothing but slither inside human orifi and induce repeated violent orgasms. If required, it can also secrete semen with a precisely programmable genetic code. Experts predict the creature will one day rule the household pet industry…

I'm finally knocked to daylight by the insistent buzz of the pager. I sit up and shake my head to get away from that hideous auction, voices still echoing. Jeezus… what the fuck is going on back there in the ol' hippocampus?

The alarm clock says 8:06 a.m. Slim's already out of bed. I yell her name but there is no reply—probably had to make an early class or get to one of her jobs. The first page of the day comes in bright and early. Crimson—a forty-year-old S/M warhorse Morgan introduced me to a while ago. When I call Crimson at her Griffintown torture chamber, she picks up at half a ring. "C'mon, Johnny," she harangues. "I'm getting sick, fuck. I'll pay for your cab. Just get down here—now!"

The torture chamber fronts as a sex toy shop on a deserted stretch of Wellington, across the road from where the Lachine Canal is blocked up at the old port. No sign identifies the premises and the window is blacked out. There's supposed to be a fully equipped, state-of-the-art dungeon in the basement. The moment I reach for the shop door, Crimson pulls it open and scans the street. She's already in costume, wearing a platinum wig and a skin-tight black PVC body suit, which shows off her skinny-with-big-tits figure—a kind of depraved Mamie Van Doren.

"You always open this early?"

"Welcome to the working world, Johnny. We're booked solid every day, right from six a.m. on."

The walls are spray-painted silver and black while the product racks display all manner of harnesses and appliances of agony whose purposes I can mostly just guess at. I pick up an item off a shelf. It's a two foot long rubber strap with an oblong bag at one end.

"What *is* this?"

Crimson looks up from counting her money. "A rat stuffer."

"A rat stuffer?"

"Yeah," she says impatiently then rattles off a monotone straight out of the manufacturer's brochure. "A live rat has its snout and paws bound. It is then zipped up in the pouch. The user has their anus lubricated and the bagged rat is inserted into the rectum. The user experiences highly orgasmic stimulation as the suffocating rat struggles wildly and goes into its death throes." She hands me the cash. "Here, one-eighty plus ten for the cab."

I carefully lay the rat stuffer back on its shelf. "Very inventive." I drop half a gram in her hand. "This is new stuff, Crimson, so go easy. I mean it."

"Yeah, it'd be great if you did."

"I'm serious."

"Sure you are. Do me a favor and stand behind the counter for a minute, will ya? If anyone shows up, tell them I'll be out in a second."

I take up my post as she disappears into the rear. Within a few minutes, Kate, Crimson's partner-in-sadism, rushes in the door, eyes still a bit puffy with sleep. She's delighted to see me.

"Johnny! Everything cool?"

"Freezing. Your co-mistress has it. I told her this stuff's stronger but go check, will ya? I don't want her going under on my shit."

"A dope hog like her? Get real. Listen, my first guy should be here soon." She comes around the counter and opens a big, leatherbound appointment book. You would expect the notations to be written in blood. "This one," Kate shows me. "Mister Konrad Schein. Tell him I'll be out in a moment, but don't come get me. He likes to be kept waiting. And if you're up to it, run his card. If I don't handle the money, it makes the fantasy thing better and he gives me a bigger tip. It's three-fifty, plus thirteen percent sales tax— so three ninety-five and change—but just make it four-hundred on the nose, that's what I do. Oh, and phone in the card first. We've had a few bounces lately. The number's right here." She points to a sticker on the card swiper.

"Who are all these characters? Mister Omar Khayyam Ravenhurst? Are you kidding? Mister Indole Ringh?"

"They're fake names for some major bigshots." She lays a grave look on me. "We could bring down the fucking government, Johnny."

"The old Profumo routine, eh?"

"Perfumo?"

"Nevermind. Go get strapped in."

Kate heads into the back lair and I hear the two of them gab from the bowels of the place before she shuts the door. A middle-aged, blue-suited clone appears at the appointed time. The guy quietly slides in but is instantly suspicious, wary of a vice squad sting designed to screw him out of the fortune he's going to make while chairing the newly struck Royal Commission on Page Counting.

"Ah, you must be Monsieur Schein," I say, my finger on his name.

"Is Maîtresse Katerina in?" he inquires nervously, eyebrows bobbing.

"Of course, Monsieur. The Maîtresse shall be out momentarily. However, she requested I see to the—ahem—*récompense* before your appointment."

"Mai oui." He takes out his wallet and lays a gold credit card on the counter.

"One moment, Monsieur, while I verify the amount."

The suit tries to restrain his surprise. A bead of sweat crawls down the middle of his forehead. "But there has never been a problem before."

"A new policy, I'm afraid. It will only take a moment."

He sucks in an anxious breath while I call the card company and give the operator the number and total amount. I notice him claw at his shirt collar. This guy's strangulation habit must be getting pretty severe. If four bills is stressing out a money-toad like him, he should go back to random blow jobs in subway toilets.

The guy's eyes are riveted on the phone as the reply takes a good long while. His lips begin to quiver. I wouldn't be surprised if he suddenly pissed himself and began shrieking hysterically. The operator finally comes back on to tell me all's well.

"Very good, sir," I smile politely. He almost faints with relief. After making up the credit slip, I push it toward him. "Sign here, please."

Kate appears a few moments later, done up in all her full-blown patent spiked Vampirella glory. "Ah, Monsieur…" she hisses.

The suit breaks into a genuine schoolboy leer, his mug flushed red. "Bon jour, Maîtresse," he grovels, wringing his hands.

She looks at me, pupils pinned, a faint approving smile creases the edges of her midnight blue lipstick. "Has everything been taken care of, John?"

I give her a solemn bow. "As you had ordered, Mistress."

"Thank you," she replies then slowly crooks a forefinger at her client. "This way, s'il vous plaît."

The clone thanks me profusely and follows her into the dark recesses for their unspeakable congress, etcetera etcetera. After they're gone, Crimson teeters out on chunky six-inch platforms. She's bathed in a dazed glow. "Fuck, Johnny, you weren't just talking horseshit for a change. I couldn't beat a pillow right now. Thanks for filling in."

"No probs. Here's that suit's credit slip."

"You ran a check on his card, right?"

"Yeah. How much does he spend in here? I think the guy's down to bus fare."

"About six or seven hundred a week."

"Jesus! This is a fucking gold mine. Better than dealing drugs."

"I know," she grins. "Just as addictive and pretty much legal." But then Crimson looks around the shop and the realities of running a small business drag her back down to earth. "Still—you don't have our overhead. We spent a fortune to get this place up and running, and we haven't finished paying off the business loan. We had to get heavy duty drainage, ventilation, sound proofing. Everything is stainless steel and custom built—really expensive. You don't get this stuff at Canadian Tire, y'know. Then there's permits, inspections, taxes, bribes." She bites her lip and sighs heavily. "No, it's not easy." A terrific thumping starts up from the basement, like a giant printing press run amok. Crimson listens to the noise. "Oh, no, not that again. It's the recirculation pump. The plumber told us the automatic models are a bad design, but you've got to have all the latest gadgets for these hoity-toity clients." The noise stops. "Hm... maybe it's all right." She grabs a rolodex from under the counter. "I'd better call the contractor, just in case. Don't want a day's worth of stuff backing up." She winks at me. "But there is a certain federal magistrate who'd pay top dollar to roll around in that kind of thing."

The image makes me queasy. "I think I'll stick to selling drugs. This is way too much work."

Crimson gives me a weary shrug. "Meh, it's a living."

I take the Metro back uptown, then the Park Avenue bus. Getting off at Duluth, I pass Bill Dodge's tiny bookstore and notice photos of some Canadian authors displayed in the window, along with copies of their novels. One of them is Elizabeth Smart. Even in this black-and-white shot of her as an older woman, she has that lascivious glint in her eye. I'd met her a few years ago, when she was in her early seventies, a few months before she'd passed away. The fact we never had the torrid, life-altering affair I've so often fantasized about has been a bitter and enduring source of regret.

As I move on, Larry the Poet turns out of an alleyway, followed by his wife, Allie pushing a pram. The baby in it has a mug like Winston Churchill. Larry the Poet is also known as Larry Priapus, actual name: Lawrence Stugatz. Word has it he's the owner of a notoriously large organ, but it's left him deeply embittered. He's been heard to cry: *They never love me for ME!*

We'd hung around for a while when I first came to Montreal, but fell out after he finagled a big Canada Council grant to launch a literary mag called *Northern Echoes*. The whole thing became too depressing to even know the guy. On the cover of the first and only issue was a drawing of some lonely, bent-over pine tree coming out of a solitary rock, the usual pristine Canadian lake in the background. Inside, the mag was ninety-five percent glossy white-space, with a pointless, four or five line poem on each page.

Larry latches onto my sleeve. "Johnny, how ya been?"

"All right."

He points at the bookstore window. "I'm gonna be in there soon. I've got a lotta new material. I'm going hardcore." He reaches inside his dingy green blazer and pulls out a crumpled paper bag covered in scribbles. "I have this incredible idea, man. I'm gonna take pictures of these poems, right? In their original form—y'know, written on bags, napkins, coasters, whatever—then print them, as is, on each page. Brilliant, right?"

"Yeah, genius."

Larry licks his chops, the bag clutched in both fists. "'kay, you listening?"

"Yeah, let's hear it."

He stands straight. "'Kay, it's called *Homage to the Annettes*. Y'know, Al Purdy's old stuff."

"I remember. Go on."

"'kay… My momma was a GASH!" he yells.

"I hate her cuz I know how!

It's not a story we like to tell.

My girlyfriend's just a gash.

OH, BABY!

So we put out at the end of a cigarette and I give this with gash in mind.

No too stiff no mo.

Honey, I miss ALL the Annettes!"

He looks up at me. "Whaddaya think?"

"Not bad."

"Fuckin' hardcore, eh?" He waves the bag in my face. "I'm writing a whole book."

"Can't wait."

"Yeah, those hacks on the Council—it's gonna blow their fucking minds!"

His wife Allie stands a few yards away, rocking the pram. She's supported the three of them by working as a waitress in all the dumps up and down The Main—and now what? Minor local celebrity as the long-time mate of Larry the Big-Wanged Poet. Her hair is hennaed a vicious burnt umber with gray roots. The wrinkles around her thin lips are ready to splinter. Yet she continues to restrain herself, a lone molecule of maternal pity spent on this post-literate. Larry picks up on it and feels her eyes burn a hole in the back of his neck. He turns in a crouch—the whipped dog reflex.

I wonder if Allie's going to explode in a frenzy of blows and curses and finally curb this love object of hers, this colorful fixture of local street culture she saddled herself with. And by curb, I mean a technique whereby the victim is beaten senseless then thrown to the pavement, has his mouth propped open so he's biting the curb, and is summarily booted in the back of the head. The most recent reports of widespread curbing come from the Thraco-Carpathian civil war. Both sides officially sanctioned this gruesome punishment in flagrant disregard of protesters in New York, London and Paris, who lay on main streets and tied up traffic for miles while biting curbs. Larry's eyes plead for back up, but I quickly move off. I snap my fingers and don't see his horrible, mewling face at my shoulder. The magic works and he soon drops away.

Continuing along Duluth, I catch sight of my Perv trick from the McGill Ghetto. He goes up some stairs and into a rundown apartment near the corner of Saint-Dominique. Paco, one of those young peg boys from lower Park Avenue, is with him. The kid's maybe fourteen or fifteen. His long black hair is tied in a ponytail and he wears a leather jacket covered in cheap chrome studs. The Perv's eyes pass over me without recognition.

Getting home, the rest of Jane's stuff is gone. A few books that were left piled on the floor next to her big lumpy reading chair, some clothes on the hallway hooks.

Okay, fine. Now that you're completely free of me, Jane, you can take all that sound advice and start attending AA meetings, sit in a circle with a bunch of 12-Step losers and memorize everyone's first name. Go ahead, Janey, maybe you can find a nice job in an office, get along with people for a change.

Of course she'll be drawn to some repentant hardcase—the sincere, stupid type who submits to taking the white AA key fob of surrender. And so, the two permanently recovering addicts exchange vows in front of their new friends then celebrate with extra helpings of coffee and cigarettes.

Well, she does have a long history of trying to save all kinds of fuck ups and losers—but only if they meet her exacting standards of victimhood. It's the whole Women's Temperance Union, Little White Mother, Protestant missionary thing. Incredibly condescending at its core, but Jane comes by it honestly. Her people have been morally strong-arming heathens and waste-cases since day one.

Okay, so we gave each other some cache, showed the world I could attract a highfalutin arts community daughter and she could pull a semi-civilized street hustler, then bottle-jacked one another into truly horrific clichés if only to show friends and associates we could move outside our comfort zones.

Trouble is, we began to believe our own propaganda—especially after she took me to her mother's seaside idyll in Terra Nova. It looked good, smelled good; the walking stick and Wellies, a couple dogs romping as we strolled along the private beach, a bit of the ol' affluence wouldn't kill me. Meanwhile, I'd hold up my end by debasing her just enough to allow her poetry to take on a harder, more physical edge, a nice tang of bitter experience.

It was Hennessy who'd pointed out the obvious flaw. Junkies and alcoholics are a lousy mix. The booze expands while the dope contracts and we ended up disgusting ourselves while viciously attacking one another's proclivities.

TWELVE

When things are going smooth, being a small time dealer is pretty okay. The days drift along, kind of the same but not in a bad way. Like on this late afternoon, we lollygag in the ground-floor draft room of the Balmoral Hotel; a three-storey dive on The Main, just south of Avenue des Pins. It's pretty empty, a few drinkers scattered around the place, a pair of teenaged girls play pool.

I'm lounging at a back table with Hennessy and Al Polo, who maintains his pretense by drinking bottled Belgian beer, spiked with shots from a flask of Courvoisier Initiale Extra. The Hen is on the nod, face on his arms. A few of my clients drop by and discreetly pick up their supplies.

Slim's working under the table as a barmaid, handling the early afternoon shift for a while now. It's not a bad little sideline, good tips. She's one of the very few people I know who actually has a job and thinking about it, those I know who do have jobs are all women.

I notice a textbook moujik sitting alone against the far wall—the big, hairy fly in our ointment. He glares at us, boring holes with beetle-browed intensity, a real barnyard animal. I've seen him here before. Let's say his name is Spiro or Gamil or Oleg or Adebayo or Chan or Jose or Guido or Ruslan or whatever the fuck. Same basic species of global hick this country's so good at attracting. Well, it's not like your hip urban intelligentsia from around the world will suddenly decide to immigrate here en masse.

Anyway, I'd estimate the moujik glowering at us is a mid-thirties nephew who arrived in the New World far too late, long after the boom times had come and gone. He's been away from his village for a few years now, but rarely ventures outside a small circle of relatives and compatriots in the city's north end. He works in his uncle's shop, accompanies the woe-ridden aunt to prayer and hangs out at his community's social club. Moujik's relations consider him too ripe to wed any of their clan's fertile young daughters. Instead he's told to settle for one of the unmarried spinsters who still burden the family, but the sight of those over-fed bovines reminds him too much of home. He aches for the exposed women he can scarcely believe really do exist—right here before his very eyes, roaming freely in the streets and bars.

Moujik had seen some of these young witches sitting out on the patio as he passed this place on the Saint-Laurent bus while going home with his aunt after visiting an ailing relative on the South Shore. From then on, he'd go with Aunt Mooka every Sunday and fight for a window seat on the way back. During each return trip northward, Moujik's face and hands were pressed to the glass as the bus went by the Balmoral patio. He'd gawk at the tanned backs and legs, the nipples straining under thin fabric, the smooth faces and curved lips.

In a singular act of will, Moujik ventures to the Balmoral alone, to sit down and order beer. He was elated to find drinks were actually served by these sirens and they were compelled to approach him and ask what he wishes. But it was Slim in particular that threw Moujik into a pit far deeper than anything he'd imagined during his feverish nocturnal longings.

Now, without ever having exchanged anything more than money, Moujik's worried grimace tracks Slim around the room. He suffers flashes of trembling fury whenever she stops to converse with a male customer. Moujik quickly finishes his pitcher and holds up the empty container to signal for another round. Dizzy from guzzling the gassy draft, his guts squirm to finally use the line his quasi-gangster cousin taught him and he carefully repeated over and over. Moujik looks up at Slim as she sets down his beer.

"Heh, leettle seester. What eez happenee?"

"Pardon me?"

"Ah… ah… nothee," replies Moujik, on the verge of fleeing. His tongue is thick, useless. He pushes money across the small table.

"Thanks," Slim murmurs and scoops the cash onto her tray.

As she turns to leave, Moujik goes to grab her by the wrist, but instead tries his mouth once again. "Me boochair," he says and whacks himself on the chest.

Slim stops and gives him a bemused smile. "Sorry, you're a what?"

"Me…" he looks about as if the words might hang within reach. "Me… cut—peeg, cheeken." Moujik's hand rapidly karate chops the tabletop. "Tahk tahk tahk." He grins, mouth hung open.

"That's great," Slim replies and moves away. Moujik's pie-eyed and mesmerized. It's a major victory.

With everyone served, Slim comes over and sits with us. She lights a cigarette and counts her float. She glances at the clock above the door, then at Moujik and mutters to herself. Maybe she wonders where he's from, imagining a sunny land of beaches, seaside cafés with fresh fish and pink sunsets on white plaster. Yeah, sure. Next time Moujik shows up, he'll have his mother and a prime steer in tow. I can see his mind race as he hatches schemes of how to convince Slim to convert to his faith. Patiently teach her enough of his language to show the kinfolk he doesn't need any matchmaking crones to capture a wife in this bleak and hostile land.

Moujik burns to know those green eyes and considers the terrible struggles to come. How he'll chase Slim through smoky dens of licentious filth, his hands still bloody from sacrificing a newborn calf. Tears will stream down Moujik's swarthy cheeks while he beseeches the holiest blood and invokes the wrath of the Patriarchs. He will beg forgiveness from his unforgiving god and drag her back to the tribal hovel.

Moujik's fevered vision stops cold when Slim hangs her arm off my shoulder. His brain seizes when she comes up close and lands a half a kiss on the corner of my mouth. I look across the bar. Moujik is gone, the full pitcher still on his table. A half-smoked cigarette smolders in the ashtray.

At 7 p.m. on the nose Morgan meets me at my place to use the phone. Every Friday around this time she gets her weekly flurry of calls from working stiffs looking to really kick off their weekend. I listen to her say "uh huh, okay" for what seems like a couple hundred times while she talks to a new john who got her message service number off some downtown concierge.

She finally moves beyond "uh huh, okay" and arranges a date, giving the john the haziest idea of who, what, where. I can barely understand her instructions and I'm in the same room. It's like some strange control mechanism—keep the trick off balance. I've asked her if it's the best business practice. She replied: "It's not like there's a shortage of these guys."

And there are indeed plenty of stories, movies, plays, skits, songs, jokes and urban myths about this kind of disaster. Usually it's some business gimp who couldn't normally find his ass with both hands, a pathetic attempt to fulfill a crappy old fantasy he's had since high school. But he ends up at the wrong hotel, wrong time. He lays down on the bed to wait for her and drifts off…

Suddenly wakes up to being smothered in the curtained blackness, panicked clawing at the bulks of two grunting thugs as their big mitts crush the pillow into his face until the struggling ceases and the muted cries die off. The miserable whining of his fat, teenaged daughter the last thing he hears before being dropped down a blind, airless well, absurd final regret he didn't book the bridal suite.

It's a perverse case of mistaken identity, the rain having smudged the hotel's name, hastily jotted down by a barely literate goombah hit man. The john floats out across the ether, briefly mentioned after the morning traffic report and ends up as filler between a government anti-racism ad and a shrimp cocktail recipe on the back page of the Lifestyle section.

"Johnny," Morgan snaps me out of my ruminations. "I gotta go soon. You're gonna meet me at the Purple Haze later—around midnight, right?"

"Yeah, I'll be there."

"So what time you seeing steroid boy?"

"At nine."

"Fuck, then you might be late."

"What're you talking about? I'm not gonna spend three hours with that baboon."

"Oh, really?" she taunts. "That baboon seems to be finding all kinds of excuses to see you for longer and longer. Maybe he's got a crush on his little Johnny."

I grin against my will and even redden a shade. "That's disgusting."

Morgan's in a good mood. She grabs for my crotch, puts on her mock pout. "Gets you hot, doesn't it? He makes Johnny *sooo* wet."

I'm laughing now and try to pull her hands off, but she won't stop with the pokes and pinches and tickles then finally pushes me onto the bed, crawls on top and keeps making fun. "It's too bad those big muscles-in-a-can mean his wiener's small as a peanut. I bet I've got a bigger boner than he does." Morgan checks the alarm clock on the night table then pulls off her t-shirt. There's an expensive black bra underneath. "We don't have a lotta time. And careful with my make-up." She hitches her white latex miniskirt and works her way up my body, reaches between us and gets my zipper and jeans part-way down. She heaves and tugs mightily.

"Jesus, lady, what the fuck are you doing down there?"

Morgan grunts between each word. "Trying-to-get-my-fucking-panties-out-of-the-fucking-way. There!"

She begins to ride me with a slow hip roll and lays the side of her face on my neck. I stroke her hair and hang onto her thigh to keep us together. "Yeah…" she breathes. "Some cock isn't bad once in a while." Morgan stops after a minute and rises a bit, undoes the front of her bra and opens my shirt so we're skin on skin. The friction makes her flush. She gets up on her wrists and concentrates on our movement, but then lets out a frustrated, "Fuck!" Jumping to her feet, she tears off her skirt and panties, hurls them into the corner then squats with knees on either side of me. "That's better," she says and slips the bra off her shoulders, laying it aside.

She's all the way naked now even though this was just supposed to be a quick screw-and-run. Her hand goes down, fingers on the base of my hard-on, wrist pressing on her clit. I feel a charge run between us and squirm side to side, almost get my pants off, but caught on one ankle. I sit up and grab onto her ass. She plants her feet on either side of my hips.

"Jesus fuck…" I say, swallowing hard and glance at my little Montreal Canadiens alarm clock. "I think I'm gonna come."

Morgan pulls my chin around. "Forget 'em, they can all wait." She leans forward, just managing to reach the clock and tosses it over her shoulder.

It lands in the hallway in a crash of tiny pieces. My pager buzzes. She grabs that too.

"Hold on a second! Don't break all my stuff."

Morgan chuckles and puts it under her bra. "Look," she says, eyes dropping. "You like to watch me do this. Look." She lifts up a bit to get her fist around me, works me in and out, rubs me against the inside of her thighs, down to her perineum and her lovin' little bum, then back up to her pubic hair and navel, all over her pussy, in and out. She makes us both twitch and shiver. I'm drawn inside her rapid breathing, the aura of warmth coming off her body, the sweet scent of her, the way she's so fucking us. Everything gets a little darker. Morgan keeps it going and going until we both positively vibrate. "Oooh, gawd…" she whispers as a thread of saliva trickles from the corner of her mouth, eyes half-shut, screwing us and screwing us.

A burning streak rushes down from my skull. "Shit, Morgan, you're really gonna make me come—like right fuckin' now!"

She rides me fiercely, teeth grit. "Okay. C'mon, baby, you can do it."

I feel cross-eyed. My hips buck. "Oh, Christ, Morgan. Fuck me!"

She howls through the final desperate barrier, crashing us together, teeth bared, gushing all over us. She panics and pulls me out. "I wanna see!"

She jams a thumb into my urethra and jacks me off madly. When she lets go the sperm burns out of me—hits her breast, her throat, her bottom lip. My groin muscles clench hard, wrench me back and forth as I cough and choke and collapse.

"Jeezus!" Morgan yells and licks her lip. "Now *that's* what I call some damn good fuckin'!"

As we're laid back, still panting and delirious, her fingers brush my cock and make me twitch like a broken marionette. She grins with those clear blue eyes. "You poor fucker. You're all mine now, wrapped right around my little finger."

"Yeah… good thing I'm not a trick."

Morgan squeezes my balls hard enough to hurt. "Don't be so sure…"

After reloading from The Man, I'm going home to make up some packages and run across Aunt Byron sitting at a jerry-rigged café that recently opened in a small parking lot on Roy, a block from my house. She's the only customer among the half-dozen tin tables. As I approach, she looks up from writing in her journal by candlelight.

"I was up at the mountain last night," Byron reports, pleased with herself.

"Me too."

"Yes, I know. I saw you with your friend, Slim. Very loving, Johnny. If I didn't know better, I would have thought you were in committed relationship."

I can't tell if she's being sarcastic. "Notice anyone else watching us?"

"Oh, a few wool-suit voyeurs. No one of note."

"So what were you doing up there?"

"Carrying out research. I believe a kind of *entente* has been reached between traditionally hostile Masonic and Jesuit forces—the grand alliance Pierre Trudeau partially succeeded at creating. If this accord is confirmed, it would of course be a historic shift in the underlying power structure."

I nod impatiently. "Of course... Well, I have some things to do. I'll see you later."

As I turn to leave, Aunt B stops me. "Oh, by the way, Johnny. That Jane woman—why do you keep referring to her as your 'wife'?"

"I dunno. It's kind of a joke, I guess."

"Really? It's not very funny."

"Yeah, I know."

THIRTEEN

Since its Sunday, the Griffintown torture chamber is closed, so I go see Crimson (whose real name is Chantal) and Kate at their apartment on City Hall Street, up near Rachel. Without their Daughters of Draco getups, all the dope-sucking, hard-assed humor and armored business acumen is set aside—they become totally different people.

In their nicely cluttered apartment full of rustic antiques and raw cotton spreads, they're one of those exemplary Montreal couples, especially when it's two women: fluently bilingual, worldly, a bit hippie in that non-sanctimonious Quebecois way. Loving and affectionate with one another, neither displays any obvious neuroses. And they don't immediately hoover up the drugs I sell them. Both snort a tiny bit then lay the stuff aside. It makes their vibe very civilized.

I'm putting together some packs at their kitchen table while Chantal sits across from me with her hair up in a knot. She wears big reading glasses and does the torture chamber's weekly accounting. Kate's more fem in her sporty shorts and light blonde ponytail. She brews some green tea and we get to gossiping. I tell them about Aunt Byron.

"So did you have sex with her?" asks Chantal.

"I don't think so… but I'm not totally sure."

They look at one another and laugh. "You could ask," says Kate.

"I don't know if I want to… It's sort of awkward and embarrassing. Better to just pretend nothing happened, even if it did."

Chantal stops her calculator entries and stares out the window. "I've had sex with a few transsexuals using a strap-on. But for a guy to do his friend after the surgery, I guess it would be kind of strange."

"Truth is I was so high and drunk, I didn't know what was going on."

Kate seems kind of titillated. "Did you have sex with him when he was still a man?"

"No, back then it wasn't like that."

"So is she beautiful as a woman?"

"Not really. Well, not at all, truth be told. She was a real looker as a guy, though. Tall and suave, very debonair, but becoming a woman… Byron's put on lots of weight and gotten kinda square, more masculine now than when she was a guy. It's all so weird. She won't tell me why she did it and she's smart enough to know it comes off like a ridiculous put-on, like Terry Jones in drag."

"Who?" they both ask.

"A British comedian with Monty Python—he was the mother in *Life Of Brian*. Remember that movie?" I put on the high, scratchy Mère Cohen voice. "'Your fahdder was a Roman, Bwian.' The whole thing bugs the shit out of me. I liked Byron fine the way she was—as a tall, charming man."

Kate and Chantal smile and touch hands. They seem so happy to have found each other and from what I hear, their relationship isn't new, maybe five or six years old. It seems impossible. Kate notices me get weepy. She jumps up and wraps her arms around my head, tits mashed into the side of my face.

"Oh, c'mon, Johnny…" she babies. "It's all right."

Chantal looks on sympathetically. "Are you that upset about your friend?"

"No, it's just… how happy you two are."

Kate kisses my hair then pours some more tea. The pager buzzes and I let out a groan after checking the number.

"What's wrong?" asks Chantal.

"It's this idiot I know, Vern, a.k.a. the Raging Skull."

"I've heard of him," says Kate. "He's supposed to be some kind of brilliant bastard."

"Naw, he's just a garden-variety asshole. I wish I could stay here with you two, be your manservant or something."

I reluctantly leave their sanctuary to go deal with Vern. Although, I have to admit, he's been pretty well-behaved since The Man anointed me as dealer. Well, why alienate a guy who can prevent your body from turning into a shitting, puking bag of gloom-wracked misery?

I step out of the cab into one of those uniquely scalding Montreal afternoons, the city drenched in a soul-sapping humidity that reeks worse than a rubby's crotch. It feels as if the sun is six feet above your head.

Vern lives in a sprawling four-storey, roach-infested apartment complex at the north end of Park Avenue, near Saint-Viateur. Built in the '30s or '40s, it's got these endless hallways, but they've been desecrated with vomit colored paint and heavy fire doors every forty feet or so. The building was once elegant, a stylish address with massive, multi-roomed suites, but like much of Montreal, it's now reduced to a welfare slum, a real 24-hour circus of winos, transients, halfwits, whores and Down East hosers. Hitting the entrance, I run a gauntlet of standard-issue loudmouths, loitering on the sidewalk to bum change and irritate passing women.

I find Vern's door wide open and walk in to the strains of him throwing up in the toilet. The barely furnished crash pad is an oven, the evil sweatbox of a reptilian ogre struggling to retain his human skin. After a few minutes Vern emerges—pale and haggard, a wet face-cloth on his balding crown. Far past the ability to speak, he lays out twenty bucks and a bunch of change. I count it then give him two packs and he gets down to business.

Just as Vern finishes up and the color returns to his face, the unmistakable thump of Michael Jackson's *Thriller* comes through the wall. Stuff in the apartment jumps around with the heavy bass whaps, the vibrations low enough to make you shit yourself if your bowels are weak. Vern darkens and storms out, heading for the flop next door. "Gonna lay a beatin' on him!" he hollers over the music.

I follow and a Warsaw Pact hick of some stripe whips open the door as if he'd timed it for Vern's arrival. There's a slim, dark haired woman in the middle of the guy's living room, her back to us. She looks pretty good from behind. The Michael Jackson fanatic raises a fey hand as if to shoo us away. Vern grabs the creep's fingers, yanks him forward and lays a head butt square in his mouth. The Sino-Pollack or whatever he is tries to pull away, his gob now bloodied, but Vern won't let go. He snaps him in for another header. The guy turns and gets it in the ear. Vern snatches his other hand and their arms are crossed over, like they're doing a Cossack dosey-doe.

The woman turns, totally bored. Some kind of classy East Asian babe in Audrey Hepburn all-black, mouth painted with gold lipstick. Vern swings her boyfriend hard to the left. The guy slams into the door post, instantly winded. She almost smiles. Vern flings the geek toward Mikey belting it out from two giant floor speakers. The guy knocks them over and trips on some wires. Mikey's cut off in mid *Thri-* . The only sounds now are the heaves and grunts of Vern working over his Samba partner.

The woman coldly examines her associate sprawled on the stained broad-loom. He blindly paws at the air as Vern drives a boot into his midsection. That flips him onto his back, down for the count. The woman sighs heavily, the tedium just killing her. Vern would have to disembowel him with an ob-sidian ceremonial blade just to get a rise out of this chick.

I raise a finger and make a loud proclamation. "In the immortal words of the wise and all-seeing Jed Clampett, 'If that boy's brain was lard, it wouldn't grease too big a pan.'" I whistle the theme song from *The Beverley Hillbillies* as we leave.

"Feel a lot better," Vern says as we return to his trap. "Couldja tell that bitch is hot for me? See the way she got wet over the beatin' I laid on her faggot? Guaranteed she'll knock on my door with some stupid pretext in three minutes flat."

I check my four-dollar Montreal Alouettes digital wristwatch. "You're on for a package," I say and press the Elapsed Time button. We watch the square numerals flash by. At exactly 2:50.34 there's a single tap on the door. Vern holds out his paw. "Fuck me," I mutter and slap a pack into it. He an-swers and there she is, one hand up against the door frame, the other on her hip, thin body slinked sideways in a long cool S.

"I require a cigarette," she tells us with an Oxford-trained accent.

"I don't smoke," Vern replies as he puts one out. "Come in anyway. Johnny here does."

"My name is Izanami," she tells us and holds out her index and middle fingers in a backward V. I slide a cigarette in place. She watches me as I light a match for her. "Merci, Monsieur."

Vern's right on her. "So, which one first—or both of us at the same time?"

She ignores his suave come-on. "The fellow you assaulted has gone to Casualty. He shall inform the police."

Vern sneers at her. "No shit? Okay, let's all phone the cops. I go first. Tell 'em I got some cockteasin', slant-eyed bitch with small tits and a flat ass in my apartment and she won't shut up and get naked."

I've always wondered if his *Ultimate Asshole* routine has ever worked. He swears by it and says it saves him all kinds of time, money and aggravation. No need for any bullshit dates, flowers, small talk, idiotic build up or fuck all else. You come on like THE Supreme Asshole and immediately pounce on any insecurity you can scope and just grind away at it. Personally, I don't have the gumption for that kind of concentrated malevolence. Like most things, it looks like a lotta work.

"Two hundred and fifty each," Izanami informs us. "Both at once, six hundred."

"Whadda you got," Vern grouses. "A gold plated pussy?"

Izanami blows a cloud of smoke at me and raises an eyebrow.

"No, thanks. I would, but I'm working right now."

"Fuck," Vern gasses. "You don't look like a pro."

"Well," she exhales, reaching out to tap an ash onto the floor. "I hold a PHD in Philology. I came to this country to complete my thesis, the Lexical Idiosystems of the Confederation Poets. Despite the board voting unanimously to immediately confer my doctorate, I have found the labor market for my skills to be limited, primarily due to the fact I abhor the over-valued practice of teaching."

Vern swings round to me. "Huh?"

"She's too smart to fuck either of us for free."

"Oh," he grasps then sits down at the white plastic garden table in his dining room. "Yeah, well, see ya later, whatever your name is."

I'm not sure why he's playing the translate-for-me dummy shtick. The fucking guy's got an honors degree in PoliSci and is a top MA candidate. Maybe he doesn't want to get into some academic pissing contest with this weird broad.

"My name is Izanami," the woman reminds us. She drifts toward Vern as he prepares to do another shot. She runs a finger along the gray scar inside his left elbow. "This interests me."

"For chrissake!" he shrinks back. "What are you, some co-dependent nutcase—a junk groupie?"

"No. However, I am rather curious about the processes involved in one's obviously intentional but self-consciously irrational attempts at creating a perpetual state of personal decay and devolution, despite overwhelming evidence to indicate highly negative medical and psychiatric consequences."

Vern looks to me again. "In English?"

"She objectively gets off on how committed you are to fucking yourself up but has no emotional interest whatsoever. And she's still not gonna fuck ya for free."

"Junk groupie," he repeats with a big miserable nod. Izanami observes as Vern gets everything ready. He scowls up at her. "You mind?"

She slowly makes for the door, but stops and lays a delicate hand on my arm, her nails the same sparkly gold as her lipstick. "By the way, who is this Jed Clampett?"

"I'm not surprised you haven't heard of him. He's a terribly under-appreciated and little-read American philosopher of the Home Spun school. Will Rogers stole his entire oeuvre. Yep, old Jed could have been America's Uncle Joe Stalin if people had only listened."

Izanami absorbs this information and stares at me for a moment. "I see. Good bye, Monsieur Clampett." She allows herself a miniscule smile before leaving.

FOURTEEN

It's been raining steadily for a couple days now, real thunderbolt hurling zingers and ugly black clouds boiling over the mountain onto The Main. I go down to McGill to drop a few packs off to Slim between classes. She introduces me to a New Yorker she knows, a hip scholarly guy called Adam. He's easygoing and quick-witted, nice looking, with long dark hair and a ready grin, plays down the fact he's up here working on his fucking doctorate. It gets on my nerves how he touches Slim so casually, loosely throwing an arm around her waist.

"Fuck you too," I mumble under my breath at her while handing over the stuff. I ignore her when she calls my name as I turn and go sulking off.

On my way over to visit Kit, an old actor friend, a blazing sun finally busts through the gray and I see my mug in a passing store window. In my black jeans, black coat—my constantly all-black shtick and my big schnozz —Jesus, I *do* look like a goddamn goat with sunglasses on. Kit's apartment is on Marie-Anne, the second floor of a two-storey slum that's a single body-check from falling into the street. Her door is open and when I go upstairs she's sitting at a dressing table with electric-orange hair in about five dozen tiny ponytails and some green slime on her face.

"What's that shit you've got on?"

"Danish bog mud," she replies and points at the forty dollars waiting for me.

I pick up the money and lay down two packs. Her place is jammed to the rafters with the rejects and refuse of countless bad musicals and dreary experimental plays. A six-foot tall cardboard reptile suit stands in one corner. A bale of garishly colored fabric ends pours from a closet. Posters and flyers of long forgotten productions cover every wall.

"I'm in the revue at The Official Opposition tonight," Kit tells me while she expertly chops a thin line and snorts it up. Freshly rejuvenated, she gives me the breakdown. "We're doing a musical version of David Fennario's play *Balconville*. Dred Blanc and his new band, Smoke Like Richard—they're doing the soundtrack—live. Buy a ticket, Johnny. It's only ten dollars." Kit stares at my reflection in her mirror as I debate the purchase. "C'mon, it'll be fun."

"I gotta work but… okay, I'll buy a pair, just in case."

Kit reaches for her bag hanging off a chair and pulls out an 8 ½ x 11 poster covered with a jumble of ransom note letters printed on bright fuchsia paper. She scrawls something on it with a silver marker and takes my double sawski. "This'll get you and your guest in the door and backstage. At least try to make the after-party." Satisfied at the sale, she regards me with serious concern. "Is this all you're doing these days? Just hanging around The Main selling drugs? I never see you at Spanking's anymore, or Club Priape. Aren't you afraid of losing touch?"

I look at her brown dollar-store slippers, her threadbare silk kimono, the bog mud. "It does worry me, but there's always someone paging."

Kit swivels back to her mirror and begins to apply some white cream to her eyelids. "It's important to have a social life, Johnny. Y'know, to be exposed to the scene. I think you ought to set reasonable hours."

"I did set hours. Nobody paid attention."

She gets patronizing. "You could just turn the pager off, you know."

"Not possible."

That gives her pause. "And why?"

"Does 911 ever turn off?"

"Well, then you should have an assistant."

"I've thought about it, but who could I trust? Everyone I know is either too sleazy, too lazy or too busy. I mean, you wouldn't do it, right?"

"Oh, god no. My schedule's already far too full." Kit thinks about it for a few moments. "Hm… I know! I have the perfect candidate."

"Oh, yeah? Who?"

"His name is Leroi. You might have met him at Tony's."

"You mean that half-Sri Lankan, half-English guy?"

"That's right. He's a very clever man, very charming—and he's good looking."

"That's important. I wouldn't work with someone who's a dog."

Kit's a chronic matchmaker and she's getting excited. "Leroi would be ideal. You two will get along famously! I'll arrange a meeting."

It's not a bad idea. I've been run ragged lately by the constant paging, never twenty minutes to myself. "Okay, ask him to meet me at the Balmoral tonight, say six o'clock. I'll have to clear it with headquarters, but maybe this can work. And if it does, I'll remember your help, Kit."

She gets nostalgic and swings around in her seat, wraps an arm around my thigh, stroking my ass a bit. "Of course you will," she smiles up at me. "You can be a real gentleman when you want to. And by the way, thanks for being so sweet when you ran into my new beau and me on the bus. He had no idea we were once involved. And it was nice to see him get a little jealous."

"I hope he's not some nut I have to worry about."

"Don't be absurd. Tim's a very sweet young man. He just asked a few questions about you, if we'd ever slept together."

"What did you tell him?"

"I lied, of course." She takes her time lighting a cigarette then grins at me. "I certainly wasn't going to tell him I used to do you with a strap-on, was I now? Tim's wouldn't understand—he's from Ottawa. Besides, it's something I'd like to eventually explore with him." She swivels back to her mirror. "All in good time."

"I'm sure he'll love it."

"All the boys do, it's only natural. Anyway, I told him you and I are friends and you'd pursued me for a while, but things never worked out. Although, I did hint that I wouldn't have minded too much if they had. You know, just to torment him a tiny bit."

"Well, I guess that'll keep ol' Timmy in harness."

Kit leans back, fingers laced around one knee, head cocked, day dreaming, scheming. "Yes, it is pretty simple. If a man thinks other men are interested, he can't keep his hands off you." She ponders that gem for a second. "It works the same way for women too."

"What, the strap-on?"

"Oh, stop," she slaps at me. "Or I just might have to throw you over the kitchen table and make you beg for it."

We're laughing and eyeing each other, maybe getting ideas about a little barter when my pager vibrates. "That's Tony," I say after glancing at the read-out. "I've gotta go meet him. I'm leaving my trenchcoat here. It's getting hot outside."

I give Kit a neck smooch as she begins to peel the green crap off her face. "All right, then," she calls as I go down the stairs. "I'll ask Leroi to meet you in the Balmoral at six."

"Tell him to be on time," I yell back up. "And break a leg!"

Even though I get to the Balmoral almost an hour late, Leroi doesn't seem to mind and we hit it off immediately. Kit's right—he's got charisma to spare. A native Montrealer, Leroi has the air of a fun-loving scoundrel who's just set the headmaster's wastebasket on fire. An Irani woman I know and her girlfriend are at the next table. Leroi's got them relaxed and flirting. You just can't teach a guy that sort of thing. It's pure gold and solid evidence of a highly adaptable intellect.

After I lay out the situation, Leroi decides he's got to relocate. Right now he lives in a time-warp neighborhood called Saint-Henri—aka 'the basement of Montreal' because it's at the bottom of that huge Atwater hill, southwest of the downtown. The whole shitty area is overrun with wannabe gangsters living with their mothers and dressed in track suits, white tube socks and loafers. Coming up here is like visiting the Jetsons.

As we walk north to meet The Man, Leroi's gawking about happily. "This is un-believable! Y'know, I was apprenticing to become a stonemason."

"Wow. Quite a future."

"Yeah," he chuckles as the light bulb over his head clicks on sunshine bright. "Early arthritis, broken hands, a ruined back and a lousy little pension. I tell ya, that working class hero stuff—it's total *merde*." He stops walking. I watch the life-altering decision harden his features. "Okay, that's it. I'm in. I'll dump the Saint-Henri girlfriend, get rid of that crappy apartment and move up here. I always knew about The Main, but I didn't really know about *The Main*." But then Leroi turns anxious, as if he's found half a winning lottery ticket. "But what if The Man doesn't like me?"

"Just sweet talk the guy. The way you did with those women at the Balmoral. You know what I mean."

He's not reassured. "But I have no experience. I've never worked retail."

"Look, you'll shadow me for a day or two and meet everybody. Plus, I'll come out with you for a couple hours when you get started."

"Really? Okay, that sounds pretty good." We continue but he halts once more. "What about Tony? He's my friend. I feel bad about what happened to him, and then to replace him. I don't know, Johnny…"

"Tony's a good guy an all, but he screwed himself going overboard on the stuff. That forced him to cut the shit so business suffered. And he shouldn't have given so much credit to absolute fuck ups. At least this way, we keep it in the family and you can help him out once in a while."

Leroi takes off his horn-rimmed glasses. His gray eyes get steely. "You're right. No fronts. Nobody. Ever." He marks each word with a flat-handed swipe at the air.

"Hold on a minute. You've got to front—but to the right people. The ones you know will pay. It's a delicate balance. You can't totally alienate these characters. I mean, you don't want some strung-out maniac rolling on you."

"Oh yeah…" he realizes, "the fucking cops! Maybe this isn't such a good idea."

"It'll be fine. You just gotta play it cool. The key thing is that since you're not a user, you'll make a pile of money for hardly any work."

"I guess… I'll give it a try for… how about two weeks?"

"Perfect. Besides, it's only part time."

That seals the probationary deal. Now it's up to The Man to give his stamp of approval, but I expect that'll be little more than a formality. We run into Aunt Byron, Al and Hennessy in front of Berson and Son, the old Hebrew stonecutters next to La Cabane. I make introductions all round and Leroi's instantly working the three of them, telling Byron about the dimpled surfacing technique used to create the rough but uniform edge around the stones. Al decides Leroi's more than worthy and tells us his party radar has picked up a big, open-bar film bash in Old Montreal late tonight and gives us the address. Hennessy's instantly smitten as well—all over Leroi, taking his arm, fawning openly. I pull the Hen aside.

"Stop it," I mumble, my back to the others.

"Stop what?" he asks, playing the naïf.

"Leroi doesn't swing that way so cut it out. He's my business partner now and I don't want you fucking things up."

The Hen raises his palms. "My apologies, darling. We certain don't want to cause any problems on the commercial front."

"Exactly," I reply and discreetly slide two packs into his change pocket. We both turn back with big smiles. "Okay," I say, slapping my hands together. "Let's go inside, Leroi. The Man awaits."

He watches Al, Hennessy and Byron as they wander off. "Un-believable."

"What?"

"That Hennessy guy's pretty weird. See the way he was touching me? You think maybe he's gay?"

"Naw, he's just nuts. Ignore him."

As I'd predicted, The Man immediately takes to Leroi, the fact he's cocky but smooth and affable. The kid has tremendous social instincts. After being approved of, Leroi has all the zeal of a new company man. We shake hands on the sidewalk before parting.

"That's it then," he says, eyeing the street. "I'd better get back down to Saint-Henri and break up with Bev." He takes out his wallet and shows me a picture. She's a nice looking girl next door, hammer in hand, ready to nail Leroi's foot the floor and put him on a retractable leash. Early to bed on Saturday nights after the pizza and hockey game, then a quick Sunday morning shtup before the weekly grocery run and laundry load. Something to live for.

"Nice girl," I say.

"Yeah, exactly what I don't want."

"Why not? You can spend your life following her around some mall, help her pick out various and sundry do-dads. It'd be a gas."

"The way I see it, you work hard, bring in the coin and be a good guy— practical women like Bev, they're all over ya. If you're a fucked-up, irresponsible mental case—sorta like you, Johnny—then you meet a different class of women, more intense."

I fling my arm around his shoulders. "Ah, you've uncovered the ancient secret, my boy. Stick with me and you'll be a wreck in no time, involved in all kinds of demented relationships that make absolutely no sense and rip your soul to shreds."

"Sounds great," he says without a hint of sarcasm. "I can't wait!"

FIFTEEN

The Montreal night hums with kinetic energy. Aunt Byron and Al silently climb the one-thousand step log staircase that goes up the steep eastern face of Mount Royal. Hennessy and I are a little ways behind them. We kibitz and gossip, play slap and tickle. Aunt B tells us to shush.

It's close to eleven and there are people all over the mountain in the steaming hot dark. A mammoth summer storm swells above the city. But right now everyone and everything sweats. I've got my shirt open and trailing as the only concession. I'd rather eat razors than suffer the infamy of shorts. The Hen's dumped his jacket and rolled up his sleeves, but refuses to undo the old-fashioned tie or remove his bowler. As we ascend the staircase, I sense the occasional pair or trio going at it in the forest and thickets spreading out on either side of us. It's too dark to see anything but I assume they're mostly men with the odd male-female coupling or tripling. Whispered moans and quiet laughter surround us. A few seem close enough to touch. I reach for Hennessy's hand and he gives me a reassuring squeeze then hangs on.

"I'm getting too old," I tell him, out of breath. "This climb is a killer."

"You're still a beauty," he flatters. "They said so in the papers."

Up ahead, I can barely see Al and Aunt Byron in their black-ops attire. By the time the Hen's hauled me up the last few steps, those two wait impatiently at the top, all business. Through the trees, some lights are visible from downtown to the south of us, and The Main to the east. It occurs to me we're not far from Pierre Trudeau's art deco pile on the southern slope.

Maybe he roams around up here at night, among the crumbling mausoleums and tilted, mossy tombstones of the mountain's old boneyards, mumbling, *"Just watch me... just watch me..."*

Aunt B leads us along the edge of the tree line at the summit. Despite her bulk, she's agile and surefooted. We make our way to a slightly lower elevation near the southeast heights, above Molson Stadium. It's so steep only a chimp or panther could sneak up behind us, but Byron's determined we approach unnoticed. After half an hour of treacherously slow going and a few wipe-outs by Al and me, Byron stops to consult a hand-drawn map. She seems to know the terrain intimately and indicates a stand of trees about a hundred yards from the massive, over-lit crucifix on the mountain's summit. "That will be our observation point. From here forward, silent running."

We crawl through some waist-high grass and lay flat just outside the perimeter of a small clearing about sixty feet across. The surrounding foliage and tree cover is so dense that you'd never notice this cozy little spot just walking by. At the moment, five or six guys hang out. Soon more begin to arrive, alone or in pairs, from a narrow pathway on the far side.

Aunt B takes three sets of cheap foldout opera glasses from her backpack and quietly passes them along. They're surprisingly effective in the dim light. Ambient illumination from the city and the mountaintop cross does help, but it's still amazing how much detail you can pick up. For her own purposes, Byron has brought a super low-light video camera with non-reflective lens and a battery belt.

The men we surveil josh and mill about. Exclusively white and Franglo, I wonder if this is the grand Masonic-Jesuit alliance Aunt B has been going on about. They range from teenaged pretty-boys, up to elders in their fifties and sixties, most of them hale and hearty. About half sport facial hair. Their expressions are casual and relaxed. Beers, wine bottles and joints go round, but there is impatience too. I check crotches and see some expectant bulges. A few wear baggy shorts, erections poking upward, others in jean/t-shirt combos. One has his belt and fly wide open, semi-erect wang hung out and primed. A couple of men are in suits, but with their ties and shirttails pulled loose, jackets laid aside.

At the edge of the clearing, a couple are already well into it, hands in each other's groins, necking with mouths wide and tongues out. One fella's pants are around his ankles. A gaggle of their buddies drift over as the pair slides to the ground. They tenderly undress one another and roll into a highly coordinated sixty-nine. That elicits a flurry of good-natured comments in both French and English. Somebody puts on a hick Joual accent and says something sarcastic. There's quiet laughter and Hennessy giggles softly, but I don't catch the joke. The whole scene has a fraternal, jocular air. Plenty of back slaps and ass grabs, tipsy chatter.

A buff young dude strips off his white tracksuit and drops to the ground next to the sixty-niners. Knees far apart, he spits in his hand and methodically jerks off toward them, really working his cock. His face is serious and focused, as if performing a dangerous and demanding task.

A balding, late middle-aged man with a red nose and a gray-haired beer gut casually jerks off as he watches the proceedings, beer bottle in hand. I study his face. He looks like a retired hockey coach and appears melancholy, as if recalling the salad days of yesteryear when he had the lithe form and boundless energy to get down on the turf with these fetching young sportsmen.

I'm not certain, but I think there are a few shadowy figures opposite us, also hidden in thick brush. More watchers? Even though most of the people we're observing probably wouldn't give a shit about an audience—and likely get off on it, I'm sure they don't want this stuff recorded. But man oh ma-rimbas, talk about your spectator sport. Right now it's avant-garde; in ten years, any money this'll be televised on Saturday nights after the hockey game. *Et la première étoile de ce soir…*

Actually, I'm not even sure why we're skulking in the bushes. We could drag out lawn chairs, sit back, relax and take in the show. Who would care? Christ, we could hold up scorecards, applaud, get in on the fun even. However, Aunt B's deadly serious about the whole deal and I guess there is something to be said for this spying-from-the-undergrowth shtick. It is giving me a wicked hard-on.

Byron nudges me toward the right. I pan over and see a trio emerging from the pathway. Zeroing in on the leader—fuck me—it's that McGill

Perv I batted around. Of course. He wears a safari suit and a pith helmet. Younger men approach warmly and defer to him, eager to shake his hand. A few give him affectionate hugs then he shares a long, tongue-twisting kiss with a tall, ruggedly handsome character that looks like Burt Reynolds in *Smokey and the Bandit*. The guy's even wearing a white cowboy hat. It's easy to imagine him crouched on the driver's bench of a six-horse chuckwagon, dirt flying as he leads the pack around the circuit at the Calgary Stampede.

The Perv is escorted by a huge, muscle-bound goon decked out in old style wrestling gear—tights and calf-high boots. His bare torso is immense, with enormous shoulders and pecs. A fez sits on his bald head and he frowns from behind a giant handlebar moustache. The strongman strides along with knuckles on hips, elbows turned out. He's got a leash looped around his right hand. At the other end is a naked boy in a studded dog collar. In the low light it's hard to tell how old he is. The youngster capers and cavorts, rubs his nipples and lets out a shrill cry.

"It's Paco," Hennessy whispers.

Christ, it is that little whore. But his face is different. Lots of make-up, I guess, but he also appears crazed, demonically high. What kind of malevolent pharmaceuticals has that bloodsucker fed the stupid kid? Paco snarls and snaps at anyone who dares get too touchy-feely with The Perv. He squirms into a small knot of admirers who surround his master, squats before him, undoes his fly and quickly gets to work. The entire erection disappears down Paco's gullet and his lips grasp at pubic hair. Others caress the kid's long black hair while he licks and slurps and devours. He eyes swing round covetously with the thing in his mouth, as if someone might try to horn in.

The strongman stands by, a firm grip on the leash, legs apart and arms crossed. He squints into the distance and ignores the lady-boys that fuss and trill over his bulk. I smack my forehead against the ground a few times then look again. The whole thing comes off like an elaborate Boschian tableau.

I glance at Hennessy and he has his face in his elbow. His shoulders juddering, I can't tell if he's silently crying or stifling laughter. Aunt Byron scrawls in her journal with one hand while she continues to stare through the camera's viewfinder with the other. Her notes appear to be illegible gibberish. Al is already gone. When I raise my eyes to the action, The Perv has shot his load and Paco's crouched at his feet, the loyal mutt. The Perv's head suddenly whips round toward us, as if prompted by a radar spike.

"He knows," I whisper and begin to rise, ready to make a run for it, terrified the mustachioed ape will attack. Still with her eye at the camera, Byron lays a firm hand on my forearm. I freeze and The Perv gradually looks away without sicking his gorilla on us. It's so hot I'm getting dizzy and lay the side of my face in the grass for a couple minutes.

"I've seen enough," Aunt B says quietly. "We ought to go."

I take one last glimpse through the opera glasses and catch Paco performing some incredible act of derring-do on the end of the strongman's long, curved erection. It's shaped like a scimitar. Paco's feet are off the ground, body impaled in a bizarre arms-to-the-rear contortion. A rough circle gathers round them. Voices rise in *oohs* and *ahs* as Paco's head lolls about.

We carefully back away on our elbows through the underbrush. The trip down the mountain is just as exhausting as the climb up. Al waits for us at the base camp next to Park Avenue. It's well past midnight now. Aunt Byron sits at the bottom of Cartier's monument and opens her journal. She notes the evening's events under the blazing lime-green sodium lights surrounding the statue.

"Tonight's luminaries included a veteran executive producer at our national broadcaster," she tells us in a calm, neutral voice. "Also, a top Arts Council factotum, along with a former Assistant Deputy Minister in the recent minority government. The man in the safari suit is a revered Ministry of Corrections mandarin."

"I know him," I say. "And that kid on the leash."

"Me too," Hennessy pipes in.

Aunt Byron jots something then carries on with the rundown. "The body guard is a high-ranking official in the Gendarmerie and the well-known author of manuals on the training of undomesticated children."

Hennessy offers a few more pointless observations. I have nothing to add and Al doesn't say much. He seems irritated and distracts himself by taking nips from his flask of Louis Royer XO. He passes it round. Hennessy and

I take long slugs, but Byron waves it off. She shows us some photographs pasted into her journal. They're cut from corporate reports and the business sections of financial newspapers, announcements of various private and public sector appointments; suited men with tight smiles and boxback haircuts. A few resemble some of the participants up on the mountain.

The summer storm that has brewed for hours shows the first signs of really busting open. Black clouds chug by, low enough to obscure the huge, gaudy crucifix on the mountaintop. Big drops come down for an instant then stop. Lightning crackles south of us, over downtown. Its thunder booms a few moments later.

While Aunt Byron packs up her journal and secures the video equipment, I see a woman I met recently—Shalini, a modern dance virtuoso. Even in the dark, I recognize her at a distance from the pronounced stride. She's only about five-four, but projects much taller with that long neck and the sweeping arch of her back—lots of pride and hardly any breasts. Late twenties, early thirties or older even, who knows—hard to tell with serious dancers. She's a scorching Habitant-Sindhi mix. The writer, filmmaker and left-wing radical Julian Samuel had introduced us during a party at his house last weekend. Morgan had come with me, but ran into an old boyfriend and they left early.

Shalini is walking a bicycle. When I go toward her, she spins round as if expecting something unpleasant. She's barefoot and wears a red, knee-length summer dress. The wind pulls it tight against her body. There's nothing underneath. She recognizes me and breaks into a grin, dimpled and easy. "Johnny!"

Hennessy echoes my name and points at the sky as he, Al and Byron quickly go toward Park Avenue. The rain's begun to really fall. I ignore him and look back to Shalini. "What are you doing?"

"Julian told me he saw you and your friends on the way up here so I came to find you. But then I ran into a man I know. We drank some wine and walked around—we... I left my sandals somewhere..." She glances about. "He asked me to watch his bike for a minute."

I look down at it. "The front tire's flat."

"Yes, I know. He went to get a pump."

"Why don't you forget about this piece of junk? It's not your problem."

Shalini examines the bike for a long moment. "You're right," she decides and lays it in the grass. The wind's picked up and bends the trees. Fat raindrops smack me in the face.

"C'mon," I say and take her hand. Both of us are fairly wet by the time we reach the first stand of pines and maples at the bottom of the mountain. The rain feels fresh and washes off some sweat. Shalini grabs both my hands and walks backward, leading me deeper into the woods, toward a picnic table at the edge of a small meadow. Teeth flashing very white in the darkness, her skin's an unusual soft, yellowy-brown color with a sprinkle of freckles on her nose and cheeks. She stops with her back against a giant elm and pulls me close.

"Julian told me why you came up here," she says, part mockery, part intrigue.

"How does he know?"

"Al Polo told him."

"Figures. Al and his big mouth."

Shalini looks round, up into the thick canopy of treetops, toward the rocky crags somewhere above us. "What you're doing, Johnny… it's a waste of time."

"Why do you say that?"

"It's all so much bigger than you and your friends. This didn't begin last week or last year."

"Yeah, well, it's all Aunt Byron's idea. I'm just along as an observer."

She grabs a couple fistfuls of my shirt and pushes her lips onto mine. The taste comes back familiar. We had a drunken smooch and felt each other up in a dim stairwell at Julian's party. Our groping stopped when she had to leave with some sulky guy.

Shalini's dress is so wet it clings to her body. I grab her round the waist, bite at her nipples and the sides of her breasts through the drenched fabric. She drags her nails down my neck. A knee comes up between my thighs, rubs hard into my groin.

I notice some movement in the bushes not far from us and squint into the blackness. "Can you believe these guys? They'll hang around through the fucking apocalypse to see one last piece of ass."

Shalini barely glances over. "I don't care, as long as they leave us alone." She gives me a bashful little smile. "You know, I saw you yesterday afternoon, walking on The Main with that blonde girl."

"Oh, yeah?"

She nods quickly, kind of sheepish. "Uh huh. When I got home I masturbated a couple of times."

"How was it?"

She's coy, playful. "It was okay... She's a very beautiful girl, Johnny."

"Yeah, I know..."

Shalini's eyes grow wide, titillated. "You're in love with her," she teases then adds a grade school sing-song. "Johnny's-in-love-with-the-beautiful-blonde-girl..."

She pulls me toward the picnic table, still giggling. We straddle the bench, face one another and her bare thighs come over mine. Her arms rise up, cross over and in a single motion, lift off her sopping wet dress and she throws it aside. Her thin naked body contrasts against the deep black forest night. She wears a fine silver chain around her neck. A small symbol hangs from it, like a sideways eighteen.

"God, look at you," I ogle and run my tongue along the ridges of her breast bone, tasting salt and sweat and rain. The storm's washed away most of the little bit of eye-liner she had on. Her fingers wipe off the rest while she titters like a ten-year-old. "Yeah, look at me!"

In the soaking dark, I lay my palm between Shalini's breasts, feel the sinew and muscle at her sternum and ribs. Rain comes down in buckets for a few moments then only in drabs then pours again as the clouds churn and thunder rips. Vaguely human shapes at our periphery flee toward civilization. Shalini pulls off my shirt and gets my pants undone. My thumbs hook around her sharp hips bones, ass muscles tensing as I raise her onto my lap. She mutters and laughs something low and husky, both hands down there to get me inside and I am hard enough to shatter. The storm rises another octave and lashes through the trees.

"Christ!" I shout. "This place is fucking dramatic!"

Shalini lifts her face to the rain. Drops bounce off her forehead and eyelids. "Of course it's dramatic. That's why I bring all the boys up here."

The rain's turned cold and goosebumps come up on her skin. She shivers as we struggle and merge and the sky heaves all over us. It's like screwing underwater. Shalini's legs come round me and one hand dives between us. I look down and she's pulling on her pubic hair. The sky's sudden flash lights up her clit for a brief instant. She pushes to and fro, mouth open and eyes shut, screeches like a cat and competes with the wind. Rain runs between us and she lays a pair of fingers on my tongue and I taste blood.

Her elbows come together, hands clasped as if in prayer, eyes fluttering. She lays back and her head falls into my palm. I push her knees all the way against her shoulders. She hangs onto my neck, mouth at my ear, mumbling in Sindhi or Urdu or who cares—creamy, filthy sounds fill my head. Her eyes go down between us, transfixed on our groins slamming together and apart. She nods encouragement and the only thing in my brain is to fuck her and fuck her and fuck her.

Shalini bites at wounds Slim left behind. The stabs of pain pull me closer and a whiplash rises in my spine. She fights to bring it on, furious and impatient now, all that lust stutters out of her at first, heels kicking at my back. Then long groans and growls, calves locked around my sides, nails dug into my arm, driving her cunt upwards. I think she's sobbing, but it might be me and I hear far-off sirens.

My head dips. I'm dizzy but determined and Shalini's lips brush mine when a bolt of lightning blasts a tree across the clearing, not twenty yards from us—and splits the thing asunder. The blinding crash of a billion watts and a mind-shattering explosion tears through us like a shock wave. We're both instantly traumatized by the near-miss and shake uncontrollably. It's the biblical castigation of a vengeful god. It's the cock shriveling naked-power-of-nature. It's blue-balls on a cosmic scale. The wind shrieks and drives the rain sideways.

"We—we have to get out of here!" I stammer, fumbling with my pants.

Shalini's black eyes are wide and terrified, trembling so bad she can barely squirm into her dress. I grab my shirt and take her hand. The last of the hardcore voyeurs sprint past us. We run for Park Avenue like a couple of Old Testament sinners.

SIXTEEN

Around dusk Leroi shows up to hand off the pager. I'm getting ready for my pre-set appointment with our most enigmatic client, the woman we refer to as The Sphinx. I'm shaved, showered and primped when he arrives.

"Look at Johnny," Leroi grins. "If you're so hung up on this girl, why don't you ask her back here? You've got a great apartment."

"It's not that easy," I say while using pieces of tape to roll hair and lint off my suit jacket. "She'd think I was nuts. Besides, you know how it is—like a doctor screwing one of his patients. It's unethical."

Leroi lies on the couch and plays around with the pager, changes the battery. "Yeah, and it could get expensive."

"That too. So what are you doing tonight?"

"The Man wants to go to a movie."

I stop knotting my tie. "Really? Just the two of you, like on a date?"

"Fuck off," he grouses. "Not like on a date. He wants to see that new Van Damme flick, *Cyborg*."

"Figures, a thyroid freak like him must blow his load over Jean-Claude, the Belgian butt-banger."

"I didn't know JC's Belgian."

"Sure, the whole country's full of pedophiles, pud-pounders and perverts. At least that's what Aunt Byron says."

"Don't let The Man hear you talk that way about Van Damme. He thinks that guy's the cat's ass."

"More like he wants to grease that cat's ass."

"Y'know, there is something slightly gay about The Man."

"Slightly? Anybody who spends that much time in the gym and creaming about himself in the mirror should just get it over with and come the fuck out of the cupboard. All muscled up like that, he already looks like a Bathhouse Betty."

"It's true. Like those biker dudes with all the leather and heavy attitude. You call them queer and they'll rip you to pieces even though they all dress like bondage fags. Weird, huh?"

"Christ, Leroi, don't you know bikers are the biggest closet homos around? What straight guy works that hard to prove he's some kind of ball-stompin' macho camacho? It's major 'doth protest too much' type bullshit."

"Un-believable," he laughs then checks the time on the pager. "You'd better go. Don't want to keep her waiting."

I dash out and hurry to the Peanut Bar in a cab. I'm totally at a loss about the Sphinx. She never whines, wheedles, begs, cons, cajoles or coys, never threatens or panics. She never asks for credit and never complains about counts or quality. She never seems under the effects or sick. The Sphinx always has exact change. Rumor has it she sleeps without heat all winter long.

I have to wonder if she even uses the stuff. Perhaps this woman is the secret Saint Sphinx who roams the streets and squares to offer pity and solace to stupid useless fucks who've sold, stolen and borrowed everything they can, firebombed all their bridges and have now lain down somewhere to very publicly croak.

The Sphinx rolls over the prone body, loaded mercy at the ready, gently kisses the abscessed vein and slides in salvation. Withered near-death eyelids open to the face that once emerged from a frozen sea with those translucent, ice-colored eyes. Pick her up in trembling hands, a face so flawless, so terrible to hold. Run with her to the temple, fingers turned blue and frostbitten. Lay that sapphire countenance on the altar before a single candle where she will thaw over countless eons while entire civilizations rise and fall. Quickly withdraw into the shadows, inspired to go out and raise vast slave armies, burn and slaughter hordes of lice-ridden peasants in her inviolable name.

When we'd met, I was convinced the Sphinx had to be from some exotic foreign land, perhaps Antarctican. Her porcelain features, aquiline nose and perfect cheekbones, the unnatural serenity of a Cathar priestess, expressions and reactions so fleeting as to have never been. But no, she's from a fishing village on the Gaspé, about fifteen hours away by bus. Still, I've got to believe some high-born Khazar or aristocratic Scyth had slipped over the side of a three-master off the coast of Bathurst, NB to leave behind his seed then swim away into the night. Or an Icelandic water sprite got hot with some Cape Breton sailors before drowning them.

Outside the Peanut Bar, I stop to pull myself together. The place is actually called Les Bobards. Its nickname comes from the big bowls of peanuts everywhere. Patrons are encouraged to crack open the shells and throw them on the floor after eating the contents.

The Sphinx waits patiently, all in black, of course, something sleek. I pause and watch her index finger gracefully rise to hook a strand of richly dyed coppery red hair. She senses my approach, ambiguous little curls at the corners of her immaculately painted lips. Her inhuman beauty makes me feel like that Moujik idiot at the Balmoral. I climb onto a barstool and she leans toward me. While passing her cheek first to one side of my face and then the other, she slips money into my breast pocket.

"Nice to see you," she says quietly.

Our fingers brush and I leave four especially generous packs in her hand.

"Imagine the story of two lovers," I say.

"Which lovers?" she asks with a trace of suspicion.

"Two lovers who are so radically perverse they get unimaginable kicks from briefly meeting once a day to barely touch hands then go their separate ways."

The Sphinx allows a soundless little laugh. Her lips part just enough to take a sip of tea. I've never seen her tongue. "You're droll, Johnny."

I grin and blush like a yokel, try to think of small talk so she won't go. "So, uh, how do you like the medicine lately?"

"You always have something acceptable."

"I do?"

"Don't you?"

"Uh, well, sure," I misfire and curse my worthless yokel brain. "But I'm in the middle of all this. It's difficult to judge the finer points."

I've heard she has some man at home. A brooder, no doubt. Grave as a dozen widows, refuses to exist beyond their gloomy apartment and sends her out in the world to live his life. The Sphinx leaves some money on the bar, gets into her coat and picks up a black patent leather purse. Before leaving, her gloved hand touches my arm.

"I think you're doing all right, Johnny."

"I am?"

"Yes, you are."

"Will you tell me when I'm not?"

"I will always be honest with you."

I watch her go out into the early evening traffic and swear to myself, zero clue about how I'd ever get anywhere with her. She impregnable as a medieval fortress. You'd have to commandeer an endless snaking mob of Roman Legions, Huns, Ostrogoths, drag out the siege engines and catapults and undermining timbers, get roasted alive with boiling oil poured from her turrets, broadswords rending limbs and maces crushing skulls...

After seeing the Sphinx, I swing by Al's. We're supposed to meet Morgan at the Bifteck. I figure we can relax there for a couple hours while my lower Main clientele slide through the place. It's become a fast tradition of ours on early Saturday evenings. The narcs only show up past midnight, too stupid to realize the bar's drug trade is all over by 10 p.m.

After Al opens the door, he tells me to wait in the living room.

"Where's Mama?"

"At church, it's Saint Mentula's Day."

"Who's Saint Mentula?"

"Patron saint of Polesitters."

"I thought that was Saint Simeon."

"No, he was a dilettante and a derivative fool. Anyway, Johnny, sit here and amuse yourself. I'm almost done."

"Done what?"

Al leaves without explanation, engrossed in a sheet of paper he quietly reads while going down the long hallway to his bedroom. After a few minutes, I hear him yell some lines—rehearsing, I guess. I sneak down there and listen at the door.

"Nicholas Flood Davin, you filthy bloodsucker! You ought to be ashamed of yourself! I want this classroom spotless, do you hear, absolutely spotless!"

What the fuck?... I peak into the bedroom. Al's leaned against the closet door, a finger pressed to one ear to achieve just the right tone. He reads from a script, hollering his guts out.

"One more slip up and you'll be the first one we rent out to those burly Dauphin miners! Do you understand, you lily-livered rodent!?"

I slap a hand to my mouth, stifle a snort of laughter. Al spins about and scowls at me. He points at the closet then puts a finger to his lips. I tip toe over and give him the twisting hand gesture like *what's up?*

"I have a client in there," he whispers. "Go wait in Mama's room. I'll tell you about it once we're finished."

I retreat into Mama Polo's simple but fanatically clean quarters. The bed has been made up tight as a snare drum and the room smells of mothballs. There's a big, ornate crucifix above the headboard. The Christ appears to be hung over. Virgin Mary statuary is on every flat surface, all with the condescending little cocked head. The Christ peers down at them with a miserable glower. *You bitches think you got woes?*

Al continues his dramatic delivery, but I can't make out specific words except for a few goddamns and bloodies. It lasts another ten minutes or so then there's some metallic clanking. Eventually I hear low conversation in the hall. Al and his "client" talk their way toward the front of the house with a genial exchange. I come out after the door shuts and find Al in the back parlor, collapsed into his wingback.

"So what was all that about?"

He lights a cigarillo and sips from a snifter of cognac. "My client is a history lecturer at the university and enjoys the odd bout of verbal abuse."

"No shit? That's a lucky break. How did you meet him?"

"I answered a personal ad in the back of *The Mirror*. Very nice fellow, actually."

"That's his name, Nicholas Blood Drubbing?"

"Nicholas Flood Davin—and no, that's not his name. Apparently, Davin was a Canadian government bureaucrat, influence peddler and alleged writer who lived in the mid-nineteenth century."

"I guess that's suitably obscure. How come you never told me about this trick of yours, Al?"

"He insists on absolute anonymity, so I expect your discretion."

"Yeah, sure, who would care? So what's he pay?"

"One hundred dollars per session; once a week for twenty minutes of admonishing him from a prepared script. I don't know who writes them, but they're not very good. Rather repetitive."

"Still, not a bad little gig, Alphonse."

"I wouldn't take a dollar less. It's an exhausting performance."

"What, just freaking out on the guy?"

"You don't understand, Johnny. He has an ear for dialogue and I can't read it like a robot—not that I would, professional ethics and all. However, he expects real gusto, projection—and that takes craft. Also, I have to help him in and out of a complicated leather and steel apparatus."

"What, like a B&D sort of thing?"

"Not exactly. More medieval, I'd say."

"You think he's one of the guys we saw up on the mountain? A couple of them would definitely fit your man's MO."

"My man's MO? There are armies of these people running around! And they're all in high-ranking positions within the government, media, the judiciary, academia and so forth."

"C'mon. Now you're spouting Aunt Byron's hair-brained theories."

"They're not 'theories.'"

"Okay, let's say every bureaucrat, cop, judge, lawyer, professor, media star and all the rest are a network of wild-eyed, baby-raping psychos. What exactly are you or Aunt Byron or anybody else gonna do about it?"

Al considers the problem for a few moments then issues a tired grunt. "Service them, I suppose..."

The Bifteck is pretty empty around dinnertime. We sit in the rear, next to the pool tables, our backs to the corner. Morgan's not here yet. Al flags down Sandy the waitress and orders us double vodkas. His eyebrows signal toward the bar at the front. Slim's walked in with a long-haired high school boy. He's a brunette beauty, dressed in a fashionably ragged black t-shirt and appears to have a nicely toned bod. Of course Slim always looks like a million bucks no matter how hard she's been carousing or what she's got on; like the worn black Levis and frayed wifebeater that shows off the sides of her tits; the ruler straight, white blonde hair down past her shoulders.

Her lad radiates pride, cannot believe his good fortune. He's cocky and yacks openly at strangers, checks to see who's noticed this fine, long-legged score of his. Slim hears his opinions on music and TV with pursed lips and might even spend enough time listening to seem civil before she drags him home.

"So, whaddaya think about this new recruit up against the boards?" I ask Al, dropping into my Danny Gallivan shtick. "He's a good lookin' kid. Scouting reports say he's got a great set of hands on him, terrific junior league record. Plays the body, loves to bang 'em in the corners. Drafted 4th overall from the Noranda Knobgobblers. Led his team in scoring, doncha know."

Al's hunched over his vodka like it's a news desk mike. He's not all that taken with Slim's young prospect. "Let's not overrate the boy, Johnny. How many young phenoms have we seen promoted to the bigs before they were ready, only to end up back on the farm team in Moncton or Val d'Or? No, it's not every rookie that can keep it up all season long. I'd wager 48 hours till he knocks on her door with something he made—a token already."

Slim picks up on our live play-by-play coverage. She sticks her tongue out at us over the kid's shoulder. She'll screw him at least once to give the oddsmakers a break. But chances are, underneath his hip young strut, he's just another whitebred hoser who'll come over the boards on fire then get caught up ice on the game-losing goal.

Slim told me that last week, pretty wasted up at the Bar Saint-Laurent, she left some guy hanging and disappeared with his buddy while the stooge was in the can. Like that Bobbo loser, like all of them, the stooge came out and saw the abandoned table and half-finished drinks. He puffed out his chest and shoved through a gauntlet of jeers. The stooge hurried down The Main and caught Slim and his pal in a laneway with their hands opening one another clothes.

The way Slim told it, she took them both home. Up in her attic, the young stooge and his bosom pal were at either end of her and grinned at each other. She saw that dumb look, like they wanted to pump their fists, slap a high-five and yell *Yesssss!* Feeling a little generous, she tried to teach these gomers a thing or two, but it all went awry.

What the fuck are you doing? Don't just grab it like it's some on-off switch. No, not like that! Oh, for Chrissake, just get off me.

She booted out the stooge and his sidekick five seconds after they'd filled their rubbers, but like all of Slim's human dildos, they were love-struck at her hostility. "Uh… can we have your phone number?"

"I don't have a phone."

Stooge's partner hesitated at the door. "Um… I guess we'll see ya round."

I notice Leroi at the end of the bar, right by the door. He's come in with a blonde French girl called Sophie. So much for his lubing The Man's JC Van Damme fixation. Sophie's got all these curvy curves, a big sweet ass and nice full breasts. Rubens would have gone gaga over her and I'm getting kinda mesmerized myself. She's yet another woman that has used Tony's place as a sort of portal. The Tone is like some unwitting pimp. He meets these incredible women because of his groovy studio, his artist gimmick, but they always end up giving him a condescending pat on the head then go off with one of his friends.

Leroi and Sophie are sitting real close, noses together, fingers between each other's thighs. Her shirt's open just enough to reveal the top half of lacy red bra. She's sassy and unpredictable, temperamental as a thorough-bred and sharp as a tack, dropped right into Leroi's lap, just as he'd prayed.

Al draws my attention to a scuffle outside the men's room. I tell him to fuck off, but when I look back at Leroi and Sophie, all I catch is a glimpse of them leaving, holding hands and laughing, a spark of red against the gray nightfall.

The Bifteck slowly picks up speed as dusk settles on The Main. The clouds break for a moment and a bright sunset bounces off the shop windows across the road. Somebody has put Men Without Hats on the stereo. As a joke, I presume. I mean, they're good guys from the neighborhood and all, but there's a limit to loyalty. Their song gets blown off the sound system with an explosion and a scream, then distorted Asexuals guitar feedback. The pool tables have gotten busy. Players write their names on a small chalkboard to reserve a spot. The shouts and banter become more excitable as the lights are turned down. In a few hours it will be packed to the gills and they'll be four deep at the bar.

A year ago the Bifteck was a tomb. The numbskull Porkchop owner had his dick in his hand and couldn't figure out how to draw flies. He'd redone the dive with curly, wrought-iron arches, exposed wood beams, beige stucco and framed bullfighting posters. He tried flamenco dancers and they immediately flatlined. Then Gypsy fiddlers—pfft. That was followed by some lowlife in a matador suit who sang Barry Manilow schmaltz while tickling a Farfisa organ. All that *and* fine dining.

Despite his considerable efforts, the Porkchop was thwarted. He'd fret, pace around and his testicles would constrict as he watched the Balmoral across the street get mobbed day and night. He couldn't figure it out. That place is a filthy hole while his establishment was classy.

Looking to replace a barmaid, the Porkchop hired a hip young babe called Marie, without giving it much thought beyond some far-fetched fantasy she'd find him beguiling. Marie advised the Porkchop to uncover the pool tables fossilizing in the back. He was reluctant, worried about the Bifteck losing its luxe appeal, but eventually agreed to try it her way—for a little while.

Marie played some of her mix tapes and a few friends dropped by. College kids began to show up and shoot eightball, drink lots of cheap draft. It wasn't long before *The Mirror* officially sanctioned the Bifteck's kitschy cool. Within a couple months the place got fairly trashed, which only added to the image and nowadays there's a lineup down the block after midnight.

So tonight the Porkchop struts around, balls first, and strokes the wad of c-notes he keeps in his pants. Of course he's convinced it was all his doing and Marie is long gone for refusing his advances. *But how can you resist me? I am the vast and conquersome Porkchop! Behold the marvel I have fashioned!*

At the bar, Slim gets antsy, tosses down her boy's shot and leads him out the door. She'll be back in an hour or so. The occasional client of mine cruises by our table. Dred Blanc stops in, that mouth-breather Hernav, even Savva's made the trek, but does not stick around. Vern and Tony score off me and ten minutes later I see them both with foreheads flat on the bar, arms hung at their sides. Fucking guys have no self-control. Aunt Byron has shown up to meet us, but doesn't even say hello. Instead, she stands at the bar with some paunchy old square.

"Well, well..." Al mutters, putting on a weasel grin.

"What?"

"Byron's having quite the little confab with my friend from the closet."

"No way!" I stare at them. "You mean that's Nicholae Claude Drivel?"

"Nicholas Flood Davin—and don't stare."

But I do because the square looks familiar. "You know, Al, I think this guy was on the mountain that night, at the fag orgy."

He inspects the man carefully. "I don't believe so, Johnny."

Now I'm sure of it. "What do you know? You left after five minutes. Yeah..." I point at them. "He was standing over a butt-fuck, blow-job three-some, jerking off."

"Well, I just hope Byron doesn't steal my business."

"No... I'd say she's hunting bigger game than that."

Byron's new friend gesticulates forcefully, worked up about something. Aunt B is entranced and quickly scrawls into her journal.

"I wonder how they met," Al muses.

"Maybe Aunt Byron's been going back up the mountain, solo. Y'know, show off the fancy new plumbing."

A bunch of heads turn as Morgan enters. She's got that natural ability to make the rest of the place just fade, and it's not only her youth. She'll be doing it at sixty. Some people are just switched on like that. She spots us and comes over with her killer smile. "I saw your friend Slim up the street. She had nice piece of under-aged tail with her."

"Yup, Slim's got taste," I agree while ordering a large pitcher.

An overweight young bonehead in a biker jacket ambles over as Morgan settles in. He's gormless and sincere, gestures widely with his beer bottle then points it at her. "Uh… I was just lookin' at you and… uh… I just wanna tell ya, you're really sexy."

Morgan's eyes drop. She lets out a tired chuckle.

"What's so funny?" Bonehead demands.

Morgan gives him a baby doll put-on, wide eyed. "That tiny hard-on growing off the end of your nose."

Me and Al grin at each other. Bonehead glares at us, suddenly full of sizzling hatred for everything he's seen since coming off the Outaouais cabbage farm. Nearby drinkers pick up on the tension and prepare to get out of the way. Morgan rests her chin on her knuckles, still with the cutesy act. "Well?"

Al gives me a nod as we get ready to pile drive Bonehead with the table, but Morgan's cut him off at the knees. He turns beet red, stiffly rotates on his heels and goes toward the men's room while gales of laughter bounce off the back of his brand new black leather jacket.

"These fucking people," Morgan bitches, mood thrown off.

She's right. The stupid asshole—I feel like killing him. Here she was in a fine humor, all sparkle and light, and he has to go and lay himself across us like a wet streak of shit.

Hennessy materializes out of the noisy jostle and drags a chair over, crowds in between me and Morgan. "I know, I know," he holds up a hand. "I'm too heavy and I'm not your brother."

"He's learning," Al grins and signals for more drinks.

A venal expression grows on the Hen's face as he scopes the room. His eyes settle on a candidate sitting on the other side of the pool tables. We follow his sight line.

"I'd make the same choice," Al confirms.

"In your dreams," Morgan shoots him down. "No offense, Alphonse, but look at her."

Yeah, look at her. She's dressed in elegant but trashy vintage wear. Dimpled cheeks and full lips done in gleaming black, there is something roguish and kind of spiteful about her. She's already blown away a squad of one-line Charlies, leaving them all an inch or two shorter.

"Okay, Lothario," I say to Hennessy and slip him an appetizer. "Here's something to grease the wheels. But play it cool, will ya, don't go crawling up to her on your hands and knees."

He zips into the toilet before I've finished my pep talk.

Morgan squints at the Hen's target. "Y'know, I've seen her around... and she doesn't seem stupid.... I'd say Hennessy's doomed."

"Then how about a wager?" Al proposes, trying to recover from Morgan's gutting. "I have twenty dollars that says he'll be successful."

"You're on," Morgan tells him. "He doesn't stand a chance."

"I'll take the Hen for fifty," I say, upping the ante.

She rubs her hands with glee. "Bring it on, suckers!"

In a few minutes, Hennessy swaggers out of the john. He beams at us then proceeds to lean against the wall, ankles crossed, trying to come off as jaunty. It is an absurd pose, a horrible cliché of body language. The woman glances at him then looks away with an exaggerated chagrin. Way to go, Hen. Shot down while you're still on the runway. I can't bear to watch.

"Ha!" Morgan gloats. "You guys backed a donkey. Okay, Johnny, give me Al's twenty in product—along with your fifty. And you can fill my prescription right about... oh... now."

But hang on. Hennessy gets a second wind, he's in there pitching. She hands him a cigarette with an impish smile. The vibe is good and getting better. C'mon, Hen! Do it for Papa! Open it up on the back stretch! She's asked him to sit down and shifts forward in her seat, chin up, elbows on the table, pushing together some nice cleavage. Hennessy leans across and lights her smoke. He babbles, a flurry of hand gestures. *Easy now, boy.* She laughs out loud, a hand to her mouth. Hey, if you can get a woman to laugh with you—not at you, you're getting somewhere.

"For fucksakes," Morgan snarls. "What a dumb bitch."

"Don't stare," I tell her.

"Yeah, yeah."

Al likes what he sees. "We're halfway home, Johnny."

"It's still neck and neck. Let's wait for the official results."

Outside on The Main another thundershower is sweeping through. The Bifteck ebbs and flows, getting packed as the music becomes louder and bootleg Bootsauce belts it out. Aunt Byron's disappeared, same with her paunchy friend. I ask Sandy the waitress and she tells me they left together a few minutes ago. Kit has peeled Vern and Tony off the bar. She gives us a tired roll of the eyes while leading them out the door.

Hennessy suddenly pops out of the pressing crowd. The black-lipped beauty waits at a discreet distance. He crouches at my elbow and a hundred bucks appears in his bony fist. I grab him round the shoulders, kiss his ear and snatch the bills.

"It worked," he says quietly, afraid to spook his luck. "Her name is Josée and she's a very nice person. We have a great deal in common."

"Ah, my young Claymore!" I crow, smirking at Morgan. "'Donkey', huh?"

"I'll take my twenty now," Al bugs her.

Morgan gives us her middle finger.

"Ignore Mommy," I say to Hennessy. "Papa's very proud of you." I brush a couple specs of dandruff from his jacket and pass him the goods. "And so is Uncle Al."

"Maybe you and Uncle Al are proud of me," the Hen whines, "but Mommy's jealous!"

Morgan's hand slowly balls into a fist, her elbow begins to cock back. I give the Hen a quick mutter out of the side of my mouth. "Better scram, kid. Mommy's gonna go psycho."

SEVENTEEN

The pager rattles its way across the nightstand and crashes to the floor, stunning me awake. The goddamn thing has become the bane of my existence. It's Slim, calling over and over like a madwoman, far too early in the morning. It takes me a few minutes to get my bearings and I'm about to go over there and see what the hell's the crisis when I glance out the front window and see her marching along Roy toward my place. I go down and open the door as her finger rises to the bell.

"I saw you from upstairs. What's going on?"

"I called your pager around one last night," she says and pushes past me. "You didn't answer."

"I was busy."

"Yeah. You were busy."

"Well, I'm here now, okay?"

After we get upstairs she pulls out a sheet of paper. "There's this weird guy that's been coming to the Balmoral while I'm working and he creeps me out."

"Oh, Christ," I realize. "The wacko who sits along the wall, across from the bar, and just stares at you, right?"

"Yeah, him—with the big eyebrows."

I'm hit with a flash of rage. "What did he do to you!? I'll murder the fuck!"

"He hasn't touched me, Johnny. Relax. But he did leave me a cheap, fake-fur jacket with a brown vinyl collar."

"Well, that alone is pretty offensive."

"The thing is, he also left me a completely insane letter and I don't want him to follow me home some night." She hands me the single page, torn from a spiral notebook. "Here, read it. The guy's really fucked up."

The letter's written in red pen, with a painfully deliberate hand, the letters gone over heavily. *Dear Alison, this is=*<u>*Your frend Avoro.*</u>

"Who's Alison?"

"That's what somebody at the bar told him my name is." I look back to the bizarro document. "Read it," she badgers.

> *I am man who give you ReaL Fur beautifl <u>jacket.</u> Ive Bin a true Friend to you- I need <u>Favor From</u> you. My reputaton is at big Risk. I need to get A lady very jelleausse- Because she's Bin IN many ways trying to <u>Distroy my Reputaton.</u> I WANT you go out with me Friday night Alison and this- ThursDay night=and this <u>coming Sunday</u>=I wan't you to go with me to her Brothers house just For one hours on Sunday 130pm. OF course I am in love with beatifull Lady <u>Rite NOW</u>- Read on Back...*

I laugh and shake my head. "This is fuckin' hilarious!"

Slim's not amused. "It's not funny. I know men are going to hit on me if I work in a bar, but this guy is nuts."

"C'mon, why don't you just break his balls? He's a geek."

"No! If I talk to him, he might keep coming back no matter what I say. I don't think he speaks much English or French. Besides, like I said, I don't want him jumping me in my laneway some night. Will you just read the stupid thing?"

> *I am fall in <u>LOVE</u> with YOU Alison!!!! But i was introduse to CONNY many times ago. She stilL thinks Im after her=and is in- so many way TRying to Distroy my reputaton. She says and so does her Family I only want her because I have <u>NO GirlFrend</u>. All this is hurtting me and my own reputaton. Call me ALISSON- tomorow at 5pm in evening <u>AVORO 955-3341</u>. I LEAVE for you beaitful 2800.00 dollar present. Avoro see you with your little boy man. Leave him! I <u>DO</u> mind if you go with other mens=Because I LOVE YOU so be good WOMan and <u>FAITHful for AVORO</u>!!!!!!!!!*

"What the hell. What's this 'little boy man' bullshit?"

Slim grabs the letter back. "Will you forget about yourself for one second?"

"You didn't fuck him, did you?"

"Don't be sick!"

"Okay, okay."

Man, all these blossoming maniacs lately, determined to crawl out of the woodwork. It's a goddamn epidemic. A tall, blonde babe like Slim gets these evolutionary throwbacks swinging from the trees. This Australopithecus goes into the bar and is convinced she shows off those long legs for him alone—the mighty Avoro.

"Can you just talk to him or something?"

"All right, tell you what. Page me next time he's there. I'll come down and deal with the guy."

"But you'll come right away, not like two hours later?"

"Slim, when do I ever leave the neighborhood?"

"I don't know. You might be on the nod or screwing somebody. How would I know?"

"Gimme a break. As soon as you page, I'll race right down there and straighten out that piece of shit."

"But don't go crazy and beat him up. Just—just tell him you're my boyfriend or husband or whatever. Y'know, so he'll leave me alone."

"Don't worry. I'm related to this type of moron. I know how to handle them."

"I hope so." She takes off her coat and relaxes a bit. "Let's go back to bed. This whole thing's really messed with my nerves. I've got a few hours before I have to be at Concordia."

"What, you're taking classes there too—McGill's not enough for ya?"

"No, I'm working in the Registrar's office."

"Christ, you're industrious."

She stops for a moment. "Jane's not back, is she?"

"Naw... She's... I don't know what she's doing... still off somewhere."

"I don't get your thing with her, Johnny. She just makes you miserable."

"Yeah, I know, you keep saying that. Do you want some tea?"

"That's a good idea. Why don't you make some Typhoo? It'll be nice and cozy."

I go into the kitchen to rustle up the tea while Slim heads upstairs and gets into bed. I think about how to deal with this Avoro freak. Hopefully he doesn't have an army of fellow moujiks at his beck and call, muscle-brained fellaheens who can quickly fashion farming implements into close combat weapons. I knew I was *right* about that asshole. Driving himself crazy over Slim, in a constant state of self-righteous hysteria, ready to unleash a hail of backhands and frothing condemnations. Every heartbeat verges on a coronary as cunt-devils mock him in shadowy bars and sloe-eyed witches prance openly on TV. He'll pound on the table at his people's social club, wave a rolled-up copy of his community's newspaper and yell about how *she learning new way in new country, heh? She suckee suckee good, ah? She play Hide Salami with welfare bum, heh? Okay, I fix…*

Not a chance, Avoro. You are dead in the water. That sleazy character living up the street? No kidding the bastard can get it up three times an hour when he's got fuck all else to do. He sleeps half the day while you scurry off to work; the god-fearing Avoro, phonetically translated name stapled to your forehead, toiling like a mule and paying penury tax to the Founding Peoples.

It gnaws at his throat, eats at him until he harasses Cousin Boscus into sitting down at Aunt Mooka's kitchen table to help him compose his heartfelt letter to 'Alison.'

EIGHTEEN

A loud bang from downstairs in the back of the apartment wakes me out of a heavy drug and booze blackout. Did I leave a window open? Maybe it's a door slamming shut in the draft. Then I hear something hit the floor down there—hard, followed by a groan. What the fuck now, a klutz B&E artist at nine in the morning? I can't be bothered to get out of bed and hope whatever or whoever it is will just go away. I almost doze off again when the bed bounces.

"Janey?"

"Even better, it's me," says Hennessy while getting under the covers fully clothed, with his boots on. "I did it," he whispers in my ear, hugging me from behind, full of excitement.

I half roll toward him and feel the fresh outside air he's brought along. "Did what?"

"I'm a certified, state-supported lunatic," he brags. "It was Oscar caliber! I tell you, there are still a few liberals left in the world. The poor woman at the welfare office, she signed all the forms with tears in her eyes. And Al Polo thinks he's an actor."

I yawn and stretch. "Congrats. Sounds like you've earned it."

"I earn everything."

Hennessy seems healthy for a change, a warm coffee color to his skin rather than the usual dingy undercoat. He scrunches up close and playful, reaches down and feels my piss hard-on, presses it against my stomach.

"Oof. My bladder's going to burst."

"Your bladder can wait." He begins to stroke me and murmurs into the back of my neck. "You know, there's something so nice about being completely dressed while in bed with a naked body."

"You say that to all the girls."

I haven't used in about eight hours and he is here now. Maybe my body's in the mood. Hard to tell, even if my brain is into it. Hennessy rolls me onto my back and with tongue and teeth on my nipples, his cool hand on my cock kind of sets it all off with a gush of libido. My perineum throbs and I begin to leak. He licks up my ribs and armpit, bites my neck. The pain brings on a burst of endorphins. He giggles and ducks under the sheet, sticks his face down there and takes me in his mouth with those sweet, sardonic lips, pushing my legs apart. He's full of daffy noises, blows strawberries against my balls, makes me laugh and gets everything all wet then surfaces, hat still on.

Hennessy rises to his wrists, grins down at me with those nicotine stained teeth, undoes his pants and zipper one-handed. I'm suddenly flushed and in a hurry, grab his skinny waist with my knees, feel how hard he is and almost choke on my own saliva. I bite my tongue as his hips twist and tease. When he finally does push, it drives the breath out of me, my eyes rolling back. Rising out of sleep to this, it's dream-like and effortless. I curl up closer, my heels against his hard little ass. We sink and we float on a lazy half-moon ride, my brain nicely shutting off for a change. Our swaying builds into a sweet rocking rhythm. And in the end, we don't come fireworks or whistling explosions. Hennessy's eyes slowly close and his breath rolls across my face, soft and warm. I feel his heat lick at my insides then look down and see myself come in long easy streaks with the ammonia smell of brand new sperm.

NINETEEN

"You were supposed to meet me at Josée's an hour ago," Morgan nags. "Where the fuck are you!?"

"At a pay phone near Savva's. I'm meeting Leroi there in a minute, then I'll come up in a cab."

"Well, hurry the fuck up. I gotta see somebody soon and I feel like shit."

"I left you almost a quarter GR last night. What did ya do, shove it up your ass?"

"Fuck you, Johnny! Don't be such a stupid asshole. Just get over here!"

"All right. Fuck."

I haven't been to Savva's place in a fair while, having gotten into a routine of meeting him at the Euro Deli for coffee every day. His apartment's street-level door is open and I can hear his stentorian pronunciations when turning to go up. At the top step, I freeze. There's some kind of full-tilt cottage industry going on. A Central American peasant girl rolls up tubes of tabloid size newspaper sheets and applies a couple pieces of tape to keep their shape. The paper tubes are carefully arranged in pyramids of thirty or forty on a long fold-out work table. A male serf concentrates on sliding variously colored plastic connectors on the ends of each. Down the hall in the living room, I can see some large pyramids, rectangles and cubes built with these things.

Savva's big Russian paw comes down on my shoulder from behind. He winks at me with his overdone rubbery smile while gabbing on the phone.

His sloshed-on designer cologne stings my eyes. He wears a pricey gray leather bomber jacket and new snakeskin cowboy boots.

"Yes, yes," he's saying. "Of course, not to worry. Sample constructions will be shipped to Hogtown as we agree. No problemska. All is moving according to schedule." He holds up a hand. "You are very kind, but do not embarrass Savva. I am only humble artist doing what is possible. Okay, please call me when you receiving shipment. Good bye, my dear Peggy." He hangs up and positively radiates. The two workies glance over at us, but Savva's right on them, his voice suddenly fierce as a rhino whip. "Eh! You! Put eyes on job! I no pay for boolshit." He turns back to me. "Johnny," he lathers. "My friend. Come into Savva's bureau."

The chaotic studio in his front room has been converted into a simple but functional office, the kind you see next to a loading dock. There's a giant calendar on one wall with various entries and tacked-up notes. Savva slides in behind the desk and points at one of the chairs facing him.

"What *is* all that?" I ask.

He leans forward and gets serious, elbows on an old blotter. "It has been very difficult. I was humiliated. Me, Savva Grudtsyn, respected experimental writer and avant gardist. After Hogtown publisher give me advance and helping me with grants, they ask me do menial labors for them!" He sneers at the assembly going on in the dining room-turned-workshop. "To make these ridiculous constructions. But Savva no stupid. I negotiate good deal."

"What is that shit exactly?"

"Hogtown publisher is also packager of children's books and toys for educational purposes. They have environmental idea to recycle newspaper with plastic connector device so children can build little house and these kind of things. I make for them various demonstration models for different expositions, capitalistic sales conference where retail parasites meet with wholesale kulaks and sign contract for this garbage, then selling them to idiotic parents. I was having no idea children's boolshit industry is so *massif*."

I thumb back at his employees. "So where'd you get the coolies?"

"Illegal Guatemalan refugees. No payroll tax, no worker compensations, no unemployment insurance contribution—and they make acceptable effort. Hogtown publisher pay me fifteen dollar per hour. I pay these *krest'yanin* three dollar per hour each. Savva making nine dollar per hour to do very little. And I getting contract from other Hogtown promotion companies so I renting small apartment across street with one guy working there. I am average eight hundred dollars every week, net net."

Despite the booming trade, Savva lets out a miserable huff while lighting one of his black and silver Sobranies. "So, other than lacking in fraternal socialistic brotherhood, why so glum, chum?"

He leans back, hands open at me. "I getting so many contract now, Johnny, beyond children's boolshit. I provide good service on schedule for excellent price. But a bizaman cannot breathe in this place. Worse than Soviet Union. Everything tax tax tax. Government apparatchiks, they torment the biznaman." He sighs heavily, as only a Russian can. "I must leave, my friend. How things are now, like this, is not for making bizness." He halfheartedly tosses a hundred bucks on the desk. I pick up the money and give him his stuff.

"So you're really gonna get out of Montreal?"

"You know I love this place, Johnny, our 'Open City', as you like to say. All my friends are here. Montreal is like beautiful, mysterious woman. Hogtown is like... I don't know—like greedy eunuch. But I must be moving there. I have accountant now. He tell me, 'Savva, you stay in Montreal, you only donkey of socialistic government, work like dog for Nomenklatura. Bizaman no welcome here.'"

We hear Leroi tromp up the steps. "What the...? Un-believable."

"Don't even ask," I say when he wanders into the office. "I'll tell ya later. Here." I hand him the pager and the small tin cigarette case we keep the packs in. "Four GRs, on the nose. Warlock, Kit and Tony just phoned. They'll be calling back in a minute."

The pager rattles on Savva's desk. "Yup, there's Warlock," Leroi confirms after checking the call. He looks to Savva. "Hey, Duddy Kravitz, can I use your hotline?"

Savva pushes an old rotary dial beast across the desk while getting his dose ready. The two Guatemalans chat and laugh in the other room. Savva's head snaps up. "Eh! You want me call immigration, heh!?" A heavy pall drops over them.

"Fuck," I mutter. "You're a bigger hard-ass than that Gletkin guy in *Darkness At Noon*."

"Today, people are very soft," Savva explains, as if he's a man long accustomed to breaking unruly churls. "Do you realizing, Johnny, when Stalin push industrialization of Soviet Union to save country from fascisti, he take these *ulicznik* from farm and put them to work with machine in important factory, give them responsibility, respect. What they do? They lie down next to machine and SLEEP! Very expensive machine become destroyed. So of course only one solution." Savva's eyes narrow. "Russians should blame themself, no the Generalissimo."

Leroi and I watch him finish his shot then rise from the naugahyde exec chair. "Okay, gentlemens, I am afraid our meeting must end. Thank you for consultations."

Savva shows us out and heads across Duluth to his other operation above a used clothing store. I give Leroi a brief rundown of the recycled newspaper constructo-kits and Savva's plans to relocate in Hogtown.

"You've got to hand it to him," he says as we stroll toward his rendezvous with Warlock. "The guy's doing it more or less legally."

"Well, he is an immigrant, with all that pent-up ambition."

"Sure, but guaranteed he'll hate Hogtown."

"How do you know? You've never even been."

"Savva's one of those talk-too-close, in-your-face guys. That'll be a huge handicap in a frigid place like that."

"Yeah, maybe you're right. He is too grabby, all the constant backslaps and Vulcan death pinch."

"But worst of all," Leroi points out, "we lose like four hundred bucks a week. I guess we'll have to wait and see if he really does go."

"Oh, he's going to Hogtown, all right. Savva's tapped a nice revenue vein and he's got the energy to mine it. Under his writer and artist gimmick, he's a total moujik and those people are relentless."

TWENTY

I slowly surface in Morgan's bed after surviving another long night of drink, drug and debauch. Well, *the dose does make the poison*, as old Bombastus used to say. Splintered recollections of noise drift past, people talking, yelling, coming and going.

At least I think this is Morgan's bed. I guess it doesn't make much difference when the whole neighborhood becomes your lie-in, but yeah... I can smell her body and floating up to the light I want to touch her as my eyes open and looking down... Aw... for fucksakes! Not *this* again! There's a goddamn giraffe puppet on my dick! I pull the thing off and hurl it across the room. When I rub my eyes, my hands come away with a mess of black and red make-up. That fucking—"MORGAN!!!"

No answer. I look in her dressing table mirror and the stuff's smeared all over my face. There's some drawings on the floor, pencil and oil stick on 24 x 36 inch sheets of newsprint. They're all of me, passed out naked with only that stupid puppet on my knob, made up like a demented clown, mouth hung open. I look like a retarded corpse.

Goddamn Morgan, she's pulled this before, desperate to get her BFA from Concordia. The problem is she's ignored some drawing credits because she can draw like others can breathe so naturally figured on leaving that stuff till last, easiest to do and so on. As usual with that sort of thing, you never actually bother and then one day, whomp, like a kick in the snatch, you've got to complete a year's worth of drawings in about a week. And she figures they can't just be any old bullshit still-lifes of fruit or puppies—that she's got to make a real impact, so I'm the one paying for it. Actually, Morgan's lost-dog pal Lindy is also on the hook. The old pooch has been immortalized on several occasions while totally conked out, including one time with her ass in a big bowl of stale popcorn, naked but for a rucksack full of stuffed toys on her back and boxing gloves on her feet. Morgan has badly abused our trust and our inebriation. You just can't go unconscious around the woman.

I make sure my stash is still under the carpet behind the nightstand then grab a wrinkled towel from the floor, wipe most of the crap off my face, but can't locate my pants in this disaster area. There's tons of clothes everywhere, open luggage, drawings, paintings, all kinds of broken junk. I'm forced to make do with a pair of oversized kelly-green track pants I dig out from one of the suitcases Morgan's got scattered about.

Holding them up with one hand, I go into the hallway and almost trip over Lindy, sprawled outside the bedroom door, face down among a bunch of rough sketches. All she has on is a dirty bunny hat with big floppy ears, tied backward on her head and an orange plastic flower is sticking up from her butt. Lindy's breathing but basically in a drug coma. I nudge her with my foot. She mumbles something but doesn't move.

I finally track Morgan down to the roof deck behind the kitchen. She's tipped back in a folding chair with a beer going; drawing-paper clipped to a wooden board, sketching a small pile of bald and tortured Barbies. She turns and half cringes up at me, trying not to grin too much.

"Very fucking funny! I should cut your dope with horse laxative."

She reaches for my hand and suppresses a giggle. "Sorry, baby. But you looked so cute. Why don't you go have a shower? Then we'll get something to eat."

"Where are my clothes?"

"I washed them. They should be dry by now." She points at my jeans and shirt hanging from a line near the end of the roof.

I grab my duds and heading to the can, pass Lindy standing naked in the kitchen. She's gawking at the bunny hat in one hand and the plastic flower in the other. A smudged cartoon penis drawn with lipstick goes from her pubic hair up to her chest. Lindy's eyes slowly rise, a jumble of rage and raw humiliation.

"Don't look at me," I tell her. "Take it up with René Magritte out there."

But getting ready to shower, I hear Morgan in the kitchen, quickly turning the tables. I'd warned her weeks ago that Lindy would move right in and take advantage—do her dope, smoke her cigarettes, drink her beer. But Morgan's one of these people who leaves the gate wide open until the chiseler she's helping goes way too far. Then, without realizing, they suddenly transit from victim to freeloader and the gig is up. Lindy crapped out after Morgan discovered that some of her stuff was missing. I don't have a clue how she keeps track of anything in this charnel house. Maybe it's some kind of multi-spatial perception that takes in the entire room in a single visual sweep, more four-dimensional grid search than photographic memory. Whatever it is, Morgan can tell when somebody's fucked with a single spec of her dust.

"I know you pawned my *Funhouse* vinyl," she's accusing Lindy. "And The Nils bootleg—and my signed hardcover edition of *The Main*."

"Maybe they got lost in all this mess," Lindy mopes.

Morgan comes down hard. "It's not a mess! I know exactly where everything is. Exactly."

For some reason, this whole thing reminds me of a guy I know from Hogtown, Paul something-or-other, an acquaintance of Al Polo's. I guess because of his unwavering ability to pull a bonehead move and end up fucking himself when things are going pretty smooth. This Paul wanker came up to Montreal for a weekend one time, so I brought him along to a big blowout house party. It was beginning to nicely take shape just after midnight, lots of vivacious women and talkative guys arriving, booze, drugs and laughter flowing. The party was in a massive two-storey apartment, above a derelict bar down at Ontario and Hôtel de Ville—I mean fucking gigantic. I'd been hanging out with one of the three women who lived in the place, an architecture post-grad whiz called Lyra. The apartment was falling to pieces, graffitied inside and out, mad murals done by Tony and other artists all over the rooms, the hallways, big hunks of plaster missing, lathing showing through here and there—a beautifully decayed, gloomy old palace—just the way she liked it.

So Paul and I are standing in the hall gabbing with Lyra, her roommates, and some other people, when out of nowhere he comes onto her like Joe Renovator, starts to blather as if he's some expert asshole, browbeats her about how she should re-do the place, what kind of R-spectrum drywall to use, stainless cupolas, thermal flying buttresses and fuck knows what other absolute horseshit he doesn't know anything about anyway. Lyra stood there and listened to his bollocks for a minute then turned her back to him and faced me, a bit of color rising to her cheeks. In a brittle voice, loud enough for Paul Handycreep to hear, she says very slowly: "Get him out of here."

Now, when a woman looks at you that way and speaks with that tone of voice, there's no ifs ands or buts. So without a moment's hesitation, I took Paul by the elbow and led him down the stairs. "Listen, man, you've gotta go."

His big fat face turned ruby red. He was stunned, mortified after suddenly comprehending he'd acted like complete jerk-off, but there's no apologizing. You pull that kinda stunt, you're finished. Paul was banished from the Queendom and began to blubber after he realized I wasn't going with him. As if. Anyway, the lesson here is a guy's got to swing with the Power of Pussy, not against it. If you try to swing against the Power of Pussy, you will always—ALWAYS lose in every possible way—even if you happen to be right, which is beside the point, anyhow. You will lose spiritually, intimately, aesthetically, intellectually, socially and you will become really uncool, a sexless blob, a strident old nut who endlessly watches 'real' war footage and starts every stupid conversation with *Apparently…* Women will sneer at the sight of you and that makes for a pretty narrow world.

After showering, I'm going into Morgan's bedroom and hear Lindy chirp like some addled squirrel monkey. "Well, I guess I'll see ya sometime…"

"Probably not," Morgan replies, having turned mean as a rectum-spreading tool.

Lindy clomps down the stairs with Morgan right behind her. The door bangs shut, the deadbolt clanks and she pounds back up, dives onto the bed spread eagle, full of relieved laughter. "Lindy's gone!"

"I hope this teaches you to stop bringing home every lost mutt you run across."

She pulls off her big t-shirt and grabs my smokes off the nightstand. "Yeah, okay, Gordon Gecko. C'mon, let's get high. I don't wanna miss my Life Drawing class. They've been bringing in this really cute model."

"Oh, yeah, how cute?"

"Mm... He can't be more than eighteen or so. I always open the windows. The mildest draft and his cock goes up and down like it's doing pushups. He gets all embarrassed and blushes and sweats then puts on the shiest little smile. It is so fucking sweet. Fuck, man, I'm surprised the whole class hasn't gang raped him."

"Jesus, you're getting me excited."

I shift to the edge of the bed to cook our shots and Morgan spreads her legs behind me. I feel her breasts, warm on my back, her pubic hair at my tailbone. She reaches round, grabs a handful and squeezes hard. "Ow! Don't! That hurts."

"I know," she pouts. "That's why I like doing it. Oh, daddy, I can't help myself, I just love to make you cry."

"You're a real little monster, you know that?"

Morgan lets out a nasty snicker, fingers digging right in.

TWENTY-ONE

I've agreed to go on another mountain mission with Aunt Byron. When I get to Al's in the late afternoon the door's unlocked, but nobody seems to be home, not even Mama Polo. I hear the shower going. It's gotta be Byron. Al wouldn't bathe during daylight, and dollars to donuts Mama's a full-on tub woman. While waiting around, I sift through the newspapers strewn on the coffee table and notice Aunt B's backpack between the couch and sideboard. I peek inside and see her diary. Stealing a look down the hall, I grab it for a quick scan. She's refused to show me this stuff, continually putting me off with "It's a work in progress," and insisting none of it would make sense to an interloper.

There are all kinds of loose pages, photos of various Montreal streets and buildings, the mountain from different angles, a postcard from Mo Wilensky's deli, a small and fairly skilled pencil rendering of Solomon's Temple on Clark Street, accompanied by various Hebrew and Greek words and phrases, arcane symbols and anagrams. The letters AA are repeated here and there throughout the journal, some done in elaborate script, some followed by a list of secret society type gobbledygook; *"Argentum Asteris, Enochia?"* and other *"names for things that cannot have names."* There are elaborate, hand-drawn maps of the pathways snaking through Mount Royal's Catholic and Protestant cemeteries, with faintly penciled-in attempts to join them in a different patterns; pentagrams, heptagons and the like. I leaf through and read snippets of factual data about Mount Royal; 761 feet high, covers a few thousand acres, the parks around the mountain were designed by the same guy who did Central Park. There are short, descriptive comments about me, Al, Hennessy, Slim, other people I don't know; photocopies from medical textbooks about rare diseases that impersonate other diseases; transsexual pre- and post-op procedures. I find a dry report on Byron's first night in Montreal, when she was at my house and we talked about having sex. Then a clinical account of the homo orgy on the mountain. Boy, she really does have a way of draining the blood out of things. But I've got to say, I'm always amazed when people can write pages and pages of notes by hand and not get illegible. My handwriting falls apart in about two sentences.

Near the back of the diary there's a faded color snapshot taped to the page… *Holy shit…* it's a young and very male Aunt Byron with the McGill Perv next to him. … Written in the white margin at the bottom: *To my good friend, Byron. All the best, Duncan Campbell Scott.*

The child Byron is dressed in cheap reformatory denims, hair almost white blonde and cut prison short. He has the ambiguous little Cheshire cat smirk that became his trademark and which the sex change seems to have erased. The younger Perv is tall and strapping—a man clearly in command, but a progressive thinker too. His arm rests around Byron's shoulders in a paternal posture. Perhaps active in the Big Brothers, a firm but friendly mentor. This Duncan Campbell Scott character appears to be in his late twenties in the photo and sports a crinkly, ginger-colored comb-over, pattern baldness already setting in. They both hold fishing rods. Behind them is the shore of a tree-lined lake, along with a small wooden jetty and a rowboat. The picture must be about twenty-five years old. Hearing somebody come out of the shower, I return the diary to the backpack.

"Johnny?"

I throw my ass into Al's wingback while grabbing *The Gazette* sports section. "Present—and sort of accounted for."

Byron appears in the living room archway dressed in a big fluffy white bathrobe and hotel slippers. "I thought I heard you come in. Alphonse has gone to an audition. He'll meet us at the mountain in approximately thirty minutes."

"Groovy. Where's Mama Polo?"

"At church. It's Saint Futuerina's Day."

"Who's Saint Futuerina?"

"Patron saint of the noseless."

"The noseless?"

"Yes, those who had their noses smited from their faces. Not a widespread practice at the moment, but a common form of punishment inflicted on early Christians who openly professed their faith." On that note, Aunt B does an about-face and goes off to get ready.

As we walk west on Duluth, toward the mountain, a gaggle of rowdy kids, maybe eleven or twelve years old, come our way. Byron stiffens as they pass, skirting around us on the narrow, cobblestone street. Once they're by, she picks up the pace. "Let's get away from those children."

"Why, you know them?"

"Don't look," she warns under her breath.

"Why not? What's going on?"

"Nothing. And it's going to stay that way."

"Byron, what the hell are you talking about?"

A couple of the kids eye us, but keep their thoughts to themselves.

"Youngsters that age can be very dangerous. And more than you might think, they are fully aware of their powers."

"Their powers? What powers?"

"Open your eyes, Johnny. One word to the authorities and they could instantly have us handcuffed and imprisoned—a quick kangaroo court and you're suddenly facing ten years behind bars. The prisons are full of men who've been Shanghaied that way—power-mad psychiatrists eliciting so-called 'recovered memories' of brutal sexual abuse. Utterly medieval and completely hysterical."

I turn and watch the kids continue along. They're over near Henri-Julien now and horse around with lots of cheerful noise.

"I don't know... They look pretty normal to me."

Byron pulls me round. "Don't look! You'll only provoke them."

155

"Provoke them? Into doing what, making fun of us?"

"Children that age are extremely malleable and can easily be turned into weapons. Abuse is a complex phenomenon and comes in many forms."

"You're losing me."

"All these youngsters need to say is, 'By the way, Father, I think I'll tell my teacher about the marijuana you've been smoking—and how you walk around the house naked and semi-erect. Should I do that, Father?' Of course the stunned parent replies, 'But I don't even smoke cigarettes and I certainly don't walk around naked.' The child smiles very sweetly and Father's jaw drops. Check Mate."

"Wow, I didn't realize how bad things are getting out in the Volks Reich."

"Go ahead and laugh, but being aware of these situations is a matter of basic research. You and everyone else always complain about conspiracies and that information is hidden."

"When do I ever complain about conspiracies?"

"Well, everyone else then. The critical data is easily accessible, but most people are simply too lazy to sift through all the media nonsense."

"Look, you're the one who's all gung-ho about nailing diddlers and the like. Why this sudden paranoia about kids?"

"It's not sudden and I do wish to see justice done, for everyone—not injustice!"

"Okay, calm down already."

"I am calm!" Byron snaps as she marches along, stiff jawed and straight backed, in a kind of militaristic snit.

Al waits for us at Cartier's monument as we cross Park Avenue. Aunt Byron's dragged along two video cameras and a backpack full of tapes, a tiny cassette recorder, some wires, mikes, batteries and other bits and bobs. I'm not sure what she hopes to accomplish during daylight hours. The voyeur and random sex activity is pretty low-key up here while the sun's still out.

"How was the audition?" I ask Al.

"It wasn't," he sours. "I don't have the correct 'appearance.'"

"What, the molester-uncle look is out of fashion this season?"

"Ignore him," says Aunt Byron, holding up a hand as if to block me from view. "He's in an evil mood."

I groan while she gives Al a collegial hug and a pat on the back. They take a broad look at our surroundings and Polo rubs his hands together in spite of the stifling heat. "So... where would you like to begin?"

Aunt B squats and consults her jam-packed diary. "First, I'd like to create some context for earlier shoots. Therefore, I believe we'll need a few scenes of the monument here, along with some long shots of the mountain and the surrounding area. Then I'd like to walk over to the Oratory and videotape the pilgrims."

"Walk over to the Oratory!?" I yell. "What are you, Sir Edmund Fucking Hillary!? We have to go right over the mountain to get to the Oratory!" I look to Al. "You'd never make it, Polo. You'll drop dead of a coronary even before I do!"

Byron's flabbergasted. "For Godssake, Johnny! You're only thirty-two years old!"

"Yeah, well, I've had a hard life."

"It is quite a way," Al backs me up. I watch him bend a knee and wince. He throws in a little bum-shoulder flourish.

"Very well," Aunt B gives in. "We'll take a taxi once we're done here."

"That's more like it," I settle down. "But you're paying."

"You ought not be so parochial, Johnny. The world is a very big place."

"Yeah, too big, if you ask me."

After some desultory taping of the mountain, the monument, the view down Park Avenue and fuck knows what else, we flag a cab. The streets on the northwest slope of Mount Royal, around the Oratory, are gridlocked with tour buses and herds of walking pilgrims, all under a blistering sun.

"What's with the mob scene?" I ask.

Aunt Byron consults her dog-eared journal. "There are some important feasts this week. Saint Veep's Day, for one."

"Great, let's party."

The driver can only get us within a few hundred yards of the place so we have to walk the rest of the way—uphill, of course. To see anything in this goddamn town you always have to climb somewhere. The huge domed Oratory looks like a lesser Saint Peter's basilica and is built into the side of the mountain; the kind of oversized candelabra Liberace would have lived in if he had been a religious nut. The Oratory came into being due to the exertions of a saintly little guy called Brother André. His heart is kept in a sacred alcove, a reliquary, they call it.

Aunt Byron's excited, unfazed by our having to fight through the dense and sweating crowd to reach the bottom of the massive staircase that leads up to the main cathedral. She buys a few postcards from an old cripple stationed nearby.

"Jesus fuck," I grumble as we're surrounded by packs of flabby white tourists, all with veiny legs and disgusting yellow-nailed feet. "Look at these suburban psychos. Fat, deformed, big horrible faces on them, wearing the worst shit on earth. Christ!"

"Don't blaspheme," Aunt Byron scolds me. "They're humble believers."

"They're fucking Frankensteins, man! You cut them open and all you'll find is rancid lard and moldy insulation!"

"For the love of God, Johnny, show a little respect."

Al stumbles under the weight of Byron's camera equipment he stupidly offered to carry. The fool looks ready to throw up. "What's wrong," I razz him. "Baggage too heavy for Sherpa Polo?"

His mouth hangs slack. "Uff... I need a drink."

Hail Mary-muttering worshippers bustle around us and get in line for the fanatic's climb up the ninety-nine steps of the center staircase. It's reserved for those who are crazy enough to do the whole thing on their knees, standing between each step. Doing this is considered an act of penance or contrition or whatever you call that Catholic s&m. No knee-pads allowed.

Aunt Byron takes off her yellow Guayabera and hands it to me, now stripped down to a turquoise t-shirt and the smaller video camera hung on her back. The unharnessed boobs flop around over a fair-sized gut. She looks like Captain Bly with tits and attracts some double takes.

"You've got to be joking," I say. "You'll *die* trying that shit—and you're not even Catholic."

"You don't have to be."

We watch a gang of Japanese sightseers prepare for the Immaculate Kneeling or whatever it's called, some of them running in place to loosen up. Other faithful stagger back down, pants torn, knees bloody and gouged, but with sunny, beatific smiles. Several who cacked-out part-way up are carried to the bottom by burly attendants. A few paramedics wait with water and oxygen masks, obviously accustomed to this freak show.

I shake my head at seeing this madness close up. "Holy fuck… This is an outdoor torture chamber. No way I'm going up there. It stinks of evil."

Aunt B's had enough. "Now you're being ridiculous. You can wait down here, I won't be long."

Al's bent over, hands on knees. He raises a finger without looking up.

"All right, you too." Aunt Byron allows, pointing at the camera bags. "Don't lose that equipment."

Me and Al retreat to the shaded side of a bus and watch her line up and genuflect. Al takes a long swig from his flask of Old Paarl Rock Private Reserve.

"You up for a little wager?" I ask him. "Twenty bucks she doesn't make it halfway."

Al takes another slug then passes me the flask and gestures at the staircase. "Very well, but I win if she makes it to that second landing."

"Deal."

It's about fifteen minutes before the lineup moves along and Aunt Byron reaches the starting point. She drops to her knees and leans forward, fingertips poised a couple steps up, like a sprinter ready to explode out of the blocks. With a word from the attendant, Byron takes off and soon catches up to some of the slower worshippers ahead. She gains momentum instead of beginning to tire and slow down like everyone else. In fact, she now flies up those stairs, kneeling and standing at breakneck speed, weaving through traffic. Some other climbers left in her dust become enraged. They yell and wave their fists, but none jump to their feet to give chase. It must be against the rules.

In what's got to be record time, Aunt B reaches the top and stands triumphant, bloody patches at her knees. She turns and shades her eyes, glances back down at us. Two men greet her up there. I recognize them from the fag orgy on the mountain—the paunchy character she was with at the Bifteck and the cowboy-hatted Burt Reynolds clone who'd shared that deep smooch with The Perv, Duncan Campbell Scott. The three of them affect a group hug then hurry into the first building—the Crypt. Al holds out a hand for his twenty bucks.

"Something reeks," I say and reluctantly give him his money.

He grins like a wily mouse. "Ah… the miraculous power of faith, eh, Johnny?"

"Fuck, what a setup. I am such an asshole."

Over three hours have gone by and Aunt B hasn't emerged. The crowds are mostly gone and the sun's moved west, all of Mount Royal now in twilight. Al and I are sprawled on the grass embankment at the side of the Oratory. I wake him out of a loud snore. He sits up suddenly, lost for a moment then gawks around. "Where's Byron?"

"Beats me. Listen, I've got business to take care of. So either we go up right now and see if she's joined the Holy Sisters of the Immaculate De-Balling or we hit the road."

"All right. Let's go see what's happened to her."

He regards the camera gear with distaste. I agree to split the stuff with him, but starting off, we both eyeball the seemingly endless staircase then sigh at one another. "Cab?" I frown.

"Cab," he nods. We haul Aunt Byron's crap down the drive to the taxi stand, load the bags into the trunk and slump in the back of an air conditioned Chevy.

Al drops me off at the Peanut Bar where I'm to meet Leroi and get the pager and unsold product. I run in almost two hours late. He's hunched over on a stool, staring at his drink. Sophie is with him, a hand on his shoulder, her face lined with concern. They hardly notice me.

"What's going on?" I ask.

160

"Nothin'," Leroi replies and pushes over the pager, along with the day's remaining stock and money so far. "There's just over two-and-half GRs left. I gotta go."

Sophie gets off her stool and waits for him, clutching her bag. Leroi turns to leave, but I grab his arm. "Everything okay?"

"Yeah, beautiful," he grumps.

"All right, Leroi, what the fuck's happened?"

He stops and stares out the front windows. "I'm not making any money."

Sophie lights a smoke and gives me a dirty look.

"Whaddaya mean you're not making any money?"

He rubs his eyes. "I'm hung up on this shit and I'm not making a fucking dollar. Even with welfare, I can barely cover my habit and my rent."

"I thought you weren't doing much?"

"I wasn't. But now I am and I'm broke."

"What about her?"

"Don't point at me," Sophie snaps, her Joual accent low and ugly.

Leroi waves it off. "She's not doing any."

"What? C'mon, don't lie to me."

Sophie gets riled. "Fuck you, you Anglo piece of shit!"

Leroi mumbles something and walks toward the door. Sophie goes to follow then turns back to me. "It's all your fault!"

"*My* fault?"

"You told him it would be so easy, so much fun. Like a big joke. You did not warn him. You don't do that to your friends. Now he'll be like you—a nothing."

On the way home, I cut through Portugal Square and go south on Saint-Dominique. Just below Rachel, Shalini calls my name out of the darkness. She's sitting on the stoop of a two-storey row house, a beer and joint going.

"You live here?"

"Uh huh. I told you I was moving in with my friend Michelle and her daughter, Suzanne."

I drop my ass next to her.

"What's wrong?" she asks. "You look traumatized."

"Me, Al and Aunt Byron went up to the Oratory."

"The Oratory," Shalini shudders. "I haven't been there in ages."

"The place is a fucking loony bin. Are you Catholic?"

"No, thank god. I used to be Muslim when I was a girl, but that wore off the moment I discovered boys."

She goes upstairs and returns with a pair of quart bottles, hands me one then lights another joint. "I don't understand why you're still following Byron around. I get the gist, but what's the point exactly?"

"Who knows. You don't make too many long-term friends, so you hang onto the ones you've got, indulge them sometimes if need be, even if it's a drag."

"That's very loving of you, Johnny. I'm kind of surprised."

"I try. Anyway, Aunt Byron's adventure is kind of interesting. I just wish there wasn't so much climbing involved."

"So what is she looking for? Does she even know?"

"No, I don't think so. She seems so determined to be someone she's not. The whole thing's kind of weird and pathetic."

The pager buzzes and it's Dred Blanc. Shalini brings down her phone on the end of a forty-foot extension cord and I tell him to swing by. She's still curious about the homo orgy on the mountain. "You never gave me the whole story."

"I thought you said we're wasting our time chasing those perverts around."

She laughs and tips back her beer. "I meant wasting your time pretending you'll uncover anything new or important. Titillation for its own sake— that's something else entirely."

"You know, Shalini, I think you're the one who's the pervert."

"We've already established that." She makes herself comfortable. "Now, how about you cheer me up with some gory details. It's been a miserable day."

So I give her a breakdown of the 69ers, the jerk-off dude, the multi-level bumfuckathon, Paco on a leash, being impaled by the Strongman Cop, the Perv and his pith helmet, the whole circus. Shalini listens, completely rapt. "Wow. I wish I'd known it was so elaborate." She rubs a hip against me, all revved up, eyebrows going. "Maybe you and I should take a little trip up there sometime."

"It's a date—and to tell ya the truth, spying on those guys gave me a roaring fuckin' hard-on."

"Mmm! Bonus!"

She begins a high, giddy laugh that stops suddenly when Dred Blanc appears out of the night. Diffident, his constantly peeved self, he looks down at me. "I hear you're making a gay porn video up on the mountain."

"Yeah, something like that."

"Cool. Need a soundtrack?"

"I'll talk to the producer and let you know."

"Cool."

He leans forward and shoves money into my shirt pocket. "Sixty," he says and checks over Shalini. Her mouth's gone stiff. Dred takes the packs I hand him, eyes still on her. "You coming to the Miami?" he asks me. "We're going on in about half an hour."

His main band, *The Fuss*, has been dropped in favor of his now more popular side project, *Smoke Like Richard*. They'd originally been called *Ra Hoor Khuit*, but Shalini told him it sounded like some Dungeons and Dragons heavy metal crap.

"Sure," I lie. "Wouldn't miss it."

He waits for Shalini to answer. She frowns at her beer bottle, engrossed in peeling off the label. "Yeah... maybe."

Dred barely nods then goes on his way, crosses the street and heads south. The dreadlocks bounce as he walks.

"What's up with you two?"

Shalini's mouth twists. She wraps her arms around her knees. "We've had a thing for a couple months now and it's been okay. But lately he's gotten really demanding about how I look and what I say when we're around his music industry associates."

"What? You're fucking drop-dead, through and through. Anyway, who's he, the Byronic Superman?"

Shalini squints down Saint-Dominique. Dred appears briefly out of the darkness as he passes under a streetlight. "That guy can be so smart and so sexy. But then he acts like such a jerk, so bloody cool."

"You're stuck on him."

"Yeah, sort of…"

"Lady, you've got that awful handicap. You're attracted to good looking assholes."

"Everyone is."

"Maybe so, but personally, I couldn't take a white guy with dreads. Like gimme a fucking break."

"The dreads I can live with. It's all the other stuff—like him going on about my lack of fashion sense."

"Your fashion sense!? But you always look great."

"I know," she agrees, genuinely puzzled. "And really, I don't even like clothes. If it was up to me, everybody would walk around naked all the time. People wouldn't be so cocky without their stupid clothes."

"What, like nudists?"

"No," she recoils. "They're gross. So determined not to do a moment's exercise and then show off the results."

"I dunno. Maybe all the coverage Dred's been getting lately has gone to his head."

"For sure it has. He puts out an okay song and suddenly his opinions on everything begin to matter. It's ridiculous. Just because someone's an asshole, we all think they might be smart."

"So he's just a plain old run-of-the-mill asshole?"

"Well, he's definitely not as smart as he thinks. The worst thing is—he only reads guitar magazines."

"Now that's unfair. Women have always read more than men, way more. If it wasn't for women, there wouldn't be a book industry. Everybody knows that."

My dumb remark helps break up Shalini's rotten mood. She leans her shoulder against mine. "Johnny, you are a very silly man."

She grabs us another couple of beers and re-lights half a hash joint. A church bell somewhere tolls midnight, but the air's still close and humid. There are more people on the street now. Bits of conversation come toward us along the sidewalk, faces briefly appear from the shadows then continue past. Shalini climbs into my lap as we keep drinking. She hoots at the nonsense I spout—modern theories on how to teach your pet to speak. I put on the authoritative idiot voice: "Researchers have found North American cats are especially promising with Hebrew, Mandarin and Urdu. However, empirical data indicates that dogs are limited to English and Esperanto."

When Shalini stands up to get us more booze, I reach under the long and loose black skirt she's got on, run my hand up between her legs. "Speaking of fashion sense, what the hell is this thing you're wearing?"

She fans it out. "No idea. It's my roommate's. I put it on after I had a shower. It's not like I'd wear it to go out."

"The latest in house frau gear, eh?"

"Now don't *you* start on me."

"No no, it's very handy." And it is. Loose enough that I can reach up Shalini's thighs without raising the skirt much. I feel the heat before I've touched her, makes my mouth water. I put a hand flat against her hard stomach then slowly trace toward her pubic hair. It's cut really short but not shaved, thank god.

Her legs part a little. I play with her, tease her as revelers walk by and cars whiz past. Nobody notices in the dark. Pretty soon she's soaked and running onto my wrists. I cup my hand and feel her pulse through her clit. Maybe it's the excitement of doing this outside with people going by, the rising moon, the dense heat—but Shalini comes with a sudden unexpected jolt.

"Whoa," she says quietly, surprised at herself. "That caught me off guard." She grabs my shoulder to steady herself. Christ, she's like a teenage boy. You just blow on it and she'll erupt. Within a couple minutes Shalini's at it again. She breathes deep and arches her spine, hands coming up to her breasts, fingertips push at her nipples.

"I think there's somebody coming," I whisper.

"I don't care," she swoons. "It's dark out."

I begin to stroke her again and she lets out a faint growl, pulls my face against her stomach. I can smell her through the skirt's fabric and drool a bit, put my fingers to my mouth. Her taste makes me delirious.

"Uh… I can't take much more of this," she mumbles. "Let's go inside." She hauls me to my feet and soon as the door closes, jams her lips against mine. "We have to be quiet," she murmurs. "Suzanne's asleep upstairs. So shh…"

"Why don't we go up to your room?"

"No, it's too hot and my stuff's still all over the bed. Let's stay down here." She glances up. "It'll be okay."

Shalini lets the big oversized skirt drop around her feet. She sits on the wooden steps, gets out of her t-shirt as I slide off my boots. She draws me close, undoes my jeans and pushes them down. I bend toward her and she pulls my shirt over my head. I stop and listen for the roommate's kid, but hear only a clock tick somewhere.

"Don't worry. C'mere." Shalini's got her legs wide apart and leans down to take me in, her mouth filling and I want to yell something, front and back brains struggling to merge. My head spins with memories of coming, Morgan's wild laughter, Shalini clawing my neck during the mountain storm, laying in Slim's bed, driving somewhere long ago with Janey. Shalini sits up and wipes her mouth on the back of her wrist. She takes me in hand and slowly guides me toward that flawless little ass. Legs rising to my waist, her heels squat against my hip bones. She nods at me with a feverish pout. I twist and circle and push in just a bit, just a tiny bit. Everything's all wet and slippery, the thick smell of sex fills my head. Almost there then draw out a little, tickle her, do it again, then some more, teasing, teasing, watch her eyes roll back, her open-mouthed smile so white against her dark skin. "Oh, c'mon…" she half begs, half chuckles. "Don't make me wait…"

Her and her snaky dancer's body, she reaches under and using heels and hands, pulls me in. We both let out low groans. Shalini's eyes go sideways, ears pricked at whether our little bit of sound was noticed. She gives me a playful shrug and her ankles come up to the small of my back. Her hand goes between us, shoving fingers in, watching herself.

I reach down. "Let me try."

"No, I'll do it. I can come so nice like this."

"C'mon, show me how."

She's unsure but takes my hand. Our fingers entwine and work together. "Turn your wrist around. I don't like pressure right on it…" Saliva runs off her lip and drips onto her breast. She sucks it back in and lays my fingers on either side of her clit. "Here, like this…no, hang on… yeah, there. Start by touching it through its little jacket." She takes a long breath. "Like that—no, down a bit. Yeah, there…"

"Its little jacket," I repeat. The way she says it makes me smile.

Shalini stops, a bit of a scowl. "What's so funny?"

I can't stop grinning. "Nothing. You. How incredible this is. How beautiful you are."

Her smile returns, shy but profane, one of those ancient Chandela temple dancers, twenty-five centuries of perfectly contorted sexing right here on these Montreal tenement stairs. She steers my hand. "Curl your fingers."

And I feel the rougher texture behind her pubic bone, a scalding central nerve that makes her jaw drop. We rock and we roll and I am totally fucking high on her, forget where we are, mind whipping round a screaming maypole. Shalini bites my hand to stifle her noise. It all leads onto a delicate verge, a miraculous tipping point. Hands now jammed back against the stairs, she spikes herself onto me. There's a long hush, a buzzing in my ears. Her entire body twists, every muscle and tendon contracting.

We don't move and I try to pant silently, my heart pounding. Both of us listen to street noises, creaks in the night. Then a young girl's voice, a little frightened. "Are you there, Shalini?"

She holds onto my arm, puts a finger to my lips and calls up with a reassuring tone. "It's okay, Suzanne. I'm right here, sweetheart. But you can't come downstairs right now. I have a friend with me. I'll be up in a few minutes, okay?"

The girl doesn't approach or say anything. We hear her shuffle off then a door closes. Shalini cranes her neck round to look up the steps. "I think she's all right." After a few moments she reaches down for my shirt and throws it on. "I'm gonna go check on her. I'll get us some wine." I watch her sneak upstairs on the balls of her feet. She returns after a bit with a cold bottle of white and a couple glasses. "She's fine," Shalini grins gently and sits next to me on the steps. "But she wanted to know where all my clothes were."

"What did you tell her?"

"That it's so hot I had to take most of them off. Suzanne's that age where she has some idea of what's going on, but can't decide if it's mysterious or disgusting."

I glance up the stairs then back to her eyes. "Listen, um... should I do my thing in the can or right here?"

Her thigh slides against mine. "Can't you wait a little longer—so we can at least get you off? C'mon, it'll be nice."

"I dunno. I guess I can wait a bit."

She kisses me with all her mouth and reaches between my legs. We both look down and I'm still hard, still ridiculous, and still completely blind.

TWENTY-TWO

I'm killing an afternoon with Morgan, Al, and Tony, sipping Sangria in one of the sleaziest dumps on The Main—a second floor dive called The Miami. I've heard even the rats wear rubber gloves and gas masks. Tony reads a paperback copy of Roger Caron's *Go-Boy!* while Al and Morgan have their noses in the latest issue of *The Mirror.* Morgan checks her ad in the classified section as Tony reads a few lines aloud. He's awestruck and grabs a handful of his own hair, those big blue eyes bulging and amazed.

"Man, I can't believe Caron's still alive! While he was in some Guelph dungeon, they'd strap him naked into this bizarre metal thing called *the machine* and it kept him locked in like a half-bent-over position. Then some sadistic jailers would strip down to their underwear and boots and beat the shit out of him with a two-foot-long leather strap full of rivets. It's straight out of some fucking freak show!"

"A fairly traditional theme," Al condescends. "Old and degenerate jailer indulges his violent sexual fantasies on the young and incarcerated. Marked for life thereafter, they continually seek out depraved carnal adventures known colloquially as…" and he puts on a low, greasy baritone "…prison style…"

Morgan grunts while perusing the competition's ads. "Men are totally fucked. Any excuse to start hitting."

A group of career students noisily crowd around the bar for the day-long happy hour. They drink straight from pitchers, interspersed with shots of low-grade rye. Hennessy and Kit are jammed among them, cadging free drinks. They're both pretty soused, Kit's hand up inside the Hen's shirt. That little roadside whore Paco scurries around the periphery, trying to drum up some biz. Nick Cave moans on the stereo. The smell of really skunky pot drifts in from the rooftop patio out back.

Near our table, a trio of squeegee punks nod out in the corner, squeegees dropped on the floor. The girl among them is face down on the table in a puddle of beer. Her bushy black mop appears to be a giant hairball with no skull attached. The two guys with her are like supplicants on either side, both slumped identically, arms hung loose between their legs, chins on chests, a wet patch of drool on their torn t-shirts. They're just begging to be immortalized in these brain-dead poses. Morgan puts down her newspaper and returns to the drawing she's working on.

"Fuck," she carps. "I've got about five dozen more of these things to do in the next few days."

"Well, leave me out of it," I tell her. "I've done my bit."

She instinctively understands perspective, shading, and depth of field, sketching the semi-comatose squeegee punks while hardly concentrating, a smoke in the corner of her mouth. Yet her work is always effortless and exact. It could be courtroom evidence.

"Anyway, I don't know what the point is," she says, working quickly.

"The point?"

"Doing this. There's too many artists now. Everybody's a fucking artist, especially people who can't draw."

"Yeah, having your kind of talent is a real dilemma. Makes you a kind of skill Nazi."

"I know. There's these weak assholes in one of my classes, they call me an 'illustrator,' like it's cute or something. I wanna kick their fucking heads in."

"You should, then draw them all broken and bleeding. You'd get top marks, baby."

Vern the Raging Skull clomps in and immediately lays his gruesome throb on the place—like a vile cosmic burp. He's got that crazy Izanami woman with him, still wearing her gold lipstick, a good looking version of Yoko Ono. The story is they came to some sort of quid pro quo where she fucks Vern on a regular basis and he allows her to follow him around and study his Ultimate Asshole way of life. It's supposed to be the subject of an as-told-to book she's writing. The whole schmear's made Vern insufferable, especially after their project got a fat Canada Council grant to carry out the required research. Of course, he promptly blew his half on getting wasted.

They wend through the bar, feeding off one another's conceit, as if they expect flashbulbs to go off. He makes to walk past our table, but stops in front of Morgan with feigned surprise. I want to hoof him in the nuts. Vern can't pull his super-jerk act with me so he goes for the hideously sincere approach. Izanami stands by taking notes then swings a fancy looking camera from around her back.

Al waves a finger. "Tisk tisk."

She lowers the camera without comment.

"Hey, Morgs," Vern comes on. "How ya doin'?"

"Don't call me that," she slaps him down. "What do you want?"

Vern won't so much as glimpse my way. Him and his lousy machinations and new post-punk haircut. He bends close to Morgan's ear and jabbers quietly, an entreaty she might plead his case for extended credit. Morgan leans in close and presents Vern's petition. I give a sober nod of approval. He steps forward and I look up at him. "Gotta smoke?"

"Sure, Johnny."

He hands me a deck of Player's. Under the table I whip out a cigarette, slide in his stuff then return the pack. "I'll do ya sixty."

"Thanks, man," Vern nods. "Really appreciate it. And don't worry. I'll have it by tomorrow, a.m., you know me, J, good for it." He and Izanami sleaze off toward the bar as the afterwork crowd begins to drift in.

But when I go on the nod for what seems like no more than thirty seconds, I hit one of those chemically induced time warps and suddenly Paco's screaming out of the toilet right behind Vern. *the fuck?*

"I want my dopa!" Paco wails. "Gimme my dopa!"

"I left it up your ass," Vern snarls. "Now go get it, ya stupid fuckin' spic!"

Izanami follows them with her camera, taking rapid-fire shots. Paco goes for the Nikon. "Okay, then gimme dat fucking camera!"

"You little prick!" Vern barks. "Keep your paws off her!" He puts the arm on the kid and body slams him into a wall. Paco disappears down behind some piled up chairs. Vern comes over and sits at our table, big feet splayed and dirty old trench-coat flung open. Izanami slides in next to him and writes furiously in her notebook, stopping to take the occasional picture.

Paco's right back on his feet, buzzing about, totally crazed, fingers pulling at his long hair. We ignore the punk and so does everyone else in the bar. He tries a weak swing at Vern, whacks him on the ear with a half-assed blow. Without rising, Vern's big hand flies out and grabs Paco's wrist. He twists the boy onto the floor, making him snivel with pain. Vern lays out the unadorned facts. "If you ever touch my girlfriend or me again, I will *kill* you."

"I—I thought we're friends, mang."

"We are."

"Then jooz gimme my dopa. Please, mang."

"I don't have any," Vern lies to him, loud and slow. He bends closer and raises his voice, like he's talking to a deaf imbecile. "I am working on a book project which requires I abuse you in a very specific way. Do you understand what I am saying?"

The whole bar's silent, even Nick Cave has shut up. When Vern releases Paco's wrist, the kid pops up and lets out a weird, reverb kinda noise. As he reaches for the neck of a beer bottle, Vern kicks his feet out from under him and Paco hits the deck, hard. The bartender's had enough. He press-gangs a quartet of beefy tattooed regulars and they carry Paco off, each with an arm or leg. He squirms and struggles and appeals his case, but patrons shrink away. The goons hurl him down the stairs without warning or comment. We hear him crash, thump and cry all the way to the street. The pricks actually slap high-fives after they toss the pathetic little twirp.

"What was all that about?" I ask Vern. "What did you do to him in there?"

"Pain in the ass," he complains. "Little pig acts like I stole his cherry. So he didn't get any dope, but he got his rocks off pretty damn good, let me tell ya. Was beggin' for a good bang, eh, Izzie?" She nods quickly while scribbling away. "Should report the illegal fuck to immigration. Get him sent back to Playa los Faggolitos or whatever stinkin' slum he crawled outta."

Morgan gives me a bleak look. "Let's go."

Tony's already wandered out back to smoke pot with Hennessy and Kit so me, Morgan, and Al head downstairs and hail a cab. Going north on The Main, we spot Paco, the boy genius. You gotta hand it to him. He's at the curb, just below Duluth, kinda smashed up but still game enough to stick out his thumb and hump for a trick. Well, the Monkey waits for no man— or woman—or any variation thereof. I tell the driver to pull over. He gives me an evil-eye in the rearview. "Monsieur?"

"It's not what you think."

He obeys and I roll down the window. "Paco, c'mere." The kid eyes me suspiciously. "Don't worry, I just wanna talk."

He sulks over, squats at the cab's back window and tries to muster a steely-eyed glare. His left eye's swollen pretty good and there's a serious gash on his lower lip. "What joo want, mang?"

"Here," I say and hand him three packs.

He's shocked but tries to remain standoffish, worried about being the butt of another gruesome gag. "Is real?"

"It's good medicine. Take some time off."

Paco can't help himself. He shouts my name, ready to run up a light pole à la Gene Kelly and belt out the *I Love Johnny* show tune. As we drive off, Paco blows us farewell kisses.

"Aw… my sentimental old man," Morgan ribs me. "Feelin' sorry for poo' wittle Paco."

"I must be getting soft in the head. Now that fuckin' mooch'll be all over me."

Al reaches around Morgan and gives me a fatherly pat on the neck. He pulls out his flask and offers a toast. We all down shots of a particularly tasty brandy. "You're a pillar of the community," Al intones. "To paraphrase the *I Ching*, the wise ruler comprehends that an occasional and unexpected act of compassion is an essential ingredient in what must otherwise be a harsh and unforgiving regime."

"Mmm," Morgan approves of the booze. She takes another sip. "Very nice, Alphonse."

"Metaxa Grand Reserve," he sniffs. "Men have killed for much less."

As the cab goes east along Duluth toward Al's place, we see Aunt Byron putting up posters on the bulletin kiosk at the corner of Laval. I catch a glimpse of photocopied symbols, no text. A jumble of various Crowleyan motifs, emblems, chemical acronyms, and corporate insignias.

TWENTY-THREE

I've had to do some hand-holding with Leroi lately, trying to keep his intake to a semi-reasonable level. His daily usage is down a bit, but he's struggling, sick of our customers' constant bitching and sick of doing so much himself. He fell right into the shit—face first. Not even a slow build up to out of control addiction—which usually takes at least a few years. Leroi goddamn well sprinted toward it and grabbed the habit with both hands. The whole deal's worn him to a frazzle in record time so I gotta provide some moral support and try to keep him earning more than he's using.

Kit pages and walking up The Main toward her place, we get to Saint-Cuthbert where a small crowd's gathered at the doors of the empty bank on the corner. Its windows were long ago smashed by various drunks and vandals then it all got boarded up and immediately covered with posters and graffiti.

We edge into the throng and there, in the middle, Larry the Poet sits at a fold-out card table. Dressed in a fashionably ratty shirt and blazer, he tosses off glib banter while signing what appear to be chapbooks full of photos. His wife, Allie stands behind him, their kid strapped into a gaily colored papoose on her chest. Leroi goes up on his toes to get a better look. "What's going on?" he asks.

"This guy's a guerilla poet. His name's Larry and he's supposed to have a huge horse cock."

"Gawd… Un-believable."

I see Al and Aunt Byron at Larry's elbow. Al seems to be indicating what kind of inscription he wants written in his copy of Larry's latest masterpiece.

Maybe it's that book of photographed poems he was talking about. I push in to get a closer look and see they're actually garish color shots of an erect penis next to a stainless steel ruler. The hard-on must be Larry's celebrated member and according to the measurement, it's exactly ten inches long and fairly girthful.

"I'm not entirely convinced," I hear Aunt Byron say while she leafs through a copy.

"Oh, yeah, what about?" asks Larry, smug as shit as he keeps autographing the books.

"Well, you could have had a steel ruler fabricated with any measurements you wished inscribed on it. There really is only a single way to verify any of this."

Larry dismisses Aunt B's doubts with a breezy chuckle. "Yeah, whatever you say, grandma."

But Byron's logic prompts some skeptical mutters from the crowd and forces Larry to deal with this credibility gap head on. "Believe me," he says to those gathered round, offering a lopsided grin. "It's one-hundred percent certified *beef.*"

An old bum near the front won't drop it. "Then why don't you have it next to something for perspective, like a toaster or a blow drier?"

"He's right," somebody else yells. "Like when they have a silhouette of a little man next to a building or a car—give ya an idea of how big something is."

"Moreover," Aunt Byron persists, "you seem to have measured from where the scrotum meets the penis, a very subjective location. I believe the accepted method for measuring an erection is from the base of the penis at the pubic bone, along the top surface. Calculating the way you have, along the underside, can easily add an inch or two, if not more."

That gets Larry riled up. "Who are you, the fucking cock police?"

"Yeah!" another dissenter pipes in. "So it's not really more than eight and a half or eight inches, probably closer to seven and a half or even seven. You're fulla shit, Larry!"

The naysayers appear to be carrying the day. Some of his signed cock books get tossed back onto the table. One sails over the crowd and bounces off Larry's head. "Let's see it!" demands a teenaged girl, egged on by her friends. Her comment elicits a wave of malicious laughter while onlookers pick up a chant. "Let's see it! Let's see it!"

Faces jam tighter as Larry takes the bait. He stands up and begins to fumble with his belt buckle. His wife yanks him backward by the collar and angrily jabbers in his ear. Larry listens for a moment then immediately secures his belt, picks up the remaining books and marches away with her and the kid.

"UN-fucking-believable!" crows Leroi. "I love it!" It's good to see him laugh again.

The card table gets trashed and kicked into the road. Al and Aunt Byron come over as the crowd drifts away. Aunt B continues to peruse Larry's book with serious interest. "I'm not saying he's a liar. However, his work does require a more scrupulous theoretical underpinning."

Al has carefully wrapped his copy in a plastic bag and stashes it in his attaché case. "I don't care what anyone says. This sort of material almost always gains in value after just a few years. Particularly when you own a signed and numbered first edition."

I take a look at Aunt Byron's copy. A big red-tinted photo of Larry's discredited monster fills the cover. The title, *Ars Canadiana*, is written sideways at the outside edge. On one of the opening pages it lists the publisher, some thank-yous, then cataloging data and a line that reads: *The publication of Ars Canadiana was generously supported by the Canada Council for the Arts.* There's a big wedge of text before the photos begin. I start reading in the middle somewhere.

Therefore, one must accept that the work of Lawrence Priapus has evolved in the context of now defunct modernist symbolism applied in the traditionally classicist sense. This results in a clearly ironic paradox which must be weighed according to the shifting mores of his still nascent neo-primitivist oeuvre, yet remains centered by its pastiche of the horror/fantasy relationship within the territoriality of the two-dimensional surface.

Not to be misconstrued as nothing more than a representational act of insurrection, Priapus's true motives emerge as a decidedly oblique fusion of painterly gesture and personal obsession carried out within a deeply abstentionist portrayal of current societal pathologies.

Aunt Byron takes back the book and pulls me aside for a private confab. "Johnny," she says solemnly. "I will require your assistance sometime in the next few days."

"To do what?"

"I am aware you know about my... *interest* in a certain personage, one Duncan Campbell Scott, a senior Corrections official."

"Yeah... I've got some idea."

"I am planning to meet with DC Scott, a kind of summit conference, if you will..."

"What good will that do?"

"It has become clear to me I must confront him. It is the only way to confirm certain historical anomalies."

"'Anomalies', huh? So... you're not going to flip out or anything, are you? Like try to kill or cripple him, castrate him? I don't need the heat."

Aunt B's face screws up. "What do you take me for? You know very well I don't believe in violence. I would merely like to have certain questions answered."

"I'll bet. What are you going to do, just waylay him somewhere?"

"No, that would be childish. I've begun negotiating the terms of our meeting and I'd like you and Al to be there as objective witnesses."

"We can't be objective. We're your friends."

"I don't mean emotional witnesses, more as human recorders of his responses and the overall tenor of our encounter."

Man, what a fantasy. I wonder how many ass rides and head jobs the young Byron had to put out for those idyllic weekends at Lake Blowing Moose with ol' Duncky. Well, if that guy really is a key player in a vast and timeless pedophile conspiracy, he'll most likely call the cops, who will of course be his Luciferian minions.

"All right. Whatever you say. Just give me a day or two warning."

"Absolutely. And I do appreciate your help."

After I send Leroi home and take over the evening shift, Slim pages from a number I don't recognize. "Where are you, with that Adam guy?"

"No, why?"

"I thought you two were joined at the hip now."

"Don't be stupid. I'm at the New York Life building—in Place d'Armes. You want to come down?"

"What are you doing there?"

"I'm working in the law library. It's on the top floor."

"Jesus. How many jobs do you have exactly?"

"Nevermind that. I'll be closing up in a few minutes. Come. Take a taxi."

Place d'Armes is pretty quiet when I get down there, only a few cabs loiter at the edge of the square. I'm surprised the front door of the building is still open but no guard at the desk. Slim's waiting when the old elevator finally crawls up to the 8th floor. Hair tied back, wearing a dark, knee-length skirt and an angora cardy, she's doing a great impersonation of a classically severe librarian, even has on a pair of cat's-eye glasses.

"Since when do you wear specs?"

"Since never. They're fakes."

Slim leads me through a set of heavy wood doors and locks up behind us. She pulls her hair loose, gets out of the cardy and curls her tongue at me. "C'mon, let's get wasted."

The library's a real throwback, right out of the 1890s or whenever this place was built. Everything's as it was, rows of leather-bound books, the ancient oak reading tables rubbed smooth, bathed with the glow of green-shaded desk lamps. Even the big arched windows haven't been updated. Out in the twilight, Montreal begins to put on her lights. We sit on a nicely worn leather sofa and I lay out a couple packs. Slim pushes money across and gets right into it, sucks up a few big hits. "Oh yeah…" she approves, slouching back. "Just what Doctor Faustus ordered…"

I do a small shot while Slim takes off her sensible librarian shoes, reaches under her pencil skirt and pulls down the skin-tone pantyhose. "I'd love to kill whoever invented these things."

The unfamiliar surroundings have got me feeling wary, especially cuz Slim's unusually playful. She throws a leg over my hips while shoving up her skirt. "You want to fuck me on my desk over there? Then the whole city can watch."

"What's going on with you and that Adam guy?"

"Nothing special, why?"

"I dunno, you just seem... kinda warm around him."

She looks out at the office buildings across the square, toward the mountain north of us. "He was down here earlier. We smoked some weed."

"So that's why you're giddy."

Slim leans back and laughs at me, fingers pushing her white-blonde hair behind her ears. "Not entirely."

"So what—I'm the afterthought?"

She slides off her blouse and lays it to one side. "I had been planning to get you two on either side of me."

"Is he interested?"

She looks young and hopeful. "Are you?"

"Depends..."

"C'mon, Johnny, don't mope... Please. Adam's not Hennessy but he's fun and he's leaving soon. Besides, my birthday's coming up."

"Does he use?"

"He might."

"I'll think about it."

She reaches down between us, opens my pants and gets her cool fingers on me. "Well..." she needles. "A cock in hand isn't two in the bush, but a girl can dream, can't she?"

That stops me cold. "Wait a second. You're being funny."

"So?"

It's like a sharp kick in the ass. "You really like him." Slim looks me in the eyes while absentmindedly jerking me off. I pull her hand away. "Stop that."

TWENTY-FOUR

That certain time of month rolls around when Hennessy visits one of his regular tricks—a big, blond super-Kraut known as Gerald. Mister Gerald to you. He's rich and heavily cultured, lives in a pair of side by side apartments in one of those 1920s buildings on Saint-Famille. It's the kind of old palace with a door between the two suites. Maybe it was some sort of long-term luxury hotel way back when.

Even though I'm now gainfully employed, I tag along since I've always played the assistant in this particular melodrama. My role is to be in the adjacent suite, listening in. I'm supposed to put the open end of a water glass against the wall with my ear on the bottom. It's a gimmick you see in old black-and-white movies and surprisingly, it really does amplify whatever's happening on the other side. Being a stickler for veracity, Gerald has actually burst in on me a couple times to make sure I'm doing exactly as instructed.

So the fantasy commences, script by Mister Gerald. I hear him enter and slam a door. His authoritative baritone mentions money. Hennessy puts on a shrieky soprano and they argue. Gerald speaks with a cruel top's voice and complains about how the Hen spent too much time on his knees in the can at Club Flex. I fine-tune my glass and pick them up loud and clear.

"Why do you continue to lie to me? Do you actually believe I'm that naïve? I allow you into my life, offer my trust and you go right back to doing the whole lineup in the *pissoir*. Very attractive, I must say. What is it, feeling nostalgic for your days as a vending machine? Don't you realize you're gambling with both of our lives!?"

"Oh stop it. There's no need to exaggerate."

"Really!? I didn't realize you're exempt from the plague!"

"Come now, Gerald, don't be so dramatic. You can be such a queen."

Then WHAM—a sudden crash, furniture dumped over, a blind-side tackle in the living room. I hear Hennessy's garbled yelps. "Get away from me, you fascist! What do you think you're doing!?"

"Yes, try to fight me, you little black bastard! I'm going to civilize you!"

It's amazing the dialogue never varies—not by a letter. And right on cue, their voices rise into a tangle of fevered curses. Hennessy grunts loud as he's bashed against the wall opposite my listening post. Okay, here's where we get what Mister Gerald calls the "unforeseen narrative pivot." Using some kind of jujitsu, the Hen flips Mr. G. around and gets him in a half nelson or hammerlock or whatever you call that thing when the guy's arm is twisted up behind his back. Mind you, I've never actually seen them do any of this, only heard it, but that's how the story's supposed to play out.

Now it's Gerald who's face up against the wall. He lets out a desperate squeal, begs for mercy, cries that he's been an awful little queer yada yada. I mean like really corny shit. The Hen tells him to shut up and begins to pound Gerald's big muscular ass. I assume Hennessy stands on an ottoman or something since he's a head shorter than Gerald—but the Hen's got a pretty good-sized wang on him so everything's tickety-boo. Anyway, they steadily gain velocity with Gerald panting just a few inches from my ear.

But their performance is different this time, more intense somehow. I don't know what's up, but they'd do Olivier proud and I'm getting kind of excited myself so I undo my pants and stroke along for the ride, quiet as a pilot fish. I wish I had a stethoscope. Trouble is, Hennessy's in a hurry. He pounds Gerald like a fucking piston. Fuck knows where he's found the energy. It sounds like he's going to drive the guy's asshole right out his eyeballs. Gerald's pretty much yelling now for all he's worth, ready to peak. My drug-impaired hard-on is still fairly numb. *Hang on a second, you guys!* But within a few moments, the whole wall shakes with Gerald's heavy moans and tear-filled howls of purple prose. As their shtick slowly comes to a gasping halt, some very fine plaster dust floats down on my head. *Goddamn it.*

I get buttoned up and give it a minute or two before going into the other apartment. Hennessy waits by the door while Gerald's in a mid-thigh James Bond bathrobe, gabbing on the phone. He smiles at me distractedly and waves goodbye.

"You didn't get off, did you?" I ask the Hen as we go down the stairs.

"Don't be absurd. It's always the same thing with Gerald. I could do it in my sleep."

"I guess he's a man of careful habits."

Hennessy hands over my fifty dollar assistant's fee and an extra sixty. "More like a man of careful trust funds."

I give him his drugs. "Well, at least you're not trolling the streets anymore. A few easy regulars isn't a bad way to augment your psych welfare."

"I suppose Gerald's a useful idiot."

"Hey, there's a lot worse out there."

"Don't remind me."

I grab a handful of his tight little butt. "You wanna go back to my place? I got all hot listening to you guys."

Hennessy's puzzled. "Really, why? Haven't you used much today?"

"About average, but you both just seemed… uh… hornier somehow."

"Hm, that's odd. It didn't feel any different. Either way, I have to see my lady psychiatrist right now, maintain my reputation as an irredeemable masturbator." He gives me a sneaky grin. "But I'll drop by afterwards."

"Okay, page me with the time you'll be over."

"Why don't you call Slim while we're at it? The three of us haven't been together in ages and that's one little bottom I know you love abusing."

"Naw, she's gone away for the weekend, with that Adam guy from New York."

"Don't sound so jealous, Johnny. It doesn't become you."

"I'm not jealous. I just don't like to think of some other guy touching her."

"Well, then you mustn't do very much thinking."

"Oh, fuck off."

"Come now," he mollycoddles. "Baby not be glum. When I drop by, I'll bring my crotchless rubber Batman suit."

"Well... I would prefer if you wore the Wizard of Oz flying monkey outfit."

"Snookums—for you, anything."

We titter like a couple of silly old fags.

TWENTY-FIVE

It's yet another sweaty morning in the Open City as Dred Blanc and I sit in a booth at Frankie's Diner, on The Main. We mull over how he's going to pay down his substantial debt when Little Sharon rushes in, out of breath. She's Dred's former bass player.

"I heard you were doing this now," she pants, dripping with relief.

"When did you get back from the hog farm?"

"This morning. I've got forty bucks."

We do the deal under the table but the matronly waitress notices as she clears away our breakfast plates. She'll expect a large tip.

"Back in a jiff," Sharon beams and waddles off to the can.

Dred Blanc watches her go then points two fingers at his open mouth, the puking gesture. "No way she gets back into in my band with a bubble butt like that. I'll go as far as ugly or stupid, but fat is where I draw the line."

"Momma Cass was fat."

"Yeah, I guess she was okay. But it was very uncool of her to choke to death while sneaking a ham sandwich. Very uncool."

It's true. Little Sharon ain't so little anymore. Not as little as when she split town a couple months ago with much fanfare about going clean. Back then Sharon was a sweet, strung-out country girl who could pass for about thirteen with her short pixie cut, cute ski-slope nose and white polka-dot mini-dresses with plastic bugs in her hair—a diddler's dream. She'd been playing in Dred Blanc's scrap metal side project, *Smoke Like Richard*, and was an incongruous match to his rat-haired dreadlocks and cellar-dweller complexion. Determined to once again clean up for good, Sharon retreated to her parents' farm outside some hell-hole called Bracebridge, Ontario. She's a serial quitter and I'm sure this time was no different. Yet again she went cold turkey and paid the price. Weeks of horrible sickness and bone-cracking spasms, guts on fire, barely able to crawl from bed to toilet and back, everything stinking of death and despair—tormented by those vivid, lustful dreams of how fucking lovely the drug can be, coming on to her like a silver tongued incubus.

Eventually recovering her strength and appetite, she quickly becomes a two-by-three barrel butt. Horrified at what her sleek little body is turning into, she goes on a diet of salad, fruit, lean meat, no butter and no bread, but it makes fuck all difference. She swims, jogs, chops wood and works like a field animal. No matter—the tonnage accumulates. It's got to be the air in those small towns, so good for you, but chock full of calories. As usual, Sharon must have woken up on one of those dreary countrified mornings, taken a look in the mirror and ran screaming to the bus station.

Ten minutes go by before she floats out to join us, shy and content. "I am so glad to be home," she purrs, sliding in next to me.

"I guess the cure didn't take, huh?"

"God," she shivers. "I was turning into a gynormous Stepford Wife."

Dred Blanc looks her over and offers a cigarette.

"No, I quit."

"Start again. You drop about a dozen kilos and we're back in business. Nobody wants a short, porky bass player."

"Get off my case, will ya? Now that I'm going back on the magic slim-fast powder, I'll be a flat-chested twelve-year-old again in no time." She jiggles her tits up and down then pushes them together. "I mean, check it out. I've got boobs for the first time in my life. I'm actually wearing a bra!"

Dred's unmoved. "And do something with your hair," he pesters. "Either real long or real short—none of this in between crap. If something isn't extreme, it doesn't count for shit."

"Yeah, yeah…"

"And get it dyed something good, maybe stripes again or that sapphire blue you had, but not this natural bullshit. You look like a sales lady, for fucksakes."

Sharon slaps the tabletop. "You got a razor up your ass or what!?"

"Hey, hey," I referee. "Just cool it." I point at Dred. "You—give her a break, will ya?"

Sharon leans against me and I put an arm around her. "Thanks," she snuggles. "You have a great bedside manner, Doctor Johnny."

"Don't jinx the guy," Dred rags on her.

"Drop that shit," I warn. "Don't even think it."

Sharon makes a face at him. "I'll say my prayers for you, Father Johnny."

"You too. No prayers, no jinxes, no voodoo, no nothing. There's enough of that crap in my life already."

Sharon's headed for la-la land. I'm jealous. That first nod after a long time clean, it's a real keeper. "Sure thing…" she breathes as her head lolls against my shoulder, eyelids at half-mast.

"I've got a gig booked at the Purple Haze," Dred tells us, still eyeing her. "It's in three weeks."

"Plenty of time," she mumbles. "I'll be a bonerack by then. You can roll me out on a gurney, hooked up to an IV." Her eyes widen at him. "Cool?"

"Actually…" Dred points at her. "That's not a bad idea." He thinks about it for a moment. "Hm… But the audience won't be able to see much of you lying down. How about you come out with an IV pole on wheels?"

"Sure, but only if you play guitar while wearing a colostomy bag."

Me and Dred nod at each other, impressed.

Slim comes in with her new guy, Adam. She introduces him to Dred and Sharon. He smiles warmly at me, that lower Manhattan Jewish hipness evident. I half-expect him to wink. No doubt Slim's told him about us in pokerfaced detail, exactly how everything works. It's not like she'll ever spare anyone's feelings, especially those she considers old enough to behave. Also, this is Montreal and the French do have some nice, civilizing influences on we non-Francos.

They sit in the booth behind Dred, hold hands across the table and grin at each other with intimate murmurs. I try to listen in, but they're too quiet. I'd love to verbally scalp the guy, force Slim to see he's just another full-of-shit fraud, my usual method for driving off the cocksmiths she gets infatuated with. But Adam's playing it friendly and open-minded, making sure I'd look like a miserable jack-off.

As Sharon and Dred fantasize about the snazzy features they'd like to have in their imaginary tour bus, Vern and Tony roll in and throw themselves into the booth across from us. Vern scrunches three twenties into a ball and tosses it at me.

"Where's Izanami?" I hassle him, passing over their stuff. "Out buying another gross of gold lipstick?"

Tony puts a dramatic hand to the side of his mouth, plays at breaking the bad news as he slips into Shmengie mode. "She very evil Nipponese woman. She stealing Vern personality. Tonsko warn him to no be trusting her."

"Fuckin' bitch," Vern grumbles. "Let her into my world, showed her how it's done, she rips me off."

Tony lays on a broad wink, still with the Eastern European moujik voice. "To be paraphrasing the great Nicholae Ceascscu; Asshole is most important part of society. Otherwise, shit have nowhere to go."

"She was nothin' special in the sack either," Vern keeps grousing. "*The Ultimate Asshole Handbook* was my fuckin' idea. Douchebag cuts me out and now it's just gonna be her name on the cover. She'll make a fortune and I'll get dick."

Tony piles on the mock sympathy, but this time he lays on an ersatz Liberace gimmick with pinhead British accent. "Dahling, I did remark that you ought to have been a more... how shall we say... aesthetically pleasing asshole."

Vern swears under his breath while going to the can to do a shot. Tony leans across the aisle. "I talked to Izanami. She's apparently found a more complex, more attractive and longer lasting asshole."

"No surprise. Vern's a middling asshole at best. He never works that hard at it."

"True. Most of the time he's just a shithead and has rarely attained what you'd call the absolute Zen of the asshole."

The old waitress comes down the aisle between us and Tony orders for both himself and Vern, our community's bush league anus. Leroi drifts in and squeezes next to Dred Blanc. He's already wasted at ten a.m., his gray eyes pinned to the nines.

"What the fuck is wrong with you?" I confront him as the waitress brings fresh coffees.

"What?" he replies, spilling more java onto the table than into his mouth.

"Why are you doing so much?"

"Am I asking you to pay for it?"

"Okay," I back off and watch his head slide down his arm onto the table-top, half-leaning on Dred, who pushes him aside.

"Is he supposed to be some kind of product advertising?"

Vern comes back out, now also half gone. Dred switches spots with Leroi and shoves him to the inside of the booth. Kit and her new beau arrive. They sit a few tables away. Kit gestures at Leroi with a worried expression. I look at her like *what can I tell you?*

Al and Aunt Byron are the latest to join the festivities, sunglassed and hard-faced. Their stoic routine is getting pretty hard to take. They glance about and since there are no empty tables left, they deign to crowd in with Tony and Vern. Tony's right on Aunt B as she peruses the breakfast menu.

"So, I hear you've been shooting some thoughtful homosexual erotique up on our sweet and sinister mountain."

Byron glowers across the table at Al.

"I never said anything."

"Sure ya did," Vern gruffs, head against the wallpaper, his eyes a pair of slits. "Told us all about the fudgestuffer Olympics you guys been coverin'."

"All right," Al admits. "I may have mentioned something."

Byron gives Tony a serious stare. "It is not pornography. It is part of an important ongoing research project which may take years to complete."

"But you gotta admit," I jibe from the sidelines. "It woulda done poor ol' John Holmes proud."

189

Aunt B gives me a black look. "My work is not for your amusement, Johnny."

"Okay, then!" I yell, pissed off at her constant lack of humor and smug little attitude she's been grooming. "What exactly is it for?"

That stops the surrounding jabber. Even Slim and Adam listen in. Byron's story has been circulating on The Main for a while now. The mountaintop orgy quickly passed into local lore and everyone's been clamoring to see the video. Some Quebecois smut king approached Al about a distribution deal. Byron was reportedly outraged, giving Al big-time shit for even broaching the topic.

"Well?" I keep riding her. "Inquiring minds are dying to know."

Al tries to calm things. "I don't think this is the time or the place to-"

"No, he's right," Tony steps in. "We've heard a lot of curious reports about this research of yours." He shifts into a rapid and effete patter. "According to those in the know, the results may be earth-shattering, a truly agonizing re-evaluation of the fundamental pillars our society is *erected* upon. Perhaps I can create a deeply moving *penile portrait* destined for our National Gallery—grant pending, *bien sûr*."

Aunt Byron flushes at Tony's sarcasm; her fingers tremble as they run down the edges of the plastic-coated menu. "I simply consider it my duty to examine the mythology of modern pederasty and discover what is at its core—how much is truth and how much is fiction and then make the resulting data available to everyone."

Tony trowels on the mockery with a Shakespearean baritone. "Ah, very noble, indeed."

"Oh, yes," I agree. "Thank God we'll finally be able to honestly appraise our inner diddler."

Sharon lets out a loud guffaw then falls back on the nod. Tony won't let it go, sticks with his David Garrick ham-a-thon. "I've got a capital idea! A guest appearance on the CBC's new smash hit, *EcoKids Rock*. Didn't you audition for that redoubtable program, Alphonse?"

Al busies himself putting milk and sugar into his tea while he tries to deflect our bullshit. "That program is a strictly commercial consideration. It has nothing to do with the scholarly efforts Byron is involved with."

Vern's forehead lands on the tabletop with a loud whack, spilling coffee and rattling plates.

"I don't agree," Tony carries on while he lifts Vern by the collar and shoves him back toward the wall. "From what I can tell, our pedo friends will be the next great media driven trend. A fortune is waiting to be made, especially by those who recant their monstrous deeds and become born-again, book-writing anti-pedo zealots." He looks away with a theatrical eye-lash flutter and Charles Laughton put-on. "Oh, sweet epiphany…"

Byron's got no rapier-sharp comeback, but her rage is palpable and rises off her like poison gas. Still, it's all too one-sided to be entertaining. After a few minutes, everyone loses interest and turn back to their conversations. The Hen ambles in and jostles past Sharon to sit on my lap.

"Here we are," says Hennessy and shoves some money into my shirt pocket. "The sixty dollars I owe you."

"Where'd this come from?"

"I was back to see our doctor friend from the Ministry of Culture. You know, in Outremont."

"Oh, yeah? Did you have to nail her creepy husband too?"

"No, just her. He's away on business."

"Lucky break."

"Well," he adds in a loud voice. "I did have to fellate her DOG."

That instantly stops everybody, even the cook way at the front, all eyes and ears on the Hen. "Look at you!" he sniggers. "What a gang of drooling PERVERTS!"

He gets a chorus of disappointed groans.

TWENTY-SIX

I spend a couple hours sitting around La Cabane with Al and Aunt B, feeling a little guilty for making her sweat in front of everyone at Frankie's diner a few days ago. I don't say much and let her run off at the mouth about her pet subject. *Heavily abridged version*: It is an unknowably complex inter-related pattern of triple-agented one-time pad dead drop black bag animal mutilation mole people cut outs via the Thelemic Ordo Templi Orientis master plan, but only on the second Tuesday of every other month at precisely 12:06:14 a.m. or with special indulgence from your local Crowleyan Therionistic Knight of the Golden Dawn or his appropriately endowed deputy, but requires the proper sacrifice be carried out during a summer solstice that falls on a Friday between 6 a.m. and 8 p.m.—but *only* if you've managed to collect and color-in *all* the pieces of Seth's Osirian puzzle.

My stifling a couple of yawns instantly turns Aunt B from leaned-forward passionate polemicist to spurned injured party martyr, having become so easily offendable lately that I'm beginning to really not give a fuck. Even loyal Al Polo looks like he might slip into a coma. Then I commit the unpardonable sin of checking my six-dollar Patrick Roy wristwatch. That provokes Aunt B into a prissy little charade where she carefully calculates her part of the bill and leaves the precisely correct amount, to the penny—minus tip and tax, course. It's all I can do not to throw the table at her.

As dusk edges over The Main, I cross the road to meet Dred Blanc at the Purple Haze. Shalini is at a window table with a very pretty young white guy, mid-twenties or so. Her fingers gently stroke the back of his hand. It's a perfectly romantic scene, the mountain's dark outline in the background, the giant cross glowing on its summit. She waves me over and her lad seems open, relaxed, not some kind of jealous scowler. In fact, the kid's an all-round beauty with his long, sandy hair. Shalini pats the chair between them. "Come, sit. This is Jean-Baptiste, and this is my friend, Johnny."

He half rises and extends his hand while the other one keeps his tie from hanging forward. "*Enchanté.*"

"*Et toi,*" I reply, enjoying his refined manner.

He goes and gets another glass then pours me a drink from their pitcher of Sangria. Shalini sits up even straighter than her usual flag-pole posture. "Jean-Baptiste is the set designer for our new troupe, Sada Yacco—and he's very talented."

He grins sheepishly, made genuinely uncomfortable by her praise. I'm liking this guy more and more. "I have little experience. It is Shalini who makes the stage shine."

She runs a hand through her short black hair, a big grin plastered across her face. She'd invited me to watch her rehearse a few days ago for an up-coming revue. It was in a huge fourth-storey dance studio on a narrow little backstreet in Old Montreal, lit only by the cloudy day outside. There were arched floor to ceiling windows down one side and mirrors on two walls. We were the only ones there and I was thinking I wouldn't be able to keep my hands off her, but seeing Shalini move like that, her lungs at the limit, the squeak of her skin on the varnished hardwood, I could barely watch and sat in a corner, knees pulled up, sobbing like a moron. She came over, covered in sweat, and crouched at my side, breathing hard and mumbling sweetly, she stroked my forehead. Her warm hand wiped away tears. "I know… It's all right, my love. I know…" When Shalini smiled, the tiny pockmarks on her cheeks puckered in the flat afternoon light. She seemed more mischievous nymph than regular human. I watched her get undressed and dance with nothing on. I couldn't look directly and caught fluid swirls of her body flash by in the mirrors. The wavering reflection hit some people across the narrow street, on the fourth floor opposite us, in their trendy design office. They were instantly paralyzed, stopping to stare at her like a bunch of fashion-conscious zombies.

"Johnny is taking part in a very unusual project," Shalini says by way of avoiding my actual occupation. "And it involves Mont-Royal."

"In what way?" Jean-Baptiste inquires with his smooth Parisian accent.

"Well, I'm not entirely sure myself," I demure. "An associate of mine—a man who became a woman some time ago—she's developed a theory about various historical aspects of the mountain."

"And they are?"

"This woman—Byron—believes the mountain and its cemeteries, various buildings that surround it—the Oratory, Solomon's Temple, the Grey Nuns convent, Etienne-Cartier's monument, some structures on the McGill campus nearby—these places possess certain powers which provoke sexual sacrilege among this country's Masonic and Jesuit elite—all men, of course."

Shalini's mouth cocks a little, as if what I'm saying is amusing but perhaps plausible.

"Ah, oui," Jean-Baptiste laughs lightly. "Men whom gather on *le montagne* to enjoy sex. But this is very normal in any city, no?"

"No, it's not about that. I've seen a group of fifteen or twenty at one of these gatherings and yes, they're very friendly and congenial. But— my friend Byron insists these meetings are a sort of hunting ground for certain men among them, members of a very old and very powerful network which has its roots within the judicial and correctional bureaucracies. She claims they've created a Masonic-Jesuit alliance to help facilitate their ancient cult. Mostly boys, but sometimes girls as well."

"*Sur la montagne!?*" Jean-Baptiste almost shouts.

"No, no—not on the mountain itself. At least not more than the occasional recreational use."

"Then where do these people operate?"

"Byron says the network has now spread to virtually all bureaucracies within the federal and provincial regimes—and this is mirrored in other governments as well."

Jean-Baptiste takes a long drag of his cigarette and glances at the mountain's black silhouette. "*Et votre ami*, she was one of these children?"

I drain my glass. "Yes, *he* was... I suppose that's why she's made it her job to uncover this supposed 'conspiracy'. I'm not really sure."

Jean-Baptiste is fascinated. He hunches forward. "And how old is this 'organization'?"

Shalini nods at me to go on as she pours another round.

"That part is rather vague—as you'd expect. Millenia, I assume. It couldn't be any other way, could it? But whether they actually exist or not... well, it's no secret that five minutes after Europeans landed on this island—sailors, merchants and priests were buggering Indian kids on the mountain."

Dred Blanc arrives and stands at my elbow like a morose butler. "I'll be back in a moment," I tell them and pray they don't take off.

"Is she seeing that guy?" Dred asks after we're in the men's room.

"I dunno. Why?"

"I thought he was gay."

"So what if he is?" Then I twig. "Oh, right, you were involved with Shalini for a while."

Dred gives me his money. "I thought we still were."

"Don't make a fool of yourself. She needs a bitchy boyfriend like she needs a fuckin' hole in the head. Anyway, you're in a band. You're too cool to care, remember?"

He takes the packs I hand him. "Yeah, I remember. Anyway, we're going on tour soon, Hogtown, Motown, and Gotham."

"Smart move. You'll be huge."

When we go back out, I'm relieved to see they're still at the table and appear glad I've returned. Dred gives Shalini a flaccid glare. She ignores him while quietly speaking to Jean-Baptiste, again with their hands joined. Dred shuffles off without a word.

"Shall we go to my apartment," Jean-Baptiste suggests after he's settled the tab. "*Pour un cognac?*"

He lives in the elegant top floor pad of an Outremont triplex. The rooms have their original dark wood paneling and plate rails. There's an eclectic mix of furniture—Italian modernist stuff and some nice Machine Age pieces, along with paintings, prints, drawings and photos up and down every wall in the *salon* style, most of them originals. He's got acres of books, many scattered around. Stage design drawings cover the dining room table and the floor around it. I instantly feel at home as Shalini puts on a tape that begins with Pauline Julien's *La Manic*. Her version's a real heartbreaker and gets me a bit dismal.

I follow Shalini into a large, messy bedroom. Clothes are thrown about, more books, most about art and theater, some old Life magazines. There's a big brass four-poster with a few pencil and oil-stick drawings on it. Shalini sits on the bed and uses her heels to push off her cracked old engineer's boots. She lays the drawings on the floor. They're all of her in various dance poses—naked, of course, body like a flying lash. "He makes me look pretty good, huh?"

"Honey, you always look good."

She grins at my adoration as Jean-Baptiste comes in with a bottle and some glasses. We camp out on his bed and Shalini lights a joint. She opens her shirt, undoes the top button of her jeans then lays her head in JB's lap. His knuckles brush Shalini's small breasts. Really, they're perfect—just like all of her. You could fit each breast into a champagne glass.

Shalini sits back up, bored but kind of agitated, pours wine, gulps it down and takes her white linen shirt right off, then wiggles out of her jeans. She gives us a hot little laugh and bursts into action. She orders us around, pushes us this way and that while we talk, gets Jean-Baptiste's pants off, my pants off, a sock here, a tie there. She pulls him out of one sleeve then the other.

"So, uh… Jean-Baptiste…" I ask, full of long-shot hope. "Do you know anything about hockey?"

Shalini groans. "Oh, c'mon, Johnny… Don't be a downer."

JB laughs. "I do not know a single thing about hockey."

"Oh, all right," she consents. "Go ahead. But the short version." She winks at Jean-Baptiste. "Johnny must really like you."

Shalini goes down on knees and elbows, wags her ass at me while her fingers and lips go at the pretty young Frenchman. She backs up against my groin and her arousal makes me woozy. She strokes Jean-Baptiste with soft chuckles and shear bliss. I look down at her smooth brown ass, crouch and lick that flawless little pink asterisk. Her laughter pulls my tongue deeper, undulating, I get the sharp taste of her. She rocks fore and aft, taking mouthfuls of JB and shoving further onto my tongue. The rush of Shalini's inside heat makes my brain squirm. Her ass comes up higher, pushing that sweet pussy at me and her voice mixes with JB's as she moves on him faster. I'm ready to faint from all this goodness, struggle back up as her hand reaches under and brings me in. Right away Shalini's riding hard. "Yeah, this is good," she says, as if deciding on a purchase.

"Hockey's full of tragedy," I tell JB while taking Shalini's hip in one hand and resting my glass on her exquisite backside. "Broken men and their broken bodies, psyches destroyed."

Jean-Baptiste swallows hard and sucks in his gut, eyes on Shalini's lips. "Perhaps you can... uh... give me *un example?*"

Shalini stops for a moment. "An example? Don't get Johnny started. He'll be crying his eyes out in a minute."

"Ah, then I must know," he insists, the words trembling out of him.

"It's the goaltenders I love most," I say. "Back in the old days, when they wore no masks." Then it hits me. Gawd damn... I've reached some kind of perfect state of being: high as hell, Shalini sliding on and off me as I blab about ancient hockey with a Gallic beauty—my personal Mandala amid all this friendly screwing. "Their teeth and noses went first, bashed to pulp. A puck zings in and cuts a guy for twenty or thirty stitches, more even. That huge ice surface would coagulate the blood into horrible black globs. They'd carry him off, sew up the poor fuck, give him smelling salts and throw him back in his cage!"

Jean-Baptiste is gasping now, holding onto Shalini's hair.

"And there were no back-up goalies then either," I continue. "One guy! Can you believe it? That was it!"

Shalini's hard breathing makes me think she'll get off first, my yammering a lot of background noise. "C'mon," she urges. "Put some ass into it!"

I toss my glass aside, grab her hips and start slamming. "I mean, it's no wonder those old time goalies were miserable. Nervous wrecks with constant nightmares about the shot that'll kill or cripple them—or worse, they'll allow too many goals and lose their pathetic job! Most of them made shit money, ripped off and fucked over by the owners!" My bottom lip quivers.

Shalini must feel it. She twists round while hanging onto JB. "Stop it, Johnny! Forget about hockey for a minute and focus on me!"

"Let him cry if he wishes," Jean-Baptiste cuts in. "Of course, what you are saying, it is the normal capitalistic control of the worker and the means of production."

"Oh, lord," Shalini grumbles and returns to getting him off.

I've done too much dope but keep at her and it's Jean-Baptiste who's first out of the gate. His hips suddenly buck, aqua eyes fixed on mine, stuttering half words. In a few moments he goes off in Shalini's mouth and onto himself, on her lips and cheek and chin. She's not far behind. Now that he's done, she gets up on one wrist. I feel her cunt and ass muscles tighten, one hand goes between her legs and she soon hisses it all out, spine arching, screeching as if she's in pain then suddenly frozen, mouth wide open and eyes shut. "Aw… fuck…"

When the last echo fades, Shalini collapses off me, screeching with laughter. She rolls onto her back and lets out a big whoop. JB's sperm runs down into the hollow of her collarbone. "Yeah!" she punches the air. "That was fun! I want more!" She pops up and fumbles at the nightstand, lights a joint. Wine spills onto the bed with a giant pink stain. She fills our glasses then crosses her legs yoga-like and turns to Jean-Baptiste. "You were saying?"

He smiles softly, fingers going to her neck. "I enjoyed very much learning about *l'histoire du hockey*."

"Uh huh," Shalini agrees. "You can see why the Quebecois love the game so much." She's stoned, fairly drunk and sated—for the moment. I take the joint from her.

"But the athletes of today are very boring," says Jean-Baptiste. "Rich supermen and superwomen who entertain *les bouffons*."

Shalini puts on a sly little undertone. "But Johnny's obsession isn't just cultural or historical. He feels a spiritual connection." She raises my left arm. "Look at his body. How about this scar? Always fresh. Very cute, no? And all these cuts and bruises—so avant-garde."

JB lowers his eyes. "I did not want to ask about something so personal."

"It's not personal," Shalini replies with a sweet dollop of acid. "Johnny's body is public property, like a street—or like a sewer. Isn't that right, Johnny?"

Jean-Baptiste tries to hold her back. "Shalini... please."

"No, we're all friends here. We just had sex. Well, two of us did." She claps like a kid. "I know! Let's slit Johnny's throat! Then maybe he'll finally be able to come like an actual man. What do you say, Johnny? Wouldn't that be nice? Ooooh, imagine ejaculating like a real live man." Her thumbs and forefingers make a triangle and surround her cunt. She spits her words at me, eyes riding up and down my body with a revolted sneer. "This," she emphasizes. "This is wasted on you—you fucking coward."

I try to touch her, but she slaps my hand away and jumps off the bed, stands just inside the door, back to us. Anger shudders out, her head going side to side. She bends from the waist, face against shins, a little slice of pussy pie glistening. Her hands lay flat on the hardwood floor and she drops into a crouch then tips forward, feet coming up, knees against elbows. Shalini's body slowly unfurls into a handstand. She takes a deep breath then goes one-handed. Fingers spread, her torso's rigid, legs straight up and slightly apart, feet locked at right angles. I glance at Jean-Baptiste. We're both spellbound.

Shalini lets herself fall to one side. A leg snaps out, foot catching the floor so her body's in a precise sideways arc. She pushes off, twists in mid-air and floats face down to softly land on those jutting hip bones. The entire length of her is arched. She rolls on her stomach muscles and rib cage, rocks from pubic bone to sternum. What she's doing seems impossible, a hallucination.

TWENTY-SEVEN

It's Black Monday at Foufounes Electrique—the Electric Ass—a sprawling, multi-level club and bar complex on Sainte-Catherine East. The place is a labyrinthine cavern, dark as a mineshaft and done up in a heavy industrial interior. Plenty of rusty chain link fences, rough-welded iron railings, concrete slab bars. The hangar-sized performance space is like an atrium. Around the sides are several floors of party rooms, drinking rooms, hallways, tiny fuck closets with couches; a real warren you can get totally lost in, completely disorienting. Just being in here makes you kind of high. If you had to spend eternity in purgatory, this would be the place.

It's around midnight and I'm in one of the crowded side bars nursing a vodka tonic and waiting for Morgan after she's seen a john. The pager vibrates in my back pocket. It's her code followed by a number. I find a phone booth in the men's room. She tells me she'll be home in about half an hour. I forget to speak into the phone. "Johnny, are you there?"

"Uh, yeah. Your place in half an hour."

I drag myself out to Sainte-Catherine. The street's jammed with traffic, neon flashes everywhere while sidewalk vendors haggle and drunked-up wastrels totter past. I see a working girl I know called Sylvie. She's talking turkey with a john who's pulled up in a low-slung, piss-yellow sports car. "Wow!" Sylvie cries. "*Est-ce une Ferrari!?*"

The guy steps out and gabs over the roof at her. Fuck, it's that Burt Reynolds clone who was at the mountain fag orgy—and met Aunt B at the Oratory. This guy gets around. The Burt knockoff gives Sylvie a manly grin as he strokes his machine. I can just hear him thinking: *You brainless slut, Ferraris are for impotent homosexuals. This is a mint-condition 1972 De Tomaso Pantera with a fully-blown 351 Cleveland. It is THE ultimate expression of European handling and big-balled American horsepower. Tim Horton died in one of these beauties, you stupid fucking hag!*

"Don't get in that car!" I holler at her. "You'll never get home alive!"

Sylvie looks around to see who's yelling—if it's even directed at her. The BR clone gestures at her to ignore the surrounding bullshit and get in. She takes another quick glance then ducks into the Pantera. I'll have to check the papers over the next few days.

A cab stops in front of me but I ignore it and walk east, beyond the clubs and pubs and bars and bistros to end up at the massive stone footings of the Cartier bridge. I'm carried off by the immense span as it ranges over the Saint Lawrence. For a moment Montreal is completely still and wraps me in the low thrum of her busted avenues, in the musky smell of her filthy waters. She gets me excited with her vulgar tongue and sultry decay.

Jean... she whispers. I lay for a while between her flaccid old haunches and there are no crowds or cars or blinking neon to camouflage her rickety tarpaper shacks, her lonesome, garbage strewn boulevards. She stares at the ruins of her once mighty factories and conjures up memories of barges lined up in the Lachine Canal—the rough men who searched out her favors. They would teem up to Rue Notre Dame to drink and fight in cavernous, overlit taverns. She gets sentimental and holds me tight. *Oh, Monsieur Jean. We were so gay. On a warm spring evening I sat on Count Basie's lap at the Silver Slipper and drank wonderful pink champagne after Le Rocket had scored in overtime and we won Le Coupe de Stanley. We danced all night in Atwater Square.*

But that was when she ruled the nation and no other place in the land merited the grand title: *City*. Nowadays, she sits on a Balconville doorstep with swollen varicose ankles and knits a woolen girdle for the winter that's always just a few months away. A gray-faced old crone, she's become parochial as a farm wife. Reduced to the moniker *Tijuana North*, purveyor of flesh, booze and drugs meant to draw horny Yanks and Ontarians for the weekend. She offers a close-lipped smile to hide bad teeth. *Entre, s'il vois plaît, Monsieur Jean. I have a beautiful apartment for you, troisième étage, and such a view of Mont-Royal. I shall tell welfare whatever you wish.*

When I finally get to Morgan's she waits at the top of the stairs, just out of the bath. "I said half an hour, Johnny, not half the fucking night."

"Sorry. There was a Class A predator outside Foufounes—he baited that woman who's always around there. I think her name's Sylvie. Then I went east for some reason, maybe to—"

"Not now," Morgan stops me. "Set things up, then you can tell me all about it."

It isn't long before we're completely stoned and laid out in her bed—a pair of naked stiffs holding hands. The whole building seems to sway and creak in the wind, like being on a wooden ship. With the first hint of dawn there are still some errant wails of drunken rage from the sports bar down the street. The volume and intensity of the shrieks makes me wonder if they're being raped with barbed-wire dildos. Goddamn boozers, a blight on civic life. Roaring engines and tire squeals soon join the beastly cries. Their racket gradually fades as the testosterone-crazed mandrills race home to the sticks to ferociously jack off while watching hockey highlights in their mothers' basements.

We try to have sex, but both of us keep nodding out and eventually give up. "This john I had last night," Morgan mumbles. "He was... kinda strange..."

"Yeah?"

"Yeah... the fuckin' guy..." she goes on with a sickening slowness then stops. After a while she starts up again. "The fucking guy... He... uh... he stuck... a gun in me..."

A nickel plated 9-millimeter automatic drifts past, liquefies, then drops into murky waters with a soft plunk. A cloud of weak anger occurs to me. "What the hell you saying, Morgan?"

"I was... wasted. I opened my eyes... and... he's sliding this gun into me..."

The gun is made of succulent white flesh, skinless roast chicken breast. It wobbles and vibrates, veins bulging. "For Chrissake... What kinda bullshit are you telling me?"

Her arm rises then flops onto my chest. "It was… um… I got… What did I get? Three hundred bucks… I think…"

The incident is told once more in fast forward then rewinds and plays through again, so quick the images shred and catch fire. "Was it loaded?"

Morgan struggles up to her elbow. "Good question. You think somebody would do that?"

"Why else would he bother?"

I see the john in a burst of garish blue light. He resembles the cloned Burt Reynolds predator at Foufounes and diligently buffs the head of his enormous knob till it gleams like a patent leather shoe. Morgan falls back and her eyes slide shut. "Apart from the gun thing… he was okay…"

"Apart from oiling his pistol with your pussy?"

"Fuck you, Johnny."

I haul myself up into a sitting position. "Who is he? I have to kill him." I keel over sideways. "But later… I'll cut off his head. That seems about right."

"He's a big guy…" she warns. "He might throw you off a balcony."

"But I just cut his head off."

And I have because it floats before me, already drained and embalmed, now a drawing room curio.

TWENTY-EIGHT

I sit with Slim and Al in the back of the Balmoral Hotel draft room. She has just finished working and counts her tips. A gray day afternoon rush hour honks and trundles by out on The Main. The bar is crowded and noisy, lots of walleyed yelling and both pool tables going, the house lights are all on. I half listen as Al pontificates. "The victim of this terrible darkness can be any man. It's a disease of sorts. Suffered by a husband, a boyfriend, a brother, a father, perhaps even you, Johnny." He holds up a hand in unbidden protest. "And yes, me too."

Slim looks up from her money, irritated. "What are you talking about?"

"The New Morality," I reply for Al. "Speaking of which, did that beetle-browed Avoro creep ever show up again?"

"No."

"Who?" Al asks.

"The moujik. You know. The guy who used to come in here and stare at her. He gave Slim some shit-brown vinyl jacket and a wacky love letter."

"Oh, of course," Al recalls. "One of our hard-working New Canadians."

Slim's eyes snap up, shocked as she looks past me toward the entrance. "Fuck... It's him!"

I turn and peer through the smoky clamor. Christ, it is that thick-necked ape! Did I make him materialize just by mentioning his stupid name? It's like he stood up out of the floor. Either way, Avoro's finally come home to roost and he's a lot bigger than I remember. His head goes in all directions, fevered and searching. Red-eyed and disheveled, he babbles like a day-pass lunatic, paws at his face, a man stricken with unending grief. Avoro the Mighty Moujik is determined to make this relationship work.

Slim and I stand as he approaches, weaving through the tables, eyes only for her. I slowly grab the neck of a beer bottle. Al gets to his feet, ready to duck out of the way—he doesn't punch above his weight. Avoro cautiously reaches out for Slim, like she'll bite. Tears well up while the heavy, unshaven jaw twists into a low guttural whimper.

"No!" That single word from Slim sends a charge right round the room. The mob of drunks rears up as if a huge, many-headed pitbull. A pair of twerps try to manhandle Avoro. He easily shakes them off and keeps coming, mumbles softly at Slim. He stinks of cheap cologne sloshed on top of work sweat.

A cowboy boot lashes out of the pressing crowd, a sharp kick that catches him square in the jewelry box, but he won't be deterred. Everyone pushes forward to see. More kicks get him in the legs and the back of his knees. A bunch of fists rain down. Avoro finally buckles, falls at Slim's feet and reaches for her ankles. A work boot comes from somewhere and stomps on his fingers.

He doesn't even flinch, only looks up at her. His bloodshot eyes plead. *I am Avoro! Translate me!*

The pot-bellied doorman shoves his way through and jams his own boot into Avoro's neck, pinning him to the floor. A chaos of bodies pile on, a downed wildebeest struggling under a pack of vicious hyenas. The door goon pulls Slim's badly mauled groupie to his feet with the help of a few rounders. They hustle him past cursing faces and errant punches. His mug is bloody, jacket in shreds, our lovelorn cuckold cries into his hands. Avoro is shoved off down the sidewalk with a couple of parting hoofs to the ass. The satisfied customers prattle on at the excitement. Slim gets a round of whistles and cheers. A table of jocks give her the thumbs up. She's flushed with embarrassment, wipes her face with trembling hands. The barmaid comes over and crouches next to her, talks quietly then looks at Al and me. "You guys want a pitcher—on the house?"

Slim shakes her head, impatient at the woman's puerile sympathy, mortified at all this ridiculous attention. "No, it's okay. I have to go."

"You sure?" The waitress stands straight and casts worried glances about, no doubt wondering when her own free-range maniac will show up.

"Yeah, thanks anyway," Slim refuses again. She gets to her feet, barely looks at us. "I'll see you guys later." More hoots and approving nonsense follow her out the door. She hails a cab, gets in and quickly disappears into traffic.

Al nods as we watch her go. "It's happening, Johnny. By late tonight the streets could be full of fire and blood."

I look at him and sigh. "If only."

Several hours later there has been no fire and very little blood. But me and Morgan have done fair-sized whacks and I begin to meditate on our tattoos. They aren't flags or eagles or skulls or the murderer's elbow-covering spider's web. No slogans done in phony gothic script on curled banners. No S/M, B&D pseudo-kink monikers that anal retentive rubber-wear women get drawn on their tits and shaved labia. And no obscure Nepalese chakras encircling the biceps and ankles of fourth-generation hippie kids. Neither do we have the crudely self-inflicted Celtic crosses and misspelled biblical quotes favored by pea-brained jailbirds.

Our tattoos are anatomically correct and follow the paths of the most easily accessed veins. *Our* tattoos evolve very slowly, scar tissue builds, time stitched along the flesh. Over years you could end up with a complete arterial cartography etched on your surface. I want to tell Morgan what our tattoos mean, but right now she has to do all the talking. Her psychic exhaust system needs a good airing and like it or not, I get to hear all the hair-splitting detail, dull as tooth decay. The hustlers, the gimps, the jocks, the suits, the dads, the wife haters and child cheaters, the fishnet sniffers and bare-faced criers, the grinders and the hagglers, all of them demanding value for money, comparison shopping, the hard bargaining of a totally laissez-faire, kick-in-the-nuts free-market economy.

Morgan limbers up her tongue while she changes out of the stroll gear, quickly converting from Betty Page to Ethel Mertz. She pulls money from every pocket, from her purse, from her panties and from her shoe. She tosses three half-empty packs of smokes onto the coffee table. My pager vibrates. I ignore the call. They'll have to wait. Morgan's ritual yack-a-thon is more important than some fool who shivers and gacks with desperate hope while he stares at the silent phone and curses me under his breath.

Morgan puts on her powder blue Star Wars bathrobe and the big-eyed bunny slippers. She goes into the can to pursue her one hobby—shove her face in the bare-bulb mirror to pick and wrestle with her flesh, satiated only after having hacked her sweet mug into a patchy landscape of red blotches. "The last guy I had tonight was new," she yells from the john.

I hear her clatter around in there with various creams and cleansers. Then the interminable pause till she goes on about the new guy. But there's no other way. Morgan must get this evening's mind-numbing events off her chest or suffer cranial vapor lock. I ease back on the couch and close my eyes. "So this new guy," her mouth finally grinds into gear. "He says his wife's really sick. Why lie to me? To make me feel sorry for him? Like I care? I mean, who gives a fuck… Anyway, he took me to a nice place so I said I'd knock off twenty bucks. I thought Holiday Inns were dumps. Who knows why—I'd never actually been to one. Strange, huh?"

"What, that they're not dumps?"

"No," her voice comes down the hall, "that I've never been to one."

"Yeah, I guess."

"Anyhow, this place was kinda nice. Who knows, maybe different Holiday Inns are different. The staff was really friendly—total pros. Y'know, minding your own business is a skill in itself. If you're tipping somebody big they should keep their mouth shut and their eyes on their shoes, right?"

"Yup, that's right."

"Anyway, that Holiday Inn was one of the few square places I've ever been where I didn't get any attitude. And you know me, I always look good, very presentable."

"Yup, always."

"The room was kinda bland but clean as hell and they had nice big towels. Fuck, I'd spend a weekend there just for fun. You wanna go sometime, Johnny?"

"Sure, baby, we'll go to one with a pool."

"That's a good idea. So anyway, this new john, eh, he strips down in a flash and just stands there, staring at me. For a second I was worried he might be a headcase. Y'know, the sorta creep that keeps saying 'I want my money's worth'. But he was totally okay, fuckin' me nice and easy. The guy had some class. I actually fell asleep. Stupid er what? Before I realize, he comes and pulls out quick then runs into the can hanging onto his rubber like he was chased and the shower's on full blast. Who knows what his trip is. So I go through his pants and beat him for an extra fifty-five bucks. I don't think he minded too much. He liked me."

"Sounds civilized. You going to see him again?"

"Nah, he's from out of town... Y'know, it still seems weird to me how you can fuck somebody—like, your bodies can be together and then you never see them again. I always think that's weird. Isn't that weird?"

"What, that you think it's weird to think that way?"

Morgan comes right out into the living room to clarify. "No, that it really is weird to never see that person again."

"I suppose, but it's happening all over the world as we speak."

"Yeah... I guess," she frowns and returns to the can to lance blackheads or whatever the hell she's doing in there. "It's the same even if you're not fucking somebody. You can be really good friends then a few years later you don't even know each other anymore. It kinda sucks."

"Yeah, it does."

Morgan goes on to give me several more second-by-second breakdowns of tonight's customers. A handful of regulars and the one new guy. She's extremely selective, having pointed out more than once that quantity just means wear and tear on her body. Better to have a few docile, well-paying steadies and the occasional out-of-town exec type with coin, all of whom must have extremely pedestrian sexual tastes.

Well, that is the goal of any sex worker, but with Morgan's youth and looks, she can still make those types of demands. The rising cost of diminishing returns begins to kick in at thirty to thirty-five and just gets worse from there unless the worker provides a truly unique service or maneuvers the john into becoming emotionally hung up on her. For males doing males, the window of gold-plated opportunity is even smaller—much smaller.

I glance at my five-dollar Motorcycle Grand Prix wristwatch and figure I have listened to enough of tonight's tedium that I can broach the delicate matter of finances. "So… uh… Morgan, think you can lend me four hundred bucks? I don't have enough to see The Man."

According to our Byzantine protocol, I can't just tote up her take for the evening, even though the disorganized pile of bills sits in front of me on the coffee table. Her voice hardens into a veteran haggler's drone. "Why are you so short?"

"Because you and me are fucking hogs."

"Why don't you just get less off him for now?"

"Like I've told ya, he won't do less than a half ounce and even that's a stretch."

There's a long pause as she makes her mental calculations. "Okay… I can let you have two hundred."

"C'mon, just give me what I need. You're gonna get it back in product anyway."

She emerges from the toilet with her hair up in a scrunchy, face puffy; that stupid quilted bathrobe wrapped tight—a low-rent Margaret Thatcher. "Johnny, I have my costs too, y'know. It's not all just revenue and profit."

"Yeah yeah."

"Don't 'yeah, yeah' me. You know I need all kinds of stuff. My human answering service, good condoms, clothes, make-up, bras, underwear. I don't wear cheap shit. In my line of work that doesn't pay. There's also my ad in the paper—which never stops."

Having made her statement, she returns to the bathroom mirror. I press the button on the side of my watch and start the elapsed time. Now I have to sit through this long silence before she'll eventually break down. I think it's meant to make me truly appreciate her contributions.

After what feels like ages, Morgan finally hollers from the can. "All right, you can have the four hundred."

I check the elapsed time. Exactly twenty-two minutes, four point six seconds. A fair bit less than the thirty-one minute, fifty-two point three second average. She must be in a good mood. The record wait is an hour ten, two point one. We ended up in a huge fight that time so now she knows the general parameters. I'm not sure how she does it without a clock in there.

Her facial mutilations complete, Morgan sits on the floor on the other side of the coffee table. She lights a smoke and gets down to the counting. I'm expected to keep myself otherwise occupied and not kibitz. First, she flattens and separates the crumpled bills into their denominations. After that's done, she makes piles of the same coins. Then comes the paper and pen reckoning. After this convoluted marathon she finally says, "Here" and holds out the money. Fuck, what an ordeal. In truth, I only need two hundred, but with Morgan you have to hedge your bets.

"We can't keep doing this, Johnny, me picking up the slack."

"What are you talking about? I hardly make a profit because of your gluttony. And that's at my cost. At retail it would be—"

"Enough about the retail!" she shouts. "I'm sick of hearing about the fucking retail! Why doesn't that moron give you some credit—demanding cash every time. It's not like you wouldn't pay him. You both know he'd squash you like a bug."

"Good idea, I'll put your mouth up as collateral. Yes, ladies and germs! She comes with a heavy-duty whine and first class tongue-lashing. Never be left speechless again!"

"You're such an asshole. I could kick you out right now and you'd be fucked."

"You'd still have to score off me."

"What, you think you're the only dealer in town?"

"No, but you know I'd never rip you off—and I deliver."

"Spare me. Okay, take the fucking money, but try to get the price down or something. Show a little spine. Don't be in such awe of that shithead."

"Right. I'll threaten to fall in love with him."

"I wouldn't be surprised if you're already suckin' his steroid-shrunk little pecker, being such good buddies an' all."

I go to the phone booth in the all-night diner across Park Avenue and arrange a meet with The Man. Wherever he is, the background is full of
primal screams and long, overwrought cries of terror—like some Satanic
torture club. "Where the fuck are you?"

"I'll be at your place in an hour!" he yells over the hysteria then cuts me off.

TWENTY-NINE

Al phones and puts on his officious voice, tells me the big day has come. I go over there and we spend a couple hours waiting around for Aunt Byron as she prepares for her much-anticipated summit with Diddler Emeritus, DC Scott. It's taken weeks of negotiations that've made the SALT Talks seem like ordering pizza. Everything had to be hammered out. The where, the why, the how, the precisely how long, the what-subjects-can-be-discussed, the agreed upon rules of engagement, fundamental policy objectives, overall security, weapons checks, aides-de-camp, start time, break time, lunch time, furniture, the pre-approved post-conference press release, the type face and point size of said press release, how the summit will be recorded, by whom, number of copies and subsequent dissemination, the kind of clothing—casual, formal or black tie and lots more besides.

It turns out Al and I won't be allowed to observe. It will be a strictly private face-to-face encounter between Aunt B and DC Scott; not even his goon Antonio will be on hand. It was agreed we may accompany Byron to the door then wait outside.

She's distracted and nervous as hell, lapsing into fairly male body language. Her face is deep in concentration as she scribbles in her journal. I feel like throwing it out a window. "Will you leave that fucking thing alone? It's just neurotic busy work at this point."

"I must record the entire process. This is carefully compiled evidence. Any board of inquiry would find it unimpeachable."

"Like I said, neurotic busy work."

212

Al gives me a *leave her alone* scowl. He lays a hand on Byron's shoulder while reaching down to shut the journal. She raises her eyes to him. "I think it's time we went," he says quietly. It works.

We hail a cab on Duluth and squeeze in. I feel Aunt B tremble next to me and keep thinking of Waterloo or Stalingrad or Marathon, some massive, bloody act of hubris. She dabs her eyes with a tissue. Al gently pats her knee. I want to let out a blood-curdling shriek just for the sheer stinkin' hell of it.

As we arrive at DC Scott's townhome, Byron now appears doddery and feeble, hands shaking. She wears a stunned expression, dry lips turned gray, eyes vacant. Scott's place gives off a sinister House of Usher air, no lights on, as if corpses are stuffed into the attic like cordwood.

"Take as long as you need," Al comforts her and points up the street. "We'll wait at the café over there."

Byron ignores the reassurance. As she passes through the wrought-iron sidewalk gate, the front door opens. Scott's house ape, Antonio, stands at attention in black pants and turtleneck. He wears a gold pendant and has grown a little Van Dyke. His new look reminds me of the flamboyantly gay theater director in that Mel Brooks movie, *The Producers*.

Aunt B stops, glances back at us then takes a deep breath. She bows her head, journal gripped firmly under her arm, and strides up the stairs, quickly disappearing inside. Absurd shit runs through my head; Byron as damsel in distress with full-on Camelot maiden's gown and flowing head gear. I want to give chase, pull her back from the abyss, wildly swing my broadsword. Antonio's limbs fly off with geysers of blood, like the stupid Monty Python knight in *The Holy Grail* who's down to four stumps but still won't surrender. The door closes without a sound and makes me think of those cheesy haunted castle doors that shut on their own after you have entered.

"I wonder if we'll ever see her alive again," I say as Al and I walk away.

"Why even think such a thing? They are going to talk, nothing more."

"I don't know… maybe Byron'll go berserk, kill Scott and that Antonio fruit. Maybe she's got a hidden weapon, a stiletto blade or a giant serrated hunting knife—or some acid to throw in their faces!"

"Stop fantasizing about what you'd like to do. Byron abhors any sort of violence."

"Oh, you never know," I keep goading. "Maybe we'll go back and find the place knee deep in gore, their guts strung around like party streamers, Byron dancing madly in the middle of it all, butt naked as the stereo blasts out Killing Joke." We both burst into guffaws.

"Johnny, I love how sick you are. A psychopath's Rodney Dangerfield."

"Hey, as Aunt Byron loves to tell everyone, 'Don't say I didn't warn ya.'"

Al grabs a bunch of newspapers from the café's rack and we take a sidewalk table. He reads *The Gazette* Entertainment section while I make a concerted effort to get immediately wasted. On my third absinthe, Vern comes flapping by with those big feet of his. Christ, you really can't get away from anybody in this goddamn village. Despite the temperature, he wears a bulky moth-eaten fur coat, like something out of the Charleston. All he needs is the straw boater and a triangular college pennant. He sits sidesaddle on the low railing next to our table.

"How come Leroi's not answering the pager?" he grills me. Al lowers his newspaper for a second then whips it back up.

"How should I know? Do you owe him any money?"

"Yeah, but-"

"Hold it right there. 'Yeah, but' doesn't cut it with Leroi. I might be a soft touch, but he's the Ante Pavelić of the small-time dealer scene."

"No fuckin' way to treat a valued customer. You got anything on ya?"

"Nada, not even personal. I'm a pig, just like you, remember?"

"Fuck," Vern gasses and grabs my drink, downs it in one gulp then makes a face. "Jeezus, tastes like lukewarm dog piss!"

Al's clears his throat. Other customers are becoming peeved at our crude banter. Vern's eager to vent on somebody, anybody. He stands up straight. "So who's got a fuckin' problem?"

"Vern," Al warns him. "Not here. Not now. We're busy."

"Doin' what!? Jerkin' each other off?"

But his blood's weak and he can't maintain the rage. Izanami's screw job has left him dry and defeated. He's not quite as big an asshole anymore. She seems to have siphoned off the essential core of his assholeishness. My empty glass shatters as Vern slaps it onto the ground. "Aw, fuck you guys," he curses and stumbles off.

The waitress bitches in French while she cleans up. I try to soothe her with a big tip. We have a couple more drinks. I lay my head on my arms. Al's moved onto to one of those huge French onionskin newspapers the size of a bed sheet. I use my lighter to discreetly set the bottom on fire. It goes up suddenly, *whoosh*—like an acetate nightgown. Al jumps to his feet, stomping and dancing on the flaming remains. He swears at me as I howl like a madhouse hyena. The waitress is about to throw us out, but I assuage her with a twenty dollar bribe, order another round and a couple Croque-Monsieurs.

The afternoon meanders along. I go into the can and do another good-sized shot, return for a few more drinks, nod out for a while, drool on myself, knock over a coffee—and still no Aunt Byron. Al's down to reading the McGill Student Union paper. "Let's go knock on the door," I crab at him. "We've been here like three fucking hours. Maybe she did butcher them."

Al twists round toward the Perv's house. It's in shadow now with the sun beginning to go down, but still no lights. I wonder if DC Scott's like one of those old world women who forces her family to live in the basement and does all the cooking down there while the rest of the house remains pristine, with velvet theater ropes to cordon off the living and dining rooms, saving it all as a dowry for some big-mouthed, hoggish daughter. "So?" I keep bugging Al. "What do you wanna do?"

He uses both hands to finger-comb what's left of his mane. "Well… Byron did say that if she failed come back out within a reasonable time we were to go home and await further instructions."

A drunken headache smacks the back of my eyeballs. "'Await further instructions'? Why didn't ya say so? What are we, a couple of heel-clickers from the bloody Luftwaffe? The goddamn schtolzer came down here to confront that DC Scott prick. Instead she's probably doing both those freaks at the same time while we sit here like a pair of shtups. You can wait all night, Polo. I'm leaving." He hesitates for a moment then joins me.

THIRTY

"Speaking of the rotten old ham," Hennessy's saying over the phone. "Al and I are going to that fascist lager festival opening in Parc Lafontaine tonight. They've put up a whole colony of giant circus tents and we've clipped dozens of beer coupons from *Le Voir* and *The Mirror*."

"Uh... I dunno..."

"C'mon, Johnny, we'll go hassle Whitey, as you like to say."

I can hear the Balmoral bar crowd in the background, some woman yelling Hennessy's name. He shouts at her to hang on a second. "So hurry up and get down here."

"Why don't you come over first?"

"Are you alone?"

"Just me."

He mulls it over briefly. "I told you, I've got Al with me. I don't want to be rude. You know how easily embarrassed he is."

"Polo can sit there and the read the paper for an hour."

"C'mon, just throw something on and get over here. We'll have fun, then go back to your house later."

"Christ. All right, Miss Manners. Gimme twenty minutes."

After I meet them at the Balmoral, Al leads the way to Parc Lafontaine. We don't go east of Rue Saint-Denis very often, so he describes the architecture and history of various buildings en route as Hennessy and I follow, his arm curled through mine; a respectable old couple taking a Sunday stroll, young lovers on their nervous first date, a wage-earning stiff and his chain smoking wife out for some cheap laughs.

When we get there *le festivale* is already going full bore. Christmas lights and Chinese lanterns are strung up everywhere. Huge blue and white striped tents that have taken over the park for the weekend. It's called *The Boulevard of Broken Dreams*, a much ballyhooed re-creation of a late nineteenth-century European traveling fair. I always thought The Boulevard of Broken Dreams was Sunset Strip, but Euros have strange interpretations of Hollywood.

This particular version features pseudo-freak shows, leashed monkeys and midget bears, sword-swallowers, caped magicians, fortune-tellers, a boy-faced dog, all the hackneyed horseshit you'd expect. It was organized by the Belgian-Canadian Friendship League, a reputed front for Saint-Jean Baptiste Society death squads. Banners exalting the trans-national beer corp that's bankrolled this jamboree are hung all over the place.

Sing-along yobs jam together at long wooden tables and guzzle dark ale. At one end, a team of grown men in lederhosen and Tyrolean hats fill enormous pitchers in high-speed relays as an oompah band hams it up. A tuxedoed em-cee with a distended belly and tiny white-gloved hands introduces a Marlene Dietrich impersonator called Anastazia. She's a six-and-a-half-foot tall drag queen full of wags and winks, brunette mane draped over one eye. The crowd's surly. They shout the little emcee down, hammer their steins on the tables.

"What on earth is this?" gawks Al. "The Beer Hall Putsch?"

"We forgot to bring our armbands," says Hennessy.

"Yeah," I add. "And our foreskins."

As we struggle sideways through the press of bodies toward the bar, the house lights dim and Anastazia glides to center stage, tracked by a single yellow spot. With thick hands on hips, trombones slide suggestively while she slowly shimmies in a skin-tight, ankle length silver lame dress. Tarantula lashes flutter as she puckers a big red smooch at the mob. They holler at her to take it all off. Anastazia slides a feather boa across her packed bosom and a long leg appears from the waist-high slit, prompting another burst of howls. A snare drum keeps time with her ass when she launches into a raun-chy, strutting cabaret number.

Hennessy has managed to claw his way to the bar ahead of us and turns around with three plastic pint glasses full of the sponsor's swill. We are debating whether to stick around when a sinewy yoga-teaching slime called Michel appears out of the crowd, sonar on high. His lacquered talons lay on Hennessy's shoulder just so. Michel scans the crowd, his painted yap all pursed and persnickety. "I *must* speak with you, my dear Hennessy."

I try to bad vibe him. He bares his incisors at me. I drop the psychic charge for something more direct. "Go apply your leeches someplace else, Cornholer."

Michel presses an open hand to his chest, appalled. "Is this Johnny's business?"

"What is your problem?" the Hen bitches at me.

"Nothin', except for this little cock-eating vampire. Go ahead, ask the parasite what he wants."

Michel gives me a thin leer. "*Je m'excuse de vous faire sentir si jaloux.*"

I cock a fist, ready to drill him in the chops. "I'll see your apology and raise you with one of my own, you smart-ass frog cocksucker!"

Hennessy grabs my arm. "Stop it, Johnny! Try to behave yourself. I'll be back in a few minutes." He takes Michel by the elbow and they squeeze their way toward the open air, heads close, conspiratorial and snickering. I want to run up behind and garrote the two-bit fruit.

On stage, the song ends and as Anastazia takes a deep bow, a spray of beer splatters her. She glares at a nearby table of baseball-capped wiggers. They give her a chorus of dog woofs. The crowd hiccups with some vague clapping and nervous snorts. Maybe she'll drop the femme fatale act, grab a mike stand and start busting heads. The emcee's quickly on stage and detours her temper with a bouquet of plastic roses. He strikes up the band and calls for a round of applause. Anastazia's confused for a moment and peers blindly into the lights. She waves regally at the mostly indifferent audience, their attention now centered on the waitresses struggling between tables, trays held aloft.

Al and I load up on more beer and battle our way out of the main tent. We make it to the temporary outdoor amphitheater and find seats near the top to wait for the next show in tonight's cultural-exchange program. I glance about at our fellow patrons. "Look at these fucking squares. Y'know, Polo, this whole shindig proves the European anti-rock'n'roll theory—in spades."

Al revs himself up for a bout of highfalutin, high-brow horseshit and trots out his eccentric professor persona. "Yes, Johnny, it certainly is tragic—but patently irrefutable. Once you cross the English Channel to the continent, they simply cannot rock'n'roll—a cultural deformity of mammoth proportions, deeply genetic and completely irreversible." He opens his flask and takes a nip of Delamain cognac. "However, one must wonder… What did ever happen to those monstrous German, French and Austro-Hungarian rhythm and blues bands? Or the Greek Motown scene? Swedish soul. Portuguese jazz. Italian honky-tonk, Spanish punk."

He's on a hot roll and has me coughing with laughter. "Yeah," I agree, "it is pretty amazing Euros have never figured out *rock'n'roll* is just an old bluesman's expression for fucking—*a rockin' and a rollin'.*"

Al's brow furrows as he ratchets up the hammery. "Nevertheless, the inability to *rock'n'roll* is only a symptom of a far deeper *malaise*. Needless to say, continentals have had their moments, like pre-war Berlin, the Paris Commune or the Jura Federation, but those were tiny minorities of idealists. In an over-arching sense, a culture would have to be incapable of comprehending *rock'n'roll* in order to produce something like… oh… the Nuremberg Rally, Nazi Monumentalist art and wartime neutrality, not to mention those Sunday morning Telelatina programs." Al pauses only to take another swig. "Look at the history of racism, anti-Semitism and homophobia in Europe—practically made into an art form—or at the very least a fully-functional bureaucratic obsession. As a result, one is forced to draw the undeniable conclusion: It is fundamentally impossible for anti-Semites, racists and homophobes to—*rock'n'roll*, if you will."

"In other words, their basic problem is they're lousy lays."

Al nods his head sadly. "Yes… I suppose so. The same old banality of evil, I'm afraid. Yes… these findings do combine to form a rather damning indictment of the entire society."

"So I guess Brits really aren't Euros, like so many of them claim."

"*Clearly.* Their ability to comprehend *rock'n'roll* remains unsurpassed—at least among Caucasoids." Al knocks back another long snort and gestures with his flask. "And yet—Europeans do make some very good wines, brandies and what have you."

"They've also got some pretty great writers and artists. But they're usually outcasts."

"In addition, we cannot forget they did create what is now known as 'classical music.'"

"Sure, but c'mon—only a Nazi mental case could fuck to that shit. I mean, are you gonna do some *rockin' and a rollin'* to Wagner or Brahms?"

"Point taken. However, one must ask if our continental friends would—"

The dark stage suddenly explodes with powerful strobe lights and horrendous noise. An earnest Germanic creep wearing a silver body suit covered with electronic percussion pads whacks himself up and down the legs, ass, head, belly while he spasms about. The speakers bash out a helluva racket with plenty of ear-shredding feedback. I'd love to flee, but we're surrounded by a crush of serious looking dupes determined to experience this event. Fighting our way out now would probably take longer than this moron's going to be on stage. The aural rape goes on for about twenty minutes. We extract ourselves before the next act and go looking for the Hen back in the big top. I check around the rollicking action. "Where the hell is that little slut?"

"Oh, probably still flitting about with Michel and his entourage of Rue Beaudry homophiles."

"Michel," I grouse. "He's no better than that dog, Heidi. What's the Hen see in these lowlife skanks, anyway?"

"Calm down, Johnny."

"I just don't get why he can't find a better quality sugar momma. He's a fuckin' babe and Heidi's nothing but an old hosebag. She was supposed to be a stop-gap—like two fucking years ago."

"They have a past. You know he was once involved with Heidi's daughter, Cynthia, may she rest in peace."

"No disrespect, Al, but all he did was fuck Cynthia a few times."

"You know that's not true."

"Well, it is kind of sick Hennessy's doing the old lady now."

"What, your morals feeling impinged upon?" He frisks himself for cigarettes and comes away empty-handed. "Let's just say they both miss her very badly. He was in love with the girl and that's brought them closer."

"Yeah, right. Heidi wouldn't cross the street for him if he wasn't so good looking. Anyway, Hennessy doesn't even like women."

Inside the main tent, the band trots along doing a polka version of *Jumpin' Jack Flash* while juggling clowns prance. They give the impression of being police informants under the red noses and goofy antics. Next, it's a pyramid of dwarves, followed by a sword-eating fool in a loincloth. Beer bellies, hard as oaken casks, bump us from all sides. A herd of drunks swarms over a tank full of writhing sausages. They shove and shout and gobble the things down. Al cups his hands to his mouth and makes like a bullhorn. "Attention! Goosestepping will commence momentarily!"

I catch glimpses of demonic little faces peeking between the crush of bodies. They're at my elbow to whisper nasty rumors then vanish. I mistake braying laughter for someone calling my name. The emcee pulls on a rubber pig's head and clambers on stage. He tells sordid, off-color jokes. At every punch line, the bass drum thumps as a big white penis unrolls from his fly. The crowd roars and claps out of time. It feels like the foreplay before Kristallnacht.

Artie de Gobineau gets piss drunk in the corner with a Mongol whore on his lap and a Doberman at his feet. Impersonators doing George Wallace, Lionel Groulx and Elvis bellow marching songs. A Jumbo John Wayne look-a-like pushes a white Imperial Wizard cone-hat back on his giant square head. *I'm a just reeelaxin…* Both Al and me are out of smokes and his flask is empty. An hour or more has passed and no Hennessy.

THIRTY-ONE

When a brain-squeezer migraine rousts me around noon, Slim has a tall glass of cool water ready, along with four aspirins. I down it all and she trades me the empty glass for a cup of coffee.

After the beer tent boondoggle last night, Al went home and I returned to the Balmoral. A couple hours later Slim recognized my boots under a stall door in the men's room. She said she'd called out my name and when I didn't answer, climbed over. After dragging me back to my place, she held my forehead as I threw up then put us both to bed.

She has even returned this morning's pager calls, letting me get some badly needed shut-eye by telling my clientele there's nothing around right now and I'll get back to them this afternoon, once inventory is re-stocked. I feel a bit guilty letting people go sick, but what the fuck. They won't have to wait all that long and exercising one's patience does build character. Her ministrations complete, Slim shows me an old yellowed paperback. *Hockey Is A Battle: The Autobiography of Punch Imlach.* Hennessy had bought it for my birthday at the Sally Ann on Saint-Antoine.

"You and your hockey hang up," she says, studying the cover. "I was reading some of it while you were asleep. This Imlauck guy was a real jerk."

"It's pronounced *Im-lack* and of course he was a jerk," I defend the legendary Maple Leafs coach. "He had to be. Players then could handle it. Not like the pansies today."

"If they're such pansies, why are you so fascinated by them?"

"I don't love these new guys with their steroids and gay haircuts. What they do is interesting because of the whole S/M, B&D, homoerotic element in contact sports but, really, I like the pre-expansion old-timers. The guys who made shit money and played hockey cuz they couldn't do anything else. Y'know, the sort of guys who looked enviously at a plumber or electrician, somebody with a real trade."

"Okay, so one of those working class tragedies you're always crying about."

"I'm not always 'crying' about them."

Slim closes the book and gives me her undivided attention. It's patronizing, but I can live with the way she does it. "All right, Johnny. Go ahead and tell me."

I sit up and face her to better describe the thing. "Terry Sawchuk is a classic example. He was a brilliant goalie, but had a wicked ulcer, like all goalies back then. Who wouldn't? None of them wore a mask, mostly because it was considered effete. All they had on were some joke pads to protect against these maniacs firing frozen pucks at their heads. Sawchuk and the other goalies, they were always one shot away from death or disfigurement or being left a vegetable. So, him and a drinking buddy of his, a forward called Ronnie Stewart... or maybe he was a defenseman... Anyway, they both played for the New York Rangers at the time. In those days, players made like eighteen dollars a week and sent most of the money back to their wives and seven kids or whatever. Basically, they were bums on skates. I mean, they lived in fucking rooming houses!"

"Just get on with the story."

"Okay. So Sawchuk and this other guy, they didn't want to waste their cash in a bar so they'd buy a bottle of some rotgut and get drunk out on the street. The two of them were boozing in Bryant Park. Y'know, on 34th, behind the Museum of Natural History."

"Byrant Park's behind the main library."

"Yeah—one of those massive Gotham buildings. Anyway, they start to play-fight and roll around—but pretty hardcore. Remember, these are tough, semi-literate bonehead hockey players. Stewart accidentally boots Sawchuk in the guts while they're grappling. That bursts his ulcer and

223

smashes up his liver and, long story short, it ends up killing Sawchuk. And *he* holds the record for the most career shutouts in NHL history. Nobody's even close and the fucking guy died with nothing, a drunk in some park!"

Slim's not moved. "They sound like clichéd losers."

"Yeah... I guess... Dream comes true for small-town hoser who gets used and abused by cigar chomping boss archetype. A few years later the player is tossed onto the scrap heap."

"This obsession of yours, Johnny, it seems kind of regressive."

"Yeah, I know. Listen, do you think continental European guys are lousy lays?"

She rubs her eyes, running out of patience. "What's that got to do with Sawcheck and his friend?"

"It's Saw-*chuk*—and it's got nothing to do with him or Ronnie Stewart. It's this anti-rock'n'roll theory Al and I were talking about last night at that stupid beer tent festival. Don't you remember? I've told you about it."

"Yeah, I suppose..."

"Anyway, the basic idea is that because continental European guys don't get rock'n'roll and since Nazis were continental Euros and fascism is a Euro concept, that would naturally mean, y'know, they don't get irony, which means they can't really rock'n'roll, and that makes them useless lays because a *rockin' and a rollin'* is really just another word for fucking."

Slim's had about enough. "Johnny... please."

"No, I mean it. Seriously, I'm asking what you think."

Cheeks puffing out, she forces herself to ponder the notion. "Um, all right... uh... yeah, I've screwed some European guys while I've been over there, and some I met here..."

"I don't mean UK guys, they're not really European."

"I dunno... as a group they're not much different than guys anywhere. We're talking straight hetero guys, right?"

"Yeah, yeah, of course, strictly hetero."

"Well, most strictly hetero men are pretty mediocre as it is. I mean, some of them are nice people—or do you mean just their sexual technique?"

"No, not only technique. Anybody can learn that, more or less. I guess whether they get the whole kind of complex structure built around what's basically attempted procreation. Y'know, the weird irony of there being so much devoted to it—your own energy, the world's. But it's not about having children. It's about identity, libido, ego, fuck, who knows, lots of shit that has zero to do with procreating and in fact, that's considered a negative result almost all the time."

"Well, you'll never wrap it all up in a one-liner. I guess that's why sex and death are endless subjects and people never get tired of them."

I'm not too satisfied with this outcome. "Yeah… maybe…"

"Sorry to poke a hole in your hypothesis, darling."

I put on a mad professor shtick with a cartoon German accent. "Ha! Zey laughed at me in Prague!"

Slim smiles with something bordering on fondness. She runs her fingers through my hair. "It's nice you woke up in such a good mood." The phone rings. We both groan. It stops after a while. "Y'know, Johnny, you really should get an answering machine." Within a few minutes the phone starts up again and this time it doesn't stop. It's gotta be Al. At about twenty rings I reach down from the bed, find the cord and drag it over.

"Johnny."

"What's wrong with you, Polo, got the DT's or something?"

"It's Hennessy."

"What about him?"

"Last night at the fair…" Al's voice is distant, exhausted.

"What happened?"

"His body… he was found under a tree—behind one of the tents. The coroner said it was a morphine overdose."

"Al, fuck off, will ya? That's not funny."

He speaks in a thin monotone, almost formal. "I just spoke with Josée, the French girl he'd been seeing. The people who discovered him are acquaintances. They phoned her. He wasn't carrying any identification. She's going to the morgue with his passport and asked we escort her."

The room suddenly drops off kilter. I grab onto the sheets as vertigo hits. My throat constricts. I can barely manage a reply. "I'll come by and get you."

225

A wave of nauseous panic hits as I hang up and think of Hennessy eluding my grasp at the goddamn Nazi beer tent nightmare, slipping away through the crowd with that hateful fuck, Michel. I want to destroy something, but my place is already pretty much empty. Slim lays a hand in the middle of my back.

"Hennessy OD'd. We're going to the morgue." She doesn't respond, just strokes my neck. I turn to her. "Are you coming?"

"If you want me to."

"He was your friend too, y'know."

"We really weren't that close, but I'll come with you."

I break into a sweat, get out of bed and pace around. I could at least smash a few windows. "Forget it. It's all right. I don't want to put you out."

"C'mon, don't be like that. I know your heart's breaking, but I don't want to be part of some ghoulish scene."

I grab my pants and look around for my shirt. "Yeah, sure, whatever you like. I've gotta get ready."

Slim ignores my anger. "I'll be at home. Come by after if you want."

"It's all right, don't worry about it."

She begins to pick through her stuff and get dressed.

THIRTY-TWO

The city morgue is in the Sûreté Du Québec building, way out in the east end on Parthenais. It's a big sand-colored rectangular block and I imagine KGB headquarters in Dzerzhinsky Square looks like this. But everything's casual, no ID requests or sign-in. A sleepy guard at the front desk points us to the Coroner's office down a hallway.

In the waiting room, we sit across from a couple of de facto dykes. The scrawny sunken-cheeked one sobs quietly, cutting loose with the occasional bronchial cough. Her brawny, stone-faced partner smokes like a Buddha, completely still but for a fat hand rhythmically rising to her mouth. They wear cheap, matching track suits.

Waiting with Al and I is Josée, the beautiful, blue-eyed French girl the Hen had met at the Bifteck and was staying with lately down in Little Burgundy. Her face is perfectly made up, pale and raccoon-eyed, with those black-painted lips. Oddly enough, her long brown hair isn't dyed or streaked. She wears a scarlet red dress made of threadbare linen, tight on her full, round ass, one side slit almost to the hip, creamy-white cleavage bulging. It's all held together with lots of stationery clamps, curtain hooks and the like. She could be the prom queen for a high school full of degenerate romantics. It also shows some real grace Josée went and got Hennessy's misery-guts sugar momma, Heidi, and brought her along.

The dykes get called in first. The big one helps up her fragile little friend, a big consoling arm around the boney shoulders. As they shuffle toward the office, the diesel dyke gives me a nod; the quick, tight lipped dip-of-the-chin a hoser guy will offer as a manly sort of acknowledgement. I return the gesture.

They come back out a half hour later and the Coroner or whoever he is stands in the doorway, eyeing Josée. She smiles at him primly. He seems to know the rest of us aren't Quebecois and appears only vaguely interested in whether we are friends of Hennessy's, relatives or just a bunch of wackos who get off on hanging out at morgues.

His office is tiny. Al and I stand in the doorway. Heidi blubbers and blows her nose while Josée sits stiffly on the edge of her seat, ankles turned up so just her high heels touch the floor. She hands the Coroner Hennessy's passport and they speak rapidly in French. I catch maybe every fifth word as he quickly fills out a form, yawning a couple times while making some routine entries. No known viruses, no infirmities or disabilities, no prostheses.

After a few minutes he shows us to an elevator. We go down a couple floors to a sub-basement and are led into an examination room. There is a body on a gurney, under a yellow plastic sheet. Once we've gathered at the side, the Coroner says something to an attendant and he exposes just the head and neck.

Oh, my wicked little Pockenello, you turn up in the strangest places. Without his newsboy cap or bowler it almost doesn't look like him. His part-wavy, part-African hair is matted and brushed straight back. I expected him to look hellish, but he's not in bad shape. The coroner compares the Hen to the passport photo and appears satisfied. I catch his question about any distinguishing marks. Josée and I both mention a hook-shaped scar on his penis—I in English and she in French. The coroner looks us over for a moment, glances at the ceiling then turns to the attendant with a Gallic shrug and signals him to remove the sheet. We all lean forward a little. And there it is, the small barbed J of a fishhook, just below his pubic bone, the flesh deeply nicked. Hennessy's skin is bluish, our bruises and old wounds now darkly outlined. A fine scar curves round his left nipple and turns into a question mark. There's a hard and calloused blister of the oft repeated cigarette burn below his navel. I feel a small thrill that the tiny sardonic arcs are still there at the edge of his lips and lay my fingers on his mouth. Without hesitation, I dive in for a kiss. He tastes harsh and waxy. Some kind of paste used to make a dental cast. Heidi's voice rises like an old police siren as the attendant and the coroner jump toward me. I grab the plastic sheet and cover him before they've hardly moved. "*C'est bon*," I tell them, quickly retreating with my hands up. The coroner and his helper stop and exhale with relief. There'll be no ID Room freak out battle, no rolling around on the floor with stuff smashing, lots of desperate cries and the deceased suffering unspeakable indignities.

THIRTY-THREE

The sun pounds as I stand over the Hen's open pit and look down at his cut-rate coffin. We're in the Protestant Cemetery on Mount Royal. Old Nick's personal fire scorches the very air, but that hasn't stopped the entire clan from showing up. It's a black leather, latex and hardware chorus, full-tilt hair going, make-up and dead white powder melts and runs in the searing heat. Heidi weeps at the head of the grave as a couple of his loyal devotees keen and wail.

Al Polo's at my side, along with Morgan, her fingers laced through mine. She and Hennessy's new French girlfriend Josée have gotten pretty tight over the past while. Too bad he didn't live long enough to really get somewhere with her, she's a dynamo. Both Josée and Morgan are done to the morbid nines, their lithe, curvy bodies sheathed in black, leading the super-hot widow stakes—and there is some heavy competition. I think about how good it would feel to fuck them down there on top of his box; a cool, slow fucking, get seriously blasphemous, a tribute to Hennessy's finest instincts.

His old professor, Gary Betcherman, has made the trip from London. The Griffintown torture chamber babes, Chantal and Kate, are also among Hennessy's black-clad seraglio, cinched right up in their hottest bondage tackle. Larry the Poet is in attendance with his wife, Allie. I know Shalini would have come, but she's down in New York with Jean-Bapiste and their new dance company. Savva Grudtsyn patrols the periphery—black suit, shirt and tie, somber as a KGB Colonel. Leroi and Sophie, hands joined and grim-faced behind opaque glasses, both nod at me reassuringly. Vern, Tony,

Warlock, Dred Blanc, Little Sharon and Kit are all here too, along with several other freaks of The Main. Wounded and wiped out from our hard-bangin' three-night wake, the entire tribe is nonetheless accounted for—except Slim, of course. I look around on the off chance she might have shown up. But no—with the rectitude of a Calvinist hanging judge at her core, she'd never be part of these preposterous theatrics. As for Jane—she doesn't believe in funerals.

Hennessy's few remaining blood relations stand on the other side of his freshly dug hole, solemn and resigned. Well-to-do high yella Haitian academics and professionals, oozing Westmount caché. The Hen's parents were doctors, both dead in the months before him. His father was a die-cut Quebec Anglo. His mother was part of the Papa Doc brain-drain, the old mulatto elite—aggressively encouraged to emigrate by machete-wielding Ton Ton Macoute PR men.

Hennessy's relatives eye our congregation of sunglassed ghouls with obvious distaste. His plot is beside the mother he claimed to have incested. A week after the old man keeled over with a bad heart, momma was diagnosed with advanced, non-smoking lung cancer. Soon as she couldn't defend her domain, the Hen was stripping the familial manse for pawn money, even asking me to help him rip out a marble fireplace mantle while the old lady cursed on her deathbed upstairs. The fool was set to officially inherit the whole pile a month from today. Well, I guess all that loot would have probably made this ceremony inevitable—perhaps for several of we mourners as well.

The presiding pastor is a bloodless old dog, mostly senile and white as Casper. He takes some ashes from a tin can, sprinkles them over the grave then recites a low-key, perfunctory service. It's Unitarian bland and clearly meant to circumvent any Catholic-style histrionics.

We wait until the official ceremony is done and the family climbs into their limos to be whisked away. That's when our kitschy mix of rites comes out. Black cakes of frankincense are lit, bottles of red wine uncorked and the first shots poured in to Hennessy. The gravediggers waiting for our rituals to end finally run out of patience, get in their truck and leave. But not before

Prof Betcherman cadges a few shovels. By way of eulogy, I read an André Breton ditty Hennessy liked:

Leave everything.
Leave your wife.
Leave your mistress.
Leave your hopes and your fears.
Leave your children in the woods.
Leave the substance for the shadow.
Leave your easy life,
leave what you are given for the future.
Set off on the road.

When I'm done, Larry the Poet absentmindedly flicks a cigarette butt into the grave. His wife Allie smacks him. "What the fuck, Larry!?"

"Oh, shit," he mutters, grabbing his head with both hands.

I look down at the Hen's cheap coffin. Not even wood. Some sort of pressboard covered in baby blue fabric. The handles are brass-painted tin. It's one step up from Emanuel Jaques' black garbage bag. The Hen's relatives could have at least spent some of that rich inheritance on a decent pine box.

The punishing heat makes me lightheaded. I get a strong urge to keel over and join him. Open the box and slip inside, grin back up at the out-raged relatives, *I'll be out in a minute*—then slam the lid shut. I teeter forward and Al's hand whips out to grab my coattails while Morgan pulls me back. "Easy now, baby."

Amulets are tossed in, other crap is tossed in. Vern plays with a loaded syringe then throws that in. I assume it's nothing but water. Heidi takes offense. "That's a bit much. It's not landfill, y'know. I mean, he did die of an overdose."

"What's the diff," Vern dismisses her. "Hen was a total fuckin' garbage can. Suck up any kinda shit that was around."

"Speaking of which," says Warlock, always eager for some bad news. "Any word on the post-mortem blood tests?"

Al Polo gestures skeptically. "Nothing yet. But if I were a betting man…"

Heidi has to stick her oar back in. "I can't believe you people don't use condoms all the time. I mean, who hasn't slept with everyone else here, except for me? I was such a fool to enable Hennessy—and now it might end up killing me. God!" She lets out a long huff. We all look at the idiot. "Well, you know," she says, trying to pull her foot out of her mouth. "It is something we should at least think about."

Morgan's head turns about one degree and her black-red lipstick parts just enough. Eyes narrow and angled sideways, she strafes Heidi. "Shut up, you stupid fucking mutt. Look at what you're wearing." Josée underlines the judgment with a raised chin and an imperious sneer. Heidi stares down at the shapeless grey dress she's got on as a couple of tears roll from behind her big dumb glasses.

Prof Betcherman peels off his jacket and grabs a shovel. He begins to hurl dirt into the Hen's grave. I take the other one and join him. It feels good to work up a righteous sweat. Tony relieves the Prof after a few minutes and goes at it like Steve McQueen in *The Great Escape*. The super-sauna humidity quickly has him panting and dripping. He hands off to Polo, who fades even faster. Then Leroi takes over from me and Savva and Vern pitch in as well. Even some of the Hen's Goth groupies help out while Josée and Morgan stand by in their dark veils and stiletto heels, flexing those flawless calves and ankles. They smoke severely and oversee the proceedings as Hennessy's hole is gradually filled.

With the brutal sun now beginning to sink west of the mountain, our ragged procession packs up for the walk back down. I don't want to leave him alone up here, defenseless. Who knows what could happen. Nothing good, I'm sure. As everyone goes toward the path, Morgan leans against me, pulls off her stilettos then takes my hand. She reaches up with a comforting kiss. "We'll come back soon and visit, okay, baby? C'mon, let's go home and lie down. You're exhausted."

THIRTY-FOUR

It's noon and scalding hot again, less than twenty-four hours since we buried the Hen. The Man called bright and early, demanding a situation report. "So, Johnny, is this going to cause any problems?"

"No, it'll be okay."

"Nobody's checking around, nothing weird going on?"

"No, business as usual."

"Good. Sorry about your buddy, but hey, you roll the dice and sometimes they come up snake eyes."

"Sure do. Especially when you're a fucking hog about it."

"Hey, everybody makes mistakes."

"True. Like John Wayne said, 'Life's tough, but it's a lot tougher when you're stupid.'"

"That's a bit harsh. I thought you and that Hennessy guy were… uh, y'know."

"Yeah, well, he blew it, didn't he?"

"You sure there's nothing you wanna talk about?"

"No. I gotta go."

"Okay, buddy. You working today?"

"No, Leroi is."

"Good, you should take the day off. But let me know right away if there's any trouble, capiche?"

"Yep, will do."

I pick up a couple bottles of cold depanneur wine and a bunch of daisies from my florist lady then swing by to get Slim. Her sunglasses might be the biggest thing she has on. A loose, almost sheer purple silk shirt hangs off her shoulders. She is nearly bare-assed with a super-short black mini and those long tanned legs, her boy's black canvas runners untied. She gets triple-takes and the undivided slobbers of wool-suited husbands who have come out to watch the weekly topless dyke soccer game in Fletcher's Field.

A more dedicated species of sociopath loiters in the tree cover at the bottom of the mountain. I can actually hear a few of them in the bushes, wheezing like overheated dogs as we approach the one thousand log steps to the top. Up these Sisyphean stairs one more time. It is like doing penance. I need several pit stops along the way. Even Slim's feeling the climb and the woman's in shape. We see a young couple going at it off to our right. They're half-hidden behind a massive beech tree. The girl straddles the guy, her summer dress spread over his lower body. Their secretive laughter sounds inviting. It prompts Slim to give me an incredibly delicate kiss.

"You taste good," she says, licking her lips. "Like cigarettes and alcohol."

We finally get to the summit and it takes a while to walk over to the Protestant cemetery. Even though it was just yesterday, I can barely remember where he's buried, but after half an hour or so… ah, there you are, my little Lord Fondleme, Earl of the Slashed Suit Lining—the outfit that served you so well all the way to the mortician who was surely flattered you showed up dressed for the occasion.

I spend some time tidying up the grave, smooth out the fresh dirt, then arrange the daisies near his head. I crouch next to him while Slim takes long swigs of wine with her eyes squinting against the sun. Sweat gathers at the hollow of her throat. She pulls the pins from her hair and runs her fingers through it, dirty blonde roots showing a bit.

"Last time I saw Hennessy was about a week and a half ago," she remembers. "He came by the bar and whined at me for forty dollars then ran out crying when I wouldn't give him any money. I feel a little guilty for not feeling guilty." Slim can't play along for sentiment's sake. Always has to combat her crippling shyness with that hard candor.

"Don't be so mean."

"I'm not being mean. I'm just telling you what happened."

"I don't care what happened."

"Calm down." Slim kicks off her runners and pushes her bare feet through the grass. She slouches back and wags a knee at me with a cocky little smirk, then glances about, discreetly slides off her panties and wriggles onto my lap so we face one another. Undoing my jeans, she shifts side to side, parts a few pubic hairs, gets me in then begins to use her ass muscles. A single button holds her shirt closed and I undo it. Her breasts brush my mouth. I lick the sweat on her chest and neck. She throws back her head, giddy and laughing. There's nobody in the immediate vicinity, but guaranteed some watchers spy from the safety of the trees, about thirty yards away. They will observe our close-up details through high-powered field glasses as the other hand works down below. Slim plays with us and she comes easily, sweetly, the way she always does if she hasn't used much. No drama required, no neurosis required. No wonder every guy goes flat-out thundering crazy over her.

As I tense and stutter her name, she twists my nipples hard enough to make me curse. Neither of us has done much dope so when she rises a bit and reaches down to jack me off, I come all over the inside of her thighs and onto her pubic hair. We both exhale long and slow as she rests her forehead against mine, talking to me very close as her thumb strokes my cheekbone. "C'mon, baby... don't cry. I'm right here."

I watch her crawl a few yards away on all fours. Going up to her knees, legs apart, she pulls up the mini. A stream of piss hits the ground. She looks at it running downhill then turns back to me with more tipsy laughter. Finished peeing, she comes over and lights a smoke, takes a drink of wine then lays back with an arm under her head. "You realize, Johnny, screwing on Hennessy's grave—it's going to become the thing to do. Who knows, we might not even be the first."

"Sure. By next week the chatter on The Main will be all about who hasn't fucked on the Hen's grave. Everyone'll be saying how it's *simply de rigeur, my dahling*. Before long there's gonna be huge daisy-chains going around his plot. Some clever fag will probably get a performance grant."

"Don't be bitter. I know you wanted him all to yourself, but Hennessy wasn't a one-man woman."

I wonder how to protect him, the sanctity of this place. Should I live up here in a tent? A hermit ragbag obsessed with guarding the moral purity of my dearly departed, and all the other righteous dead. Rant and rave when a hearse drives up with the remains of a hypocrite CEO struck down during a particularly restive stockholders meeting. I will be there, in the background, a faint shadow of disgust, harangue from the trees and upset the mourners. Drown out the good reverend's platitudes when they try to bury the venal bastard near my beloved...

"No! They're all lies! That stiff was a tyrant! He never really cared about the secretary he kept loyal with two lousy fucks and twenty years of promises! You wouldn't even let her show up today! She's down there at the bottom of the mountain with a potted plant, crying her eyes out! May your tongues swell up and burst and your galls fill with stones!"

"My God, who is that?" asks the horrified widow, a gloved hand at her garishly painted mouth.

"Must be one of the malcontents from the latest round of layoffs," grimaces the Managing Senior Pederast and next in line to take over from the stiff delivered into the hands of the Lord this day of ashes to ashes, lawyers to embalmers, accountants to executors. A squad of company goons are dispatched with weighted nets to bring me in alive. "Use the tranquilizer gun. We must know what he knows."

Getting home after doing the dinner-time rounds, I sit in the kitchen to make up some more packs. Quarter grams, tenths of a gram, half-tenths. I listen to the fridge rattle, voices echo up from the street and I recall forgotten bedtime stories of me and Hennessy and a brainy, dark-eyed woman called Wander, way back when, in Hogtown. She had us both in her bed for many months and taught us the how of everything, her body an exacting and sometimes blunt instrument. Her lessons were often excruciatingly painful and occasionally injurious, but there was no other way to know. She would sew up and bandage our wounds then reward us with a walk along College Street.

At first both Hennessy and I had relied on sneering youth. Wander was older, in her late forties, much wilier. She came at us through our own skin, our early twenties flesh that could handle a lot. As these things do, our obedience came without perceptible degrees. Wander had pulled the oldest trick in the book—made us believe it was our idea.

Hennessy and I always shook our heads, marveling at her skill. A snap of her fingers, a slow wink, a way of crossing her ankles, a hand on her hip. Pavlov was a piker compared to what she could do because our salivating was not just a physiognomic reaction. And as with most things, it was the anticipation that really made the high. Sure, both the Hen and I had been around a lot of cunt, but Wander taught us the specific intricacies in bright, unmistakable daylight. All the finer details, from beneath her toes right up to behind her ears and the top of her scalp; what applies to all women—and more importantly—what doesn't.

At Wander's fiftieth birthday a man appeared, in his mid-sixties, attractive, erudite and obviously very wealthy. She had a big diamond on her ring finger. Her new friend was completely informed about our situation and warmly shook hands with the Hen and I. The night became melancholy and drunken. Wander finally used her teeth to break the scarlet ribbon she had tied around each of our wrists so long ago. She put them in her purse then told us to beat it. As we stood to leave, I stole a cigarette butt from the ashtray, stained with her lipstick. It now lies with Hennessy, in his breast pocket.

After waking up with a brutal dope hangover, I'm stumbling around the kitchen trying to make coffee when I hear Slim call from out in the street. I let her in and she looks pale, summer tan suddenly gone with the turn in the weather. Her hair is bleached white-blonde again. I can practically see through her.

"I called last night a few times but you didn't answer. I can't stay—just wanted to see if you were all right."

"Thanks, I'm terrific."

Slim's jumpy and distracted, meanders around the living room, picks up books, plays with the string on the blinds, opens and shuts them, lights a cigarette then doesn't smoke it.

"Slim, you're getting on my nerves. You wanna tell me what's going on?"

She taps on the windowsill then pulls her hair into a ponytail and lets it go. "I got a grad scholarship," she says without a trace of pride or happiness. "To do my Master's."

"Where, McGill?"

"No, The New School in New York."

"I'm impressed. That's a hot shit, big-brain school. But I didn't know you were such an ardent lefty."

She sighs, annoyed. "I'm not an ardent anything. I want to go there because it's in New York." She stands at the front windows again and stares at the mountain. "I applied last year and got accepted conditionally six months ago. It's gone through now."

"So when are you leaving?"

She turns to face me. "I'm not sure exactly—soon. I'm going to live at Adam's. He's supposed to have a great place on East 14th. I guess we'll share for a while, see how things go. Maybe it'll be all right."

"Yeah, okay, I get it. You're serious about this Adam guy and you're gonna go live with him. Whaddaya want, my blessing?"

She comes over and takes my hand. Her chin rises, teeth softly pulling on my bottom lip. "C'mon, Johnny. He's not so bad."

"Yeah, he's just great, a real hero. Congrats."

I watch her walk around some more and touch the walls, her finger leaves a line on the dusty bookshelf. "I'm not going down for a couple weeks, so we'll have a chance to do something."

"Do something? Yeah, sure, we'll go out on a date."

Slim comes back and runs her knuckles along my jaw. "A date with our clothes on," she smiles, already halfway out of town. "That would be novel."

THIRTY-FIVE

I've been going gangbusters since the hordes of first-year students began arriving in Montreal for "Orientation" at McGill, Concordia, UQAM, Dawson and the rest. Frosh-week freakouts, frat-house fandangos, The Main's overrun with all these kids who've never lived away from home, squads of them roaming about, gorging themselves on Montreal's infamous tenderloins, getting royally shitfaced and screwing each other into oblivion. Leroi and I don't sell to them directly, but Tony, Vern, Kit and even Hernav are all doing a booming sub-contractor biz.

It's late on a Saturday night-early Sunday morning when I'm hit with a flurry of pager calls from after-hours clubs. I run out of product and call The Man. He answers with an unusually breezy manner. It makes me nervous. Everything he does makes me nervous.

The Man's downtown apartment building has all the 24-hour high-security trappings. Video cameras cover each approach. The liveried gorillas who guard the place eye me through a barrier of potted palms in the marble-lined lobby. An elegant queer at the front desk asks for my name then calls upstairs even though I show up here regular as rain. After I am declared secure, one of the goons escorts me to an elevator. Another camera observes me from the top corner of the stainless steel box. It goes to the correct floor on its own.

The door to The Man's suite swings open with the solemn weight of a walk-in vault. Whenever I show up he always seems to be just out of the shower or gym, barefoot and wearing a plush bathrobe over colorful track pants, expansive hairless chest on display. I almost expect him to make his pecs dance.

I take off my boots and follow him across the ivory white carpet to a sunken living room. I hand him an envelope full of cash. He casually thumbs through it with a sneaky grin. That usually means he's got some instructive tale to relate. Maybe the story of a former associate now stretched out in a hospital bed and going through an agonizing reappraisal of his lifestyle choice.

"Uh, I'm a little short," I say then quickly add, "but only two bills."

The Man's grin vanishes and his big hamhock mitt reaches out and pulls me so close we are cheek to cheek, standing together on the top step of the sunken living room, as if contemplating a tranquil sea.

"Why?" he asks, voice stricken. "Bad fronts, Johnny?"

"Uh, maybe a few."

"Is the whore a problem?"

"Don't call her that, please."

"I'm sorry. The girl."

"No, she works hard, makes money, covers for me once in a while too."

"Let's figure this out," The Man reasons. "How much have you and the girl been doing?"

He must feel my ear get hot, the minor convulsions up my back. "I'm not sure… but not much."

The Man pulls me tighter. His jaw nudges mine. "I don't think that's true, Johnny."

My bowels get watery. "Y- you think I'm lying?"

"No… I think you are confused. Don't you stay at her place a lot?"

"Uh… a couple nights a week, I guess."

"Maybe I should talk to her."

"Naw, I'll take care of it, keep tabs on everything. No more fronts to anybody."

"Fronts aren't a bad thing, Johnny. You know that. It's how you reward your solid customer. The problem is all the fucking leeches hanging around. The broads, the buddies, the good friends. All of them wanting to get on the inside, lay on the sentimental mooch. It's fuckin' disgusting." The Man's voice drops to scarcely a whisper. "But whores especially, Johnny, they can't help it."

I laugh nervously, too loud.

"You think I'm being funny?" His hint of anger cuts me off in mid snort.

"No, no. I—I just don't like talking about her that way."

"Sorry, but she is a whore. Nothing personal, but a whore looks at the rest of the world like a mark, a john, a stooge."

"Uh, can I ask you something?"

"What?"

"Can we sit down?"

The Man releases his grip and disappears down a long hallway. "Have a seat," he calls back. I squat on the edge of the black leather sofa and gawk at my reflection in a big, smoked-glass coffee table. A worried looking goat in a dark and rumpled suit jacket stares back.

The Man's suddenly behind me. He tosses a baggy onto the coffee table. "Twenty-five grams, cut and ready to go. Keep a lid on yourself and you can make up the four hundred out of that."

"Ya think I can put together a few packs here? The whole mob's been lighting up the pager like crazy." I feel the big bug vibrate and pull it off my belt.

"Who is it?"

I hesitate then look at him. "Uh… the girl."

"Is she working?"

"No, she's at her friend Josée's. They're both kinda sick."

The Man smiles apologetically. "You can't make up any packs here, but hop in a cab. You'll be home in no time. Why don't ya call her first?" His tone makes the question irrelevant. "Here," he presses a button on the phone console. "I'll put it on the speaker." He takes the pager and dials Josée's number. Morgan answers on the first ring.

"Johnny!?" Her voice booms through the apartment.

"Yeah."

"Where the fuck are you!? You sound like you're in the bottom of a toilet."

"I'll be there soon, babe, half an hour or so. You guys just hang tight."

"Wait!" Morgan shouts. The phone speaker crackles. "We'll come to your place."

The Man shakes his head once, eyes closed. "Naw," I tell her. "It's uh, it's not happening there. Just wait at Josée's."

"Johnny, what's wrong? Is that steroid case giving you a hard time over a few hundred bucks? You make all kinds of money for him. Don't let him—"

"Morgan, I gotta go. See ya soon, okay?"

The Man lingers next to the phone, playing with the volume.

"What the fuck is it!?" she keeps pressing. "Why do you sound so weird? Are you at his place?"

"No, I'm at a phone booth!" I yell. Sweat drips inside my shirt. "Now hang the fuck up!"

"Why don't you hang up, asshole!? You been shooting blow or what the fuck!? Or maybe suckin' that greaseball's cock!"

"Morgan! Jesus! Please, just hang up!"

"Okay! Hurry up then!" And she finally slams the phone down.

"Nice girl," The Man chuckles.

I grin like an imbecile. "Heh heh, she's uh… she's pretty stressed out right now."

He pats me on the back while we go to the door. "Tell ya what, Johnny. Front her whatever she needs. I like her balls, more than most guys. We'll open a special account."

He catches me off guard. "Really? That could be a lot. I mean, she's a total pig for this shit."

"She's working, her ass makes big money, right? She'll be good for it."

"You're serious?"

"Yeah," he repeats with an easy shrug. "I know her type. It'll be all right."

The door thuds shut.

THIRTY-SIX

The warm weather's pretty much gone now, accelerating downhill toward autumn and then winter. I haven't seen or heard from Slim in a couple weeks and assume she's already left for New York without a word, the fucking bitch. So I'm surprised when she phones and says preparations have been keeping her busy, but now it's time we went on that date. Slim tells me she's borrowed a car even though she can't drive so I'll have to take the wheel.

It's a banged-up old Mercury sedan, covered in rust spots and gray primer. She doesn't say who owns it, but the plate is valid and the back seat's big enough for a fatso orgy. Best of all, the front seat is the old bench style so Slim can curl up next to me, my arm around her, molesting her bod while I keep one hand on the wheel. I lost interest in cars when they stopped making them like this.

She wants to go to the wastelands at the bottom of île de Montréal, so we rumble down Atwater hill on bald snow tires, through Saint-Henri and Pointe Saint-Charles. Going below the city center, the car's radio drifts into weak static. We roll through dead neighborhoods—even in the middle of the day, middle of the week. A few stragglers here and there, most store-fronts and apartments for rent or boarded up, some are burnt-out hulks. We pass blocks of abandoned and vandalized factories and warehouses.

A young hood struts along a lonely, weed-grown stretch of Grand Trunk Road. His long shag hair-do swings across the back of an acid-washed denim jacket adorned with a BTO logo drawn in blue ballpoint pen. Chin up, he glares at us fiercely as we go by.

We circle through Pointe Saint-Charles for a while then into the dumpy, clapboard side streets of Ville-Emard and back up to Saint-Henri. Here and there we see the odd inbred prol enter or exit a depanneur with a bagged beer. A few rickety trucks go by, a bucktoothed kid on a broken bicycle gapes at us. We watch a rusty locomotive with no freight cars struggle across the Augustin rail bridge and disappear into the mist coming off the Saint Lawrence.

Slim tells me to stop next to the ruins of the old Redpath sugar plant. It sits on the south shore of the black-watered Lachine canal and reminds me of a gutted fortress, pillaged and burned to the bricks. A few cicadas buzz in the overgrown lot, no people anywhere in sight. Inside are high ceilings and ancient leaded factory windows, all of them busted or torn out. Dust hangs in the stale air and smells of decaying wood and kerosene. We pick our way around collapsed beams, the rusted out remains of giant engines and missing pieces of staircase. It is a precarious six-storey climb to the top.

Slim leads me along a catwalk into a small room full of broken glass and dismantled pieces of who knows what machinery. A beat-up wooden office desk is against one wall and an empty doorway steps out to nothing. Perhaps there was a balcony at one time. Maybe this was some manager's private office. The doorway perfectly frames Mount Royal, its almost flat summit, the city crawling partway up the southern slope.

Slim wraps her arms around me from behind and kisses my shoulder. I have my hands on either side of the missing doorframe, just crumbling brick now. Peering down, it's a long fall to a big, haphazard pile of various detritus jumbled up with charred beams and twisted metal.

Slim pulls me backward and leans against the side of the desk. She undoes her faded, threadbare jeans then gets out of the old Chuck Taylor t-shirt. I slowly untie her black canvas runners and slip them off, lick each sweaty foot from heel to toes. I work her jeans down, one leg at a time and hang them off a nail. Slim opens my shirt and gets my belt out of the way, reaches in with both hands. She makes a face like mock-surprise then leans back and her feet come up, legs parting.

And those beautiful arches wrap around my cock, toenails painted electric blue, she begins to slowly jerk me off. Personally, I don't get the foot and shoe worship stuff, it seems corny. Like, what—you're gonna stuff a whole shoe in your mouth? C'mon.

But when you're with a stunning babe and you get to fuck her drop dead gorgeous feet... now *that* is sublime... Slim's toes go over the head of my cock. She lifts my balls on the top of her other foot, tickling me. "I can feel you laughing," she smiles.

Her heels hook round my thighs and pull me near. And there it is—her head inclined a little to one side, the timid half smile that only appears when we're this close. Slim goes back onto her elbows, those long legs come up, her soles now against my collarbones, ass rising. Her skin looks warm and easy. "Johnny..."

"Aw, Slim... Where are you going?"

I hang onto her hips, so slight in my hands and right now there are no cuts or bites or bruises. It's a slow and sweet, lackadaisical kind of screwing, like nothing's ever been easier for anybody anywhere. We both turn to watch the mountain through the broken doorway.

"How do you know about this place?"

"Hennessy brought me."

THIRTY-SEVEN

It's been almost a month since Aunt B disappeared into DC Scott's house and nobody's heard a word. For some reason Al isn't alarmed. I offer all kinds of possible scenarios while we sit around his kitchen eating Mama Polo's perogies. The old lady's in seventh heaven as we wolf them down as fast as she can slide them out of the pan onto our plates.

"Maybe Aunt B's chained up in Scott's basement and they're doing experiments trying to get her pregnant."

"Very amusing," Al scoffs as he spreads on some blueberry preserves. "I realize Byron's become quite the gossip magnet on The Main and I was instructed to keep this to myself, but I'll make an exception for you, Johnny, since you do have a personal interest."

"Yeah, go on."

Al grins at having the upper hand in the scandal stakes. The fact Aunt B paid an extra six months rent on her room doesn't hurt either. "Well…" he draws it out. " I did receive a short dispatch three days ago."

"Okay, enough toe dipping, Al. What's the story?"

"From what I understand, they have a great deal to work out, but their talks are progressing well. Byron sends her regards, by the way."

"I don't get it—she's staying there?"

"Yes, that would seem to be the case. Spiritual healing can be an intense and sometimes mysterious process. There is no handbook, my friend."

"I wouldn't trust that DC Scott creep. He's a total psychic vampire. The lights probably dim when he walks into a room. Let's go over there with electric cattle-prods and do some strip-searches."

Al barely rolls his eyes while pouring us some tea as Mama Polo stands by, beaming with satisfaction at the devoured food. "We'll give it a few more days," he mollifies me. "Then we'll call round and make some inquiries. Fair enough?"

I decide a little direct action is necessary so I buy a pair of mid-range binoculars and make a beeline for ol' DC's abode. Weird, but it seems to get dark in the McGill Ghetto faster than any other part of town. Perhaps due to the heavy tree cover. Or maybe because the mountain hovers over the north end and the apartment towers at the south end lining Sherbrooke Street cast huge shadows, dwarfing the rest of the neighborhood.

Scott's place sits on a corner. The lights are on for a change, but he has wooden shutters on the lower half of the ground floor picture window and they are closed. I need to find a higher vantage point. The best bet is an old redbrick student triplex across the intersection. It's got a wonky old fire escape tacked onto the rear. There doesn't seem to be anyone around, so I quietly climb to the second floor and try the binocs but it's still too low. I go up to the top and there is a jerry-rigged shed on the back of the building. It's closed in on all sides with rusty, corrugated tin walls and roof. But there's a square cut out of it that seems to swing open like a portal. Getting inside the small shack, the damp heat is oppressive and the place reeks of stale beer empties and raccoon shit. The sunset leaks between a few gaps in the tin walls. There's a door that goes into the apartment proper. I cup my hands at the window and see the place is dark, like nobody's home. If the lights come on, I should have time to take off. The sun is now low enough that I don't feel too obvious swinging open the portal.

A big bay window at the side of Scott's house sticks out from the second floor. From this height, using the binocs, I can see right in and it takes me a little while to get oriented as I slowly scan about but... oooh, yeah... we got us some pay dirt. I catch glimpses of Aunt Byron and her old pal moving around. It's not the room where me and Scott had our little encounter, but similarly furnished; expensive antiques and do-dads on fancy side tables, an art deco floor lamp, Persian rugs on a darkly varnished hardwood floor, varied and well organized bookshelves.

There are several Canadian atlases, political, historical and geographic. A whole shelf of government reports with manila covers. Things like the *1973 Royal Commission for the Investigation of Numerous Eyewitness Accounts And Second Hand Reports Regarding Under-Aged Prostitution And Coercive Bestiality Within Canadian Communities Of Fewer Than 5,900 Registered Inhabitants.* Presiding Chair, Duncan Campbell Scott Esq., Queen's Council. Then there's the *1982 Special Intergovernmental Probe To Investigate The Launch And Subsequent Disappearance Of Previous Commissions, Tribunals, Probes, Panels, Committees, Boards And Other Various And Sundry Inquiries And Studies.* Presiding Chair, Duncan Campbell Scott, Esq., QC. These publications both come in two volumes and appear to easily total over a thousand pages each. On the shelf below is a leather bound copy of *The Full And Annotated Gradual Civilization Act, Made Law In Her Majesty's Loyal Province Of Lower Canada, 1857.* Then there's stuff like the *1982 Curriculum, Alberni Residential School of Crypto-Psychiatry* and the *1971 Curriculum, Mount Cashel School of Geloscopy.* Next to these are some hardcover novels by Margaret Atwood, Carol Shields, Alice Munro and Margaret Laurence's *The Stone Angel,* all with spines that look perfectly unopened. On a lower shelf there's a big coffee table edition of *The Last Spike* and something entitled *A Hagiography of the Good Works and Undying Pursuit of the Salvation of Heathen Souls As Carried Out by Master Nicholas Flood Davin With Such Noble Endeavors Recorded by the hand of Certain Parties whilst He was in the Service of Her Majesty and Our Lord Jesus Christ.*

Panning across the floor, I see a man's bare feet. Moving up a set of shaved, muscular legs—it's DC Scott's pet stooge, Antonio. He's naked but for an old style jock strap. One of those off-white things made of mesh and elasticized fabric with a thin red stripe. The head of his hard-on pokes out the side. For such a big guy he's got a sleek little pecker on him. There's not much of a bag bulge either. Maybe those stories about steroid side effects are true. Antonio casually curls a barbell with—uh, let's see... a fifty-pound weight at either end. Not too bad at all. A sheen of sweat covers his artificial orange tan. His eyes watch one bicep then the other as he works out.

I track to Antonio's left and find Scott and Aunt B on a black leather sofa, their backs to me. DC has his arm casually draped behind Byron. They are dressed in matching beige sweaters and gray slacks. Byron's head slowly reclines onto DC's shoulder. He gently strokes her cheek. I notice a small tattoo on Scott's hand, similar to Byron's *Arcanum*, except his reads *Arcanorum*. All they're missing is the de-coder rings.

Scott points a remote at the TV. I have to hang precariously out of my perch to see what's on and… fuck me—it looks like the video Aunt B shot that night on the mountain, when good ol' DC had shown up with Paco and the strongman cop. Byron's so-called "damning and irrefutable evidence."

The video is grainy black and white, but fairly clear considering she shot the thing at night. Just beneath the screen, I catch a glimpse of black hair. Paco. That fuckin' kid is everywhere. He's on his stomach, right under the TV, completely naked and eating from a bowl of pretzels. Chin resting on knuckles, he's fascinated with his star turn on Mount Royal. I zero in on the screen again as Paco watches himself being impaled by that enormous, scim-itar-cocked police boss. The kid turns to Aunt Byron and DC, all smiles, says something and laughs.

Back to the action, the camera jiggles, goes blurry then black. When the picture returns, it closes in on—wait a second—it's me and Shalini at the picnic bench that night! Tough to make out very much since it must have been taped from a good distance, maybe sixty or seventy feet away in the stormy dark. Fuckin' Aunt Byron.

There's a sudden cut to an overexposed, hand-held image, just the top ridge of the mountain with the sunset blasting over its summit. The camera tilts downward to a tree trunk right in front of the lens. It takes up half the frame. The rest is a telephoto shot of Slim and me screwing at Hennessy's grave. Jesus Christ…

That gives way to bunch of short mountain scenes: A postman with a mail bag over his shoulder. He stares down at some guy in a Hydro Québec uniform on his knees, giving him a blow job. The next scene is a pair of teenagers feeling each other up among a litter of beer bottles and chip bags in the Catholic graveyard. Then Slim again, this time with that Bobbo geek. He goes down on her between a pair of birch trees, the log staircase in the distance behind them. I can't believe she brought that asshole up to our mountain. The shot jumps to Savva with Vern's fuckmate Izanami, sitting on a bench. She's in Savva's lap as they face each other, both dressed all in black. They go at it under her skirt in broad daylight. Some kids and parents play in the background. Geez, even Leroi's in this public fornication montage, banging his sexy French gal, Sophie, the back of the Oratory dome visible above the treetops. Then Shalini again with the hips of a long-haired white boy working between her legs. And Shalini once more, getting it doggie style from a big African guy while she goes down on the pussy of a giggling dance friend. The occasional passersby strolls past some of these scenes without reaction—except for the odd bashful smile or smart-ass comment. Next, it's me and Hennessy, then Paco again—with Vern. Both have their pants around their knees. This time Paco's pitching and Vern's catching. There are more shots—men, women, some I vaguely recognize from The Main, a couple of dogs stuck together. It all goes by faster and faster until there are only flashes of each scene. The images eventually fade to black. Yes, very artistic, Aunt Byron.

My neck and shoulders are killing me from holding this awkward spying position. I climb down from my perch on the edge of the portal and check the back door window of the apartment I'm semi-invading. It's still dim in there, nobody seems to be home yet. I crouch down and mix up a shot on the floor of the shed. It's getting dark, so I end up with a few bloody misses before finally hitting a vein.

When I zero back in on DC Scott's TV, the scene has moved outdoors, to a pine forest and lake. It has the washed-out color of old Super-8 film and looks to be the same locale as that snapshot I found in Byron's journal. The POV is from the front porch of a log cabin. Two figures trudge up a shallow incline from the water. A twelve or thirteen year-old Aunt Byron and a younger, more virile DC Scott. Byron wears a blonde crew cut and looks like fuckin' Opie. Scott still has some crinkly red hair, but you can tell it is just dying to fall out. He wears big aviator style tinted glasses, a lumberjack shirt, and chinos while Byron's dressed in the same reformatory denims. He holds up a fish, a perch maybe—two or three pounds. DC lays a paternal arm over Byron's shoulders.

There is a jumble of blurs, feet, ground, then a naked young Byron cannonballing off the small wooden dock, cheeks puffed out. Far in the background, the tail end of a black and red Chevy two-door with those cool horizontal rear fenders. A big splash and Byron surfaces, silent shouting at the lens. Cut to DC Scott behind the wheel of the car. He waves at the camera with a made-for-home-movie laugh.

Then a flash of numbers, negative scratches and Scott appears—on his knees, madly wacking off, face horrified and covered in sweat, under a lime green spotlight in a dark room—like he's being forced at gunpoint. His mouth distorts, teeth clenched and eyes squeezed shut as he ejaculates but continues the demented, high-speed masturbation. A blurred figure passes before the camera. Scott flinches as if anticipating a smack to the head. I swing the binocs to him and Byron on the couch. They seem mildly amused. Paco is sprawled on his back now, one arm behind his head, other hand playing with his small, semi-erect prick while he watches DC's act on the tube.

There's more. Man 'o' mannequins, this home movie is a *Quo Vadis* epic. The new scene is another forest—day time—and could be the same clearing from that orgy night on Mount Royal. A group of maybe a dozen white men stand in a circle, from late teens to mid-sixties or so. The camera slowly moves across each of them. None gazes directly at the lens. All are well-developed specimens—no spindly-armed feebs in this crowd. They wear nothing but soft leather loincloths. Some of them sport full beards while the rest have several days growth. Each holds a rough wooden spear decorated with bits of feather, wire and trinkets. They thump the base of their weapons against the ground in rhythmic unison. Their gathering looks like some reclaim-your-lost-warrior-soul Robert Bly circle-jerk.

The giant police boss strides out of the dense forest. In daylight you can really see how huge this guy is, built like an NFL lineman. About six-seven, two hundred and eighty pounds of bearish muscle and bone. His bald head reflects the sunlight and a big, fiery red handlebar moustache is curled up at either end like Simon fucking Legree. An elaborate chrome and leather cock harness restrains his untamed beast. It struggles and throbs against its fetters. His only other article of clothing is a pair of gleaming black police boots. The circle parts to let him through then closes. The boss goes to the center and the camera tracks laterally as he slowly turns to take in each participant. The effect is dizzying and I almost lose my balance.

They begin some kind of solemn rite where each neo-warrior steps forward and pounds his right fist against his chest. *I swear eternal fealty till death do us part, ten bags full, mine liege.* The big cop does likewise. The first guy to be inducted is the Burt Reynolds look-a-like. No cowboy hat this time, he thrusts his spear forward. The police boss grasps the thing then thrusts it back at him. I feel like laughing out loud. Their little ritual ends with a nice, manly hug. They embrace with fists thumping each other's backs—not with an open hand. Clearly, no overt hanky-panky is allowed during this grave liturgy.

The next guy steps forward and—Christ on a short crutch!—it's *The Man!* Now I really want to cut loose with a full-blown screamin' cackle. I can't believe it—what is he doing with this crowd? And here I thought the stupid fuck was just some illiterate Park Ex Gino who'd pulled himself up by the cockstraps. But there he is, in all his muscle-brained glory. Being only five-five or so, The Man has to really reach up, arms extended, like a kid begging to be picked up by Daddy. It is rather awkward. The cop is forced to crouch and lift The Man right off his feet to perform their ceremonial cuddle, and then set him gently back down.

After the final warrior gets his snog, the camera tilts skyward for a cornball shot of the sun-dappled treetops and endless blue cosmos bla ba-bla ba-bla. That seems to be the end of tonight's feature presentation as Paco ejects the tape. I sweep round and notice Antonio is gone. Aunt Byron and DC Scott have their heads together, noses rubbing, warm smiles and slurpy little kisses. Yuck.

THIRTY-EIGHT

Slim will leave town tomorrow morning. University transcripts were long ago verified, US paperwork done, scholarship money in the bank. She will move to New York to be with her good guy, Adam. From what I hear, he really loves her and really wants to take care of her. Slim's gone through lots of men in this town. Some fondly recalled, most forgotten. Today she seems cheerful and excited, kinda rare for her. She's eager to get high when I show up to say my farewells

"Do me a favor?" I ask. "Don't turn into some middle-class housewife with a moral streak."

Slim looks up from folding clothes into a small suitcase and ignores my barb. "We're still going to be friends, right?"

"Yeah, yeah. I know it's time for you to go. I can't say I like it, but what the fuck. You've run the course here, right?"

She takes me lightly by the hips. "So you'll come and visit?"

"Sure, why not."

"Well, then you do me a favor."

"What?"

"I know Jane's been gone for a while now, but if she does come back, I don't think you two are the best match. Maybe you're too hard on each other."

"You think Jane's hard on me?"

Slim's head falls to one side. "C'mon, Johnny. I don't really know her, but you're hard enough—" She doesn't finish. "Anyway, I just want you to feel a little bit of peace."

"What, like you do now?"

"Don't do that. It's not fair."

"Yeah, you're right," I sag. "Here's a gram till you can score in New York. I'd better go before I say something stupid." I put the stuff on top of the dresser and don't take the money she's left.

Slim pulls me close again, her wrists on my shoulders and gives me a very soft kiss. "You'll be okay, right?"

"Stop asking me that."

"And you will come visit sometime?"

"I said yes, didn't I?"

Slim can afford to be sweet now like she's never been. I smile and don't tell her I'd rather slit my own throat than see her happily domesticated.

"And you'll write?"

"Yeah, I'll write."

She's in no mood for anything bleak. "C'mon, this might be our last chance for a long time." She pulls me toward her bed, already barefoot with unzipped jeans and sleeveless t-shirt, so I get her naked in about fifteen seconds. We stand together listening to the street outside, my hand stroking her back.

"Hennessy was right," I say. "It is nice to have someone completely naked in your arms while you're still dressed."

We stay like this for a while. Her neck and shoulders and breasts, her little bum and flat belly in my palms and on my fingers. But what do I say? *Don't go. Stay. Stay and what? We'll be good together. No, really, we will.*

Slim lets herself fall backward onto the bed, arms out and giggling as she watches me bounce around on one foot trying to pull off a boot and a pant leg. After doing half a circuit of the room and almost keeling over, I stand at the bottom of the bed, finally free of everything. There's lots of fondling and easy necking. We share a cigarette and a beer as tongues and hands go everywhere and into everything, the painless familiarity of one another's skin, the way she tastes and smells and moves, the way her thin lips tug at my mouth. Slim makes a circle with her legs and draws me into it sideways, cradles me with one arm. "C'mere, sweetheart..."

She reaches for the bottle of lube on the floor next to the bed, flips open the cap one-handed and squeezes the clear gel onto me, from navel on down. Her fingers crawl around and eventually go under, make me sort of nuts as she slowly works in her middle finger then crooks it forward to draw a long shiver from my throat.

"I'm gonna miss you," I murmur, arms hung around her neck. I rest the side of my face on her shoulder and she gets another finger in, the two of them in and out, thumb hard against my perineum. A prickly rush runs over my scalp. I go to pull away, but she holds me tight and gets a third finger started, making me cringe.

"Ow... that hurts..."

"Shh..."

She slows down and her ring finger joins in, then her pinky. The four of them curve together to slide and slide some more, working me open. Slim looks down at what she's doing and distraction makes her suck back saliva. She bends forward and her tongue touches my nipple. I can barely speak.

"Uh... this is too much..."

"Shh..."

"Stop saying that."

"Shh..."

Then comes her thumb, pressed into her palm. I swallow hard and lift my hips to make room. She pushes gradually, this way and that way, gradually again, involuntary tears run down my face. Slim's up past her knuckles now and things blow up in my head, voices from somewhere, nose running, a strong urge in my bladder. The reek of everything inside me, the smell of how soaking wet she is. Her hand squeezes me deep, shreds me right up the seam.

"Don't do this to me... Not now..."

"Shh..."

I drool openly as motor control slips away, slack jawed, my head rolls. She moans and her whole body sways with the rhythm of her hand as it consumes me up to the wrist. Slim leans forward, mouth coming down over me as her fingers grip my core. My whole body throbs around her wrist, a wrist so thin and so fragile. Her tongue curls along the length of me, builds me up to ruin, to crumbling memories, to minutes and hours, agonizing and unbearably true. A howl breaks somewhere in my chest, brain banging against skull as her mouth yanks a searing orgasm from my guts, making me twist and writhe and thrash. I see a blur of my come flow from her between her lips. I'm filleted right open and fall back against her leg. Slim's face rises, those green eyes boring in as come runs onto her chin.

"Uh… *Jeezus*…" I mumble. "Maybe I will come down for a visit…"

For a long while we don't move and she just caresses, forcing my cock to stand up. It feels as if there's more inside me, as if my poor old prostate refuses to let everything go. Slim's hand slowly emerges, then the knuckles, then her fingers. Her voice slurs and stumbles. "I gotta fuck you…"

It takes a lot of effort to throw a knee over my hips. I'm still aching as she grabs the base of my hard-on, helps me get harder. She looks down between us, aims it for her pussy and sinks right down the length with a chuckling groan. Now it is a simple matter of labor. All tenderness pitched aside, she rides me hard, both hands working on herself. There's a killer in there somewhere and Slim is determined to drag it out, preferably kicking and screaming. I feel her entire body ripple, her teeth crushing out garbled obscenities. It takes doing, it takes time, it takes severe concentration, it takes an unbroken tempo, and finally, it is the sound of relief, of ejecting a sweet serrated thorn from the soft underbelly. She pulls me along for the ride as we come like a pair of rutting young curs.

Laying around afterwards, we luxuriate with warm smooches and dreamy half-word promises, a bit of armor peeled away for a few minutes. While we're getting high, a grief-stricken woman down below on The Main begins to call. "Gamil… Gamil… Gamil…" No one answers. Her voice takes on a seagull's insistent cry and lulls us into an uneasy nod.

Slim's hand is flat on my chest as we lie next to each other, eyelids heavy.

"Don't forget what I said about Jane," she mumbles.

"Yeah, it'd probably be better. I don't know how to make up for anything."

"You don't need to make up for anything."

"Yeah, I do."

Slim lifts her head a touch, looks at me, irritated. "What are you talking about?"

"I knew how bad things were going to be."

She sours at me breaking our spell, but asks anyway. "How bad what would be?"

"Hennessy. I knew. At that fucking beer tent. I knew what would happen."

Slim rolls away and wraps her arms around a pillow. "Don't be a martyr, Johnny."

"But I did know and I did nothing but let him walk away with two grams of my fucking dope cuz I was jealous of that stupid little prick, Michel."

"Stop it. You couldn't have known."

"It was the same with Jane's abortion. When we got to the clinic, every nerve told me it would be a disaster. Not because it was an abortion. It could have been anything, a fucking appendectomy. I just knew it would all go wrong. *I knew.*"

"C'mon, don't do this. Not right now."

"But it's true. I didn't say shit cuz I was thinking about scoring. I wanted to get it over with, get her home and go score. I should have taken care of her. I knew it was the wrong day, wrong time, wrong place."

Slim sits bolt upright, green eyes flaring. "Then go tell Jane!" she shouts.

"I did tell her! It didn't matter by then."

She grabs my hair and slaps me hard. Her fists and palms come down in a fury, forcing me to flinch and turn. "Don't lay this on me, you selfish asshole, you fucking fraud!" She throws herself onto her side and curls up facing the wall. I reach for her, but she jerks away. "Don't touch me!" Her back shudders as she begins to cry.

Slim doesn't stir when I get out of bed about an hour later. As the sun rolls over Mount Royal I put on my clothes and go out the back, down the fire escape. Out on the Main, the woman's voice calls once again. "Gamil... Gamil..."

258

THIRTY-NINE

It's a bright and noisy afternoon—as if the whole street's in my apartment. The Man was supposed to drop by ages ago to re-stock the pharmacy. I've called him repeatedly for hours. Nothing. Maybe he's at one of his *au naturel* circle jerks. I can't get a hold of Leroi either but that doesn't mean much. He could be anywhere, not having to carry the pager today. I'm tempted to go by The Man's apartment without an invitation, but—well, I don't really need a broken nose.

Still, I get paranoid visions of evil narcs, welfare project shootouts and savage beatings in the Champ-de-Mars catacombs. I have a tiny bit left for myself, but I'm terrified things have gone dry because when they do, everybody usually goes dry all at once. If a drought hits, even the best hustlers are suddenly reduced to peddling semi-opiated snake oil. It certainly adds weight to conspiracy theories about Québec's Biker-Mafia-Rotten Cop Triumvirate. Where the fuck is that asshole? My patients are going rangy. Tony's the latest to have several bouts of pager fever before I phone him back yet again at the ptomaine snack bar in his building's lobby.

"Johnny," he hushes, as if waiting for biopsy results.

"Still nothing, Tone."

"Fuck, man. Why isn't he answering?"

"Maybe he OD'd on steroids, turned into the Missing Link and ran off into the forest. How the fuck should I know!? Quit paging me!"

"Sorry, but you think maybe something's happened?"

"Hey, don't bad vibe the thing, man."

259

"Oh, god no!"

"Well, let's not dwell on it. He'll call. He has to."

"I dunno, Johnny. I've had a really bad feeling lately."

"Tony, will ya fuckin' cool it!"

"C'mon!" he breaks down. "You gotta have something!"

"I told ya. Nothin'. I'll call when I'm back in shape."

"I'll be waiting," he whimpers.

"You do that."

I hear him carefully replace the receiver as if it might crumble in his hands. Maybe The Man's pulled a Tony on me, summarily fired my ass without prior warning. It is true that complaints about my service have piled up lately. As with most things, I started out all gung-ho, but the daily grind has made me kind of lazy and unreliable. I've heard some of these malcontents now refer to me as "The Quack." Fucking traitors. I should cut their stuff with ipecac. The phone rings. I take a deep breath.

"Yeah?"

"Johnny…" The Man croons.

I check my watch. Five hours late—right on the nose. What a cocksucker. "I was about to call the cops, report you to Missing Persons."

"Missing Persons," he laughs, low and smooth. "So, I guess you need to see me."

"Nah, you took so long to call everyone's kicked."

"Yeah, funny. I'll take care of ya, but first we gotta do something. I'll be by in a couple minutes."

Hearing The Man beep his horn, I go downstairs and he's driving a minivan with Leroi in the front passenger seat, looking kind of spaced out. He barely acknowledges me when I get in the back and The Man puts the pedal to the metal, flapping on about somebody who owes him money. He swears all kinds of dismemberment, repeats favorite phrases as we go down Coloniale - stuff like "Rip his guts out" and "Really make him know." He finally shuts up as we get to Sherbrooke and head west. At Jeanne-Mance, we turn north and stop at the corner of Prince Arthur. The Man throws the car into reverse and deftly parallels parks. He's the only person I know who never has to look for a legal spot in areas that are normally a driver's nightmare—like the McGill Ghetto. Wherever he needs to park, someone pulls out as he arrives or the spot waits for him, invisible to the hapless losers that circle the block for hours.

The Man briskly leads us to the building on the northeast corner. It's semi-run down, about twenty-stories tall. The target is a small time con artist known as Marcel Le Mouse. He cut a deal with The Man to start his own franchise servicing the downtown office crowd. Unfortunately, as often happens, Marcel became his own best customer. Final tally: He owes The Man just over twenty-seven hundred bucks and hasn't paid a dime. But that's not the worst offense. Rather than agree to a regular, if punitive, re-payment schedule, Marcel went into duck-and-dive mode. He offered The Man various stories, theories, assurances and what-ifs. Then Marcel committed the unpardonable *faux pas* of ignoring The Man's calls.

"Okay, we're here," he tells us as we exit the elevator on the top floor. The Man points at PH4 then stands back and fires the flat of his big right shoe square at the door. It pops open as if on a spring.

We hear Marcel begin to yell "What the fu—" but his voice cuts off when he appears in the apartment's entryway. Marcel races into the can and locks up. He screams some shit about calling the cops. The Man calmly informs him the phone is in the living room and why doesn't he come out and let's have a nice reasonable chat.

After a few minutes, Marcel works up the balls to crack the bathroom door. Perhaps he expects the muzzle of a shotgun to be jammed in his face. But no, the three of us quietly wait for him. He slowly joins us with a nervous titter. "Heh heh. Good joke, eh, guys?"

The Man smiles tiredly and with considerable sympathy. "Marcel, Marcel, Marcel…"

Marcel opens his mouth to deliver what could be the finest oration of the decade—but we'll never know. It lasts about one word before The Man grabs his balding mullet and drives him face first into the booze bottles and cut-glass decanters sitting on a big mirrored wall unit.

Marcel lets out a pained yowl and starts to beg as he lays prone on a throw rug among the broken glass, his nose gashed and lip split open. As the white shag collects some red splotches, The Man takes a straight-back chair from the kitchenette and slams it onto the living room floor. He again seizes Marcel's hair and lifts him into the interrogation seat. The Man becomes a high-speed dervish and has Marcel duct-taped to the chair in a matter of moments.

"I'm gonna leave your mouth open," he explains, "to answer my questions. Check?"

"Check," Marcel mumbles through a froth of blood.

"You got any cash hidden in this apartment?" The Man points at the floor to indicate which apartment he means.

"No."

"Any other valuables here—jewelry, antiques, collectibles or anything like that?"

"No."

"Any bank safety deposit boxes or other places where you got cash or valuables stashed? Like apartments and houses of girlfriends, relatives, buddies and all them."

"No."

"You sure?"

Marcel tries to speak through his busted face. "Yeah—but if you lemme—"

The Man surprises him by doing a couple of rapid-fire tape circuits and seals his mouth. The eyes pop wide with the realization he just might be killed by this steroid-pumped maniac. Leroi glances at me. I look past Marcel out the balcony's sliding doors. In the brilliant sunlight there's a majestic view of downtown. To the east I can see the colossal reach of the Cartier Bridge and even the ocean-going container terminals way out at Pie-Neuf.

The Man walks slowly around the two-bedroom pad. He too admires the view. "Hey, Johnny. I can see your house from here."

I grunt at his shitty joke. Continuing to stroll about, he works his hands into his deerskin gloves, the ones with little pockets of sand sewn into the knuckles. He inventories items.

"This Nikko sound system—good make. Take it to the car," he orders us. "Same with the TV. Toshiba. And that computer over there."

Me and Leroi look at each other and sag. The Man shouts from one of the bedrooms. "Holy Fuck!" We go in there and he has one of those clear acrylic stands that holds a collectible sports card. "Look!" he shows us. "A signed Mike Bossy rookie card. You know what this fuckin' thing is worth!?"

The bedroom obviously houses a boy. Marcel's son, no doubt, probably part time. There's no sign of a woman anywhere.

"Leave the card alone," Leroi tells him. "It belongs to the guy's kid."

"Fuck the kid! Marcel shoulda thought about his kid before he tried to screw me."

"Leave the kid out of it," I join in.

The Man eyes us, and for a moment I think he might have me and Leroi chaired and taped right next to Marcel. But he backs off, though not entirely convinced. "This card's worth like two, maybe three bills, easy."

"Don't take the card," Leroi badgers.

"Yeah," I add. "Or you can carry all that shit downstairs."

"What a couple of weeps. The kid's probably some spoiled piece of shit."

Leroi's unmoved. "Will you just forget about the goddamn card?"

"Okay, okay," The Man complies, putting it back. "You guys wanna act like little pussy faggots, go ahead. But next time some fuckhead won't pay his tab, don't come crying to me."

The Man marches into the living room and takes it out on Marcel. He lays a flurry of right crosses and left jabs into the guy's face and body. Marcel emits muted screams and groans. His eyes swell up dark red, blood leaks from under the tape. The sand pockets in The Man's special beating gloves have split one ear horizontally and shredded Marcel's bottom lip. There are a couple of nasty gashes on his forehead and bald spot. The Man's blows get so rough he finally sends Marcel and the chair to the floor. It looks like the guy's knocked right out, maybe even dead. Leroi and I watch for a few moments.

"C'mon," I say and motion to him to grab hold of the TV. The thing's an awkward bastard.

"He's a psycho," Leroi mutters under the weight of this big hunk of crap. I drop my end out in the hallway. The tube doesn't shatter, but one corner of the black plastic casing splinters.

"What the fuck are you assholes doing!?" The Man hollers and comes out to see what's happened. "Don't break the fucking stuff!"

"So who said we're goddamn movers!?" I yell.

A few doors open down the hall. The Man throws a shit-eating grin in their general direction. "Moving day! You know how it is!" The doors shut without comment. "Okay, forget the TV. Just take the light stuff, like the stereo and computer."

"What are you talking about?" Leroi complains. "All that shit's big and heavy too. You should have brought a hand cart."

"Christ, you two are a couple of real fucking girls. Okay, just take it down a bit at a time. Can you handle that much?"

Back in the apartment, The Man lifts Marcel and his chair off the floor and gives him a breather. He checks out the kitchen and finds some prime steaks in the freezer, tosses them at us. "Here, take these too." A Braun coffeemaker and bean-grinder are piled on the counter, along with an un-opened set of Ginsu knives and some other chachkas. After our fifth trip to the van, nothing else will fit. The place is now half-empty and fully trashed.

Marcel's pitched forward and breathes noisily through a crushed nose. The only thing holding him up is the duct tape. The Man pulls out a hunting knife and cuts him loose. Marcel slides to the floor, a pulverized mess. The Man points at him. "Okay, that's it for now. Here's the deal. Four hundred a week, plus interest, till we clear this up—aside from any other business we do. Capiche?"

Marcel moans. The Man quietly closes the apartment door. Waiting for the elevator, the three of us stare at the busted TV we have left out in the hall.

Back at my place, Leroi paces around, highly agitated. "I can't believe what we just did. What that insane asshole just did!" He stops and massages his temples. "Johnny, I gotta quit. I can't do this. I'm a normal person." I can see his mind grope for a way out. "First, I'll uh... I'll go into a rehab.

There's a place I heard about on the West Island. Fuck, I can't believe I got hung up like this. I knew it would happen. I'm so stupid! It's UN-fucking-believable!" He walks around some more and the ideas continue to flow. "Then I'll go live with my mother in Sri Lanka—or maybe go to Sophie's hometown with her, in New Brunswick. I'll get some kind of job. I could go back to doing stone and cement." He considers the options while gazing out at the mountain. "Well, maybe not that—but something."

The pager buzzes on the coffee table. Leroi picks it up and checks the number. "This fucking thing! You know I feel it vibrating in my pocket sometimes—and I don't even have it on me! I mean, is that fucked up or what?!" He goes toward the door then turns to me. "Sorry to cut out on you like this, but—"

"Don't worry about it. I'm not long for this bullshit either."

"Yeah, man, you've got other skills. You don't have to do this." He loiters for a moment, unsure of what to say. "Get out, Johnny. That guy is a monster." He repeats it slow. "The Man is a fucking monster."

I don't say anything as he leaves. Standing at the window, I watch him walk along Roy toward The Main. With a rediscovered spring in his step, the relief rolls right off him. The Man is a monster. The Man is a monster who never gets a parking ticket.

FORTY

I find a letter in my mailbox. The address is in Slim's blocky, all-caps handwriting. Hard to believe she's already written. It hasn't been that long. On the front of the envelope: 'St. Johnny Rugmuncher.' The return addressee: 'S. Rug.' It's a pretty sweet little peace offering and gives my heart a nice thump.

Hey Sexy—

It's so great to be in NYC again, this time as an inhabitant. You just can't help but love these wide and echoing canyons, the whole larger-than-life thing. Montreal seems pastoral next to this city, but I do miss the mountain. I've been binging too often lately. Adam complains I go out too much. I guess he's used to this town so it's no big deal to him. I'm still getting acclimated. He gets kind of morose and quiet sometimes and it's hard to take, so I need to get out on my own. Some of his friends took me to a nightclub full of college kids. I was so high and drunk I can't remember the name of the place or where it was, or what band was playing. It was really packed and I could feel people stroking my ass, but would anyone even look at me? I was so pissed I almost clobbered one of them. The guy I tried to pick up necked with me a bit, then said he had to get some sleep because he needed to go to school in the morn. Gad. Just as well. I was so wasted I probably would have puked on him.

There's a big DA and X scene here. I finally gave in and got really high on X. It was weird to have such a throbbing body stone because I haven't done those kinds of drugs in a few years. I was sick most of yesterday. The whole thing was pretty stupid. My companions killed the drug hangover by dropping acid, but I declined. I can't keep up with them. Anyway, classes have begun so I have to remain somewhat lucid. I've been trying to cool it with the J, but you know how that goes. At least it's cheap down here. Not of that notorious Montreal quality, but not bad.

Like I said, Adam has his moments, but overall he's good and his place is really great. Lots of his friends live in the same building or on the same street so there's a nice communal feel. I like to fuck him a lot and he's certainly got more brains than the last one. We've had some pretty hysterical arguments about my tendency to um—wander a bit. Our fights are pretty juvenile, but he seems to enjoy them.

I've been thinking about you. It seems to me we were getting closer all the time, but I never knew where it was headed. It always felt like something was just beyond reach. We'd fuck each other frequently for a while then things would drop off for weeks or months at a time. I guess we both had too many other involvements to concentrate on each other very easily. But I've also been wondering what the real diff was between me & Jane re: you. Was it just that she is dead set on her utopian ideal—stomps right in there and bangs out her territory? Was it about your guilt re: that nightmare abortion you went through together? I have never been clear about your feelings either way. Maybe you're absolutely in love with her and its complete sacrilege for me to think of myself and Jane in the same sentence, as if I'm just a distraction.

I do think you and I are buddies and I tend to believe you feel the same, but I wish we hadn't parted snarling at one another. I definitely did not need to hear all that stuff, at least not on that particular day.

And your monologues about a lifestyle change—they were strange. Sitting on the edge of the bed in only a shirt, staring into the kitchen, your profile seemed like a horse or some kind of reptile mashed flat. It was like your skull and your bones were really pressed up against your skin. You were sort of sad, not quite defeated, but powerless in a way. I never thought until then I might be more content than you. Why is it such a conflict for you to try to take what you want, even if you might be wrong about it? Me, I still imagine being with you, even cohabitation maybe. At times it's felt like some kind of balance was possible

267

between us. No jealousy, no fucking insanity. But for whatever reason it's all re-
mained at arm's length. It really is too bad. Maybe we're both too self-centered or
just too lazy.

Hopefully, you're back to your chipper self, probably bouncing Morgan on
your knee and my meanderings are making you queasy or you'll just think I've
flipped my lid. I don't care. I don't live there anymore and I don't have anything
to hide. Anyway, we are still friends, right? Maybe you can come down sometime
for a visit.

My cunt and my asshole say hi.
XO
S.

Slim. So filthy yet so prim, remote yet occasionally loving. And her blasé
little backhand: "It really is too bad." Yeah, no shit. I pace around the apartment and re-read those lines. "Buddies"? Sure, real good buddies. I find
some paper and fire off a response, something along the lines of: *Yeah, cool.*
No probs. We shoulda, we coulda, we might have even woulda—but gee, we
didn't. Oh well, it's maybe kinda sorta almost perhaps could be too bad. Yeah,
sure, no sweat, whatevs, let's be buddies, bosom pals. With anybody, with every-
body, yeah. It's all totally cool, right?

I also use the word 'disingenuous' and have to look up how it's spelled.
I march over to The Main, buy a stamp then slam the letter into the mailbox, making a few people jump. Walking back home in an angry huff, I
think, *what difference does it make?* The apathetic slut probably won't even
read it. I imagine Slim getting my letter: She yawns at the first line, then
has trouble keeping her eyes open for the second and passes out during the
third. It drops from her hand to be trampled by all of Adam's cool friends
and nobody ever bothers to pick it up and see what it is because it's torn and
dirty by then. A lightning bolt epiphany slaps me in the head: *I'm* the creep
women talk about when they mention some guy they've hacked off after a
short suck-fuck-and-duck affair.

I don't want to go home and just mope around, so I make my way up to
Mario's Duty Free Depanneur to pay down my tab and buy some smokes.

With any luck, Mario has managed to get on his feet and open the store. I saw him at the bars late last night, completely hammered and ready to brawl. The pager buzzes a few times in my shirt pocket. It's Kit and Tony in quick succession. I call them from the lobby of the 4040 Building. Kit cheers me up, makes me laugh out loud by sweetly promising to "bang the mother lovin' ass off ya—but only if you'll trade me for a quarter GR. C'mon… you're getting the better end of the bargain, ya hot little bitch."

"Geez… you really do know how to turn a girl's head."

I agree to drop by and front her the dope, but take a rain check on her tempting offer. Next, Tony's wheedling. "I'm on the way, Tone—about fifteen, twenty minutes. I gotta see Kit first then we'll go to Mo Wilensky's for lunch."

"Groovy, Mein Herr. Hey, listen," he catches me before I hang up. "Has Leroi been sleeping with Sophie?"

"Who's Sophie?" I deke.

"C'mon… Y'know, the French girl I'm seeing."

"Oh, yeah… She's quite the sassy little gash, eh?"

"Your language is pretty base, Johnny, do you know that?"

"Yes, I do know that. It's an affectation, which is meant to help bolster my credibility as a street personage and petty drug dealer. As to your in-quiry, I have no clue and even if I did, I would not thusly betray the young woman's privacy. On The Main, discretion is the better part of keeping doors open and beds accessible."

"Yeah…" Tony grumbles, not amused at my rap. "I think she might be seeing some other guys, maybe just using me to get into what she thinks is a scene and have a whole bunch of experiences in a short time, like a summer project or something."

"It's a grand ambition and makes me fondly recall my own days as a gay young roustabout, the burden of time leveraged much lessly on my brow than hence—or some such horseshit. Anyway, she's young, good-looking, smart, well read, has that sexy French vibe, her libido's healthy. She's having some fun. What exactly is the problem? Oh, right…" I feign and put on a weepy Bugs Bunny voice teasing a lovelorn wallflower. "You want Sophie to be your wittle girlfwend. Awww… How touching. Tonicus, the sensitive type."

"Shut up. What's so bad about that? You're always going on about your 'wife.'"

"It's the Power of Pussy, Tone. You can't force it, unless you plan on becoming a rapist. It just happens, like contracting a really sexy strain of dengue fever. You just deal with it and if you survive, it'll be as a broken husk of your former self, but with some incredible memories—until you go senile, that is. Is that what you want?"

"Yeah, actually, that is what I want. I've never had a truly overwhelming, totally insane relationship that breaks my spirit and crushes my soul and does all those things to her too, both of us left forever scarred and wondering years later what may have been."

"Wow. I think you're finally catching on. Well, if you do want that kind of madness, you've got to stop throwing yourself all over these women like a wet blanket. That'll drive away anybody, a dog even—a wino."

"I know," he admits. "I can't help it. I always feel like such a fool around women. I don't know what it is."

"Okay, listen. I'm dying for a smoke and I'm just down the street from Mario's. I'll be at your place shortly to offer more sage counsel. In the meantime, don't throw yourself out of any ground floor windows."

I go into the dep and Mario's manning the counter while Warlock loiters about, keeping him company. "No wisecracks about my wife," I warn them.

"Oh, puh-leez," Warlock titters. "The lovely Ms. Jane has been gone so long now I'm sure you'd need a photograph to distinguish her from all your other *affaires de l'amour.*" He draws out the French bit with a lugubrious Charles Aznavour flourish.

Mario howls and punches me in the shoulder. I'm about to lay into Warlock when a Park Extension Greek Shithead we know bursts in with a giant pistol held at eye level. He's got bad shakes and jabbers at Mario for money. Warlock and I just stand there, stunned. I'd heard this guy recently held up the shop for petty cash. Once, twice, okay, but Mario's not interested in a third round and the gun makes zero impression on him.

"You betta go home," he growls.

Greek Shithead holds out his free hand and dances in place, a frantic hotfoot jig. "C'mon, Mario! Just gimme what's in the till!"

Mario's eyes fall on Warlock, then shift over to me. He sighs heavily. In a flash, he whips out a two-foot-long machete and leaps over the counter with a Hindi war cry, scaring the piss out of all three of us. Shithead shrieks and bolts out the door. So much for the hand-cannon. Mario's first swipe gets him on the back of the thigh, a long gash that instantly gouts blood. Shithead runs for his life as Mario gains on him. I rush outside ahead of Warlock.

"Mario! Forget that asshole! You'll be charged with murder!"

Shithead flies down Duluth toward The Main, about sixty yards away, dropping the gun as he goes. Mario's right on his tail, hits him with slashes down his back and ass. More blood flies.

"He's finished," I tell Warlock. "Mario's gonna kill that stupid fuck!"

Warlock licks his lips as we watch the crazed pursuit. "Or at least maim him terribly!"

Cars and passersby slam on their brakes, shocked faces gawp at the high-speed butchery and vibrant trail of blood. A gaggle of teenagers hoot in delight. Shithead makes the corner at The Main, barely slowing down, and disappears southbound. Mario follows and a few moments later we hear a bunch of horror-stricken screams. A minute or two passes and nothing. Finally we see Mario stalk back toward us. His shirt-front is covered with blood and he looks solemn, still gripping the machete.

Warlock's pink-faced with excitement. "Perhaps Mario's decapitated that fellow!"

"Naw, he'd be carrying the guy's head."

We hear sirens approach. Cops, meat wagons, fire wagons, hot dog wagons, news gimps, the whole panoply's on the way. A mob has begun to form, people already feverishly retelling the tale. Neighbors gather on the long wrought-iron stairways of the surrounding tenements, casually drinking beer and creating a kind of amphitheater. A small group of men stand protectively around Mario. He won't let go of his weapon. Traffic quickly jams up in the narrow streets and clogs the intersection. The blood's turned black on the sidewalk, even blacker on the road. I think there are some small strips of flesh left behind, like sushi.

Ambulance lights and more commotion draw another crowd down at The Main. I can see some paramedics shove a blood soaked bundle into their truck. Mario's object lesson in vendor-client relations has straightened me right the fuck out. I need a shot—bad. I'm hit with a bout of the dizzies but manage to stay upright, shove my way through a knot of eager bystanders and walk north toward Tony's. Half a block up Clark, I vomit into some bushes. More gawkers stream south to catch the aftermath. They make disgusted faces at me then continue on, pointing at the streaks of bloody sidewalk dead ahead. An ice cream truck is the first to arrive on scene and a lineup instantly forms. I bend over and puke some more.

FORTY-ONE

It's been a week or so since Mario carved up that Greek Shithead, but man, it's still giving me nightmares. I heard he survived his haircut. Amazing, considering the blood loss. Add that to the hole in my days where the Hen used to be and with Slim leaving town, fuck, it all feels like battle fatigue.

Looking for distraction, I've been tempted to knock on DC Scott's door, see what's happening with Aunt B, maybe try to sell them a remote-controlled, four-legged butt-banger. When I go by Saint-Famille and Pine to deal with Vern and Hernav, Vern tells me that while shoplifting steaks at the trendy La Cité supermarket on Lower Park, he spotted Aunt Byron going in—not more than twenty minutes ago. I knock ten bucks off his pack for the info and Hernav wants the same. He wears an idiotic Axl Rose hide-the-baldness bandana. I slap it off his head and into the street.

"Hey, man!" he whines. "What did ya do that for?" When he bends down to grab it, I boot him in the ass, almost driving him head first into the door of a passing car. "Shit, man! What the fuck's with you?"

"Just be thankful I don't give you rat poison, you worthless streak of piss."

Vern chortles and throws an arm around my shoulders. "That's the way, Johnny. Take it all out on the weak and the stupid."

"You guys are nuts," Hernav sulks. He goes off with a few cautious over-the-shoulder glances. I give him the throat-slitting gesture.

At La Cité, I watch Byron from a distance as she browses among the fruit and vegetables, a woven basket hung off one arm. The two-faced hag wears a long Indian peasant skirt, a crisp oversized white t-shirt and some kind of Tajiki embroidered vest, hair wrapped in a green silk scarf. It's another one of her well-to-do arts community hippie dyke ensembles.

"You fucking Judas," I ambush her.

She's not fazed and continues to feel up some ruby grapefruits, dropping a couple in her basket. "Johnny, please. Don't be childish."

"You duplicitous cunt. You pulled all this bullshit so you could once again be Duncky's most prized human pet. You're in love with that fucking bloodsucker. You always have been."

Aunt Byron's drops her guard an inch, beseeching me. "You don't understand. Our relationship is extremely complex. I began by wanting revenge, yes, but I have grown beyond that. Vengeance is not enough to live on. Human lives are not monoliths."

"What about sneaking around shooting me and Shalini, me and Slim—and everybody else on the mountain? You couldn't just leave the fucking mountain alone, could ya? You goddamn lowlife, I should fucking well stab you."

She glances away, eyebrows raised. "Very well, you surveiled us. I'm not surprised, but my intentions weren't at all puerile."

"No, of course not. You stupid bitch, look at yourself. You're not a woman, you're a fat fucking joke."

Byron drops the front, expression hardening. "If you can't live with your own failures, don't take it out on me. I know you're heartbroken, but doing this won't help."

"What—Hennessy? Is that what you're judging me on?"

"I didn't say that, but you can be your own critic and I'll do the same for myself. Whatever I am or whatever I was—at least I'm now willing to admit things are not black and white."

"Do you really think he'll choose you over some hot young piece of multi-cultural ass?"

Her back stiffens. "There's no need to choose. We can be a family as well as anyone."

"A family!? That guy needs a family like Dracula needs a garlic enema!"

She ignores my crack. "There's much more at stake here. Duncan will soon be hosting a major conference for the institute he's founded. I'm integral to the process. I've helped negotiate with various levels of government about the funding and purview."

"What purview, to promote diddling as a fashion statement?"

She takes a breath and pushes past my taunts. "The institute's goal is to examine cases of child abuse—of all kinds—and ascertain which are based in fact, and which are not. We then offer victims—on both sides—legal advice and representation, if merited."

"You're completely fucking insane. What about what he did to you?"

"Aren't you listening? I don't want to spend my life settling scores. We've all changed—except for you."

"Jesus!" I laugh, loud and bitter. "You'll go along with anything that suits your pathetic fucking agenda!"

Our angry exchange has drawn the stares of other shoppers. Aunt Byron's face tightens into a thin smile. "I think it'd be best if you simply left us alone."

"You started this. You showed up in Montreal and asked for help. You dragged us up the mountain. And I'm not the one watching videos of you having sex!"

Byron pretends to yawn, fighting off public embarrassment. "So what is it you want from us—money?"

"Fuck you," I snarl and walk away.

FORTY-TWO

Al pages me around dinner and rather than call, I walk over after seeing Kit, Warlock and Sharon. It's been miserable days lately and it'd be nice to scarf down some of Mama Polo's good old-fashioned grub. But when I get there, she opens the door all fretful, wringing the corner of her apron. "Mister Yonee, a girl callink for you many times. She very upset." The phone rings and Mama Polo points down the hall. "Is her again, for sure."

Morgan sounds crazed when I pick up.

"What the fuck is going on?" I ask her.

"Where have you been!?"

"Out seeing—"

"Forget that! Just come get me—right fucking now!"

"Why, what—"

"Johnny!" she yells, on the verge of a freak out. "Hurry up—and come up the back!"

"Okay! Where are you?"

She gives me an address in the east end, off Papineau. Al's ensconced in his wingback after dinner, nose in the paper and drinking the tea his mammy just made. "Is Morgan all right?" he asks while burping and digesting.

"I dunno, I gotta go see."

"Oh, I'm sure it's just one of her little conniptions. She does seem to enjoy them."

"Yeah, keeps things fresh, I guess."

Mama's all over me, wants to shove blynai and smoked pork down my throat. I take some to eat on the way.

The apartment's on the second floor of a crappy duplex, south of Sainte-Catherine. Halfway down the block I find the lane that leads to the back of the dump. Morgan lets me in with furtive peeks up and down the alley. It's desolate, just a couple of kids playing with an old tire. She puts a finger to her lips and motions me to follow into the front room of a bare little flop with minimal furniture. It's a classic trick pad, nobody lives here.

"So what the problem?" I whisper.

"I have this regular B&D trick. We always meet here. Things went really bad."

"How bad?"

She points at the hallway closet.

I look at her. "What?"

Morgan grimaces, fear mixed with disgust. "I didn't know what to do."

I approach tentatively, reach for the doorknob from a distance and wouldn't be surprised if a shrieking mental case leapt out at me. If I am being dragged into some bass-akwards role-playing scenario, I'll wring her fucking neck. She would pull that kind of stunt if the john paid enough.

"Holy shit!" I yell, stumbling backward.

It's a guy trussed up in an elaborate harness made of black leather and chrome chains, stainless steel padlocks, and industrial cable. He's on his knees, chin on chest, his entire head wrapped in a rubber zipper mask, sheathed in shiny PVC from the waist up. A dog collar is tight around his throat, locked to a steel shaft that goes down to a complex genital clamp. A short chain runs from the rear of the collar and cranks the handcuffed wrists halfway up his back. His ankles are manacled together and hooked to the cuffs with a thick leather strap. A woven steel cable is looped around the back of his neck. The two ends go under the guy's crotch, meet in the crack of his ass then separate and hook into loop-bolts in the closet's ceiling. Fuck me—what a contrivance. There are thick smears of lube here and there, mixed with plaster dust. I can see where he's smashed holes into the closet walls trying to free himself. He just hangs there from the apparatus and does not appear to be breathing. Morgan hovers behind me, knuckles at her teeth.

"Did you help him get into this fucking thing?"

"Well, yeah, he can't do it by himself. Maybe you should get him outta that shit, see if he's alive."

"Why haven't you done it?"

She makes a squeamish face. "I don't wanna touch him if he's dead."

"I thought you didn't do this kind of over-the-top bullshit."

"Well, he pays a ton and it's usually pretty easy. I don't have to fuck him or anything."

I squat down and examine the rubber head harness. Small padlocks secure the mouth-zipper and dog collar. Morgan hands me a ring of tiny keys. I try a few and find the right ones then carefully pull off the head gear.

"JESUS FUCK!" I shout and fall on my ass, quickly back-crawl away.

"WHAT!?" Morgan jumps, ready to bolt.

"It's the fucking Man!"

"What man?!"

"The *Man* man!" I turn to her, a rush of panic hitting me. "What the fuck are you doing with The Man!?!"

Morgan bursts into tears. "How should I know this guy's The Man? I've never *seen* the fucking Man!" Her eyes widen with sudden rage. "Hey, did you sick him on me!?"

"No! Are you nuts!? He must have followed me to your place!"

She sneers at the prone shape. "The sleazy asshole! Serves him fucking right!"

My mind flips to the terror of supplies cut off, dire sickness and despair, once again reduced to those hideous codeine tabs and eating handfuls of anti-diarrhea pills. The cushion of Morgan's money-making ass provides a bit of cold comfort, but how long would that last. I haven't got a lot of stuff left and wonder how much money The Man had on him—and how much product. No, he wouldn't carry a lot of it, even for convenience sake. Well, maybe a little for her. I notice his clothes laid out nice and tidy on a chair in the corner of the front room, along with a black gym bag—for all his toys, no doubt.

Morgan comes up behind me to take a closer look. "Will ya just see if he's alive or not."

It's pretty clear she's already made her prognosis. The eyes are open but glassy. A red ball-gag is jammed in his mouth. I touch the throat and can't feel a pulse.

I rub my eyes one-handed. "Jesus fuck…" I look up at her. "How long ago was this?"

"I dunno, a couple hours."

"A couple hours? Why didn't you call me?"

"I did call you, about a thousand times! At Al's place, you fucking idiot! I couldn't page you. There's a phone here, but I don't know the number and I was afraid to ask the operator."

I look back at The Man. My temples throb. "So how did it happen?"

"How do you think it happened?! It was an accident! He started having some kinda seizure and I couldn't get him undone. The more he panicked the tighter it all got. I kept telling him to relax, but he spazzed out on me." Her face falls into her hands. "I'm fucked! It's all gonna be my fault."

"Well, why didn't you just take off?"

"I dunno!" she whines, panic clawing at her. "Isn't that like murder or manslaughter or something? Anyway, I didn't want anyone to see me leave."

"Great. Instead they see me arrive."

The butt plug and cock strap which are part of his getup have thankfully prevented bodily evacuation. A blue hard-on bulges straight up, the head coated in a crust of semen. Without someone who's really adept at releasing this B&D style Gordian Knot, things could get very ugly very fast—and Morgan's not mechanically inclined.

She throws herself face down on the single bed in the corner. Everything feels very still. Some children babble out in the street. Morgan's voice comes up muffled. "So what are we gonna do?"

"Is anybody supposed to show up?"

She turns to face me. "I don't think so. This is his fuck pad. He's got a girlfriend somewhere."

I get to my feet. "You were smart to stay here. We'll wait until it's totally dark and just leave him where he is. Does anybody else know you're here?"

Morgan sits up, eyes flashing around. She pushes the hair from her face and wipes off some mascara. "No… just you."

I think about her calls to Al's place, the phone records. It could all add up to a backroom beating somewhere down the road. "Okay, it'll be dark soon. We'll wipe the place down and go. Not much else we can do."

Morgan grabs The Man's t-shirt and whirls round like a manic maid. I go through his stuff and catch a heavy whiff of his trademark *Shrieking Mongoose* body spray. I find a ring of keys and take them, but there's no wallet and no money or dope. *No money.* The Man walking around with *no money.* I look over at Morgan as she buffs the night table and phone. The small apartment's quickly wiped down. She finishes off a light switch. "I think that's it."

During the next twenty minutes or so Morgan stands at the kitchen sink chain smoking while I check several times for a heartbeat or pulse. I sponge him off wherever we might have touched. It doesn't seem possible anyone could come back to life after that long so I almost shit when I hear some gurgling as an awful stench rises from his mouth. Again I listen for a heartbeat. Still quiet. Maybe it was just some post-mortem burping.

I turn off the kitchen light with my elbow then fumble for the right key to lock up. Morgan raises her chin, eyes narrowed and sliding toward the closet. She looks up at the ceiling. I grab her by the ribs. Our mouths knock together, biting lips. She drops her bag and jams up her skirt, ass slamming against the kitchen counter and hoists herself onto it. I undo my pants and rip a hole in the crotch of her black tights. She grabs on and shoves me in, dry, pubic hair caught and pulling.

I keep a watch on the closet door as we fuck and imagine The Man as he comes busting out of that shit, chains and harnesses, cables and hunks of plaster dragging after him. Morgan lifts her ass right off the counter as we pound together. She holds herself up on the edge, legs hooked around me, boot heels kicking. She hisses and lets go, grabs onto my shoulders and we sink to the kitchen floor. Genitals bashing, we come in slow, grinding waves. I pull out and reach down between us, look at our come on my hand—a bit of blood mixed in. I lick some from my fingers. Morgan's eyes go to the hallway as her lips close around my thumb, sucking away the rest. I roll off and pull her to her feet. She pulls her skirt down then goes to stand by the back door.

I take a last look around as she grabs the knob with her sleeve. When we come out the laneway and walk toward Papineau to find a cab, a few dole goons eyeball us from their stoops, but it's completely dark now and they won't recognize shit. Besides, guys like that never talk to the cops for fear of being cornered for their own unpunished deeds. Morgan glances out the back window of the taxi. I turn but there's nothing, nobody follows us. She lays her cheek on my shoulder as I wrap my arm around her. "You're gonna have to be The Man now, baby."

"Oh, yeah?"

She lifts her head and looks me in the eyes. "Do you know where he was getting it?"

"Sure, these Turkish guys in Park Ex. I was there with him a couple times, but I don't know if they'll deal with me."

"Just show up with money, they'll deal with you."

"Easy to say. They only do ounces and up. I've got about six grams left. I gave The Man my float this morning. He was supposed to see me today for the reload. We're fucked unless you wanna work some triple overtime."

She opens her bag and shows me a big whack of hundreds, fifties, and twenties, all wrapped in blue elastics.

"How much?"

"Seventeen thousand, nine hundred and twenty dollars," she whispers. "I'll give you seven grand."

Fuck me. She actually sat there and counted it while that animal was dying in his closet. "Any dope?"

Morgan's hand comes out of her leopard print bomber jacket. There's a baggie in her palm, four or five grams. I give her a big, face suckin' kiss and shake my head in wonder. She gets comfy and puts on an impish little grin.

He'd asked me about Morgan a few times after hearing her ball-breaker routine over the speaker phone and then offering to give her big dope credit. Perhaps he'd prayed she was the woman who would finally take him as far as he needed to go. When they first met, Morgan would have seen she was swimming with a house-broken shark and he just might swallow her whole. I'm sure she knew who he was, even if he didn't tell her. But the potential payoff had to have been too big to resist. How did he explain it? The way he explained anything—directly. *No, I'm not gonna fuck you. I need your help with something. Here, let me show you.*

Was there tenderness as she assisted him with getting into all of his hardware? Did she burble loving little clichés? Did he blush when he got erect? No, it had to have been a fairly mute encounter with him issuing abrupt but even-tempered orders. He had a goal. Morgan was merely an assistant, like Houdini would have had. The Man's ego demanded she be very attractive— and skilled in her way—but not exactly unique.

So how far in advance had she planned to one day stand back, watch and wait as he struggled madly, his ferocious strength only making things worse? Did she coolly go through his pockets while he let out mute cries of panic, unable to speak or shout or beg, eyes imploring? What was the safe signal? Two taps? Three?

FORTY-THREE

Everything aches. I'm feeling too ragged to walk up to Portugal Square and meet Warlock, so I take the Saint-Laurent bus for the half dozen stops. Falling into a seat, I find the Business section of today's *Gazette*. There's an advertorial about the DC Scott Institute for Social Justice. I've seen the ad here and there lately, but haven't bothered to read it. The institute has a chichi designer logo and some PR tripe broken up by a photo of a benign looking DC, the same soft little mouth in the middle of his nicely trimmed beard. Further down is a shot of a starry-eyed Aunt Byron, head tilted just so, another dyke scarf wrapped around her head, a video camera poised on her shoulder. She's described as the Institute's Associate Director and Media Liaison.

When I find Warlock in the square, he's feeding pieces of raw hamburger to a couple of two-foot-tall northern ravens, having stopped in Montreal on their migration south. They're huge, severe looking creatures with judgmental faces on them, the demeanor of executioner judges. You can just imagine those piercing eyes stare down at you from the bench, an unswerving conviction your very soul must be flailed to bloody tatters.

The ravens are perched about ten feet up, on top of the sawed-off obelisk in the middle of the square. Warlock tosses the hunks of meat with a deft wrist action. They snatch it without much ado. No doubt the squadron of pigeons that usually hang around here split the moment this pair of orthinological heavies showed up.

"Friends of yours?"

"They don't need friends."

He's right. Northern ravens are far too cool for friendship. They're black as a void from top to bottom, even their feet and talons, and make vampires look fey. Fangs are nothing compared to those hooked beaks that could rip the sinew from your back.

"So…" Warlock starts on me. "I see you've become something of a *cause célèbre*."

"Give it up. I'm not forgetting the forty bucks you owe. And I don't want it in Confederate dollars or whatever you've dug out of your sarcophagus this week."

"No need to fret, Johnny. I'm solvent at the moment."

"So what then?"

"Your erstwhile wife's book."

"Book?"

"Yes, book. It's a traditional form of printed communication. Her debut effort is causing quite a sensation from what I understand." Warlock slowly twists the knife with immense pleasure. "You're mentioned quite a few times, name unchanged."

Bile rises up the back of my throat, a migraine kindles in my neck. "Where did you hear all this?"

"Take a look for yourself at Bill Dodge's bookstore. But you'd better hurry. I hear they're selling at a fairly rapid clip."

Finished feeding the ravens, Warlock methodically wipes his hands on a monogrammed hanky then brings out his monogrammed wallet. He removes four brand new twenties and I give him two packs. The ravens lift off with those massive wing spans. They rise up in a lazy, sweeping arc and head south toward the river.

"Yeah," I grunt. "More small press crap nobody will remember."

Now Warlock really does smirk for all he's worth, having a great time. "Perhaps it will be you that's forgotten. Just think, it won't matter what you did or didn't do, whether you're hurt, upset, or none of the above. If what she's written is truly memorable—and I believe it just might be—your life won't mean anything once you're far in the past and her work is still being read. I think you ought to feel privileged she's trying to keep you alive."

He gives me a final heaping spoonful of smarm. "Now, why don't you run along and go see what all the fuss is about?"

"I don't have time for that bullshit. I've got a business to run."

At Bill Dodge's bookstore it's right there in the window display. *Calamity*. A few copies are tastefully posed on a piece of black cloth. On the matte black cover is a sepia-toned photo of our broken down old street, Coloniale, looking southwards from Napoleon toward Pine. The title and Jane's name have been designed to seem like cracked and peeling gold flake. I stand there for a while staring at it. Bill Dodge notices me from inside the shop, taps on the window and gives me a knowing smile.

FORTY-FOUR

Autumn's almost done and Jane's book is turning into quite the sensation. I don't feel any malice toward her sudden stardom—even if she did use my real name. Reviewers have been going overboard, claiming she's single-handedly made poetry relevant again. I've seen her face on a few magazine covers, heard her smoothly answering questions on CBC radio and caught a little bit of her on the bar's TV. She was being interviewed on some arts program and looked confident, beautiful, relaxed. Her replies weren't pat or earnest, she was quick-witted and amusing. I'm proud of her.

For me, the past while has been strictly rote. Sell, reload from the Turks and check the papers for any word of The Man and his bound remains. No mention so far. Maybe his body is still in that closet; perhaps having paid a year's rent in advance. That is something he would do.

Morgan has gone kinda mute since then, concentrating on school. She's pared her working life down to a few extremely passive, extremely well-paying regulars. We haven't had much sex since leaving The Man behind. Each time has been sort of automatic, as if it's just another task on her to-do list. When we were together last she tried to palm me off with a weak hand job and we ended up in a huge fight.

But she was dead on about the Park Extension Turks. They remembered me from earlier meetings and the shift was seamless. In this particular trade, someone's sudden disappearance is not unusual. For all they care, I might have gotten rid of The Man myself to step up the wholesale ladder. As long as it doesn't bring any heat or affect their biz, it don't mean shit. Like well organized criminals anywhere, they are deeply conservative and insist on absolutely no boat rocking.

The phone's ringing when I come up the stairs, shaking off the weather. First thing I hear at the other end is some distorted PA announcements then Morgan comes on with a cough and a runny-nosed snort.

"Johnny!" she sobs.

A spasm of terror runs up my back. Now what. "Where are you!?"

"I'm at the airport."

"What are you doing at the airport?"

"I'm leaving!"

"Leaving!? Where the hell are you going!?"

"A rehab in Minneapolis. Sorry, Johnny, I have to go."

"Why Minneapolis? Why not here!?"

"Cuz it's a really fuckin' good rehab—and it's not here! I'm sorry, Johnny, I really like you and everything, but I have to go." She sounds drunk.

"Morgan, will you stop this. Let me come get you."

"No! I don't wanna end up like Lindy!"

"But Lindy's thirty-five years old!"

"That's only fourteen years away!" Her voice breaks. "I have to go. I'll try to call ya."

"How the fuck can you leave with all this shit going on!?"

"I gotta go, Johnny. I said I'm sorry. You know how it is."

"Wait, Morgan! Don't hang up!"

"You're cool and everything. We had fun…"

"Morgan, wait!"

And click. I listen for a few moments then a dial tone comes on. I actually look at the receiver. She was the one telling me I have to be The Man and all that bullshit, and now she bails, the stupid cow. I think about rushing out to Dorval, but instead call airport information. A woman tells me there's a flight to Minneapolis, through Chicago, but it's boarding in fifteen minutes. She says there's another plane in an hour, connecting in St. Louis. Okay, I'll go racing over to Minneapolis, scour all the shit hot rehabs—and do what?

It's true, she is only fourteen years younger than Lindy.

FORTY-FIVE

These grim days of early winter have been dragging slowly toward Christmas. After that joyous milestone, we can look ahead to several bracing months of Arctic gales and waist-deep snow. So I'm feeling shitty enough as it is hauling my ass through the afternoon slush, making deliveries because nobody wants to come out into this frozen December filth. I got another letter from Slim today. It took me a while to open it. I didn't believe she'd bother writing after what I'd sent her. Just touching the envelope, I felt the acid. And this time there was no cute'n'dirty address, no tongue-in-cheek 'Hi Sexy' intro.

Well happy fucking return, asshole. I got your epistle. Now you suck on this. What the fuck is wrong with you? 'Kid-stuff desire'? 'Taking your anima out for a little exercise'? No wonder you bitch about the facile so much. Self-hatred's stronger than any other—and always within reach of self-pity. Why do you croak about your trumped up anthem of depravity when you're really just another washout? No, not calculated, never. In your undying quest for intensity, maybe I'm just a little too fallible, you contrived prick.

In spite/because of your mind fucks, I do bother to wonder about it—about us. Your fetishism, my aching gut, rage that could just as easily be indifference. Oh, well. I guess we all have to stand in as an archetype for some sorry bastard. But the least you could do is effect something before you turn tail. God knows there must be more sublime disinterest than this same tired trash I dish out to every boring Joe.

I don't know what your plan is (I don't have one, you'll whine—me, I don't want nothing). I don't know whether you think you want to fucking give birth to me or snuff me out. But either way you do dick. Your flaccid malevolence goes about as deep as the layer of skin you scraped off my face last time you felt the call. Maybe my letter made you feel like your head was on the block. Or fuck, I don't know, maybe you're sweating over that Honeymooners re-run you called home. Yes, I do happen to wonder about how much you would do, make me do, I would let. Of course I want a hand in my own destruction. Otherwise, I would just step in front of a train and die like a stupid cat.

Shalini phoned me early this morning, saying she'd been away on tour for the past while. We agreed to meet for dinner at La Cabane. She apologized for giving me a hard time when I'd last seen her, that night at Jean-Baptiste's. She told me it was just the red wine bringing out her nasty side. Even so, I've only used a tiny bit all day while waiting to see her and I'm feeling kind of crazed.

Cutting through Carré Saint-Louis, I see Aunt Byron and her boyfriend, that DC Scott creep, strolling along the square's tree-lined paths, like they're some joyful retirement commercial. Somebody told me their institute has opened a richly upholstered head office among the substantial greystones that surround the square, so I guess this is their little lunchtime constitutional. They are dressed in matching designer parkas and Byron wears a pair of groovy après-ski sunglasses, her arm through his. Her hair's dyed ashy blonde and done in a horrible ringlet perm. She laughs with her man as he relates some amusing anecdote. I can't stand it and walk the other way.

Going past one of the Indian restos on Prince Arthur, Shalini sticks her head out and calls me in. She's been having drinks with a dance friend and the girl's valet. Shalini gives her a slow, lingering kiss goodbye on the neck, just below the jaw line. The bland little escort closes his eyes and goes up on his toes, but gets only a non-contact peck on the cheek.

After they're gone, Shalini gets into her coat and scarf while I yammer about the Aunt Byron fiasco, the video of us—of everyone on the mountain.

She laughs it off as juvenile, adding she doesn't mind the free publicity. Her nonchalance gets me aggravated. I tell her about my bitter correspondence with Slim. That makes her pause and look at me with surprised admiration.

"Actually writing angry and passionate letters to one another. I'm a little jealous."

We scurry through the sharp and icy wind over to my place. The house is freezing. The rads clank and emit a pathetic hiss. Shalini makes tea and brings it up to the bedroom. We huddle beneath the tented duvet with a flashlight and get undressed. "Maybe I'll set DC Scott's new digs on fire," I grumble. "After I've chained them all to their desks."

Shalini holds the flashlight under her chin for the old monster movie effect. "Very dramatic, darling, but he's fairly well known now and you'd be a main suspect. That would probably mean prison and we'd all miss you."

Her humor catches me off guard. "So what can I do?"

"Regroup and move on."

"But I hate what Byron's doing to my mountain."

Shalini gives me a generous laugh. "It's not your mountain."

"Well, our mountain then."

"It's not our mountain either, my love. It's just the mountain. It'll be here long after we're all gone, don't you worry."

"But I am worried. Byron's video will end up everywhere. Then all the squares will show up and crawl all over Mount Royal with their stupid festivals, ruin the whole thing. Or some parents group will go on a morality campaign. I know the Quebecois don't give a shit, they're too sophisticated for that. It's these fucking Canadian hypocrites. They'll want public decency cops behind every tree. *Hey, you there, get that cock out of your mouth! We'll follow you home and tell your wife and boss!* Y'know, that kind of nosy bullshit."

Shalini chuckles while crawling into my arms. I hear the pager buzz on the nightstand as the day changes to early evening out there beyond our covers, cars honk amid the rush hour commotion. I ignore the pager and cradle Shalini as she dozes on and off. Having kept my intake to a minimum today, I am feeling kind of electrified—ready to prove a thing or two.

I work my fingers between her thighs, but she turns her hips and pulls my hand up to her cheek.

"I'm going away."

"Where to?"

"Europe."

"When are you leaving?"

"The tenth, four days from now."

"For how long?"

"I'm not sure—several months, I think. The Quebec consul in Paris has organized a tour for our new company. France, Belgium, Switzerland and Austria—maybe England. We'll see. I'm also going to study and teach over there."

"Well, that is what you wanted, right?"

Shalini's eyes are shut, the back of her head in the crook of my elbow. "Don't sound so bitter, my love."

"Why not?"

"You should be happy for me."

"I'm ecstatic."

She smiles, eyes still closed. "I've been dreaming of trains lately. The old kind, with the nice wood-paneled compartments. It'll be exciting to perform almost every night."

I gently stroke her throat, feel how well it fits in my hand. She murmurs and nuzzles close, eventually falls asleep. After a while I roll her lengthwise and lie next to her, try to zone out. Shalini's bum pushes into my stomach, but I last about ten minutes. My head is too full of voices, trains, pages and pages of hateful letters blown down the tracks.

I slip out of bed and stand at the front window for an hour or more, naked and shivering. The apartment shudders in the wind, a bitter, early December wind that harkens the beginning of real winter. It's a razor sharp bluster that charges down the Saint Lawrence river valley from the north Atlantic to make all of Montreal brittle and hard.

I smoke and watch dusk lay down over the mountain. Shalini mumbles in her dreams behind me. Then out of nowhere, I hear the squawk and scree of countless sirens cut through the city's rush hour. Far off to my right, a

convoy of flashing red and blue lights races up Mount Royal's northeast-
ern slope. I grab the binoculars and try to recall what's over there. The
Oratory, a Metro station, a few hospitals, the University of Québec—the
École Polytechnique. Fire trucks, cop cars, ambulances, some military ve-
hicles, black vans, all fly up Chemin Camilien-Houde toward Côte-Sainte-
Catherine while more of them bottleneck at the bottom, where it meets
Park. I check the sky for aircraft or missiles, pillars of smoke.

Shalini wakes up and yawns. "What are you doing?"

"There's something happening on the mountain."

FORTY-SIX

The papers and radio shows are full of outrage, accusations, questions, explanations, kneejerk psychiatric evaluations, demands for resignations and top officials vowing to never again be caught napping. But out on the street things are very quiet for a Thursday morning—barely any traffic or people. Al called at the crack of dawn to say he's leaving for Vancouver immediately with Mama in tow. It's a genetic predisposition to flee at a moment's notice, as soon as the radio begins to play marching music; suitcases always standing ready in the closet, tickets and counterfeit passports in the utensil drawer. I went down to the bus depot to say goodbye.

"We're getting out before the border closes," Al told me. Then he looked around at the shabby old station, commuters and travelers trudging by. "This town's had it, Johnny—at least for a while. Welfare in BC is two hundred a month more. Besides, the film industry's moving out there. I have to think of my career."

"That you do."

"I'll get in touch once we're settled. You know you're always welcome."

We hugged and Mama Polo cried. She clung to me for a moment with her little hat pinned on and her old lady smells, a hanky crushed in her tiny fist. "Good bye, Mister Yonee. You are such nice man. Please coming to see us."

I watched them get on the Grey Coach and settle into their seats. Al leaned across his mother and slid open the window. "At least go see her," he yelled over the bus starting up. "You owe each other that much!"

The phone rings a bunch of times while I lie in bed, watching the mountain. I don't bother answering. It rings again about an hour later and startles me out of a heavy nod. I reach down onto the floor and grab the receiver. "Yeah, what is it?"

"It's me."

"What do you want?"

"Dred phoned. He said your friend Shalini told him you wanted to talk to me."

"I never told her that."

There's silence. I can hear traffic honking in the background. "Well, do you want to talk?"

"I guess. So how's it going down there?"

She draws a breath. "Y'know... New York's always great, even if you aren't." I hear her moving around. "How's that Adam guy?"

"There's no more Adam guy."

"No Adam guy?"

"No. No Adam guy, no nobody guy."

We go quiet again. She lights a cigarette.

"Did you move out of his place?"

"Yeah, I lucked into a cheap little rent controlled apartment at West 48th and 10th. This woman who's gone to New Mexico for a couple years, she sublet it to me. It's a climb to the fifth floor, but it's pretty nice."

"Isn't that Hell's Kitchen around there?"

"They don't call it that anymore."

"Too bad."

"So you want to come down?"

"And do what?"

"I dunno. See if we can get along."

"And if we can't?"

"Then we can't."

This time I light a smoke, look around my pad, out at the mountain. "Well... when should I come?"

"Whenever you want. I'm here."

"How about tonight?"

"Sure. Call me when you've got a ticket." She gives me a phone number. "Leave me a message if I'm not home. I'll call from school and check."

I phone Shalini's, but it's busy for over an hour. I finally get dressed and trudge through the slush up to her house. Her roommate's daughter answers the door.

"Shalini's busy right now," she dismisses me and tries to lock up.

I shove my boot in the way. "It's important."

"Who are you?"

"Tell her it's Johnny."

"I said she's busy."

"Suzanne, will you stop this and tell her I'm here."

Her face pinches. "How do you know my name? Oh, you're the man from that night on the stairs. I don't think she likes you."

"She likes me fine."

I hear Shalini up in the house. "Who is it, Suzanne?"

"That man from the stairs." She turns and stomps up. Shalini comes down and pulls me inside, closes the door.

"Listen, why did you get Dred to call Slim and tell her to phone me?"

"Because you're in love with her and I heard from a mutual friend down there she'd broken up with that Adam guy."

"Christ almighty. Do we live in some kind of klatch nobody can break out of no matter where on the fucking planet they go?"

"Stop it. What happened, are you going?"

"I dunno. I guess so."

"Just go. Then I won't have to feel bad about leaving you here."

I pull her close. My forefinger strokes her nipple. It gets hard. "Fuck, Shalini, I'm gonna miss you."

"I know you will, my love, but this isn't the place it was—even a few days ago." We both look down at her hand in mine.

I pack a few clothes, some letters and photos, a couple of books, along with two extra pairs of sunglasses. I grab the pager and walk down to see Octavio. He's crowded in behind his fruit, palms held over a propane heater. "Johnny," he greets me. "Buy some blow, will ya? I'm slow today, *tabernac'*."

"I don't need any blow. Listen, I'm leaving town and you gotta take over my pager. You got a line on this kinda shit?"

"What about your boss?"

"He's away on a trip."

Octavio comes out of his shed and I hand him the pager. He checks it out, already counting his profits but suspicious of any leg traps. "So where did he go?"

"Didn't say, but he's not coming back."

"Oh, like that, eh? *Tabernac'*."

"Yeah, *tabernac'*."

Octavio shrugs. "The wop won't be too happy but, eh, fuck him. I been thinking about going freelance."

"So you gotta a line on this shit? I don't want to leave my people high and dry."

"Sure. I know these Turks up in Park Ex."

"Of course. Same guys I get from. All right, but go easy on my customers, will ya? They're not greaseballs or shitheads."

"Don't worry, Mama Johnny. I'll take good care of them. So where you going?"

"New York."

Octavio gives me the revolutionary drug brother handshake, as Hunter S called it. He hammers me on the back. *"Bonne chance, mon ami!"*

Continuing my goodbye rounds, I stop at Mario's depanneur. Both him and his brother Harry are there. When I tell them what's up, Mario comes dancing over, feigning left jabs and right hooks then grabs me in a bear hug, pinning my arms. "You go make something strong with that woman," he says, nose an inch from my chin. "Don't be no fucking pansy. You gettin' too old for da pansy."

Harry throws his long arms around both of us, making it a somber threesome. He nods down at me and Mario. "That girl, she want you and you want her. Like the man say, don't be no fucking pansy."

A customer blunders in, a half-cocked giggle at our manly triad.

"Whachoo laughin' at?" Mario growls. "Get thee fuck outta my premises." The customer backs out, suitably stricken.

I take a cab up to the cemetery. I'm tempted to do something big, a real headline snatcher—dig Hennessy up and take him with me. A swirling arctic wind blows around the knee deep snow. The driver almost gets stuck back-and-forthing along the narrow, icy graveyard lanes. After lots of my shouts and bad French, we find his plot. The cabbie keeps the engine running while I tromp over to say goodbye. The Hen senses me struggle toward him, brooding from six feet under. I push crusty snow and ice off his tombstone and lay down a bunch of hot-house daisies then glance back at the taxi.

Listen, Hen, I gotta go. I don't have time for a quick screw. There's this train—but—I'll be back some time. C'mon, don't look away like that. You know I really did believe we'd grow old together. I was sure of it. Never a doubt we could live through anything, no matter how ridiculous, how painful or embarrassing. But then you had to go. Over nothing—a drunken, greedy miscalculation, all your good looks trapped in a pointless forever.

You've broken my heart and it breaks worse every day, grays my hair and lines my face that I didn't look behind those goddamn beer tents, maybe twenty feet separating us as you slouched under that tree and slowly stopped breathing. I was this far away, my love—this far.

And yet, I treasure the privilege of having been part of our little bit of unshackling, all of us on The Main, in our big dumpy apartments and drunken, drugged out love affairs. It was our Golden Age, everybody in one another's pants, casually winning the war for our own hearts and minds. It was perfect. More than perfect, it was easy. We could bet everything and always win. For once success took no effort, no sweat of the brow. We won by not winning, by debauching and sleeping late, by filling the bars and sexing all over the mountain, our victories constant and gentle and irresistible.

FORTY-SEVEN

It's a few minutes past noon, but Windsor Station is quiet. Even the PA announcer sounds half-asleep. I buy a ticket for *The Adirondack*, a milk run that goes through Albany and arrives in Manhattan at ten after midnight. I dump a handful of change into a pay phone. It rings for a while. Nobody answers and there's no machine. I feel the pager buzz in my shirt pocket. Reaching for the little bastard, I remember I don't have it on me. My boarding call comes over the speakers as a trio of black porters push carts full of bags and boxes down the ramp to track level. A tour group falls in behind them.

I try calling again a few minutes later. It rings a long time and I'm about to hang up when she knocks the receiver off its cradle. "Sorry, I forgot to turn on the answering machine."

"You still want me to come down?"

"Yeah—I think so."

"I've got a ticket. The train gets into Grand Central just after midnight."

"Are you going to be on it?"

"I don't know. Should I be?"

She doesn't say anything for a minute then takes a breath. "I'll be there to meet the train."

After she puts down the phone, the PA issues a final call for *The Adirondack*. I look out the front doors of the station and up Rue Stanley's steep incline. Mount Royal fills the top of the street.

Acknowledgements

Many people made important contributions to *Mount Royal*, often without realizing just how important; whether by reading and commenting on various drafts, proofing, helping me recall and/or verify certain incidents, places and dates, or simply through their encouragement and support.

So I'd like to offer my deepest thanks to...

Lisa Dempster, Fernando Pereira, Richard Stevenson, Gudrun Lock, Claire White, Mark Heffernan, Tom Roach, Leroy Bakelmun, Heather Dowd Burgess, Jason Papadimos, Jeff Ostofsky, Dr. Kumar Gupta, Joan Yolleck, Renata Jes Kos, Rhonda Sussman, Romas Maslaveckas, Deborah Federico, Diane McCauley, Mark Thibodeau, Morena Tursi, Araina Nespiak, Panayiotis Pantazidis, Julian Samuel Kahan-Singh, Benoit Pintel, Vera Frenkel, Gillian Robinson, Mohammed al-Abaya, Vlad Cekota, Wanda VanderStoop, Sandra McLelland, Parvana Pratibha Israni, Ireni Stamou, Susie Showers, Linda Aretz and Alison Campbell... along with The Gonidis Clan: Joyce, Wil, Holly, Morgan, Kiron & Moriah, everyone at The Painted Lady, the Trinity NN mob, Ashwin and the gang at King East, the Junktion Riders, my old Montreal crew—and to all good sex workers everywhere.

And special thanks to Halli Villegas and everybody at Tightrope Books.

Basil Papademos was born in Toronto and has lived in Montreal, Vancouver, the US and various cities in Europe. After writing the underground novel, *The Hook of it is*, he spent several years writing for television and the Internet. Basil currently resides in Bangkok.